PRAISE FOR
# TROUBLE THE WATER

"In her brilliant new novel, *Trouble the Water*, Rebecca Dwight Bruff skillfully uncovers an American odyssey, long lost in the camouflage of history. It is the unlikely journey of Robert Smalls, born a slave in Beaufort, South Carolina. While suffering the heartache and horrid indignities of chattel slavery, Smalls dreams of freedom for himself and his family. In what has to be one of the most daring and nail-biting escapes ever attempted in the low country, Smalls succeeds in changing the lives of many while becoming a Civil War hero and a paragon of civic leadership. Bruff gifts her readers a stunningly dramatic narrative. Gripping, heartrending and at last, inspirational. A testimony to hope through the darkest of times and a testimony to the triumph of the human spirit, not soon to be forgotten. Kudos to Rebecca Dwight Bruff!"

—**JEFFERY BLOUNT**, author of *The Emancipation of Evan Walls*

"There are white stories and there are black stories. Rarely do we encounter a book that so beautifully weaves the two into an inspirational American story."

—**JONATHAN ODELL**, author of *The Healing* and *Miss Hazel and the Rosa Parks League*

*Trouble the Water*
by Rebecca Dwight Bruff

Published by

 köehlerbooks ™

210 60th Street
Virginia Beach, VA 23451
800–435–4811
www.koehlerbooks.com

# TROUBLE

# THE

# WATER

A NOVEL

REBECCA DWIGHT BRUFF

VIRGINIA BEACH
CAPE CHARLES

*Trouble the Water* is a work of fiction, inspired by the extraordinary life of Robert Smalls, who was born into slavery in Beaufort, South Carolina. In this novel—except where noted in the author's end notes—the characters and their thoughts, conversations, relationships and actions are a work of the author's imagination.

*Wade in the water, wade in the water children,*
*Wade in the water,*
*God's gonna trouble the water.*

African American spiritual

# PROLOGUE

Before this decisive night, I'd not fully appreciated the subtle line between inspiration and insanity. But now, with all our lives at risk, I found myself navigating that most perilous edge.

Only the enslaved can fathom the price and the cost of freedom—life or death itself. Not only my life, but that of my wife, our children. And not just my family's, but those of my crewmates. Would we live an unknown future of freedom, or perish to the dark and watery depths? Men. Women. Babies. Fifteen lives hanging in the balance, entrusted to me.

Every moment, every experience, every longing led here. Every work-weary day, every sorrow-soaked night, every step on every road, every hurt and every hope, every echo of the cry of every slave I'd known, every whisper of every distant dream.

*Tonight. Now. Or never.*

My plan was either brilliant or foolish, valiant or vain—a dream hope-filled and desperate. Our crew was capable. The weather was in our favor. Our plan, solid. It seemed that God might be smiling, opening the Red Sea.

*We succeed or die. No in between. Triumph or tragedy. Freedom— or nothing at all.* We'd spent a long day loading the *Planter* with weapons for Confederate soldiers all along the Eastern Seaboard. Captain Relyea told me that when we finished he'd leave her in our hands until we sailed early the next morning.

My thoughts were as heavy as the 200 pounds of ammunition and the big howitzer we heaved aboard. We were loading guns for men determined to keep us in chains, piloting a boat against federal soldiers willing to die to see us free, keeping guard on this little cotton steamer turned rebel warship while the captain and officers went ashore—against orders—to eat and drink and sleep with their women.

As Captain Relyea left the boat that evening, I tipped my cap.

"See you in the morning, sir. Rest well, sir." I busied myself with the lines, keeping my hands moving and my eyes averted, lest I reveal my nerves. I looked up, startled to see the first mate, Mr. Hancock, returning to the boat.

"Forget something, sir?" I asked.

"No, boy. Just decided it's probably best for one of us to stay aboard. Damn protocol, you know."

My heart stopped. "Of course, sir."

Alfred, working on the deck behind me, had heard. I hoped his expression wouldn't betray us. As soon as Hancock slipped down to the stateroom, I whispered, "Say nothing to the others."

"We can't do this now!" Alfred said, panic in his eyes and voice quivering.

"We must. Say nothing!"

"Are you mad? How?"

"We'll lock him in his stateroom or kill him if we must. This is our only chance."

Alfred inhaled deeply and sighed. "Yes." He nodded. "God help us all."

"Say nothing," I repeated, and he nodded again. I knew this good man would die beside me if we failed.

* * *

Evening fell slowly. I watched other crew members arrive and worried how to keep Hancock concealed until we shoved off. My stomach knotted like the heavy lines holding us on the wharf.

Alfred had to get to the engine room, but if he went down too early, Hancock would have questions. Our timing was critical. We waited. But every minute lost pushed us into deeper risk. Our plan hinged on exiting the Charleston Harbor and passing Fort Sumter at her watery gate before sunrise.

Two of the crew arrived and I busied them with checking the big side-wheels.

Almost an hour passed. Lamps along the waterfront were being lit, the tide was shifting, and my heart raced. *Already an hour behind.*

As the curfew bell rang, Hancock emerged from the engine room. *I should have locked him into the stateroom; what was I thinking?*

"Boy, I'm headed home after all. Looks like we're all set for morning, and it's dull as hell staying on this boat. See you in a few hours."

I nodded. "Yessir."

I heard Alfred exhale. Our eyes connected; we said nothing.

* * *

William, Sam, and Gabe, along with their women, waited on the *Etowah* just a few minutes away, up at the northern wharf, along with my own sweet Hannah and our little Liddy and Robbie. They'd all board the *Planter* from there. Our other crewmen were finally aboard, but we were already behind schedule thanks to Hancock's brief bout of responsibility. As Hancock strolled away from the boat, Alfred hurried to the engine room to start the boiler.

I grew up on the water and knew that these tides would soon be against us. If we passed Fort Sumter in daylight, running against the tide, we'd never make it. It was that simple. If the guns at Sumter didn't put us on the ocean floor, we'd be captured and executed. At least I'd go to the bottom of the Atlantic on my own terms.

A few minutes later we slipped, silent as mist, out of the southern wharf, and made our way toward the *Etowah*. We agreed that if we were stopped, we'd say we were under orders to retrieve additional supplies before sailing out of Charleston's harbor. We could only pray that we'd be believed.

But another obstacle appeared when the wind shifted, clearing the clouds. We had hoped for fog; a clear night could be disaster, making our smoke and steam visible. Worse, if the breeze pushed our steam over the city, people would fear fire. The entire population of Charleston had become watchful of smoke after the blaze that destroyed much of the city back in December. Anyone seeing smoke would call the alarm, and the response would be swift.

It was too late now; we were moving. The rest of our crew was waiting, and our hopes were now in God's hands.

When we slipped softly into the dock on the northern wharf, Hannah and the children, along with our other crew members and their women, moved in beautiful silence onto the *Planter*'s deck. I saw the terror on the women's faces when they boarded. Hannah whispered that she'd done her best to calm them, but the longer they waited, the more anxious they'd become. In a moment of divine brilliance, she'd insisted on a silent prayer.

I'd married an amazing woman but wondered what the other mothers and daughters thought. They had no reason to trust me as I herded them down into the hold and told them I knew God would use them, and all of us, for glory. I told them to keep praying.

Then I locked them in.

Past midnight and under cloud cover, we headed out into Charleston Harbor. We maintained a slow pace to avoid notice, but I itched to hit full steam. Alfred and Brother John, feeding the engine coal, kept us at a low, steady speed, customary for the early morning departures through this harbor. We flew the Stars and Bars at full mast, with the South Carolina palmetto and crescent below her. We'd passed this way dozens of times at this speed, and even at this time of night. But nothing about this was routine.

As we approached Fort Johnson, two miles offshore, we gave our customary passing signal—two long blasts and a short—and kept steady. Fort Johnson was well armed; I'd taken some of the guns there myself, on this very boat, and I knew those guns and cannons could sink us with ease. We passed without incident, and I realized I was holding my breath again.

I called down to the engine room. "Full head! Full head o steam!" John and Alfred fed the engine, and I felt our speed increase.

I leaned against the cabin window, just as I'd seen Captain Relyea do so many times, arms crossed over my chest, his straw hat pulled low over my forehead. I'd even practiced his limp. But I'm certain his heart never beat with such nervous ferocity.

Fort Sumter was about a mile ahead, where the harbor narrowed and then opened into the broader ship channel, the only way in or out. Opposite Sumter, on the north side of the harbor's narrow mouth, lay Fort Moultrie. Before the war began, a boat this size could pass between the two forts without coming too near to either of them. But last year, the rebels built an enormous floating log boom, forcing every vessel to pass within range of Sumter's cannons.

I knew Sumter was using small watch boats as well, and I wondered if I'd see them before they saw us.

We continued on, and a light fog returned, for which I gave thanks.

I called for the signal.

Gabe shook his head. "Not yet!" he hissed. "Are you trying to sink us, after we've made it this far?"

Under other circumstances, I'd have disregarded him, but he was right, and I swallowed my pride.

A mistake like that, and pride like mine, was a fatal formula.

Eight long minutes later, he gave me a nod.

"Signal to pass!" I called.

"Signaling!" he responded, giving two long blasts. The third followed, short and hissing. I held my breath again—and prayed. Silence. The pause was too long. My stomach climbed to my throat.

We waited. I'd never had to repeat a signal at Sumter. If they'd not heard, and if we passed without being cleared, they'd fire on us. But if they had heard and we repeated the signal, they'd send a guard boat to find out why we repeated.

At last, we heard the signal to proceed, and a voice from across the water: "Kill us some damn Yankees, boys!"

"Ay!" I called, and waved my ungloved hand. Gabe went pale.

We kept moving, steady, and finally we were out of range of Sumter's big guns—but not out of danger. The most perilous moments lay directly ahead. The Union's *Onward*, heavily armed, saw our Confederate flag waving in the clear first light of morning.

I went cold as their cannons pivoted toward us.

# PART I

*It's not what you call me
but what I answer to.*

African Proverb

# CHAPTER 1

## BEAUFORT, 1839

Trouble came the night they hanged the runaway. That's what everyone called him: *Trouble,* because that's what Lydia called him. She said they told her to name him Robert Henry, "but he come on a night full o trouble."

They hanged Ruben down by the arsenal for trying to escape. He'd gotten far, but the dogs were too good, and old Barnwell Rhett was too determined.

*Trouble.* Sounded to some like a curse, foreboding and ominous. But for Lydia Polite it was a promise. You had to know Lydia. She knew tribulation and suffering but turned her face toward endurance and hope. She said the road to glory passed right through trouble— not around. That night, hope and suffering would merge through her loins.

\* \* \*

Three weeks before delivering her own child, Lydia brought another baby into the world, serving as midwife to the missus of the big house.

Jane McKee feared pregnancy and childbirth, and her fears grew in proportion to her girth for nine long months. When her water broke on that chilly March morning, she stood, paralyzed, looking through the upstairs bedroom window, down to the yard, where her eyes fell on the magnolia tree and then the camellia, whose pink blossoms had opened just days ago. She'd told her husband, Henry, that she wanted to name the child Camellia if she delivered a girl, but he'd laughed.

"What kind of name is that, Jane? That's a flower, for God's sake! We'll name her for my mother or yours, of course." And that was the end of that.

She knew that Henry hoped for a boy, that he longed and prayed for a son. Henry had buried his father four years earlier, missed him profoundly, and yearned to carry and advance the family legacy. Henry itched to fish and hunt with a son, and to someday leave him with the plantation, the wealth, and the respected name with which his own father had left him.

Still standing at the window, wet down her legs, the first contraction came, and she gasped, more from surprise than pain.

"Lydia!" she called. "Lydia, quick! I need you!"

Lydia, twice Jane's age, had in fact been Henry's childhood caretaker on the Ashdale Plantation. She climbed the stairs slowly, her own womb heavy, to Mrs. McKee's room.

"You be alright now, Miss Jane. Let's just get you comfortable now." She guided Jane by the elbow, and helped her onto the bed, noticing the trail of blood-tinged water that followed them, knowing she'd be the one to clean it up.

"Lydia, tell Henry to call Dr. Johnson immediately!"

"Yes'm." Lydia nodded. *This gonna be a long, long day, honey. No need for hurry. First baby never hurry outta his momma.*

Lydia trundled back down the stairs to find Mr. McKee. Not seeing him in his parlor, she looked out the back door and found him talking with George, pointing toward the barn. His favorite mare would be foaling soon. He wanted a filly, as he was eager to breed what he hoped would be the finest hunting horses in South Carolina. A healthy filly would be far more lucrative and far less trouble than a stallion.

George saw Lydia watching them and directed McKee's attention to the house.

"Mr. Henry, it look like Miss Jane might have that baby today. She's asking for you."

"I'll be there right away, Lydia. In just a moment."

"Mr. Henry, she wants you to call for Dr. Johnson. Mediately, she say."

Confident he'd send George for the doctor within moments, she shuffled back into the house. *Too old for this. And these two, maybe not old enough.*

A cry of pain from upstairs interrupted her thoughts. "Comin, Missus." She remembered to pick up the heavy scissors before climbing the stairs again. No point in having to make extra trips up and down, no matter how long this day lasted. That deep ache low in her back warned that her own labor wasn't far off.

*Long day ahead, for sure. Ain't no pain like a baby comin through. And Missus, bless her heart, she's a tender one.*

Lydia found Jane sitting up in bed, smiling, with a book on her lap. "Why, Miss Jane, you look like you goin to a garden party today! How you feelin now?"

Jane laughed. "It's not so bad, Lydia, not like the misery I've been warned of."

"You just getting started, sweetie."

"I know. The wailing and gnashing of teeth will come later, I'm sure."

Nine hours later, as the sun dropped below the horizon, Jane McKee delivered her first child. In a fog of exhaustion and pain, she heard Dr. Johnson declare the child healthy. "Your daughter," he said, laying a wet and wailing bundle in her arms. Her heart sank.

*But Henry wanted a boy.*
*I don't know how to be a mother.*
*Everything hurts.*
*And Henry wanted a boy.*

∗  ∗  ∗

Three weeks later, the night I came, Lydia wept and gasped and moaned through the hours. As the first glint of morning light broke across the water of the Beaufort River, her contractions gave way to release. She screamed and pushed, finally delivering me, her second son. She was alone in the dependency house on Prince Street, save for the old midwife offering both hope and wisdom for what was sure to be a difficult birth.

Lydia was forty-four, or at least that's what she guessed. She couldn't be sure; none of the slaves from the Lady's Island plantations knew their birthdates. But Lydia knew that she was born a few years after a man named George Washington had become important (though she didn't know why) and she knew she'd seen at least four decades of life, every day of it in the heat and beauty and toil of the South Carolina lowcountry.

Lydia's tears came from pain and fear, of course, and hope. Childbirth was hard, dangerous, and often fatal. Many newborns and young mothers were buried in the soft soil of Southern plantations.

Lydia had given birth long ago and had faith in her body, faith that it could endure. She was small, but strong; tender and fierce. Her rich brown skin bore scars from childhood, before she belonged to the McKees. Her eyes, dark and gentle as a doe's, shone with the wisdom born of suffering, love, and hope. Lydia had endured it all. Most of life was about enduring. *"But we glory in tribulations also: knowing that tribulation worketh patience; And patience, endurance; and endurance, hope."*

She'd heard that from the balcony of the church in town—a thousand times, surely. *Tribulation.* "Just a fancy word for pain and trouble," her sister insisted. "Fancy word don't make it not hurt all the same."

Lydia preferred the fancy word, the way it sounded, the way it gave dignity to pain. Henry McKee and his wife, Jane, used such fancy words, but not in fancy ways.

Mrs. McKee was a kind woman; her husband owned the plantation across the river and sixty-three slaves, including Lydia, having inherited them from his father. The McKees took care of their slaves—for the most part. Lydia thanked God for that, but still wondered about the tribulation of being owned by another person. She'd never known anything else, but it never made sense to her either. *It can't be right.*

*Tribulation.* She clenched the bloody bedsheets in pain and relief, pushing toward life. Her mama used to say, "Life can find a way even when there ain't no way." Maybe tribulation was about pushing on, finding a way. This baby was finding a way, that was certain.

\* \* \*

Phibe, the midwife from the plantation across the river, came to help and almost missed the birth.

"Girl, this baby be ready!" She rolled up her sleeves and laid her leathery hands on Lydia's heaving belly. "George mighta told me c'mon fast."

"I sent him minute my water break," Lydia said.

George, the McKees' barn slave, took the McKees' best mule across to the Ashdale Plantation to fetch Phibe. On most days, he could get from the house to the ferry in just a few minutes, but today he had to skirt the main road where the constable's assistants talked and laughed as they assembled the scaffold. George's stomach turned. Ruben almost made it. Ruben did make it, till he got found.

The hammering of the nails echoed the hammering of George's heart. He'd watched as the buckra—the white men—brought Ruben back to Beaufort. He watched as they dragged him from the boat.

Could've been worse, maybe. They might've skinned him or burned him alive long before Beaufort. They might've dragged him all the way back behind a wagon or a horse, or he might've pulled a wagon himself. They might've taken bits of his flesh, or his eyes, or ears or hands or feet, executing him part by part, making an example of him, showing the others what happened if they ran. That probably would've happened if he'd been a Charleston slave or a Baltimore man. There were thin mercies here in Beaufort; they brought thin comfort.

Ruben sat alone now in a dark cell, listening to the construction of his own scaffold; in a few hours he'd carry his own noose, and step off into his own death.

George took a deep breath as he led his mule onto the ferry, and a breeze brought the faint, sweet scent of honeysuckle. Seemed like he was always either holding his breath in fear or exhaling in relief. He couldn't stop thinking about Ruben—the dreamer. Ruben always imagined what might be, always talked about how things would change, always believed he'd find a way.

But Ruben's desire extended beyond himself. His plan was to go north, to Pennsylvania or New York or somewhere far off, and find a way to bring the rest out with him. He dreamed big.

George held the mule's halter, wondering what Ruben dreamed now that the gallows were being nailed together, now that the rope was being strung. He'd known Ruben for as long as he could remember. He knew Ruben would walk with his head held high, all the way up the steps, ignoring the taunts of the buckra, unafraid of the whip. Ruben's courage came from some deep place, maybe from the ancestors, a place George wanted to find for himself. They were as unlike as brothers could be, George thought. He'd always been the one to hold back, cautious and careful; Ruben was the fearless one, the strong one, the sure one.

The ferry bumped against the dock on Lady's Island, and George waited for the other folks to leave before he led the mule over the wooden ramp to the grassy landing. It took an hour to get to Phibe's cabin on the plantation, and by the time they returned together to the house on Prince Street, day had turned to night under a crescent moon.

* * *

Phibe heard Lydia before she saw her. Limping through the door of the backhouse, the old midwife began humming, and let her eyes adjust to the dark.

"George," she called out the door. "Light me a light here."

George lit a small lantern and brought it to the door, and Phibe set it on the old crate that served as a table. She resumed her humming.

The lantern cast a weak light around the little room, and the bent old woman opened her basket for her birthing tools, and a small jar of sugar, and another of ash.

George set a kettle to boil, and Phibe soaked a long strip of cloth in the hot water, then wrung it out and hung it on a nail in the wall next to Lydia's mat. She poured the sugar and the ash out onto a banana leaf, and stirred them together with her finger as she continued to hum.

Lydia gasped again and groaned. She felt her belly tighten, and then a searing, burning, tearing pain.

"Aaagh!"

Phibe took Lydia's hand. "Squeeze tight, girl. Squeeze hard!"

Blood. Water. Blinding fierce pain. A moment to breathe. Relief. And then the gripping contraction, again. Burning. Tearing. Bloody blinding pain. A breath. Relief.

Again.

"Aaagh! Jesus! No!"

"You bout done, honey. This baby jus bout here. Squeeze tight. Push hard."

Lydia pushed, screamed. Tears ran down her face, and she clenched Phibe's hand and she pushed again, and then felt the give of her flesh and the birth of her child and the relief of her agony. She sighed, deep, deep. She felt and smelled the warm blood beneath her.

I emerged from the warmth of my mother's womb, gasping and trembling.

"Well, looka there." Phibe laid me on Mama's belly. "You got you a big boy, Liddy. Big boy."

Mama shook her head and smiled. "How in the wide world? I'm jus too old."

She trembled again with another contraction, expelling the placenta, bloody and whole.

Phibe wiped the blood and mucous from my head, with extra care around my eyes. I squeezed them shut, then wailed. Phibe wiped me clean, head to toe, admiring my size and Lydia's strength.

"Now we gonna make sure he let go right." Phibe dipped her small knife into the boiling water and stretched out her hand from my belly to measure and then sever the umbilical cord. She rubbed the sugar-and-ash mixture all over and around the cord, all the way to my belly, and then took the placenta and wrapped it in the banana leaves.

I shuddered in Mama's arms, and cried out, loud, demanding. Mama nudged her warm and heavy breast and she winced as I found her nipple and nursed with fierce urgency. My intensity amused her and, for a moment, diverted her attention from the searing pain and the pool of blood beneath her.

"Nursin baby, nothin sweeter," she said.

Phibe smiled and kept on humming. She'd attended hundreds of births, and this one was quicker than most. But there was more blood than most, too. She'd seen strong women collapse, and most were younger, if not stronger.

Mama shifted her weight to let Phibe attend to her torn and bloody flesh. Pulling the blood-soaked sheets away, the old woman pushed a balled-up cloth between her legs.

"Hold your knees together, Liddy," she instructed, and wrapped a band of cloth around Mama's thighs to ensure the compression. "Now you lay still, hear?"

Mama heard Phibe's voice as if it were far away in the trees, heavy and thick as the morning mist, and she tried to focus on the old, wrinkled face, which struck her in that moment as beautiful.

Her thoughts turned to the mother of the man who, that same night, was being hanged at the Beaufort Arsenal. Against all odds, he'd made it beyond Baltimore, on his way to New York. But he'd been captured by the bounty hunters and brought back as "restored property," and the inevitable execution followed. She knew—they all knew—that every mother of every boy child was just as likely to bury that child as see him grown. She knew that every mother of every girl child was almost sure to see her daughter sold or raped—or both.

She knew that birth meant life, but it also meant suffering, pain. And as she wept that night, her heart broke for Ruben's mother, and for Ruben himself.

*  *  *

Mama felt exhaustion in her bones. There was too much blood this time and I came so fast and so hungry. Miraculously, I was not only healthy, but also stout and strong, with a head full of black wool and a cry that reminded her of an ancient song. She remembered her own mother's voice, singing the songs of Guinea, the rhythms of hunters and warriors and weavers, the anthems of strength and power.

From Sierra Leone they had come, our Mende ancestors, chained in the dark and filth of a hundred ships. Her mother had survived, and her mother's sister and one brother, but the rest of their family had died either of fever or at the hands of the traders after they reached the other side of the Atlantic. Mama's mama told stories and sang songs, keeping alive memories and myths.

"We are Nyame's children, we are Anansi's friends," she'd said, "and we will spin our way to a new life. You'll see."

Nyame, creator of the world, god of the sun and the moon, connecting earth and sky, gave all wisdom, and the people spoke of him with wonder, and with trust. Anansi, the clever spider god, created possibilities out of impossible problems. Nyame made the rain fall, the night dark. He worked in ways mysterious and magic. Anansi wove webs of surprise and laugher. Mama often thought of Nyame and Anansi when the preacher at Beaufort Baptist told stories of a man who came to earth from heaven, somehow connecting the two distant realities.

* * *

Mama named me Robert Henry, as she'd been instructed by Mr. McKee, who had chosen Rachel for a girl. Our owners liked Biblical names for the females, believing this would imbue them with a degree of righteous obedience. Boys more often carried names that echoed the owner's or his family's heritage. *Robert Henry*. She couldn't imagine calling me that. She closed her eyes and asked the ancestors for my basket name.

*Trouble.*

She opened her eyes and smiled. *Trouble*. Yes, this was a night of trouble, a season of trouble. She'd call me Trouble, and she would let my name remind her, every time she spoke it, that hope might live, someday, on the other side of trouble.

So, she named me for the man who owned her body but thought about the man who held her heart. Her lover walnut dark and iron strong; her owner pale and thin. She knew that she mattered to them both. And she knew that neither of them could protect her, or her child, from the tribulation at hand.

As she nursed, she listened to the crowds just a few streets away. The April breeze drifted in through the open window and carried the sounds of the waterfront. She heard the deep voices of the marshal and his assistants as they finished the business of the hanging, dismantling the platform as if they were tidying up after a lawn party. And she heard the crying and singing of the slave women.

Slave men had been prevented by curfew from being present, but they knew what the women witnessed that night; they knew it wasn't the first nor the last of the hangings.

On the night she gave me my birth, Mama prayed to Nyame and to Jesus and to her ancestors and to all the wild spirits of the dark, and she sang her pain and fears.

"If there be glory in pain," she cried, "this boy, this boy, I know he be glory."

*   *   *

Phibe carried me out into the dark night and stood in the yard under the old oak. An owl called and another answered. The commotion from the hanging had ended, and a quiet lay over the town like a blanket. I slept in her arms, and she wondered what would happen to me if Mama didn't wake up. I'd go back with her to the plantation, and one of the aunties would have to find a way to nurse and protect me. My chances would have been slim, for sure.

She tucked me against Mama's side, and then took the banana leaf-wrapped placenta back out to bury it under the oak, where George had prepared its shallow home.

"We can least give this boy his roots here," she muttered into the silence.

*   *   *

Mama emerged from the fog of sleep late the next morning, to the sound of my hungry wailing. She felt her milk come in and wondered how long she'd slept. Raising herself up on her left side, she tried to sit up and felt the torn and bruised flesh beneath her. *Bone tired.* She knew fatigue, and she knew pain. She knew she could and would survive this.

*Something about this boy.*

She sensed , somehow, that I was charmed, chosen. Why or for what she didn't know, but she knew as sure as she knew the pain, as sure as she knew the fear and hope that rose with each new sunrise.

"This little man so hungry!" Phibe said as she placed me in Mama's lap.

*Have to be strong. Have to grow this child up.*

As I nursed, Mama hummed, prayed, dozed, dreamt.

* * *

Two months after Liza Beth's birth, and a month after I arrived, Caroline Rhett delivered Peter, the fifth son and seventh child of the Robert Barnwell Rhett household. Caroline's ability to produce healthy children, and particularly an abundance of male children, was legendary. Mrs. McKee wanted to like Caroline, wanted to not carry the resentment she felt for the town's social leader, wanted to not always feel inferior. She longed for Caroline's approval and friendship, and status.

"The Rhetts have a new baby," Henry McKee announced as he pulled off his coat and handed it to Mama. "I just saw Barnwell down at the bank."

"How many does that make now?" asked Mrs. McKee.

"Seven. And this is boy number five. Lucky man."

"Poor Caroline!"

"Poor Caroline nothing. Barney says she delivered inside of three hours. The woman is astonishing."

"She may be astonishing, but she's got seven children under the age of ten. I don't know how she stays on her feet. I'm exhausted with one!" She paused. "She has plenty of help, of course. But still."

"Five boys." McKee whistled. "Well, we're just getting started, my dear. We'll get to work on a boy right away."

Tears welled in Mrs. McKee's eyes. "Henry . . ."

"Damn it, Jane. Stop it."

"I'm sorry . . . I only . . . I know you wanted a boy."

"Of course I wanted a boy! What good is a girl, really?"

Mrs. McKee and Mama looked at one another, wordless.

# CHAPTER 2

Mama and I lived in the backhouse—the dependency, they called it. It was hardly a house; we shared its two small rooms with George, the McKees' barn slave, and it sheltered our bed and blankets, our fire and cooking pots, the few clothes we had, and a dark wooden box holding a very few personal possessions belonging to my mother. I loved to sit with her and listen to her stories about the ancestors. She let me hold the small carved figures, a king and a queen, and whispered the legends of our past.

Our ancestors lived many generations ago, and were living still, she told me. If we were home in Africa, we would honor them at their graves with fruit and other gifts, and we would thank them for their provision and their wisdom. She said that even though we were far away, that we could honor them still by listening to them and choosing to be strong and bold even in the worst of days, even when we felt weak and afraid. She explained that Life chose us and enfolded us in the great circle, and what we gave to Life, Life would return to us.

Most of our ancestors, she said, worked hard and fought bravely, and loved their own ancestors and their children too. They gave themselves to Life—to the land, and to the forest, and to the rain and the wind and even the wild beasts. And the land and the forest and the rain and the wind and even the wild beasts gave back, and everyone had enough.

But some were not so strong or good or brave. They gave in sometimes to pain or greed or fear. They took more than they needed of the earth, the rain, the forests and the beasts. And when that happened, the earth and rain and forest and beasts took back, and life became hard or lonely or short.

The best of the ancestors, she told me, were not only strong and good and courageous, but they were also wise and allowed Life not only to give, but to teach. She spoke of the great powers of courage and love and forgiveness.

"You can choose how you think," she said, "and you can choose how you speak, and how you treat people. All of us have a good heart, and all of us have an evil heart, and you must choose which heart you will feed. If you feed your good heart with love and forgiveness, with song and laughter, with suffering and hope, it will be enough, and will grow larger and stronger than your evil heart, and it will stay peaceful within you."

\* \* \*

The house on Prince Street was my home from the beginning, as were the shimmering rivers and tides, the marsh grasses and grand oaks, the fields of rice and cotton around us. In our room out back, my mother told me stories too dark to repeat and too important to forget.

I played in the yard with the McKee children, and it wasn't until I was five or six that I understood that we were not part of the same family. I knew, of course, that my skin was dark and that theirs was light. I knew that my mother and I slept in the quarters in back, and the McKees slept in fine beds in the big house. I knew that they were warmer in the winter and that sometimes they ate when we were hungry. And I knew that Liza Beth and Hank knew who their father was. I wished that I knew mine. I wished George was my father, or Henry McKee; they both raised me and taught me and protected me. I enjoyed their attention and I seldom doubted their affection.

This home and these people—this life—all of it was tangled together like the Spanish moss in the live oak trees. Even when we were unaware of it, we were part of each other's stories.

* * *

I recall sitting with Mama in the yard where she was mending a dress for Mrs. McKee. I held the buttons and a spool of thread.

"Trouble," Mama said. She paused to let me know this was a serious talk. "Trouble, life is a frail thing, like a thread. It break easy, and it don't hold much all by itself. But you pull it through something strong, like this wool, or you twist it up with more threads, like how we sew on these buttons, or you coat it good with wax, then it be tougher than you know."

"Yes, Mama."

"See that web there?" She pointed to the big spiderweb stretching from the lowest branch of the pear tree to the skinny one above it.

"Yes, Mama."

The spider's web sparkled, each individual thread damp, made bright in the morning light. A big dragonfly had got stuck in it.

"Mama, that dragonfly can't move."

"That's right, baby. He done."

"How, Mama?"

"All those teensy threads, they nothing all alone. Can't even see em. But that little spider, she's clever. She catch the big bug. She spin the web, and wait."

"Why, Mama?"

"Baby, all God's creatures got to find a way. Some creatures big and mean. Some little and clever. Spider find a way."

Then Mama told me about Anansi. She was a fine storyteller, and even though she insisted I speak the king's English—"just like Mr. McKee, son, so people take you serious"—she eased into the old sweet rhythms of her own early years when she told the ancient stories.

"In Africa, where our ancestors stay," she began, "there live the spider god Anansi. He the most clever creature in all da world—so clever, in fact, dat sometimes he grow big like a man and sometimes he be tiny as a spider, and he can move, if he want to, from da earth to da sky and back again.

"One day, Anansi leave his home to go find some tasty food for his family. He know his wife like somethin chewy, and he know his babies like somethin juicy. Suddenly, he hear a big noise and he look all round and he see a leopard with the antelope, holdin it in her big teeth. Anansi, he look round and he see a big beehive fallen from a big branch, and now it be on da jungle floor, just beyond da leopard.

"'Oh,' he say to himself. 'My babies would love some honey! If only I can get past da big leopard, I could fill up some pods with honey and take it to my babies!'

"Just den, ol leopard look up and she see Anansi, and Anansi be afraid. But ol leopard, she not fraid of some little spider, and she go back to her bloody feast.

"Anansi, he hurry past ol leopard to da broken hive, and he think, how he gonna gather up a bunch of good sweet honey without get all stung by all the bee? He look round for some empty bean pods and he find one just da right size to fill with honey, and he pull it to da hive. He accidentally bump da tail of ol leopard, and she flick her tail, and it startle up all dem bees and dey begin a swirl, all full o anger and fear.

"Anansi, he sit patient and watch da bees torment that leopard's tail and backside. Ol leopard, she jump up and scramble off to get away from da bees, but dey follow her. More dat leopard swat with her front paw and her thick tail, more them bees attack. Da battle tween da bees and da leopard just last a few minutes, but dat's when Anansi fill his pod with fresh honey from da hive, and he carry it home to his babies!"

Mama finished her story and got real quiet.

In a voice soft and low, she said, "Baby, we got to be clever like Anansi. Dis ol world full o leopards and bees."

# CHAPTER 3

A hard look, even in a flawed mirror, reveals both truth and distortion. I looked hard. I watched and studied every grown man in my small world, but I didn't recognize my father.

"Mama," I asked once, "why won't you tell me? Is it Uncle George? Is it Mr. McKee?" But she raised her hand to me, and my cheek stung, and her voice shook as she spoke.

"Don't you never ask me such a thing again. Don't you never!"

"But, Mama—"

She spun and grabbed me by the shoulders, and her eyes flashed with anger—or was it fear?

"You listen to me now. Ain't nothin good outta questions like that, you hear me? You leave that alone now. You just leave it lone."

She turned and left me with my questions and confusion.

\* \* \*

One morning around that same time, I walked with Henry McKee to the river's edge, an easy stroll under the live oak canopy of Prince Street, and then a turn down Carteret Street.

Mama made me practice saying "*Mister* McKee," instead of *Masser*, the way George said it. She said I'd best learn to speak fine.

"Where are we going, Mister McKee?" I asked. I knew, but wanted to try on what I'd been practicing with Mama.

"Time you learn to catch a fish, boy!"

Mr. McKee, a gentle and good-natured man, loved his daughter, but he mostly wanted to do the things a father did with a son. I'd heard him say it a dozen times to Mrs. McKee: "Jane, this house needs a boy!" And I'd watch her smile and shake her dark curls.

We each carried a willow pole and a pail. At the pier, Mr. McKee stopped. "Lookee there. Tide's up. All the way up. Won't last all morning, though—let's go get 'em."

The water shimmered in the morning sun, licking the heavy wooden posts under the boardwalk. Out over the river, three pelicans soared high, then dipped low. I watched as one of the big brown birds folded its huge wings and plunged into the river, disappeared—I counted to five. It surfaced with a river trout in its odd beak and tossed its head back. I could see the fish squirming in the leather pouch under the pelican's beak. With a gulp it was gone.

"Good fishermen, aren't they, boy?"

At the end of the pier, Mr. McKee tied a light rope to the handle of the pail and dropped it into the water. Moments later, he lifted it and showed me the tiny fish he'd scooped up, just an inch or two long.

"Now, watch me first; then you can do one in a minute." Mr. McKee held a little fish in his right hand and impaled it on the barbed hook in his left hand. "Just make sure the hook's on real good, right in the middle."

The baitfish squirmed, and a pale liquid oozed from where the hook went in. Mr. McKee dropped it into the water and handed me the pole. "Hold that a minute; let me get this other one baited."

We each held our poles and watched the river's life in a comfortable silence. More pelicans, a hawk far off. Something big splashed a time or two downriver. We watched for dolphin, and for snakes; only a fool wouldn't watch for snakes.

We watched the water for a long time. Then I heard Henry McKee speaking, and I wondered who he was talking to.

*Of books and boats I sing:*
*And this old town of note,*
*Where each man had a library*
*And every man a boat.*

*Plantations all had muscled crews,*
*A landing and a boat,*
*Each lad was taught to sail and row,*
*But also how to quote.*

*On summer morns they loved to read;*
*On summer eves to float,*
*Woe to the man who had no books*
*Or chanced to have no boat!*

*For Beaufort was a strange old town*
*In those old days remote:*
*One had to have a library;*
*One loved to have a boat!*

"A library and a boat, boy! Old Barnwell has his priorities!" Mr. McKee laughed, and I nodded, trying to imagine such a world for myself. "Old Barnwell" owned an enormous plantation, held public office, and ran the college in Columbia. And he was Peter Rhett's uncle.

Peter Rhett was a month younger than me but bigger and heavier. His father, Robert Barnwell, was a man before whom no colored man, slave or free, would choose to stand. Peter seemed more like his father than the other four Rhett boys—angry most of the time and hot-headed. The Rhetts held dozens of slaves and enormous power in the Lowcountry.

Thinking about Peter made my stomach hurt, so I tried to imagine having both a library and a boat. My effort was interrupted by a splash just in front of us.

"That's it!" Mr. McKee said, smiling at me and jumping to his feet.

His copper-red hair blew in the breeze and his blue eyes squinted in the sun as he reached for the pole. His lean frame belied his strength.

I watched Mr. McKee hold the fishing pole in both hands, right above left, and he gave it a sharp snap back, away from the water. The line went tight and the tip of the pole bent, and I wondered if it would break.

Mr. McKee pulled the line in and a fine gray speckled fish thrashed on the hook.

"Trout," he declared. The fish was almost the length of the man's forearm. "That's fine eating."

Mr. McKee's energy was contagious, and I stared at my own line, wishing hard for a fish to take the hook.

Mr. McKee baited his line again, and leaned back on his left elbow, enjoying the warmth of the morning sun and the light breeze. It would be hot in a few hours.

"Think I'll catch one, sir?" I asked.

"Patience, boy. Sure you will. Just be patient."

"How do you know?"

"Just know."

"What about gators? And what about big fish? Real big fish? What about sharks?"

I'd heard a story of a boy who'd gone fishing on a boat and fallen overboard, and a big shark ate him. All the boys talked about it for days, and the story eventually included details regarding the boy's limbs, in pieces, retrieved from the shark's belly a week later.

Mr. McKee smiled. "Well, son, we're pretty lucky here. Gators don't much like these salty rivers. You've got to watch for them in the ponds, like that little pond over on Ashdale. But they don't show up here much. Just once in a blue moon."

I tried to imagine a moon gone blue.

We both watched our lines in the water.

"Do you know what a shark looks like?" Mr. McKee asked.

"No sir."

"Would you like to see one?"

I pondered that. *Close enough to see one is close enough to get eaten.*

"Not today," I answered, trying to sound brave. And just then the pier shook, and we heard a piercing, screeching cry and turned and saw the tail of a small deer being dragged into the water by an alligator on the water's edge under the pier. The collective weight of both animals collided with the pier's post again.

Twice the gator and deer surfaced, and then the water under the pier grew still.

That evening after sunset, I looked into the sky, and watched for a moon gone blue.

# CHAPTER 4

Jane McKee didn't want to disappoint her husband with another girl. After another year of Henry's determined efforts, she was expecting again.

Mr. McKee's desire for a boy had grown, rather than diminished, as if mirroring his growing affection toward me. "Such a smart and inquisitive and charming boy," Henry often noted to Jane, George and others.

Mrs. McKee wondered, on occasion, who my father could be. She shook her head, violently, when she wondered *that*. *Impossible.* And yet—Henry paid such attention to me, took such delight in our time together. He so wanted a son.

She swept the thought into a far corner of her mind and picked up her pen.

*January 17, 1844*

*Yesterday I went with Mrs. Fuller to the Beaufort Ladies' Society meeting, in the home of Mrs. Rhett. Such a grand and lovely house! Caroline never disappoints when she entertains, and this was as fine a tea as any ever hosted, here or anywhere, with cakes and biscuits of all variety, and all the ladies looking royal. We all know, of course, that Caroline practically sold her soul when she married Barnwell, and he's not even a true Rhett anyway. Still, it was a nice morning, and something to break the monotony.*

*Caroline invited a visitor, a Northerner, Mrs. Warner, to speak to the ladies and she was most interesting. She's a writer, from New York City, so of course her life is full of extraordinary people and events. She told us so many fascinating stories about her life in the city and her life as an author. She also suggested to us that we keep a diary, a record of the comings and goings of our lives. She says, with great gusto, "This will help you to notice life!" and that we'll find that our own lives, even here in little Beaufort, are also full of interesting people and events. I don't know about that. Nothing ever seems to happen here. South Carolina is so terribly slow and sleepy. But for some reason, I like her idea of "noticing life," so I've promised myself that I will keep a diary, for a while, at least.*

This new habit of keeping a diary intrigued Jane from the moment it was suggested. It had never occurred to her to record her observations and ideas and thoughts. Until then, in fact, she'd not pondered the possibility that she possessed her own observations and ideas and thoughts, but now that she recognized the activity of her mind and the world around her, she was eager to make note of it.

*What do I think?* She dipped the nib into the ink. She'd had to ask Mr. McKee for a pen to use, and when she explained why she wanted it, he'd smiled, amused.

"What will you write, though? It's not as if the household needs to be documented!"

"Well, perhaps I'll notice something interesting, or curious. Perhaps I'll record my ideas."

Now, sitting at the little mahogany desk at the window of the upstairs bedroom, she paused. *What* do *I think?* She found it easier in the beginning to write about the people she'd encountered or the places she'd been during the day.

As the pregnancy progressed, she discovered questions that seemed to grow along with her unborn child, and most of her questions needed to be kept close to her own heart; most never even made it onto the paper. She wondered—and worried—about her ability to be a wife and mother.

Only seventeen when she married Henry, she was fortunate in that she liked the man, eight years her senior. She knew that wasn't the case for everyone. And she liked the little world in which they lived. Henry was prosperous, and though they weren't as affluent as the Rhetts or other of their Beaufort neighbors, they lived in comfort and gentility.

But she wondered, sometimes, *Why do we have no choice in our lives? Why must our fathers and our husbands determine everything for us?* She could never bring herself to write these questions in her diary. They were too forbidden. And she had to confess; even if she were given the opportunity, she had no idea what she would choose for herself. Perhaps they were right, fathers and husbands and preachers. Perhaps the men were ordained to be the heads of the households and the heads of the social structures.

She read her Bible occasionally now, more than she'd read it before, and found that, although she'd been told it held the answers, it provoked more questions still. *Who is made in the image of God? Who are the faithful sheep that feed the hungry and liberate the captive? And who is this God who flooded the earth, ordered wars, demanded that a father sacrifice a son?* As the tiny life grew slowly within her, the questions swelled with it.

Some days, the questions swarmed, bothersome and aggravating, and she had to swat them away like mosquitos on a summer day.

As the pregnancy progressed, the young mother grew ill, and

then gravely ill. She was frightened, and wondered if her husband was more concerned about having a son than a healthy wife. Sometimes she wondered how he felt about Lydia and her boy, Robert Henry, and she dreamed occasionally, when she had taken the laudanum, of the little boy sitting on Henry's lap and calling him *Papa*. She knew it was ludicrous to wonder. Lydia was almost twice Henry's age. But Jane also knew that it was not infrequent. She swatted the thoughts away again, and eventually they quit coming back.

Near the end of the pregnancy, the thoughts and ideas and questions and mysteries of life grew, and she began to recognize the substance and power, if not the beauty, of her own mind.

*March 2, 1844*

> *Our little Liza Beth turns five tomorrow, and she is becoming quite the handful. She reminds me of her auntie Elizabeth, my own stubborn and beautiful little sister. They're both so headstrong and willful. And Liza Beth looks so much like Elizabeth, too, with those dark curls and big eyes. She's got her father's inquisitive nature, and if it weren't for Lydia, I just don't know what I'd do. Lydia's own boy, Trouble—well, his name is Robert, but everyone calls him Trouble—he's only a month younger than Liza Beth, and he's certainly curious himself. He's earned his name, that's sure enough. He's a good boy generally, especially for a colored child, and if he weren't a darkie, he'd be a clever child, I do believe.*
>
> *I'm so pleased that our Lydia has experience with children. She seems to know just what to do with Trouble in every circumstance, and is teaching him to be a little gentleman, even insisting that he learn to speak properly. And though I'd never ask for her advice, I do find myself watching her as I struggle to manage Liza Beth. Just last week, Liza Beth fussed through*

*the night, flailing and screaming with night terrors, and Lydia settled her right down. I'd have no rest at all without Lydia.*

*April 7, 1844*

*Desperately ill for days now . . . cannot stomach any food, and growing weak. Henry has called for Dr. Johnson. Lydia is caring for Liza Beth.*

*April 12, 1844*

*Dr. Johnson has provided laudanum and assures me that the morning sickness should subside in a few more days. I fear I'm failing to "notice life" in this condition, even though it's the creation of life causing such misery.*

*October*

*I do not know today's date, but I know it is Sunday. The bells at St. Helena's have rung and I hear the sounds of carriages, and people conversing, and sometimes a bit of singing. This gives me some reassurance that the world is going on, even though I've not been part of it for quite a while now. Thankfully, the horrible sickness has passed, but Dr. Johnson insists that I remain in bed. I am dreadfully bored, and am struggling to "notice life!" and put it in my little diary here. I am, however, noticing the life growing in my womb, and find the small pinches and kicks a source of joy.*

*November 3, 1844*

*Have been in bed now for 7 weeks, and preparing for the worst. Dr. Johnson says this child may come any day now, and will be far too small to survive. Caroline Rhett came to call yesterday, and told me that she had had a difficult expectancy a few years ago, and was praying fervently for me. She has seven children; I wonder how difficult her pregnancies could have been! It seems that everything comes easily for her. Henry and the doctor are in the hallway, but I can't hear what they're saying, and I am frightened.*

*Caroline and some of the other ladies have been visiting frequently, trying to soothe and distract me with news and gossip. I learned today that Mrs. Fuller still finds Beaufort "backwards and dull," according to Mrs. French. And yesterday, I was informed that Mrs. French is cold and "very reserved, terribly reserved," according to Mrs. Fuller. I don't know what to make of either of them. Rev. Fuller is as popular as any man has ever been here in the Beaufort Baptist pulpit, and Rev. French is as warm and kind as any clergyman I've ever met. They both make it tempting to leave our traditional Episcopal pew, though I'm sure Henry would never consider it. And besides, those Methodists of Rev. French's flock are a bit tedious with their insistence on caring for the poor.*

*December 5, 1844*

*Our little one arrived two days ago, and while he's terribly small, he is also terribly loud and strong. Dr. Johnson said he expects little Henry—we're going to call him Hank—to be just fine. Oh, such relief! My tears of pain and fear have become tears of joy and my spirits are rapidly lifting. My Henry has been so strong, but I see his fatigue over these past weeks, and today I see his relief. He's delighted, and a bit impressed with himself, to have the son he's so long wished for. Oh, my hopes for our little Hank, oh my prayers.*

# CHAPTER 5

"Trouble!"

Liza Beth, bossy and curious, summoned me to the back porch to announce that she was going to be a big sister. She stood on the top step, hands on her hips, and looked down at me. "We're having a baby. And I will always be older and bigger!"

Always full of sound and drama, she was. Mama said she was born that way. The gentility of both her parents seemed to have eluded her. She waited for the arrival impatiently, ready to assert her newfound status.

Finally, after long weeks of concern and Liza Beth's nagging, Mr. McKee emerged from the house, smiling and laughing with Dr. Johnson.

"Henry, that boy announced his arrival with all the vigor of babies twice his size! I expect him to do just fine. But if anything troubles you or Mrs. McKee, you send for me, right away."

"Thank you, Doctor! I can't tell you what a relief I feel. And Jane, too. We're mighty grateful to you."

"Well, you both get a little rest now, and I'll drop back by in a week or so. Just watch, like I said, for any sudden changes."

My own relief was unspeakable. I jumped and laughed and clapped my hands, and while I knew that it was not the case, I felt in my heart that this new baby was my brother—my very own brother—and that I had a chance to be protective and brave. I resolved to be the finest brother this or any baby could possibly know.

Sitting on the back steps, waiting for Mama, I wondered what the new baby was like. *How little is he? What does he look like?*

And then I wondered: *How in the world did that baby happen?* This question had not previously occurred to me, but now it seemed to be the most urgent mystery. *How did that child get into Mrs. McKee? And how did he get out?*

*   *   *

Henry Howard McKee arrived the winter before Liza Beth and I turned six. Everything about little Hank was sweet. He was born small, and though he was healthy, I always thought of him as delicate.

I remember only fragments of days and moments from that season of his arrival. Mrs. McKee spent weeks in her room before Hank was born, and more weeks afterwards, and it seemed like everyone tiptoed and whispered. Mr. McKee was quiet and didn't smile much; he would go into the room for a bit, and then come out looking a little lost. Mama stayed in the room long hours at a time.

One day a few weeks before Hank's birth, I overheard Mama talking to Liza Beth. They were in the kitchen, and I was outside, just under the kitchen window, snapping peas.

"Babies are hard work, child. That's why your mama needs to rest so much."

"But doesn't she know that I need her too? How can she just lie there like that?"

"Honey, someday you'll know all about babies. Till then, just trust Lydia. Your mama, she doin hard work just lyin there."

Liza Beth was quiet for a few minutes before she asked, "Lydia, how many babies have you had?"

It was quiet again, and then I heard Mama's voice, low. "I've birthed three babies, honey. One's just about grown now, and one's in heaven, and Trouble's my baby boy."

*What? Mama? Other children?* She'd never told me this. *A grown child? A sister or a brother that I never heard about?*

*And one in heaven?*

*Why? How?*

I thought about my mother's tenderness, the way she spoke to me, the way she held me. I imagined her holding an infant, rocking, nursing, singing. *A dead baby.* That thought undid me; hot tears ran down my face and I doubled over sobbing.

The kitchen door opened, and I looked up to see Mama, with Liza Beth standing behind her. Mama's face showed her surprise.

"What in the world you cryin bout, son?"

"You got a baby in heaven, Mama. A baby in heaven."

"Oh, honey, that was a long time ago. I shoulda told you bout that little angel."

I couldn't breathe; the sudden weight of my own heart terrified me. *How could Mama endure such a thing?* She was without doubt the strongest and most capable human being I knew, but she was first a mother, and I knew the depth of her tenderness and the power of her love. I couldn't imagine the hole of sadness within her.

For the first time, I tasted the flavor of helplessness. I'd failed to prevent that baby's death or my mother's loss. I'd borne none of the weight of such grief. I resolved in that naïve way that children make resolutions to never let such a thing happen again, not to Mama, or to Mrs. McKee, and not to my baby brother Hank.

Each evening, I fell asleep beseeching the God of Beaufort Baptist Church to protect all three. Surely, my concern and my prayers and my vigilance would be adequately resolute and robust. Surely my steadfastness would safeguard this baby, even if I had failed my mama and the infant she'd grieved.

* * *

George and I walked out to the chicken coop for eggs. He was always *Uncle* to me; all the adults were auntie or uncle.

In the house and around the McKees we spoke "white." The McKees expected it, and Mama insisted. But alone and around the barn we used a lot of Gullah, the language our folk brought from Africa. *Biddy* meant chicken; we called a turtle *coota*; when we said *buckra*, we meant the white man.

"Uncle George, how do eggs get into biddies?"

He looked at me like I'd asked him to lay an egg himself.

"What dat, son?"

"How do those eggs get in there? And how do they get out?"

"Lawd. What's it matter? Dey give us eggs ever day. Dat what matter."

"But how? I know you know."

He stopped walking and grinned down at me and shook his head. "Lawd, boy. Well, I guess they got some tiny little eggs—like little seeds—in there, and then someday they get big and they jus come out."

My memories of George begin with the distinctively pleasant aromatic blend of tobacco, horse, leather, and sweat. To this day, when I step into a barn, I think of him. He spent most of his days in and around the barn, or with the horses or wagons, or over on Ashdale with the field livestock. I don't know what Mr. McKee would have done without George, who seemed to be able to fix anything, animal or machine. He did his work quietly and unhurried. His patience with the animals was infinite; his patience with children was generous; his patience with the McKees was gracious; and his patience with the folks in town was reserved.

George seldom spoke in past tense. I knew he'd belonged to the McKee family since his own childhood but never heard him talk about people or events. He watched out for Mama and me as if we were his own kin, and many years passed before I understood why.

"Uncle George, tell me! How do babies get into mamas?"

George stopped and looked me right in the eyes.

"Well now, you gittin to be a big boy and full o questions. And I guess you got a right to know; you gonna need to know someday." He paused and flashed one of his rare smiles.

"Well," he said. It seemed to me he was hunting for words. "You know how sometime that ol rooster jump around and play with those hens?"

"Uh huh."

"Well, when they playing like that, that ol rooster, he's helpin that ol hen make those eggs hatch."

"Uh huh," I said, but I had no idea what he was talking about.

"And that's kind of how it work with people; a rooster and a hen play a little bit and a good egg'll hatch one day."

We got ourselves a basketful of eggs and headed back to the kitchen.

"Uncle George, does it hurt?"

This time he didn't look at me at all. But I heard the grin in his voice.

"No, son. No, it don't hurt one bit."

# CHAPTER 6

## WINTER, 1845

Liza Beth's response to the arrival of little Hank was mixed. The baby's presence both fed and threatened her remarkable appetite for attention.

As I wasn't allowed in the house, I had no opportunity to see the child I'd worried over. Mama assured me that I'd have plenty of time with him soon enough.

Meanwhile, there was much to do and see in and around the barn and yard with George. The oldest of the mares had recently foaled twins, increasing my curiosity about how baby animals got in and out of their mothers. The new foals were endlessly entertaining, awkward, skittering and dancy on their skinny legs.

We'd had foxes in the chicken pen too, and the bloody mess they left behind was fascinating to me. I'd seen animals butchered for meat, and I'd seen Mama break a chicken's neck, but the raw mess of scattered, bloody feathers, broken eggs, and pulled-apart bones was new and thrilling to me. I was drawn to the savagery and wondered what it was like for the foxes. Did they feel powerful and bold?

Liza Beth came out of the house as I was coming toward it. "What are you doing?" she asked.

"You have to come see," I said, "but you might not like it. It's not for girls."

She took the challenge and went with me to the pen. A faint aroma of fresh blood and flesh floated toward us before we turned into the gate. With the carnage in full view, she stopped and gasped. And vomited.

I thought she'd be angry at me, or upset by the gore, but after she emptied her belly, she wiped her mouth and looked at me with wide eyes.

"Oh! Oh, look at that. Those foxes! Look, Trouble!"

She walked into the pen and among the bits of chicken as if inspecting a battlefield. Her capacity to appreciate this surprised and impressed me. A great deal of time and energy was being invested in the construction of her gentility, but it seemed she resonated more with the appetite of the fox than the domestication of the hen.

"Do you think they eat them while they're still alive?" she asked.

I hadn't thought of that. I wished I had.

\* \* \*

Mama called me to go with her to the market, pulling me away from the henhouse and its gory intrigue. We finished the shopping and began the short walk back to the house, carrying coffee and tea, flour and beans. The towering live oaks draped in Spanish moss on both sides of the lane touched overhead. A blanket of tiny green leaves covered the brick walls along the way. "Resurrection fern," Mama called it.

We rounded the corner onto Carteret Street and saw an agitated crowd, men mostly, gathered around the whipping tree.

*Wuh-psssh!*

"Aahnng!"

The whip, the scream. Again and again. The whip. The scream. The whip, the scream. The whip the scream.

Whippings weren't uncommon in Beaufort, but they weren't daily either, and they always drew the attention of folks on the street. Owners believed they served as a warning to disobedient or stubborn slaves. By being present, the enslaved stood in solidarity with the suffering.

Mama and I stopped, and I tried to see past the people in front of me. I heard the cries and the screams, and the voice sounded familiar. And then I saw—it was Indie. I'd not seen her in weeks. A wisp of a girl, she was tied with her arms stretched around the old live oak, her right cheek pressed up against its trunk, the flesh of her back exposed and already striped with blood. Indie, my friend. I'd seen grown men whipped and beat. I'd seen men and women in the stocks, even. But Indie was just a girl—helpless.

I pushed into the crowd. "Indie! Indie!" Four white hands grabbed me by the arms and shoulders and threw me to the ground. I kicked at the legs, thrashed against their boots.

"Stop it! Stop it! You're hurting her!" The man swinging the whip turned from the bloody child and raised it again, this time at me.

*Wuh-psssh!* Across my shoulder. *Wuh-pusssh!* Searing sting, the warm blood, the scent of manure, the weight of the boot still on my neck.

"Enough!" Henry McKee's voice. "That boy belongs to me. I'll take care of it from here."

"Better teach the little shit his place, McKee," a man snarled.

"Better mind your own damn business, Rhett," McKee replied, grabbing me by the wrist and yanking me to my feet. "Let's go, boy."

\* \* \*

When we got home, Mama spoke finally, quietly.

"Moses," she said. "Son, you need to know about Moses."

I didn't understand; I was thinking about Indie, and how I was glad her face was turned away from me so she couldn't see that I saw.

"That be your story, son. Moses."

# CHAPTER 7

## 1846

Some weeks after Peter Rhett turned seven, Barnwell Rhett summoned his fifth son the same way he called his dogs. "Let's go, son!" he said, slapping his leg. It was never a question, or an invitation, always a command. Peter followed him, like a puppy hungry for attention and trying to keep up, along the long wooden dock on the river.

The Rhett house faced the water to catch the breezes, and looked out to the dock, built long to accommodate the rise and fall of the tides, where his father's new boat waited. As they neared, Peter seemed to study me and Mr. McKee.

Peter watched me sometimes when my mother and Mrs. McKee lingered talking in the street or at one of their gates. I noticed how Peter observed Liza Beth and me—how we laughed and played and fussed almost like siblings. Even then, it was obvious Liza Beth McKee was the song of his heart.

The Rhetts stepped onto the new boat, the father barking at the son to sit down, touch nothing, pay attention. The elder Rhett had commissioned the boat to be built up in Charleston, where he spent most of his days running the newspaper, and where he kept a much bigger house and boat. The Beaufort place served as a vacation house, and a place to keep Mrs. Rhett and the seven children out of his way.

Peter did as told; he sat, touched nothing, paid attention, and watched Mr. McKee and me step into the boat. He appeared surprised that his father let a slave boy on, but apparently both adults were all right with it. I watched everything, said nothing, and sat on the port side, a little removed from the rest of them.

"She's a beauty, Barney!" Mr. McKee humored Peter's father, turning slowly around in the boat and whistling. "A real beauty!"

"Just like the big one in Charleston," Rhett said, "exactly half the size. I think she'll do here. Shallow draft, perfect for the tide changes. We'll see if she can find the fish."

Peter's father considered himself a fisherman, despite his lack of success. Never encumbered by patience or logic, Mr. Rhett expected the fish to come to him, the way his dogs and children did when ordered. Mr. McKee, on the other hand, had a reputation as a fine fisherman, and hunter, too. His task today was to guide them to successful fishing and make Barnwell Rhett believe himself an angler.

The morning mist, just lifting, gave way to that soft early light that artists struggle to capture on canvas. Decades later, Peter would acquire one of those fine paintings, but at the time, he took the magic morning light for granted. So many things, he assumed, just *were*. And would always *be*.

Mr. McKee made fishing look easy, elegant. He baited and cast effortlessly, showed Peter and me how to hold the hook, how to toss the line, how to watch. He mitigated Peter's father's clumsiness as far as that was possible, and by late morning we'd all had a fine day and stepped off the new boat with several meals for both households. Peter's father had done most of the talking, but Peter was most attentive to Mr. McKee's repartee. Peter, of course, spoke only when addressed, and I, feeling the heat of his hostility, never said a word.

I pretended not to listen to the men's conversation.

"I've had another damn runaway, Henry. I just don't understand 'em."

"Just the price of doing business, Barney. It's been a long time since that last one."

"I thought that'd be the last one, ever. Seems like a good hangin' should send the message."

"They forget, I guess."

*Hanging? Who hung who?*

*       *       *

When they got back to the house, Peter took a deep breath and, at last, mustered the courage to ask a question.

"Father, did you hang that man?"

"What man, son?"

"The man you talked about on the boat—the one who ran away."

"Oh, that! No, son, he wasn't a man; he was a slave." He laughed at his son's naiveté.

"Did you hang him yourself?"

"No, of course not. The constable hung him. But I'm the one that made it happen. Son, in this life, you've got to be the one to make things happen, or the things will happen to you."

They'd gone into the library at the front of the house with its book-lined walls. Peter's father got up from his desk, where he'd been making notes. He was always writing down some idea or another. He strode to a shelf that held a dark wooden box, shiny from age, with a brass latch and pulled out a small, flat metal square. It had a hole punched in one corner, with a leather cord pulled through, and some letters and numbers stamped on it: *CHARLESTON 479 FARRIER*. Underneath that: *RUBEN*.

"That was his tag when I bought him. Look here . . . says *Ruben*. I guess that must've been his name. I never can remember all their names. And this—" He pointed at the number, above more lettering. "This is his number—479—and says he was a farrier. That's why I bought him; needed a good blacksmith and Charleston always has the best."

In Charleston, slaves who were hired out by their owners were required to be registered every year, and to always wear their tags. It served as something of a tax receipt and identification, showing that the slave was authorized to work and to move around in town, within prescribed hours and locations.

Peter turned the tag over in his hands, felt the edges worn smooth.

"You can have it if you want," his father said. "No use for it now."

And he waved Peter out of the room.

# CHAPTER 8

## BEAUFORT, 1847

Unlike Liza Beth, I found Hank to be a great deal more interesting and fun as he got older and more mobile. Curious and busy, always touching what he was told not to touch, constantly exploring where he was told not to go, he kept his mother busy. By the time he was three, Liza Beth complained that he no longer acted like a baby.

Mrs. McKee grew exhausted and frustrated, trying to keep up with Hank and run the household. She had yet another baby on the way. She leaned on Mama but soon realized that if Mama was watching Hank, too many domestic tasks went neglected. So, I was enlisted to do what I'd secretly hoped for—to watch after Hank, to be "in charge" of him.

It was an odd arrangement. Looking after a busy three-year-old was quite a lot of responsibility, and I was eager to accept it. It was complicated, of course, because I was his slave and he began to learn that he had power over me. But he was a sweet boy, and good-natured, and I wanted so badly to be a big brother to him that I welcomed the duty.

It was easy. Hank adored me and I adored him. He loved to follow me everywhere, and I loved that he wanted to. We both believed the arrangement to be to our own advantage. I wanted to be essential in the McKee household and sought to be esteemed— even if only by a toddler. I took my role seriously and watched after the little boy with both attention and affection. The role of guardian gave me extended access in and around the household and the community.

* * *

Our neighbors on Prince Street included the Dukes and the Johnsons and, over on Craven Street, the Rhetts. The Dukes owned my friend Indie, about my age; their boys and those owned by the Rhetts were sent to the fields young. Sometimes Liza Beth and I would take Hank in his wagon and find Indie, and we'd play through the mornings, almost oblivious to the realities beyond us. But I understood, even then, that while we all inhabited the same town, we lived in separate worlds. If not for Mr. McKee's affection, I too might be in the fields.

One evening, after supper, I went back outside with Liza Beth and we played in the yard while Mama bathed Hank and put him to bed. It was spring, with the days growing longer. We decided to go find Indie for a game of tag in the evening shadows.

"You know you ain't s'posed to be out runnin roun after dusk!" Indie's mama fixed a stare on me, and we sprinted down the street. Of course, I knew about the curfew, but it made no sense to me.

I ran ahead of Liza Beth to hide behind a big oak and I waited there to jump out and scare her. When I heard her footsteps, I threw myself out, hands waving, and yelled, "The haint gonna get you! The haint gonna get you!"

Her eyes flew wide and her hand covered her mouth, and I saw she was looking not at me but past me. I felt two massive hands on my shoulders.

"Boy, you gonna wish it was a haint. Let's go."

I recognized the growling voice of the deputy constable, and smelled the bitter tobacco on his rough, heavy hands.

"You get on home, now, miss," he snarled at Liza Beth. "This boy's coming with me."

His huge fist clutched my neck and I struggled to keep up with his long strides as he dragged me down the street. When we got to the jail, he shoved me in, and when I hit the floor his hard boot slammed against my ribs.

"You nigger boys think you can break curfew? Not on my watch." He banged the cell door shut, and I lay on the cold floor.

I tried to sit up and vomited from the pain and fear. I leaned into the corner of the cell and closed my eyes.

Mr. McKee's voice drew me from my fog of aching agony.

"Trouble. Trouble!"

I tried to focus, but I saw two of him.

"Trouble, get up. Let's go."

He pulled me to my feet, and the pain stabbed through me, but I refused to cry or moan.

"I've told you, boy. How many times have I told you? You've got to come home at dusk." His voice was neither scolding nor warm, and I wondered if he was concerned or simply annoyed. Maybe embarrassed.

\* \* \*

While Liza Beth and Peter and the others went to school every day, I began taking on more serious chores around the house and barn, and I didn't see Indie very often after that.

Sometimes little Hank and I would find things to do together. We both were drawn to animals. I preferred the horses and mules and cows, while Hank prized the small and furry creatures—the bunnies that snuck into the garden, our fat old housecat, Missy, and the countless kittens she produced, the squirrels that played and stole the pecans right out of the trees. Little Hank, he even liked the mice that nested in the barn.

I took Hank along with me most mornings to gather eggs or to carry firewood for Mama, or to help George in the barn. We especially liked the barn, full of animals and smells and tools, ladders to climb, wagons to play on and in and under. And we both relished being with George. He seemed to understand everything young boys were curious about, and he was capable of fixing anything. Neither father nor brother nor preacher nor police intrigued or instructed, captivated or corrected two boys as completely as George. Despite his efforts to deny and hide it, he adored us too. Our curiosity and laughter added a kind of light and music to his dark, sad days.

Hank's affinity for small creatures demanded attentiveness, and George taught me what to watch for.

"Careful, now, when you in da hay. Mice won't hurt none, but da rat can bite, and da snake can bite bad." He taught me to keep Hank out of dark corners or deep hay, how to redirect the little boy's attention and energy, and how to appreciate the safer wild creatures.

Hank liked rabbits best. "Bunny!" he'd shout when he spotted one on the edge of the garden, or in a neighbor's yard. I made a game of it, and each day we'd count bunnies, looking for them everywhere we went, trying to spot and count more than the day before.

"Uncle George," I pleaded, "could we build a little rabbit pen for Hank? I could help him find some rabbits and teach him to take care of them."

"Ain't right to pen up a wild thing, son."

"But they're not really wild. And he'll lose interest after a while, and we can let em loose. Please, Uncle George."

George said no to me, but Hank came to him, crying. We began building the pen the next day.

The construction of the pen consumed all three of us. George measured, cut, and nailed the frame while I tried to help. Hank counted nails and dreamed up names for his bunnies.

"Uncle George, you ever heard of the exodus?" I asked, while I held a board for him to cut.

"Why you askin, son?" George was seldom surprised anymore by my questions. They seemed to come out of me from every direction and with no warning, like the horseflies in the barn and apparently just as annoying.

"Heard the preacher talkin bout exodus and Moses, but I don't know what happened. Mama said ask you."

"Your mama know as much as I do." George paused while he nailed a corner tight. My mama was wise and knew that sometimes a boy would listen to a man better than he'd listen to his own mother.

I waited. Always seemed like the more something needed to be said, the longer George hesitated to say it. When he spoke, I knew to listen hard.

"Well, now. Let's see . . . First off, they say it happened long time ago. Egypt. You know where Egypt is?"

"No sir."

"I reckon I don' know neither. Somewhere yonder, somewhere farther even than where our folk come from, way cross Africa." He straightened up and stretched and wiped the sweat from his eyes. "Guess it's hot there too, like here."

"But what happened?"

"Well, now, those Egyptians had the Hebrews a-workin for em. Slaves. Bout like us. Ol Moses, he was one a them Hebrews, but he weren't no slave boy. He had it pretty good in the masser's house. Jus like he was parta the family or somethin." George paused again. "I ain't rememberin how that came to be.

"Anyhoo, Moses, he grow up, an he see a Gyptian beat down one a them Hebrew slaves, an he think, 'Now wait a minute here, that slave be one a my people,' and it make him real mad, and he beat that Gyptian bad."

I liked that. "Good!"

"Well, now, not so good. He beat that fella so bad he die, and ol Moses have to run and hide."

That made no sense to me. "But the Gyptian was the bad one! Moses oughten not have to hide!"

George exhaled. He looked up into the top of the magnolia tree, as if the answer were resting there. "Thing is, son, sometime a man do the right thing, and he gotta run for his life."

"Where'd he go? What happened?"

"He went off somewhere, long place off, for a long time. Tried to jus forget about it, and jus live a quiet kinda life. But sometime that don't work neither." He let me ponder a minute. Hank had climbed into my lap, sleepy.

I whispered. "What happened?"

"This part's kinda confusin, but Moses was jus mindin his own bidness, and a tree started burnin, and when he went to see about it—" George had warmed up his story-telling heart and found his dramatic rhythm. "God spoke up."

I'd never heard George say such a thing. *Is he serious?*

"Moses!" George bellowed. He startled me, and Hank's head popped up, and I settled him back down.

"God say, 'Moses, you gotta go help the rest a them Hebrews get outta there!'

"But Moses say, 'I don think I can do that.'

"An God say, 'Who you think you talkin to? Now git on up and go take care a all them.'"

I whispered again. "Did he? Did he go help em?"

"Well now, I guess it depend on who you talk to. Finally, he did get em all outta Egypt. But then they was all lost for a awful long time. And some of em didn't like it one little bit. Things was real bad for everbody."

I sat quiet, and let that sink in.

George sat on a barn stool and looked at the hammer in his

hand as he spoke. "Jus member, son. Sometime you do the right thing, and nothin good'll come of it. Cept you know it's the right thing. Sometime you do the hard thing, and nobody preciate it. But it got done. Some folk'll tell you, mind your own bidness and watch out for your own self. Some folk'll say watch out for the other ones, help em get outta Egypt."

"What do you say, Uncle George?"

Hank slept peacefully in my lap. Mosquitos buzzed around us, and I waved them away.

"I dunno, son. I guess ever man got to find his own best way . . . I jus dunno."

When we finished the pen, Mr. McKee helped us capture our rabbits. Hank named his Benjamin. I named mine Moses.

Hank and I were close as could be, and when Mrs. McKee said they be gone a spell to visit family in New Orleans, I knew I'd miss that little boy.

*Jane McKee's Diary*

*November 7, 1847*

*Yellow fever. My God, of all the things that could happen. Mother is desperately ill, and Elizabeth too, and her sweet boy James. I'm confident that Elizabeth and Mother will be fine, but poor James, only five and now so frail.*

*We'd been told that the threat had passed, that the folks along the Mississippi and especially in New Orleans were in jeopardy, but not here. It's simply awful. I do believe half the town is ill. No one is out on the streets, thank goodness. Apparently only the mosquitos are thriving.*

*November 22, 1847*

*This morning we said our final goodbyes to little James, and to Mother.*

*November 27, 1847*

*My greatest fear—little Hank burns with fever this morning. Dr. Johnson has been called, and the rector from St. Helena's—I can't bear to see him so listless and pale.*

*November 28, 1847*

*Dr. Johnson tells us to pray for the best, and prepare for the worst. The rector tells us to pray regardless, and trust God in all things. My heart tells me to hold on to hope. Hankie seems improved today. Is that just wishful thinking? Perhaps God listens to a mother's pleas . . .*

*December 1, 1847*

*I'm relieved beyond words. Our Hank is fine, and recovering his strength by the hour. Thank God. And yet, I find my heart full of questions and doubt. How, why did God not let sweet James survive? How am I to console my sister? She prayed for her child, as I did for mine. How will she feel when she sees little Hank, as she longs for her boy? The rector tells me all things are God's will, but how? How can God will one mother to embrace her child, and another to bury hers? What kind of God is that? And what kind of Christian am I to ask such questions? May God forgive my dark and doubting heart!*

# CHAPTER 9

## SUMMER, 1848

From the yard I could just see and hear Mr. McKee, and I tried to look busy with the rabbit pen as I listened. He finished his coffee, pushed back his chair, and looked out the back window. "Good day for a ride."

Jane McKee was silent. There were no good days, even in the spring, even when the azalea bloomed. Her grief hung everywhere, like the moss on the trees.

"I think I'll take Trouble with me today. He should be learning the horses now."

"Another day with Trouble. Why must you spend so much time with that boy? And, Henry, we should quit calling him Trouble. He'll live into it if we're not careful."

"His mama called him that before we did, Jane. He's earned it, that's for sure. He's nosier than a puppy." Henry walked out into the yard and called me. "Trouble! Let's go, boy. It's time to saddle up."

I'd waited so long, wondering if he'd take me along one day. "Mama! I'm gonna ride today!"

"Son, you listen to Mr. Henry. What he tell you to do, you do that. And you listen to Uncle George, and you watch him. That man, he knows his horses. You watch him."

"Yes, Mama."

"Old George, he ain't got much need for folks, but he sure love his horses and his dogs. You watch him now," Mama said. I sensed her gratitude for both Mr. McKee's affection for us and for George's unwavering concern and commitment to us; both served as a kind of protection. Mr. McKee gave me both attention and skills, and George watched me with a ferocious loyalty, determined to protect me, and keenly aware of the difficulty in doing so.

"Yes, Mama!" I flew out the door and into the yard, eager as a colt, and ran to the side fence where Mr. McKee was tightening a boot buckle.

"Trouble, do you think you can handle a horse?'

"Yessir, Mr. McKee, yessir."

He chuckled. "We'll see." He told me, years later, that he'd learned when he was a boy himself that the character of a man was never more transparent than in the treatment of an animal, a woman, or a servant.

\* \* \*

George Jackson's stable. Everyone called it George Jackson's stable. And everyone knew that George Jackson's stable, like George Jackson himself, was Henry McKee's property. But George ran the stable with such pride, and handled the horses and mules with such care, and provoked the envy of so many others, that they all referred to it as George Jackson's stable. It was home to Beaufort County's finest horses and mules, and no one knew that with more certainty than George Jackson himself, though he'd be the last man to say it.

I'd watched George handle every one of these animals almost every day of my life. I watched him measure the grain and the hay and carry it to the trough for the draft horses, and to the stalls for

McKee's geldings and his prized mares and the fiery stud. I'd peered through the barn door the morning that George helped Annie, the oldest mare, drop her twin foals, and I'd watched again when Mazie foaled a stillborn. George cried silently at every birth, and the whole household sensed his pain when an animal had to be put down.

I followed Mr. McKee to the barn where we found George bridling McKee's favorite mare. A thoroughbred from Kentucky, Lexi was a big bay, almost sixteen hands, and though she'd produced half a dozen foals, she had the heart and strength of a three-year-old.

"We'll put you on Mazie," George said to me, without taking his eyes off Lexi. Mazie was short and round and gentle. George called her a Marsh Tacky, and she would teach every child in the McKee household how to sit a horse, simply by being a smart and reliable old mare. She stood patiently as George slipped the bridle on and then took it off again so that I could do it on my own.

"Just slip it up over those ears. That's right, hold the bit just so in your left hand, let her open up and she'll take it in her mouth."

George picked a saddle from the rack and carried it on his hip over to Mazie, then swung it up onto her back.

"Right here," he said, making room for me beside him at Mazie's left shoulder. "Stand right here and show me how to tighten this cinch." George smiled, knowing that I'd watched this routine hundreds of times and knew exactly where to stand and what to do.

"That's it." George nodded approvingly as I tugged the cinch once, then again, then waited for Mazie to give a big exhale before tugging once more. I pulled the cinch down, then across the buckle, and slipped the end under the saddle strap.

George gave Mr. McKee a leg up onto Lexi, then did the same for me on Mazie. The patient old horse shifted her weight and let me adjust to the new sensation of muscle moving beneath me.

"How does that feel, boy?" asked McKee.

"Fine, sir, just fine."

"We'll start out easy and take the path down along the Point. It's nice and flat. Just let her have her head there."

\* \* \*

We left the yard, turned left onto Prince Street, and the horses clopped lazily toward the Point, winding along the river's edge. Mazie had a gentle, rolling gait, easy enough for me to learn.

The path narrowed along the curve of the riverbank, smooth and fragrant under the canopy of old oaks, and then opened into the soft marsh grasses.

"Watch for gators, now. Snakes too," McKee said.

I knew how to watch for the cottonmouth, its blocky head and thick, dark-banded body. And I knew how to spot a gator, too. A small one could kill a dog or a boy. A large one could bring down a deer or horse. I'd heard terrifying stories about alligators and water moccasins both; every child in Beaufort knew they could strike unprovoked, fierce and deadly. Every family possessed a legend of the death of a favorite dog or horse or child. I watched, especially where grass and water met, for the slightest subtle quiver, ever alert for the silent threat.

George rode with us, easy and elegant as if he'd been born on a horse. Like all good horsemen, he could feel the animal's energy and he imparted his own to the horse. He knew how to give a horse what it needed and how to coax the best from the beast.

Today, he wanted Mazie to teach me how to ride, and he wanted to teach me how to trust and respect the horse. A boy who could learn to respect the strength and power of a dumb beast would grow to be a man who knew to respect the strength and power of other men. And his own.

# CHAPTER 10

## 1848

When Liza Beth began leaving for school each day, Peter Rhett began showing up at the McKee gate with determined consistency. I was usually already in the barn, milking or feeding the chickens, but I kept my eyes and ears open.

"My father always says that you either make things happen, or someone else will make things happen to you," Peter had told Liza Beth. Peter was becoming like his father, demanding and brazen. I watched him once on the top steps of the front porch, one foot a step above the other, right hand on his hip, trying on his father's posture. Looked stiff to me, like living inside a wooden body. Those Rhetts always seemed to stomp around where you could walk just fine.

Peter had eyes for Liza Beth; no one could miss that. And he claimed her about every morning on his walk to Mrs. Chatham's schoolhouse. The McKee home wasn't directly on the way for Peter but close enough for him to pass through the iron gate with its obstinate latch to collect Liza Beth. At the top of the steps, he'd take a deep breath and knock on the front door and wait.

"Good morning, Miss McKee," he'd say with a smile and bow.

Sometimes Liza Beth rewarded him with a bright smile or a laugh, or a "Good morning." Sometimes she'd hand him a book to carry for her. Sometimes she ignored him altogether. Her inconsistency never affected his constancy.

At midday, when they returned from school, he'd open the gate for her, and she might or might not thank him, or smile, before running up the steps and into the house. They looked to be made for one another. Liza Beth, slender and pretty, with those big brown eyes and dark hair, and Peter, an inch or two taller, and shoulders growing broad, with his father's blue eyes and red hair—they were quite a pair.

On one warm October morning, I watched as Peter paused at the gate, bested the latch, whistled. But when the front door opened, it was Mr. McKee rather than Liza Beth.

"I'm sorry, son, but you're going to have to walk alone today. I'm afraid our girl is under the weather this morning."

"What's wrong with her, sir?" he asked.

"Oh, nothing serious. No need to worry."

"I wasn't worried."

"That's good, Peter. Off to school now."

Peter's smile evaporated, and he turned toward the street with downcast eyes, which landed on the neighbor's flower bed. Inspired, he was at the gate again, clutching a handful of lilies. He reached for the latch, pulled his hand away, then reached again. Maybe he was remembering, *Son, in this life, you've got to be the one to make things happen.* He opened the gate, took a deep breath, walked through. At the top of the steps, he took another deep breath, and knocked on the door. Mama opened the door and smiled.

"Well, lookee here."

"Could you give these to Liza Beth for me?"

"I'll see she gets em. Don't you need to get on to school now?"

He turned without speaking, stomped down the steps and slammed the gate behind him.

* * *

Liza Beth and I had learned just about everything we knew together. We'd learned how to throw a ball, and how to skip a flat rock on the water. Like puppies in the same litter, we chased squirrels and rabbits and cats. Mr. McKee taught us both how to tie a knot, to catch a fish, to watch for snakes. He showed us how to choose a perfect peach from the tree, and how to catch a lightning bug in our hands at dusk. Liza Beth and I, we'd taught each other how to snatch a piece of pie from the kitchen rack before our mothers ever saw us, how to climb the big oak behind the house, how to whistle with a blade of grass.

Now I watched as she read from the book in her lap. I listened in wonder as she slowly unveiled the story, as she transformed the spots of ink on the pages into an adventure for our ears and minds.

"Show me how to do that!" I insisted. "Show me!"

Liza Beth hesitated. Peter Rhett had just arrived, regular as sunrise. She didn't move from where she sat at the top of the front porch steps.

"We should go now," he said.

"Not yet. We have some time still." And she patted the step next to where she was sitting, so I sat.

"First," she began, "each one of the letters—these are all letters, see?—each one has a sound. See that one?" She pointed to the *S*. "It sounds like *ssss*."

It looked to me like the shape of a snake, so the sound made sense. "*Ssss*," I said.

"This one"—she pointed to a *T*—"that sounds like *ttt*, like the first sound of your name!" It was clear that this was fun for her.

"*Tt*," I made the sound. "Trouble!" *My name has its own letter!*

"Liza Beth, have you lost your mind?" Peter shouted. "You can't teach him to read!"

"Of course, I can, Peter. It's not that hard." She paused, but couldn't resist. "You're learning, aren't you?"

In one swift move, he leapt up the steps and grabbed the book from her. His face reddened, and his eyes turned cold.

"Of course I can read!" he hissed. "But not him. You can't teach them to read! It's bad enough the way you've taught him to talk!"

"Peter Rhett, give me my book!" She grasped for it, but he held the book the same way the Baptist preacher held his big black book on Sunday morning, arm stretched high, like a treasure, just out of reach. He pivoted toward me.

"Are you crazy?" he laughed. "Or are you just stupid? You can't read. You can't ever read."

The way he said "ever" meant "never."

It wasn't the first time Peter spoke sharp to me, but it was the first time I cared.

"Why?" I demanded. "Why can't I read?"

"Because you're a stupid negro boy, don't you know that? Don't you know that?" He was shouting again. *Neegro.* That's how the preacher said it, down at the church, like the word both explained and excused the way the world worked.

Then he looked at Liza Beth and little Hank, and I knew that he was parroting both his father and the school's teacher when I heard him say, "These *neegro* children may not read! It's against the law! You'll go to prison forever if you teach a nigger to read!" He put great emphasis on both *forever* and *nigger.*

The front door flew open. "What in God's name is going on here?" Mr. McKee demanded.

Peter threw the book down and stomped away.

"I'm sorry, Papa," Liza Beth said. "I was showing Trouble how to read, and Peter . . . he . . . he reminded me that I'm not supposed to do that."

She apologized to him, not to me.

That was the day I realized I was in a prison already.

I was nine years old then, I think, and that was the day I determined I would indeed learn to read.

I would learn to read, and I would learn to write, and I would learn to cipher numbers, and I would learn to be a man, a real man, a man who would come and go as he pleased, a man who had a little money in his pocket, a man who had some say in his world.

I would be a man. I would learn to read.

*   *   *

Not long after the Peter Rhett incident, I saw Mrs. McKee writing in her private book as she did every so often. I wondered about the secrets in there; I wished I had secrets I could put to pen, and a book to write in.

*Jane McKee's Diary*

*April 3, 1849*

> *It's been over a year now since Mother and little James passed, and I can't seem to move through the dark to find light anywhere at all. Last Sunday was Easter, and the rector spoke of resurrection and eternal life, but I feel as if their deaths have brought me eternal death.*

> *Hank asked me what "'surrection" meant, and for a moment, I thought he'd said "insurrection." It's on everyone's minds—well, not insurrection, of course, but secession. The men seem to talk of nothing else. Really, since Barnwell Rhett called them all together a few years ago, they talk of the Northern aggression constantly and I fear it may come to a true struggle. Henry is impatient with my questions, but I want to understand this situation. We've been blessed, clearly, but this*

*talk of our way of life being threatened—well, I don't know exactly what that means, but I know enough to know that it would be awful to lose it.*

# CHAPTER 11

## BEAUFORT, 1849

Every Sunday morning, the Reverend Richard Fuller strode across the front of the sanctuary and stepped into the pulpit of Beaufort Baptist Church, his authority flowing behind him like his black robe. He was certain of his place, certain of his position, and thoroughly certain of his power. Law school had instilled confidence and divinity school conviction, and as he stood before the congregation, he recalled the scripture "He looked upon them with compassion," and smiled.

Rev. Fuller was not a man given to humility, and he found quiet, but deep, satisfaction in likening himself to Jesus. He gazed upon the sanctuary of Beaufort Baptist Church as planters and businessmen and their families filled the pews on the main floor, while the balcony teemed with slaves—men and women, children, servants all. The church had long been home to both races, providing both a fragile social ballast and a thin veneer of balance when tensions flared.

Across the street at St. Helena's Episcopal, Dr. Joseph Walker processed solemnly behind the acolytes, down the center aisle of the stately sanctuary, and then climbed into the raised pulpit to call his flock—white and wealthy—to worship. Walker, noble and inspiring, had led the congregation and the entire town through a fine season of stirring revival, and, as is true in every era, the piety of the privileged shone bright. Sons of the American Revolution, planters and businessmen, the wealthiest and the most influential, gathered on Sundays, kneeling to pray, lifting their open and upturned hands to receive the Eucharist, bowing their heads in gratitude for their abundant blessings. These took seriously their role in preserving the fine reputation of their beloved community.

A few paces north, the Methodists came together in Wesley Methodist Church, named for the energetic and ambitious evangelist who'd come from Oxford for a season or two, eager to offer Christ to the sea-islanders of the Southern colonies. His legacy took root, and Rev. Mansfield French watched after the faithful of Wesley Methodist, encouraging them to be people of action, to "do all the good you can, by all the means you can, in all the ways you can, in all the places you can, at all the times you can, to all the people you can, as long as ever you can."

French, while less charismatic than Fuller and less regal than Walker, loved and nurtured his small congregation, provoked them to good works, and struggled mightily with Christendom's silence on the issue of slavery in America. Like Fuller, he welcomed and encouraged the slaves to worship, and like Walker he trusted the decency and dignity of the gospel to steady the ship in stormy waters.

\* \* \*

My earliest memories of church weave a tapestry of music, movement, and food. Early in April, on a fine clear morning, when it was still cool in the lowcountry and irises were beginning to bloom, Mama helped me dress in my "fine pants," the trousers reserved for Sunday. They were a deep-gray cotton, buttoned up tight just under my knees. The buttonhole was too snug for my fingers, and Mama hummed while she helped me with it. I had a fine white shirt, too; it was a little too big and had once belonged to one of Mr. McKee's brothers. Smooth and light, unlike the rough shirt I wore other days, and a bright, clean white, I believed it made me look older and bigger than I was.

Mama put on her Sunday best too, a dress she told me once belonged to Mr. McKee's mother, deep pink with a flowery pattern, over full petticoats, with a high collar and long sleeves that puffed out above her elbows, and a long row of buttons at her wrists. It seemed to me a person could melt under all those layers and ruffles, and I marveled at my mother's strength. I imagined her a queen, like our ancestors in Africa.

We stepped out to the street, and walked the short distance to Charles Street, where great crowds gathered from every direction. From the plantations on Lady's Island came the field slaves, hundreds of them, by rafts and small boats. They too were in their Sunday finest, though for most it meant simply the least dirty and least ragged of their few choices. A great palette of faded browns and blues, they moved with pride and purpose, singing and clapping as they came.

Men and women and children came together; the biggest and strongest among them guided and sometimes carried the smallest and the weakest. Young mothers carried toddlers on the hip, and infants on the back. Young men, strong and hard-muscled, walked alongside the grandmothers and grandfathers, honoring their age and wisdom with patience and presence. Shy children clung to parents and bold ones played with one another as they walked toward town.

From the farms nearby and from the planters' homes they came, in pairs and threes and groups of four, striding together toward the church, a rising tide of humanity moving up and through town to the church on Charles Street. As the procession grew, the volume grew, voices blending together, footsteps finding rhythm, hands clapping.

The deep bass tones of the men seemed to lead the song, and the song led the people. They moved forward, but there was a side-to-side sway as they moved, and the mass of people filled the whole street, bending and waving as one, like the tall grasses in the salt marsh.

Two deacons—Sam Webster, a slave from the Rhett Plantation, and Jimbo Parks from Mr. McKee's plantation, Ashdale—led the throng. As they neared the front steps of Beaufort Baptist, they turned to the crowd, raised their hands and voices, and rallied the people to even more enthusiastic singing. The music was palpable. We could hear it, yes, and we could feel it, smell it, touch it, and it touched and moved us.

We moved toward the church, white and imposing, and flooded up the front steps, half a dozen steps up, then a broad landing, then another half dozen steps to the two massive white columns of the entryway.

Deacons Sam and Jimbo led us right through the front doors of the church, held open by two smiling men. I recognized one as Barnwell Rhett. The other I didn't know.

The procession slowed as the people sang their way into the church, two and three abreast. The white folk were already inside the sanctuary, in their pews, standing and clapping in time with the music, smiling and pointing. I didn't know then, and don't know still, if they were amused or proud, or some curious mixture of both. Their welcome seemed sincere, and the feast that followed the service a couple of hours later was fine and generous. And yet, something seemed out of kilter to me even then. Some of these were the same people who slung the whip just yesterday, who bound the child to the tree for an offense as small as crying, who lobbed stones at field hands.

We wound our way across the front of the sanctuary, passing right in front of Rev. Fuller, who stood smiling at the altar rail, and we flowed up the central aisle, still singing, swaying, clapping. I noticed the gleam of the heart-pine pews and wondered which slaves had spent the week polishing for today's spectacle. The floor had been scrubbed too, but by the time we all marched in, it was covered with leaves and sand. At the back of the church, we took one of the two grand sets of stairs that led up to "the gallery," where we took our place and watched as the crowd continued to enter before we finally settled in for a long morning of preaching. These procession days only happened a few times each year, but they infused high energy and enthusiasm into the congregation.

In those years, Beaufort was home to a great many more colored folk than whites, and the church was full of both. As I look back on it now, I see the genius of Rev. Fuller—how he found a way to steady the ship in the uneasy waters of this small town: keep the slaves gathered, moving, singing; keep them fed; soothe the white conscience, if it wants soothing, with the image of dark souls saved. "Keep your friends close, and your enemies closer," the saying goes. Keep everyone close and enclose them in the language and fervor of righteousness.

* * *

We sat in church every Sunday, every single Sunday, but we never heard much about Moses. No, but that preacher sure talked about the apostle Paul. Good old Saint Paul, every week, saying, "Slaves, obey your masters."

I wondered who St. Paul was, and figured he must be a white man.

Every time we went up in that balcony in that big old church on Charles Street, and sat down to listen, Rev. Fuller held up his big black book.

"The word of the Lord," he said.

"Thanks be to God," said the people.

And then everyone would sing.

*Afflictions, though they seem severe,*
*In mercy oft are sent;*
*They stopped the prodigal's career,*
*And forced him to repent;*

*"What have I gained by sin," he said,*
*"But hunger, shame and fear?*
*My father's house abounds in bread,*
*Whilst I am starving here.*

*I'll go and tell him all I've done,*
*Fall down before his face;*
*Unworthy to be called his son,*
*I'll seek a servant's place."*

*'Tis thus the Lord his love reveals,*
*To call poor sinners home;*
*More than a father's love he feels,*
*And welcomes all that come.*

"My brothers and my sisters," he'd say as his hands grasped both sides of the big pulpit, like he was holding it steady, or maybe it steadied him, and he'd survey the room in silence. He'd start with the planters and their families on the main floor, taking his time, and then he'd look up at all of us in the balcony, and he somehow conveyed both affection and gravity.

He spoke, finally, with a voice heavy and deep. He liked to repeat the words of the songs, to remind us that hunger, shame, and fear could be avoided, but only if we remained obedient.

"What have I gained by sin," he recited, with great dramatic pauses, "but hunger, shame and fear? My father's house abounds in bread, whilst I am starving here." He made it sound personal, as if he himself had known sin and hunger and had found salvation right here in Beaufort Baptist—and bread, too.

"God has granted us another day, a day of life and breath. Thanks be to God!"

"Amen," said the crowd in quiet unison.

"Oh, how God loves you, each and every one, and gives each one an ordained place in the Kingdom! Created of ivory—" He smiled upon his white flock. "And created of ebony—" He looked up into the balcony benevolently. "How he needs you, every one of you, to give your best to the Kingdom."

He said it was God's own word, that God himself insisted that we work hard, and not simply obey our masters, but do it with gladful hearts. That's what he said: *gladful hearts.*

Sunday church was a diversion, that's for sure. As much as we disliked the imposed hours of worship, and as irrelevant as it seemed to our lives, it was a small price to pay for a few hours of relative rest and safety and the chance to be with one another.

Rev. Fuller took full advantage of this.

\* \* \*

After church one Sunday, Mama was feeling particularly inspired and told me the story of the frogs in the kettle.

"One day," she said, "the missus was hungry and there wasn't no meat at all, no pigs, not even a skinny chicken. So, she sent the slave boy down to the creek and said, 'Bring me home some big bullfrogs. Don't you come back with that basket empty; you bring back some fine big frogs.'

"So the boy, he go and he catch the frogs; first he caught just one, then he caught two more, and then when he caught two more after that, he come home.

"And the missus say, 'Fill that big kettle with some nice cool water, and put them frogs in there and they be so happy.'

"So the boy put the frogs in the nice cool water in the big kettle, and sure enough, they were happy frogs.

"And then the missus say, 'Now put that kettle on the fire, and let that water warm up nice and slow.'

"So, the boy put the kettle on the fire, and the water surely did warm up nice and slow, and those frogs never seemed to notice a thing. The water just got a bit warmer, and they was just fine. And it got warmer still, and they was just fine. And then the water, it got plenty hot, but those old frogs were just comfortable as ever and before they knew what happened, they'd done been cooked up."

Mama liked to tell a story and then just let it sit. I thought for a long time about the frogs in the kettle and wondered if St. Paul had somehow got himself stuck in a kettle. Maybe he just didn't know what was heating up around him. Maybe Rev. Fuller, too.

# CHAPTER 12

## 1850

After Indie's whipping, not a day went by that I didn't think about the story of Moses, and the people who came out of Egypt. I wished I knew more about it.

And there wasn't a day that I didn't think about learning to read, too, but I didn't know who to ask about that. I kept hearing Mr. McKee's words: "Of books and boats I sing . . . a library . . . and a boat." I wanted both.

From the gallery at Beaufort Baptist I would watch Rev. Fuller and the people below reach for the hymn book again and again. When the music started, their heads went down, all of them, as they looked at the pages of the book to do their singing. Up in the gallery, we just sang. We sang with our heads up; we learned the words when we heard them, and they seemed to live inside us, in our heads and hearts, in our blood and in our bones. We knew the words, but it was more than that. We knew the songs, the heart and strength of them. The sweet mixture of word, music, rhythm, rhyme; we knew the soul of the song, the core of the music.

We knew the songs, and our mothers sang them quietly as they nursed us, our grandmothers hummed them as they cleaned or cooked or sewed; the men sang them in the fields to give pace to their work and to quiet the pain in their backs. We knew the songs, and the songs knew us, and the songs shaped us, and we shaped and reshaped the songs. We sang different than the white people downstairs. They sang plain and gentle, with their noses in the books, as if they could keep the song contained. We added texture, changing rhythms sometimes, varying the voices, emphasizing both the pain and the promises. We changed the words to make them ours.

We knew they were the songs of the church, but the people downstairs didn't know that we had made them ours. We liberated the song, and somehow, eventually, the song helped to liberate us.

So, I watched the people below us as they reached for the hymn books. They opened the books and they opened their mouths, and I knew they were reading the words that we all sang, and I wondered what they found in those words, in those tunes. I saw only the backs of their bowed heads. I noticed how still they stood when they sang and wondered how a living being could stand so still when they were making music. *How do they keep their feet, hips, shoulders from swaying? How do they keep their hands so still?* Music moved and washed all around us. *Why stand so still?*

I would watch the stiff singing, the hands holding the books and the heads bent down. I knew I could do it backwards. I could find a page with a song that I knew, and I could find the marks and I could figure out which marks meant *Holy Holy Holy*. I could figure out which marks meant *Lord God Almighty* or *Jesus* or *Emmanuel* or *Alleluia* or *Amen*. I knew the words and I knew that if I could find the marks, I could learn to read.

I thought about this for a few weeks as I watched the people sing. They turned to a page with a designated number. I knew my numbers. They sang the words of the song. I knew those same words. The process was clear, and with every Sunday that passed

I was more certain that I could accomplish this. What I couldn't sort out, though, was how to get one of the books—how to make it mine for a while.

* * *

On a sweltering Sunday in August, late in the morning, as the preacher carried on again about slaves obeying masters, I watched the McKees from my place in the gallery. It was one of the quarterly procession days, and we'd sung our way to the Beaufort Baptist Church along with most of Beaufort. The McKees customarily attended St. Helena's Episcopal Church, but on these special days they joined just about everyone else in town for the spectacle of the procession and the celebratory music and the great gathering of all the people in one place.

It felt to me more show-like than worship-like, to be honest.

Liza Beth sat next to her mother amid the crowd on the main floor, and I knew she must be as bored and sleepy as I was. Hank was on the other side of Mrs. McKee, his little head against her shoulder. I thought, while I was watching them, that even though Hank was several years younger than me, he would not only read and write soon, but would someday run his father's businesses. We had just sung "Jesus thou art all compassion," but I was wondering, *How does compassion work in this hard world?*

The sanctuary was stifling. We rose to our feet for another song, and then there was a great commotion below us, an ominous crack, the sound of stone on stone.

And a shriek.

Phineas Hinton, the aging and towering patriarch of the Hinton clan, stood too quickly and fainted, cracking his head hard against the pew in front of him and then the stone pillar on his way to the floor, where he lay with a pool of blood growing around his head.

Someone called for Dr. Johnson; he was on the second row, left of the pulpit, and already on his way across the room. The McKees, like everyone else, jumped to their feet, straining to see what was happening. Rev. Fuller held both hands high and shouted, "People! People! Let us remain composed!"

But all hell broke loose, right there in the church. Mrs. Hinton was on the floor with Phineas, crying and hollering. Those folks nearest them were making it hard for Dr. Johnson to get through; and those of us in the gallery finally had something interesting to observe.

All the orderliness of Sunday morning had turned to chaos, and as is so often the case, opportunity emerged. A few of the slaves nearest the stairs were down and out immediately, headed toward the river where they could catch a cool breeze. Most of the children were already ahead of them. Two couples a few years older than me made eye contact and headed into the shadows of the upstairs hallway.

As for myself, I saw that this might be the time to find myself a hymn book. I slipped out the side door, and down the stairs to the sanctuary floor. Hank and Liza Beth clung to Mrs. McKee, who was trying to avert their attention and steer them from the bloody spectacle. I shoved my way through the confused tide of people pressing toward the door and pushed directly into the path of Mrs. McKee.

"Missus!" I got her attention. "Missus, let me help!" I reached for Hank's free hand and gave Mrs. McKee my most reassuring smile.

"I'll follow you, Missus," I said. "I've got Hank."

Mrs. McKee nodded, and Hank and I fell in just a step or two behind her. Liza Beth was crying and threatening to faint. She had a leaning toward drama and was trying to absorb as much as possible while at the same time making her own noisy contribution.

While Mrs. McKee was occupied with Liza Beth, I used my free hand to reach into the rail on the back of the pew and liberate two of the slim hymn books and drop them inside my shirt. I couldn't be sure that no one saw me, and I was afraid to look around for fear of drawing attention to myself. But if anyone saw anything or said anything, I would tell them that Hank told me to bring them. "Only doing what the young masser say," I would say.

I looked up to see Peter Rhett watching me. He glared. His left eyebrow arched. He had a way of using his eyes to make his threats, and he was making one now. He was two pews to my right moving toward the center aisle and facing me. Hank was between us. Maybe he hadn't seen anything.

"Hank," I said firmly, "stay close to your mama." I knew that the closer I was to Mrs. McKee, the greater my probability of getting past Peter Rhett.

"Boy." I felt him say it as much as I heard it.

I didn't turn or look. I acted as if I'd heard nothing, and I wondered if he could sense my fear. Of course, I knew that he knew that I had heard him. Ignoring him was sure to enrage him, even if he'd seen nothing. But I also knew that he couldn't get to me without leaping over two pews, and the only person to be feared more than Peter Rhett was Peter's mother, who was just behind him.

"Boy." Louder this time.

I turned and looked, not at Peter, but at Mrs. Rhett.

"Good morning, ma'am." I smiled. I forced myself to look Peter in the eye. *Did he see me take the books?* I felt sheltered by Mrs. McKee, but I wondered just how far she would go to protect me. She loved my mama, no doubt about that, but me? I couldn't be sure.

*Jane McKee's Diary*

*January 25, 1850*

> *This morning I overheard Lydia and George talking about Trouble. It seems they think he's unaware of his good fortune to work here at the house along with his mother. How could he not understand and appreciate that? My goodness, don't these people understand how much we do for all our coloreds? Like Henry*

*always says, what do they think they'd do without us, without this way of life? Thanks to us, they have a place to live, and work to do, and food to eat! Honestly, they'd not make it a week without us—most of them can't read nor write, and can't put together a proper sentence to save their lives. Lydia and Robert, of course, are exceptional. They're brighter than most, and they pay attention and they've learned a bit of civilized life. George too, to a lesser extent. But those hands in the fields, they have no skills at all. They should be grateful!*

*There's an awful lot of talk from the North about manumission. Henry and Barnwell and some of the others are quite concerned. It simply makes no sense. The men are right—do those Yankees have any idea what would happen if we suddenly had no one in the fields to cultivate and harvest the rice, or our remarkable sea island cotton? Have they given no thought to the ways commerce would be interrupted in our harbors, and in theirs? These people should visit Charleston and see for themselves! Why, over half that city's population is colored, and, as Henry says, the wheels of commerce would come to a screeching halt if they were all suddenly let go! And what of them? What would they do? Where would they go?*

*Henry says the Yanks aren't malevolent, but naïve.*


*February 3, 1850*

*Lydia has come to me to ask for Trouble to be sent to Ashdale for a season. She says he should be exposed to "conditions of reality" for his own edification. I'll have to speak with Henry, of course, and I told her as much, but I don't believe he'll agree to such an arrangement. For one thing, those field hands are so unrefined and coarse. Most of them are uneducated and some are just terribly filthy. They would be quite a negative influence. I don't see how in the world that could be edifying, but Lydia feels quite strongly about it. And of course, Henry's affection for the boy—I just don't think he'll want to do that.*

*As much as I disagree with Lydia in this instance, I must confess that in most circumstances I do believe she is quite clever. If she were a white woman, she'd surely be esteemed for her wisdom and steadfastness. She has become, over these years, almost a friend to me, almost a confidante. And she is a fine mother to her boy, and has been from the very beginning. He can be a handful, for sure; his pet name fits him well. He was only six or so the first time Henry had to go fetch him from the jail for ignoring curfew. He wasn't trying to be impudent, but he's never really been able to comprehend the way things are. Just because the other little boys don't have to go home before sundown, there are perfectly good reasons why he and all the colored boys must.*

*The first time this happened, he simply wanted to keep playing; he wasn't disrespecting our authority. The next time it happened, he seemed, again, only to want to remain with his playmates in the yard. But the third time, even though he insisted that he just wanted to play, I detected a spirit of rebellion, if only a touch. Maybe his mother is right; maybe he needs a lesson in reality. Henry laughs it off. He says Trouble is just a smart boy, smarter than most of his kind, and making the most of every moment and opportunity. It's odd. Sometimes Henry almost seems to be proud of that boy. I don't know. Anyway, for his own sake, I sure would hate to see him become rebellious. And for Lydia's sake, I wouldn't want to see him come to harm. I suppose they've all got a bit of defiance in their blood though.*

*February 9, 1850*

*After all these years with Henry McKee, there are times I just don't know that man! What is he thinking? Honestly.*

*Two nights ago, I told him about Lydia's request. I told him I think she means well, but that boy will only pick up bad habits and bad ideas. He'll practically become a savage.*

*"Good heavens, Jane, that's a bit severe now, isn't it? He's a smart boy, and it might do him good to taste a bit of the more difficult life. Might clarify his perspective some, help him see how good he's got it here."*

*"Or it might turn him."*

*"Turn him what, Jane?"*

*"Turn him against us, Henry. It might turn him against us."*

*I tried to explain my fears, how even though we're good and fair to our slaves, Trouble would surely be exposed to more difficult conditions. And he'd likely encounter other slaves from other plantations, slaves whose owners are harsher than us, slaves whose lives are far more unpleasant. He'd get ideas. Just last week we heard that some of the field slaves had a copy of a book by that Frederick Douglass fellow, a fugitive! The ideas. What if Trouble got ideas like that?*

*Henry might as well have been deaf, and I mute. He heard not a thing I said. Why in God's name does a man never listen to his wife? They think us less capable, less wise. To our husbands we're no more than property.*

*"He'll go next week. Another hand in the cotton will be good, and he won't be missed much here."*

*There are days when I swear I do not know this man.*

# CHAPTER 13

SPRING, 1850

When my mother told me I'd be going to the plantation, I thought she meant just like the other trips to Ashdale. Mr. McKee and George had taken me along with them every week or two for a couple of years now, and we'd checked on livestock and the field hands, and then come back home by sundown. No, this time Mama said I'd be staying for a while.

"How long a while, Mama?"

"Maybe a year, son. Give or take some."

"A year? A year in the fields? Mama, no, I don't—"

"Son, no discussion."

"Mama!"

"NO discussion, Robert Henry."

*George. Is this his idea?* He'd scolded me, severely, a few days before, just because I'd hurried through the weeding of the little flower beds next to the house. He said I'd missed some weeds, that I was being lazy. I tried to explain that I'd been quick, yes, but I'd been careful, and I'd hurried in order to do something that Hank wanted right away. But George was angry and edgy and unbending, and said I'd better learn how bad things could be. *And now he wants to send me to the fields? He would betray me because of weeds in a flower bed?*

* * *

The day we went over to Ashdale, it was just Mr. McKee and me. George was put to work repairing a door on the barn. As angry as I was, I really wished that George was with us; I needed his quiet, steady presence.

We dismounted at the main house, and a boy about my size took our horses for water. I realized I wouldn't see Mazie again for months. I'd thought about how it would be to not see my mama, or George, or any of the McKees. Leaving little Hank hurt most.

A few days before I left for the plantation, I took Hank for a ride in his wagon. It was a Sunday afternoon, and I pulled that little boy all over Beaufort. We went down by the waterfront and threw some bread on the water for the fish and ducks, and when we finally came back up Carteret Street to Prince Street, we smelled supper cooking. Mama was fixing chicken and grits, and sweet potato pie. I knew I'd get a plate of anything that was left, and I was hungry.

"Big dinner tonight, Hankie!" I said.

"Why?"

"I'm going on an adventure, that's why!" I told him, trying to convince us both that it was a good thing.

"Can I go?" he asked.

"Not this time, my man." I lifted him off the wagon and swung him around to the steps. Then I remembered my hidden hymn books. "You run in and get ready for supper. I'm gonna put the wagon in the barn."

I watched Hank trot to the kitchen door and bump it open, and heard him tell his mother, "Twouble's gone go to a 'venture, Mama!"

* * *

The day I stole the hymn books—after we got back home and Mrs. McKee got Liza Beth settled down and convinced her that the blood from Mr. Hinton's head was not the same as the blood of Jesus—I'd found them each a home. I put one under my blankets, tucked back in the corner where I slept. Nobody would come across it there, and if Mama found it, I knew she'd ask me about it in private. I took the other one out to the smoothed-out place in the yard where Hank liked to play with his wooden toys and wagon. He had a box on his wagon where he kept some of his favorite things. It was like a treasure box to him, that wagon, and he was proud and protective. It was old and dark and smoothed by the years. It and many of its contents had belonged to his grandfather, John McKee. He had an old toy gun in there, and some "magic rocks," a whistle, a few feathers, the skull of a squirrel, and a slingshot, among other things.

The hymn book fit perfectly up against one side of the box, and almost disappeared there, being brown and flat just like the inside of the box itself. Hank would probably not notice it, but if he did, he'd assume it had always been there, like so many of the other contents of the box, and being too young to read, he'd ignore it.

The next few days passed like all the others. I spent the mornings helping George in the barn, and the afternoons helping my mother with house chores. Work in and around the barn was my favorite. The smell of hay and manure and leather, the whinny and stir of the horses, the fussing of hens. I liked all that. I liked the simplicity of the work. The horses ate, and then soiled their stalls, and they were satisfied. I fed them, brought fresh water, mucked the stall, and it was gratifying. We gave something to each other. After that first ride on Mazie, I'd learned the personalities and needs of each of the horses, and they'd become my friends.

George was my friend too, in his own way and on his own terms. He seemed both ageless and ancient to me; I was sure he knew everything that could be known. His economy of conversation was itself a gift and a lesson. He had little need for small talk, but when he had something to say, I knew it was something I needed to hear. He often spoke in proverbs, but only when necessary.

One day, I asked George—quietly, as I knew we could both be punished just for having the conversation—"Uncle George, do you know how to read?"

I'd known him my entire life, and I knew that when he narrowed his eyes, he was suspicious and wary. It was his signal that we were venturing into dangerous territory.

"Read? No, son, I don't know nothin about readin." His eyes went squinty.

"I sure do want to learn to read," I told him.

"Ya learn to cut down da tree by cuttin em down." He finished filling the water pail and lifted it and walked away.

*  *  *

Now I wondered what else I'd be learning. I knew I'd been lucky to avoid the fields. I knew enough to know it would be miserable, and I felt my gut turn, and my heart rose into my throat. I pulled the wagon to the barn, retrieved my hymn book from its hiding place and headed to the little backhouse to get my few belongings ready for Ashdale and plantation life, whatever that was.

Mama and Hank were both on my mind when we arrived at Ashdale, but not for long. The overseer, Mr. Palmer, was waiting for us. Palmer had a reputation as a hard man, and he looked to me like he'd earned it. Sinewy lean, with chiseled features and dark eyes, the man seemed incapable of any expression other than a scowl. Even when greeting Mr. McKee, from whom he received his wages, he refused cordiality. I'd never liked Palmer; I doubt he'd ever liked anyone. And here I was, under his watch. My legs trembled. I kept my eyes focused on the ground in front of me and tried to remind myself that Mr. McKee was a kind man and would expect Palmer to be decent, if not kind.

But I'd heard about Palmer from some of the field slaves and knew better than to expect anything but unforgiving toil. Before ever even stepping onto the field, I felt an insidious fear rise up.

*Jane McKee's Diary*

*June 22, 1850*

*Lydia came to me today and asked what I write in my "little book" here. I told her it was just a way of noting things that seemed to matter, or things that made me think; just my way of noticing life. And, truth be told, I do notice life more since I've been keeping this. Anyway, as Lydia stood in the doorway, it was clear she had something on her mind.*

*"What is it Lydia?"*

*"Missus McKee, you known me a awful long time."*

*I nodded. We'd known each other most of our lives, it seemed. I waited.*

*"I took care of Mister Henry when he was just a boy. I been with your family longer than I can count."*

*"Lydia, what is it?"*

*I hold great affection for Lydia, and it was true that she's belonged to the McKees since Henry's childhood. It occurred to me that she might want to ask for her manumission. Rumor had it that some of the slaves to our north were asking outright to be released, and Henry had mentioned it again recently. I braced myself for the question.*

*"Missus McKee, I need to tell you somethin'. And ask you somethin. Somethin real big, ma'am."*

*"Good heavens, Lydia! What is it?" I wanted to sound stern enough to make her think twice before asking for something outlandish.*

*"Missus McKee, could your write somethin' in your book for me? It's real important to me, sure is."*

*"Lydia, what in the world are you talking about? What do you want me to write for you?"*

*She looked past me, out the window, over the trees. "I need you to write it down about Ruben. About what happened to Ruben."*

*She paused. I waited.*

*"I been carryin it here in my heart, every day, carryin the love and the sorrow, and it just get heavier every day. Maybe if I tell you 'bout it, and you write it down, maybe then I can carry most o' the love and let go some o' the sorrow, an' it won't be so heavy. Maybe if you write it down, Missus, maybe it might be a way for Ruben to still live a little bit, even if it's jus' in that book of yours."*

*Her gaze remained somewhere beyond the trees. The ache of her voice, the simple poignancy of her words caught me by surprise.*

*"My goodness, Lydia. Of course. Come sit down, and we'll begin."*

*Lydia sat on the low bench under the east window and fiddled with her hands in her lap while I turned to a clean page and inked my nib.*

*I wanted to give her a moment with her thoughts, so I busied myself with putting the date on the page. I was eager to hear what she might tell me next, but just then the door banged open and little Hank burst into the room, crying.*

*"Hankie, dear! What?"*

*"My bunnies, Mama! My bunnies!" He was on his hands and knees, searching under the bed.*

*Suddenly, two rabbits flew out from behind the bureau. Hank dove to capture them and missed.*

*Henry finally heard the commotion and bounded up the stairs to rescue us. The rabbits were relocated to their pen, and at dinner we had a good laugh.*

*"That, my dear," I said to Henry, "is why Trouble belongs here, and not out in the fields."*

# CHAPTER 14

## ASHDALE PLANTATION, 1850

The plantations were all different, but they were all the same. Some had produced indigo, some rice; some fine sea island cotton that in a good season was more valuable than gold. Some plantations covered thousands of acres, some hundreds, some less. Some turned on the backs of 400 slaves, some 250. Ashdale used sixty-two. Some drivers and overseers were white, and some were slaves. Some owners and drivers and overseers were ruthless and some simply inhuman.

Fieldwork stole childhood and humanity and gave nothing but backache and heartbreak. Every plantation's spring rains cultivated the mosquitos that brought misery and sometimes an awful sickness. Every plantation's slaves suffered the summer's relentless heat, and the winter's icy chill. Every plantation's value was measured in its production rather than its people.

On Ashdale, like every plantation, slaves began work by dawn every morning, and stayed till dusk.

\* \* \*

Palmer called to a lean-muscled boy, older than me, almost a man.

"Jeffrey! Get your ass over here. We got a new boy and you got some work with him if you think you want your supper tonight. See that he's in the cotton in the morning, and make sure he knows what he's doing."

That's how I met Jeffrey, who looked at the ground when he said "Yessir" to Palmer. He herded me through the evening routine before opening the door to the shack where two dozen men slept—or tried to sleep—every night.

We ate supper; it was unlike anything I'd ever eaten at the McKee house. On Ashdale, as on most plantations, the cook slaves worked together to provide something for everyone to eat, just to have something in our bellies before we tried to sleep. Albert and Sadie, Ashdale's cooks, didn't have much to work with, that was plain. On my first night there, I got in line with the other men, as the women and girls formed a separate line—two long, dark, hungry ropes moving toward a big wooden table set out in front of the cook house. Albert served the men. Sadie served the women. They each held a big ladle, and as each hungry slave stepped up to the table, they dipped it into the big pot, and sloshed a ladle-full of watery grits into a tin cup. The Ashdale slaves were luckier than some. I heard stories of slaves eating from oyster shells, or sometimes sharing a few spoons and a common pot.

That first night's dinner failed to fill my belly, and I tossed on my mat most of the night, getting up several times to go to the woods to relieve myself—unpleasantly. In the morning, the pattern was repeated, but streamlined: everyone received a crust of hard bread. The process was efficient, and all hands were in the fields at · daybreak—*deyclean*, the Gullah-speakers called it.

Jeffrey carried a long-blade machete, and as we walked the cart path to the field with thirty others, he warned, low-voiced and urgent, "Stay close by me, boy. The field ain't like that house you been at. Watch what I do, how I do it."

I nodded. "Alright."

"Don't stop till the man say stop. I don't care what for. Don't ask for nothin. Don't ask no question atall."

"Alright."

"And you keep your eye off the girls. Leave em lone."

I'd watched some girls the night before, across the yard, and I noticed one in particular, noticed too how my breath came fast when I watched her move. She sat with an older woman and another girl, each of them mending a cotton sack, talking quiet, keeping their eyes on their work, needles busy. She hardly moved, but I noted the subtle bend of her wrist, the lift of her hand, the tilt of her head. I couldn't see her eyes, and, goodness, I wanted to see those eyes.

*Wuh-psssh!* A bullwhip snapped within inches of my right foot. "Pay attention, boy!" Palmer shouted. "You look where I tell you look, and I'm telling you right now look at the house yonder." He pointed to the shed at the edge of the clearing. "You'll be staying over there, come sundown."

"Yessir."

"You better watch yourself there, boy. I don't want no trouble with you."

"Yessir."

I couldn't think what sort of trouble he thought I'd find, but I worried I'd stumble into it somewhere anyway.

\* \* \*

The long days got hot early, and stayed hot late, with the humid air steaming energy from the workers under the sun's boil. Only the mosquitos thrived. But the fields refused to wait, and Palmer refused to allow the workers unscheduled rest.

Thirst, miserable thirst, never relented, and there was no remedy. Like most everyone else, I kept a small pebble in my mouth to keep the spit coming. At noon, we took a spell, tried to find a patch of shade under an oak on the field's edge, and on the good days Palmer handed each slave one slice of dried meat. I learned it was called jerky, and found it distasteful at first, but soon came to appreciate it. That became a pattern. The distasteful, the painful, the miserable—endure or die.

On that first Saturday, I learned more about the rhythm of the week when we finished work midafternoon. Palmer rewarded the Ashdale slaves with the luxury of stopping before sundown in order to clean up and rest before Sunday church. His vocabulary contradicted reality; neither reward nor luxury defined the experience. The reality of the Saturday work schedule simply took us from the field to Palmer's house, where he and Mrs. Palmer and the four Palmer children put everyone to the tasks of chopping wood or plucking chickens for their Sunday dinner. Some of the older women, snapping beans or shucking corn, found a few moments to sit while they worked, having learned the delicate balance of sitting as long as possible in order to get some rest without sitting so long that they would be punished for being too slow.

Palmer must have heard that I was good with horses because he assigned me barn work, which spared me, at least a couple hours a day, from the fields. Late that first Saturday afternoon, as I finished feeding the horses and mules and stepped out of the barn into the heavy afternoon heat, I almost collided with a big fellow I'd seen in the fields the day before. Something about him seemed familiar. Broad-shouldered and muscled, the man carried a half dozen hoes and shovels in his huge left hand and a basketful of corn in his right. He saw that I had both hands free and, without a word, swung his big basket my way and I took it.

"This way," he said.

I followed him to the shed next to the barn where he put the field tools away, and then to the yard of Mr. Palmer's house. He motioned for me to set the basket on a low table in the shade and nodded at two stumps for us to sit on. He tossed over an ear of corn and took one for himself, and we began shucking, stripping those big, protective leaves and checking for worms, then pulling off as much of the silk as we could.

We'd gone through about half the basket before he spoke again. "Where'd you come from, son?"

"I'm from the McKee house, in Beaufort." I answered straightforward. He struck me as a straightforward sort of man.

"That's what I thought." After another minute or two of silence, he said, "Pretty easy over there, is it?"

"It's alright," I said.

More silence.

"How's Lydia?" he asked, when he finally spoke again.

"How do you know my . . ."

He smiled, then laughed, and that's when I saw it. In the laughter, I saw my mother's eyes and her smile, both.

"How do I know your mama?" he finished my question. "Our mama. I heard bout you long time ago. Wondered if I'd know you when I see you. Sure nuff, you're her boy."

Stunned, I couldn't find my voice, but the man suddenly became talkative enough for the both of us.

"My name's Abram. Abe. They call me Abe."

"I'm Robert. They call me Trouble." I struggled to comprehend. "We're brothers? You're my—"

"Your brother? Well, I guess I am!" He laughed again. "Or at least we're half-brothers! Who's your papa?"

"I wish I knew that," I said. "Who's yours?"

"Man named Polite. Lawrence Polite. Never knew him. She said he got sold off to a planter in Mississippi when I was real little. Said he was a good man." He paused. "Said he was real fine lookin." He threw his head back and laughed at himself again.

Abe said he thought he was twenty-one or twenty-two, which made him about ten years older than me. I remembered overhearing Mama all those years ago. *"One's just about grown up now."*

We finished shucking the corn, and I followed Abe to the back porch. Mrs. Palmer sat in a rocker, overseeing her yard. Abe sat the basket down on the top step. "Here's your corn, ma'am."

"Good God," she drawled when she looked up. "You boys look like you could be brothers."

\* \* \*

Abe and Jeffrey both watched out for me as best they could, but they couldn't protect me from the other boys—boys about my size who'd grown up doing hard field labor, boys who resented me for being a house slave instead of a field slave. None of them were any bigger, but they outworked me the first day and made sure I knew it. The next day I went out strong, determined to keep up. Watching a boy in the row next to me, I saw that he had a rhythm for picking. Bent low, with that long cotton bag over my shoulder and dragging behind me, I pulled the fresh white stuff from its sharp, dry stalk. All day long. I found my rhythm, and I kept up. My hands were raw and bloody, but I kept up. My back ached, my feet ached, my head ached. But I kept up.

On the third day in the field, the biggest of the boys turned to me. "What you think now, boy? What you think now? This is real work, that's what it is. Real work. And you up there at the house, chasin chickens an playin with the baby, and eatin like a king! Even talkin like a white boy! What you think now?"

"You're right," I said. "This is real work, sure is. I got nothin but respect for you, Tommy."

"We'll see bout respect," he said, not even bothering to look up from his work. "We'll see how it goes."

I'd been aware of the resentment. I'd heard the murmurs in town. I'd heard that the field slaves thought the house slaves were oblivious to their experiences, indifferent to the ragged, harsh reality of their lives. I'd even heard how some of them said Henry McKee was my daddy. And I'd dismissed it. Until now.

Until that summer on Ashdale, I thought all the slaves were in the same boat.

* * *

As hard as I worked, I knew I wouldn't earn the respect of those boys, and I knew I'd better watch out for myself. I could probably hold my own in a fight, but I didn't want to find out, and by midday, every day, I was too damned tired to fight with anybody.

One evening, as we carried our tools back to the workhouse to clean up, Tommy started in on me again. "What you think now, city boy? How you like our fields? You wanna trade places with me, Bobby?"

I took a deep breath. "Don't call me Bobby. Name's Robert."

"Bobby. Little Bobby. We got ourselves a Robert already, member? You ain't half the size of Big Robert over there." He used his hoe to point across the path at Robert, who was, in truth, enormous. Big Robert heard his name and looked our way. I'd seen him on that first day, and even though I heard he was peaceful enough, I'd kept my distance. Now I tried to direct a smile his way without revealing my fatigue or fear.

Big Robert nodded in our direction. Tommy pointed his elbow at me and said, "Hey, Robert. This little cracka say his name is Robert. You think we need another Robert round here?"

Robert shook his head with a sad smile, not looking for a fight. But Tommy was.

"Hey, Robert. This boy thinks he's as big and strong as you. What do you make a that?"

Robert wagged his huge head and stopped walking, and faced us straight on. It crossed my mind that Big Robert could kill me if he wanted, with just a swing of his shovel. Or his fist. The man stood absolutely still for a minute. I held my breath.

"He ain't so big," he said, finally. "He smalls."

He turned back up the path with his tools. I breathed a sigh of relief. Tommy howled with laughter. "*Smalls*! Our little man Smalls!" And I was Smalls from then on, to everyone on Ashdale.

Later, when I thought about it, I was glad to finally have a last name of my own.

# CHAPTER 15

One evening, after our so-called supper, Abe nodded for me to come sit by him. He was leaning against the east side of the shed for a little relief from the heat, next to a handful of men with their backs resting against it.

"We got us a shout tonight, Smalls," he said, smiling at the new name.

"Alright." I'd heard about the shout, but had only a vague idea. "Tell me bout it."

Abe sighed. "City boy. Just come on with me. Meet me back of the wagon house, sundown."

I'd heard Mama and George talk about the shout—how most of the slaves would stay in their quarters, in case the overseer looked in, while a few slipped away for an hour or two. Everyone knew the risk of leaving, and some had decided it was too dangerous. George told Mama, "Ain't no point in making a hard life harder." But Mama shook her head and smiled a sad smile and hummed a tune she said she'd learned as a child, with her mama, at her first shout.

Under a new moon, a handful of men and boys walked without speaking along a sandy path. Away from the fields, and under the oaks and pines, the scent of life refreshed my spirit.

We walked about twenty minutes until we came to a small clearing, the grass matted to bare, sandy patches, obviously a place where people gathered frequently. As we arrived, so did another handful of people, stepping into the clearing from the opposite side, and then another little group, and another. Folks were quiet, whispering a little, and sharing big smiles and hugs. Looked to me like there were some men awfully glad to see their women, and women glad to see their men. At some signal that I failed to see, everyone got down low, sitting on the ground or squatting on their heels around the perimeter of the little clearing. A man I recognized from town stood in the middle. Everyone was pressed real close.

"Children!" he whispered as loud as a whisper could be. No one spoke, and the night was full of sound—frogs calling, and a few birds, and little deer in the trees.

*   *   *

I remembered another man, some years before, at the little Wesley Methodist Church in town, when Mama and I slipped in and out on a Sunday when the McKees were at St. Helena's Episcopal and thought we were at Beaufort Baptist. I was too young to understand the risk or Mama's courage.

The man moved like a king, strong and sure, full of purpose and strength. He stood next to Rev. French. I had never seen a white man and a black man stand together like friends, like equals.

Rev. French spoke first, addressing the small crowd. "I'm glad you're here this morning, and it's not lost on me that you are taking no small risk. We will be quiet—but we will not be silent. And we will be brief, but we will not cease to be about this work."

French continued. "Mr. Douglass is on his way to Baltimore, and then New York. He's kind enough to take a moment this morning to speak to us." He nodded at Mr. Douglass and stepped away from the pulpit so all eyes were on the handsome black man.

He began. "Know this, my brothers and sisters, know this: A day will come, a day will surely come, when freedom will prevail! Just like the Hebrews of the exodus," he said, "the dark waters of oppression will be pushed back, and God will make a way where there is no way!"

"You must be wise," he said, "and careful. And you must be bold. And above all, you must never lose hope. We are a people in exile, but we are citizens of hope, and there will come a day—there will indeed come a day—when we will live, free and strong, in hope!"

He took a deep breath and a long pause, and he looked across the little congregation, and then up toward the window shining bright behind us. "For I know the thoughts I think toward you, saith the Lord, thoughts of peace, and not of evil, to give you an expected end. And what is that end? A future. A future with hope!"

I don't remember what else he said that day, but I never forgot the man. I wanted to be a man like that—strong and fearless, full of hope.

He finished, and the church emptied, quickly and quietly.

"Thank you, Mr. Douglass," I heard the preacher say as they slipped out the side door. "I know this stop was unexpected on your part, but my conscience would not allow me to forfeit the opportunity."

I stopped and looked up at the two men, and Mr. Douglass smiled. "Learn to read, son. Once you learn to read, you will be forever free."

\* \* \*

In the clearing, the man in the center of the circle whispered, "If you wanna be ready, you better be ready!" It sounded like something George would say. "Maybe God gonna make a way where there ain't no way, and all God's children wanna be ready."

He whispered to us how a woman—some kind of angel, almost—was leading people out, taking them north, and he told us that maybe she'd be among us sometime soon, maybe in weeks or months. Most everyone had heard the stories about singing in the night, a coded summons to gather. "Steal away," they'd sing, low and wistful. "Steal away, steal away, steal away to Jesus. Steal away, steal away home, I ain't got long to stay here."

Maybe the owners thought that meant somebody was about to die, going on to heaven. Music, like words, carried more than one meaning. For many of us, music was the message that didn't require reading.

Most everyone knew if you heard "Swing low, sweet chariot, comin for to carry me home," it was time—time to slip out, to get on that train. Even if we could escape, some couldn't imagine leaving. On Ashdale, everyone had food to eat and a place to sleep, and even though Palmer was mean, he wasn't murderous.

On the rare times anyone spoke of escape, they chose veiled and hypothetical language, talking about *other* people, ever alert to the possibility of betrayal.

Some folks thought the risk was too great. "Just how you think they gone get long, with no place to lay down they head, no food, no nothin? They ain't got much, but they got more than nothin."

Other folks thought escape was the only option. "They want the buckra tellin em where they can sleep and what they can eat, and who they can touch, and what they can say? No sir! Let em starve first; you know they gonna go first chance they get!"

As for me, I just wanted to be back at the McKee house. The McKees were good to me and to my mama, always kind to both of us. We ate good food and wore clean clothes, and maybe our room behind the house was small and dark, but it was so much better than the men's shack on the plantation. I missed being around George and the horses, and I missed fishing and riding and hunting with Mr. McKee, and I missed little Hank and even Liza Beth. "Ebry frog praise e ownt pond" was the old Gullah expression—an odd way of saying we seem to prefer what's most familiar to us. My life at the McKee house was plenty alright.

And yet, it wasn't all right. How could it be? *Doesn't every man have a heart and a mind? Don't the gods give everyone a soul and a fate? What would the ancestors say?* "*Stand up! Be a man! Belong only to yourself, and the life that you choose!*"

That's the kind of man I wanted to be.

All these thoughts were in my head when I felt Abe's elbow in my rib, and he nodded toward the whispering man in front of us. The man prayed with his whole body—on his knees, hands raised over his head, fists clenched, head thrown back, eyes closed. Then he opened his hands, stretched his arms out wide, shook a fist, nodded and shook his head. Circled around him, following his lead, the people did the same, fervent and yet almost silent.

"Yes, Jesus," one would whisper. "Make a way, Lord!" another would moan. It was a pleading, and a prayer, but I knew that it was also a promise, a contract. We didn't know what the future would bring, but we knew we were in it together. And that night, for the first time, I felt connected to these folk, like I was responsible to them somehow.

\*   \*   \*

Later, back in the men's cabin, awake on the floor, I tried to pray. When I went with Mama to the Beaufort Baptist Church, the way the preacher prayed, we just heard the preacher's words. But at the shout under the trees, everyone prayed their own words, encouraged when they heard the prayer words of the others. I tried to think about Jesus, wondered what he would say about this white world that turned on the backs of the black slave. Rev. Fuller didn't talk much about Jesus, except to talk about his suffering on the cross, how nobody ever suffered more, how glad everyone should be that Jesus took all the suffering and bled and died. I thought, *If Jesus took all that suffering, how could there still be so much all around?* Mostly, Fuller talked about St. Paul and about obedience, and serving without complaint. He said that God put men in authority, and everyone better obey.

The preacher at the shout seemed to be talking about changing how this world worked.

Mama had told me about other gods, Anansi and Nyame—far-away gods, gods that seemed to want good things for the people. She honored those gods, and she also honored the Jesus God; she might even say she worshiped them all. She told me that any true gods, wherever they were, whoever they belonged to, had to be on the side of goodness, had to be on the side of kindness. She said she didn't see how a god could choose evil. Only a devil could do that. She said sometimes she felt God's touch in the church in town when the song was alive, and sometimes she glimpsed God when she saw people together, watching out for each other.

"I don't know much about God, baby, but I know I want to choose goodness. I know I want to hold my head up and know I ain't hurt nobody. We don't get to choose much, but I know if it's a choice tween good or evil, I want to choose some good. If it's a choice tween kind or cruel, I want to be kind. If it's hope or pain, honey, I be choosin hope."

I wanted to choose like my mama. I wanted to choose my own way. Day after day, I did what someone else told me to do, but I could still choose my thoughts, couldn't I? I could choose my own words, couldn't I? And maybe with practice, maybe if I got good at choosing those things, maybe that would help me choose other things well.

I drifted to sleep, thinking of Mama and her words, and in my dream she sang:

*Wade in the water, wade in the water, children,*
*Wade in the water, God's gonna trouble the water.*

*  *  *

The hours became days and the days became weeks, and the warmth of May became the searing heat of July, and I grew strong and tough. My hands turned to leather, and a full day of hoeing or pulling only made them harder. I could lift or pull as much as the other boys and more than some. I'd proven myself, for the most part, in the field and the barn, and while I missed Mama and Hank and the McKees, I knew that this was changing me, shaping me, teaching me. Of course, I believed it to be a temporary arrangement. Had I thought it permanent, I'd not have been as optimistic.

Witnessing and experiencing the reality of the field slaves hardened my body and my soul. I saw things no boy should see, things that ought never happen at all. Nightmares from the smell of burning human flesh would haunt me for decades.

It happened in July, at the end of a day so hot the mosquitos didn't even want to bite. The heat covered the fields like hot, wet blankets. We'd heard that we might finish the day early, something about the Fourth, but it didn't happen, and by the time we got back to the work shed to clean the tools, the heat had wilted everyone's energy.

Jeffrey and a boy named Jimmie were putting wood on a fire so that some of the women could make a new batch of soap. Jimmie was small, younger than me. It was too hot to make a fire, and miserable to stand near it and make it hotter still. I was feeling glad that I didn't have to help with it this time when I heard a shriek that turned my stomach—a wail of pain and fear. I turned and saw Jimmie on his back in the fire. Jimmie's mouth was open and gasping, his eyes wide and terrified, his clothing aflame. Jeffrey reached into the flames, and his shirt caught fire too, and then I saw Abe and Big Robert pull him away, and the wood gave way under Jimmie, and his screaming stopped.

Summers in South Carolina were like the Bible's hell itself. I wondered if cruel white people burned in hell; I wondered if their melting flesh smelled the same. I wondered about Mama, and the McKees. Their hot, humid summer days and nights were nothing like the hell-fields of the plantation in July.

*Jane McKee's Diary*

*July 19, 1850*

*This summer's heat is stifling, more so than previous years, or perhaps I'm simply not up to it any more. Well, it's just too hot to do anything at all. Everything seems to be wilting in this oppressive oven. Even the children have slowed down, except for Hank as his bunnies entertain him so thoroughly. He's completely unaware of the heat, or the mosquitoes or anything else. He adores those little creatures. Yesterday he told me he named one of the new babies Trouble, because he misses our boy Trouble so much.*

*I suppose Lydia was right. Trouble probably needed some hard work; that's just about the only way to keep these folks in line, especially the bright ones. He's a big boy, and we sure don't need him getting uppity.*

*When Lydia heard about the accident on Ashdale—that poor boy falling in the fire—she went silent on us. For almost a week, she worked, and hummed a little, but she didn't speak at all unless I asked her a direct question, and even then she offered only the briefest of responses.*

*July 27, 1850*

*Liza Beth and little Hank just wear me out so. Thank goodness baby Will sleeps the warm days away. Liza Beth says she's bored, because it's too hot to go out, too hot to go and visit her friends, and too dull in here with Hank and me. We've got*

*all the windows open, and manage to catch a bit of breeze, but
I do understand her restlessness. She seems to be growing up so
suddenly too, with fits of sullenness and emotional outbursts, and
then such childish regression. She won't be a child much longer.*

*Hank, on the other hand, almost relishes the heat. He loves
exploring the garden, finding little bugs, watching the squirrels
and raccoons and our occasional little deer, and of course his
beloved rabbits.*

*Children certainly have it easy these days. Why, when Sarah
and Elizabeth and I were girls, we were never idle enough to
be bored. We worked hard at our chores, and truly did our part
around the house, always busy. Children today simply don't
realize how fortunate they are.*

*This morning I overheard Lydia and George talking about
the boy who had the accident on Ashdale.*

*"Liddy, it wasn't nobody's fault. Bad things happen, you
know that."*

*"Course I know that, George. But I tell you, when somebody
build Hell, bad things gonna happen, even if they don't mean
for it to. They done build Hell all round us. It's where we live.
Sure as anything, bad things gonna happen if you livin' in Hell."*

*I've never heard Lydia speak so coarsely. My goodness. Well,
she doesn't understand, can't possibly understand. We've built
a perfectly lovely way of life, and she certainly has the benefit
of that. And her boy too. Sometimes bad things do happen,
especially where carelessness or ignorance abounds. Why, we all
grieved that boy's accident, of course. These things happen. I
suppose I need to have a word with Lydia.*

*July 30, 1850*

*Such a difficult season we've had. This beastly oppressive heat
and the accident on the plantation, and now we've received word*

*of Caroline Rhett's death. I'd had a sense that she was unwell, and I'd wondered how she managed the burden of two households, all those children and life with Barnwell. She slipped in and out of Beaufort and in and out of our lives the way the egrets come and go, floating over the high grasses but hidden upon landing. She was like that, beautiful and delicate, and elusive. I pray for those children, especially Peter. He seems a bit unmoored.*

# CHAPTER 16

Every week or so, I saw George or Mr. McKee briefly when I was in the barn tending to morning chores. George would look away, mostly, and Mr. McKee usually stayed at the opposite end, barely making eye contact as he spoke to Palmer.

One morning, early in August, I think, George waved me over and whispered as he was shoeing one of the plow horses.

"Little Hank be sick, real sick. The missus is real worried."

I pictured the little boy's smile and could almost hear his laughter. Every day in the fields, I'd thought about Hank and wondered what he was doing, what he was getting into, who was watching after him. I wondered how much he'd grown, and what questions he was asking, and how his bunnies were doing. I missed him bad.

*Jane McKee's Diary*

*August 1, 1850*

*Something is terribly wrong with Hank—I've sent for Dr. Johnson, but we're told he's still not back from his trip to Charleston. Oh heavens!*

*His color seemed off. I asked him how he felt, and he told me he needed to feed his bunnies. But when he came in from the rabbit pen, I saw that he had blood on his upper lip.*

*"Hankie, what happened to your lip?" I asked.*

*"Nothing, Mama. It's my nose."*

*Another little summer cold, I thought, and he's irritated his nose to the point of bleeding. Later in the afternoon, though, I knew it was far more serious. He told me he felt cold. Chilled? In August? And yet, he had no fever.*

*And then more blood, from his nose and then from his mouth, and even in the chamber pot. The next morning he was too weak to get out of bed, and I sent for Dr. Johnson, only to be told he wouldn't arrive home from Charleston until dusk.*

*Henry and I sent Liza Beth next door for the day, concerned that Hank's illness might be spread to her, and we sat at his bedside throughout the day. We coaxed him to take some cool water, but it seemed that even his mouth had become tender and bloody. So listless. He slept, but restlessly, uncomfortable, and kept reaching for his leg, as if a gnat or fly were pestering him. And finally, finally, oh how could we have missed this? Finally we saw the oozing wound above his little ankle. His stocking and trousers' leg hid two small punctures, now exuding a blood-tinged watery fluid.*

*"What happened here, Hankie?" I asked. "Does this hurt?"*

*He shook his head, wearily. "No, Mama. It hurt when it bit me, but it doesn't hurt now."*

*"When it bit you?" Henry made no attempt to hide his alarm. "What bit you, son?"*

*"It was just a little ol' snake. One of those little garden snakes."*

*Dr. Johnson arrived as the sun dropped and the room grew dark. He told us later that the venom of even a small cottonmouth can be fatal to a child.*

*I remember nothing of the next few days, and at the end of the week we laid our Hankie next to Mother and James, in the cool shade of the grand live oaks at St. Helena's Episcopal churchyard.*

*Lydia sent George for Trouble, and the three of them stood at the edge of the graveyard through the entire liturgy. They bowed with us as the rector prayed, and they watched with us as the little box was surrendered gently into the ground, and they walked with us back to the house, sad and silent.*

*   *   *

Hank's death changed everything, for all of us. Such a little boy, but his passing left such a giant empty place. I was called back from Ashdale, and plenty grateful to be off the plantation. But I hated the reason. Sometimes I wonder, *If I'd been there with Hank, could I have prevented the snakebite?* And sometimes I wonder, *What if it happened while I was watching over him?*

I'd longed to be a big brother, and I'd failed. Mama told me that the rain falls on the just and the unjust alike. I suppose that's true enough, but he was a sweet and special boy, and all our hearts broke hard that summer.

Mrs. McKee stayed in her room for weeks, and Liza Beth was sent to spend time with family in Charleston. Mr. McKee took to the water and the woods, spending long days fishing or riding, quiet and alone except for my presence. He took me with him everywhere, and in those long, sad days I learned the subtle and powerful rhythms of tides and the mysteries of shallow, fish-filled creeks. We never spoke of Hank, but I watched a father's heart ache, and I learned something of the cost of love and loss.

And I discovered I was created to be on the water.

# PART II

*And the Lord said, I have surely seen the affliction of my people which are in Egypt, and have heard their cry by reason of their taskmasters; for I know their sorrows;*

*And I am come down to deliver them out of the hand of the Egyptians, and to bring them up out of that land unto a good land and a large, unto a land flowing with milk and honey; unto the place of the Canaanites, and the Hittites, and the Amorites, and the Perizzites, and the Hivites, and the Jebusites.*

*Now therefore, behold, the cry of the children of Israel is come unto me: and I have also seen the oppression wherewith the Egyptians oppress them.*

*Come now therefore, and I will send thee unto Pharaoh, that thou mayest bring forth my people the children of Israel out of Egypt.*

*And Moses said unto God, Who am I, that I should go unto Pharaoh, and that I should bring forth the children of Israel out of Egypt?*

*Exodus 3:7–11*

# CHAPTER 17

After Hank's death, Mr. McKee decided I should stay on at the house in town. He said I was more valuable helping George than I could be back on the plantation. I spent plenty of time around the barn, and even more with Mr. McKee. Sometimes he took me when he went riding or hunting and I'd help out with the horses, but most of the time we were on the water. We spent hours fishing or crabbing, or just watching the birds, riding the tides silently. I spent less and less time with Liza Beth and recognized that the paths of our lives would move us ever farther from one another as we grew up.

A full year passed, and life around the McKee house began to feel kind of steady again. One afternoon, Mama sent me to the chicken pen with instructions to select, kill, and pluck two nice big biddies for a special meal. The McKees were expecting guests for dinner, and my mother was an inspired cook. She could make a meal of anything. She occasionally let me help her in the kitchen, which turned out to come in handy, on down the line.

"Son, peel these potatoes." "Son, skin us a rabbit." "Son, shuck some corn." She taught me how to chop and peel, and how prepare the greens, and she'd long ago showed me how to kill and pluck a chicken. So, I slipped into the pen and looked for just the right birds. We had several big browns, and I decided to catch the biggest among them.

In the late evening, when the chickens roosted, it was a simple enough task to take one. They were quiet, and you could just slip your arm under and around them, and they didn't mind a bit. But in the early afternoon they were feisty and belligerent and just plain mean. I moved slow and quiet into the midst of the flock, and the squawking commenced. I reached for the chicken I wanted and just missed. She flapped and squawked and ran, and all the others did too. They screeched and hollered, dust flying, and I ran around just like those chickens, trying to catch that big brown hen. We ran from one corner of the pen across the yard to the opposite corner, and then down the fence line, a blur of dust and noise. I dove into the mass of moving feathers, determined to grab that chicken. When I finally landed my prey, my hands and feet bore the wounds of a hundred pecks and clawings.

I carried that big old hen by her feet out of the yard and behind the shed. Holding her feet tight in my left hand, I held her head between the fingers of my right hand and jerked hard. The neck snapped, the wings flapped, and the legs trembled, and in that moment of surprise, I dropped her, and for a few seconds she ran around in a tight circle, with her head hanging from the top of her neck. The she twitched violently and flopped on the ground.

I was covered with dust and chicken shit and splattered with my own blood, and went back into the yard for the second chicken. After a few minutes and another war, I had two fine, plump dead hens hanging by their feet in the yard next to the kitchen. I set a kettle of water to boil, then found a pail to set underneath them, and slit their throats to bleed them. When the water was hot, I dropped both chickens in and counted to 100. I was good at counting and was very pleased to have the opportunity to use this skill.

As I closed the back door of the kitchen, thinking I'd go wash the blood and feathers and grime from my hands, I heard the rattle of a cart's wheels out on the road in front of the house.

Peter Rhett was sitting on the bench of a little vegetable cart. He'd harnessed two boys, like mules, to pull it, and he was swinging a horsewhip over their heads. The boys were bigger than me, but not much. They dripped in sweat, and one had an open wound under the harness strap. Even for Peter, this was extreme.

"Smalls!" he shouted. "This is what we'll do to you, boy!"

* * *

Peter noticed his father's keen interest in the treatment of slaves, and he'd heard his conversations about the importance of keeping them in their place and avoiding rebellions. Their race was so inferior, Barnwell Rhett insisted. White men were "obligated to God Almighty!" to manage them carefully, for their own good and for that of their owners. The senior Rhett feared slaves would turn on people, even kill. He'd seen how strong they could be, and how they appeared almost emotionless in that strength. He saw, too, their wily cleverness.

The McKees' colored boy, Trouble, was a perfect example, Peter thought. He had watched him take a book from the church, and Peter wondered what else he was capable of.

Liza Beth insisted that Trouble was harmless, that he'd never hurt anyone. She was naïve, and Peter worried for her, wanted to be her hero. He would prove himself to her and his convictions. The opportunity came when one of his own house slaves dropped the milk can he'd been hauling up from the barn. The slave was a scrawny boy who worked with another about his size, mostly around the barn.

When he dropped the milk can, a few drops of milk splashed out, and he quickly righted the can and looked around to see if anyone saw. Thinking he'd gone unseen, he continued across the yard to the house, but Peter intercepted him.

"Spilled it, did you?"

"Jus a little, masser."

"Think you can just dump the damn milk all over the yard?"

"No, masser. It was jus a little."

"Take that to the house and come back to the barn. Right now."

He nodded, and Peter savored the power he had and the energy it gave him. Felt good. His father would be proud.

When the boy came back to the barn, Peter ordered him to find the other boy, and told them to pull the cart out of the barn, the little one they used for hay and vegetables. Peter had them take their shirts off, and made them each stand just ahead of the T-shaped tongue while he hitched a draft harness around their necks and shoulders. They looked at one another, eyes wide and afraid and confused, and Peter discovered his appetite for control and dominance.

The cart was already loaded with hay, and Peter climbed on the bench and took the reins and drove them up to the Point, headed toward the McKee house.

*What will Liza Beth think?* he wondered.

\* \* \*

When the cart neared the house on Prince Street, Peter called out: "Miss Liza Beth McKee!" She didn't come out, but I did.

The cart stopped just outside the gate, and the boys both bent to rest their hands on their knees. Gasping, they heaved for air. They kept their gazes low. I felt their humiliation, if not their pain.

I picked up a shovel, the heavy one leaning against the shed, and walked out to the gate

"Let those boys loose, Mr. Rhett."

He laughed. "That's right, Smalls. You tell me what to do! Who the hell do you think you are?"

"You're on McKee property, Mr. Rhett, and Mr. McKee don't tolerate such a thing. Let those boys loose."

"You speak for McKee now, do you? Well, do you fight for him too?"

With that, he jumped down from the cart seat and lunged at me. I swung the shovel and struck him hard, hard as I could, on the left shoulder. I heard a crack, like the sound the chickens' necks had made earlier, but louder, and he howled in pain and dropped to his knees.

"Goddamn you, Smalls! You broke my damn arm!"

Peter writhed and screamed, and I told him I'd break his other arm if he tried to move. I freed the two boys from the cart harness.

Mama and Mrs. McKee were both halfway to the gate, having heard the shouting and Peter's wailing.

"Mama, these boys need some water, and something to eat."

She hurried the boys, silent and wide-eyed, into the yard.

Mrs. McKee bent down to Peter. "We'll get you home, Peter. You'll be alright."

Peter glared at me, and through clenched teeth said, "Your nigger's going to pay, Mrs. McKee. He's going to pay."

Her eyes told me she believed him. And that she was afraid for me.

*   *   *

There was nothing Mr. McKee could do for me this time. I spent that night in the jail, and the night after that. The first night is a blurred memory of fists, and a whip. When I woke in the morning, what was left of my shirt was stuck to what was left of the flesh on my back. The constable's deputy brought me a cup of water and some stale bread and grumbled something about how he hated to think what would happen to me next. I'd been put in a cell with two others, an old man and boy just older than me. The two of them had been caught stealing a chicken.

"Just wantin to feed the babies," the old man said. Mama had told me that the field slaves seldom had meat or chicken, and sometimes didn't even get to eat the vegetables that they harvested for their owners. They got by on squirrels or maybe fish. It never occurred to me that a man might need to steal to feed his children. I couldn't deny how much I'd been sheltered from the realities that most slaves faced daily.

Midafternoon on the second day, when the sun was high and the cell hot as an oven, Mr. McKee came to fetch me. He and another man were talking, and I tried to hear, but they kept their voices low. A couple of times I heard him laugh, and he sounded a little nervous to me. A few minutes later, he raised his voice, and the other man did too, and then they both spoke quietly again. Mr. McKee had always been awfully good to me, but I worried that he would decide I was too much trouble now. But Mrs. McKee witnessed the boys hitched to the cart; surely he would listen to her. *Surely he will take my side. Surely he won't let me go to the gallows for this.*

The more I thought about it, the less sure I was of my own future. I imagined being led through the streets, hearing the taunting of Peter Rhett, walking up the steps of the platform to have the noose dropped over my head and tightened around my neck. I imagined seeing my mother in the crowd, weeping.

I sat on the floor of that cell, my back stinging from the sweat, and let hot tears run. I closed my eyes and prayed to God that my mother would be all right in spite of everything. I prayed that if her heart broke, she'd find some comfort in knowing I tried to do the right thing by those boys. And I prayed that Peter Rhett would leave her be. My prayers were interrupted by McKee's voice just above me.

"Trouble, look at me."

I looked up and struggled to my feet.

"Yes, sir."

"That was a mighty serious blow you struck. That Rhett boy is hurt bad."

"Yes, sir."

I wanted to tell him about the boys strapped to the cart, treated like mules. I wanted to tell him how it made my blood boil, and how I couldn't stand to see it. I wanted to tell him how Peter Rhett deserved more pain than he got, and how, if I was going to hang for it, I wished I'd swung at his head instead of his arm.

"The judge is going to let you come with me, but only under the condition that you leave town. Son, this is serious. Real serious."

*Leave Beaufort? What does that mean? Where will I go? And how did he do that? Why would the judge let me go?*

"Yes, sir."

The deputy constable unlocked the cell door and motioned me out, and I followed Mr. McKee down a dark hallway. We left by a door on the alley side of the building and walked back to the house on Prince Street in silence. I wondered if Mama knew I was being taken away; I wondered if Mrs. McKee came to my defense.

### Jane McKee's Diary

*September 22, 1851*

*Henry is on his way to Charleston today, with George and our boy, Trouble. A hasty decision it was, and a hasty preparation, but necessary. Trouble beat that Rhett boy half to death two days ago. It wasn't unprovoked, but he ought to have known better. Henry convinced Mr. Rhett and the constable to spare the boy and remove him from Beaufort. And so they've gone already, and I'm glad for it. The boy's becoming dangerous. We thought his time in the field would fix him of that, but he seems instead to have grown more rebellious. It breaks my heart, though. He's a smart boy, and I've always been fond of him. Perhaps we unwittingly brought this on ourselves; perhaps we were too patient with him.*

*I'm glad Peter's mother, bless her soul, wasn't here to witness any of this. What Peter did to those boys was harsh, yes. But, he says, in his defense, that they'd been surly, and he was simply putting them in his place. Perhaps old Barnwell instructed him to, I don't know. Still. It's as if he had to make sure everyone saw. And then Trouble's reaction.*

*Lydia, I'm sure, is relieved, as he'd surely be brought to justice were he to stay here. She's tried so hard to raise him well.*

*People will talk, I'm sure. They'll wonder why Henry is so protective of this boy. They'll speculate. That might have bothered me once. But I don't care now. Let them say what they will. No mother should lose her son too early, and I don't want to see Lydia lose this boy. Henry's protection is the right thing, and I told him so.*

*In truth, I suspect Henry is the one who will miss him most. He and Trouble spent so many mornings fishing, and riding, and hunting. In a way, Trouble helped Henry learn how to raise a son, and now Henry has neither the first son nor the colored boy.*

*Happily, our little Will is healthy and growing fast, and soon Henry will have his son after all, a boy to ride and hunt and fish with.*

*Perhaps it's all for the best. Charleston is booming still, and Henry says Trouble will surely bring us more revenue by working there than through any means here. And I hope he'll appreciate what he had here with us. He's a clever boy; I just hope he matures and settles down before he does something even worse. I pray for him. In spite of everything, he is ours.*

# CHAPTER 18

The walk from the jail was less than half a mile, but it felt endless that evening.

"Go wash up," Mr. McKee told me when we got back to the house.

Mama met me at the edge of the yard and didn't say a word. She didn't need to. I saw in her eyes that she was angry—and relieved. She looked me over good, shook her head slowly, then turned and motioned for me to follow. She warmed some water and helped me pull the blood-and-sweat-soaked shirt from my back, taking bits of skin with it. It hurt bad, but not as bad as knowing how frightened she'd been for me, and worried.

She soaked a rag in the warm water and gently, tenderly, cleaned my back. In a voice low and quiet, she began to sing.

*I feel like goin on,*
*I feel like goin on,*
*Though trials mount on every hand,*
*I feel like goin on.*

She sang, and my tears came again. I didn't want her to see me cry, and I didn't want her to know how scared I felt. But I knew she knew.

George waited a bit before coming out of the barn.

"You lost your mind, boy?"

I couldn't answer.

"You lost your mind?" He kept his voice low, shaking his head, but his words bit hard; I'd never seen him so angry. "You lucky you not already hangin. You think you provin somethin? All you gonna get is dead, and take us with you." He never took his eyes off mine, but I knew better than to look away. He was right.

"Damn fool." He turned, walked away. Maybe he was right about that too.

Later that evening, I heard Mr. and Mrs. McKee talking.

"Jane, we really don't have any choice. If he stays in Beaufort, there's sure to be more trouble, that's certain. And besides, in Charleston, he can be put to work and we're likely to make a good eight or ten dollars or more, every month. It's best for everyone, especially with the rice market falling off as it is."

"I know, Henry, but what if he causes trouble for James and my sister? James doesn't have your patience, you know."

"Don't I know it!" said McKee. "But I've told Trouble plainly that if he causes any problem, any problem at all, that James and Eliza will put him out, and if there's trouble beyond that, I'll be forced to trade him."

"Oh, surely he knows you wouldn't do that!" Mrs. McKee sounded incredulous.

"Well, I don't know; I'd hate to see it come to that."

It hadn't crossed my mind until that evening that the McKees could or would trade me. Or maybe I'd be sold. I heard about the Charleston slave auction from some of the men in the fields.

I determined in that moment to stay on the clean side of trouble. I knew one thing for sure: Belonging to the McKees was far better than belonging to most anyone else. Sometimes I wondered if it might even be better than being free, because I knew they'd watch out for my mama and for me. I didn't know if I could do that by myself. But whenever that question slipped into my head, I heard Indie's screams as she was whipped, and I saw the terror in Jimmie's eyes when he burned, and I promised myself that if I ever got a chance, I'd take it. I'd find my way free.

\* \* \*

We left Beaufort an hour before sunrise the next morning. We rode all day, with plans to spend the night roadside and then ride a second long day. George drove the wagon, and Mr. McKee and I were on horseback. Mrs. McKee had decided that no trip to Charleston should be wasted, and she expected Mr. McKee and George to return with a wagon full of supplies, including some nice silk for dresses for Liza Beth. She'd heard about a machine invented by a man called Singer that could stitch fabric faster than the fastest slave. I heard her ask Mr. McKee to bring one back. Mr. McKee was distracted, and I didn't know if he heard her at all.

I was scared, wondering what lay ahead. Fear has a way of intensifying everything. I seemed to hear and see and feel and smell every detail of every moment that day. I worried I'd be taken to the slave auction but was too scared to ask.

We rode that first day mostly in a comforting and familiar silence. Mr. McKee and George were quiet by nature, and quiet by habit when they were out on horseback or in the wagon. They'd taught me to listen for snakes, for foxes, for gators if we were in swampy patches or along the river. They'd taught me to listen for other riders or wagons, or gunfire. Many years later, I realized the great value of the ability to listen, to notice, to learn in wordless places.

We rode along the road north of Beaufort for a couple of hours, and then the road bent a bit east, and we followed the Harbor River for a long while. As we got farther and farther from home, I tried to memorize every trail and creek and swamp. I wanted to know this part of the land the way I knew my way around Beaufort and her rivers and marshes and creeks and tides. For some reason, it felt important to know and remember it all.

The lowcountry grasses along the river waved and rolled like the ocean, and changed with the tides, and smelled like life itself.

By late morning the day had grown hot; sweat ran, and the salt stung my back. The pain reminded me that I'd broken Peter Rhett's arm, and I smiled. I'd do it again if I had the chance, and I hoped I'd someday get the opportunity.

From our right, just as we passed by a row of big oaks, gunshots rang. Three in quick succession, and then another two. By the sound, we knew they were some distance away and the shots of hunters, probably someone looking for a rabbit or possum or deer. For a moment, I wondered what we would do if someone fired on us. The thought passed; no one would fire on Henry McKee.

We rode through the afternoon along the Ashepoo and crossed it late, as the light turned the marsh grass to gold. A welcome breeze moved the warm, humid air a bit, bringing no small relief to our horses. Mr. McKee had a cousin out here, a man with a rice plantation, where we'd spend the night.

"Another two hours, boys, and we'll be at Strong's place," Mr. McKee said.

"That's good," said Uncle George. "I need to take a look at this axle and wheel when we stop. Feels like it need a little work."

Suddenly we heard a thunderous crack, and George's mule reeled and lurched, and the wagon fell to a halt over its broken axle and landed hard on George's right leg, pinning him to the ground. Startled, the mule fought against the harness. Mr. McKee was already off his horse. I jumped down from Mazie and tied her reins off on a tree branch and did the same with Mr. McKee's horse, and ran to the wagon. Mr. McKee tossed me the reins to the mule.

"Hold her steady," he told me. "I've got to get George out from under there!" I grabbed hold of the mule's halter.

Leaning into the wagon frame with all his weight, Mr. McKee shifted it just enough for George to roll to his left and pull himself out from under it. He moaned a pain-filled moan.

I've since learned that the large bone of the lower leg is called the tibia. I learned that day that a broken tibia can pierce the skin.

After I unhitched the mule and tied her off, Mr. McKee sent me to the back of the wagon for the blankets we'd used the night before, and he used his knife to tear wide strips from them. He told George to lay still and he knelt at George's feet and gave his broken leg a quick hard tug to straighten it out. George winced. My stomach turned and I had to look away. Mr. McKee used the blanket strips to wrap the leg tight and snug. I watched as the cloth turned brown-red above the wound and wondered at George's ability to remain silent.

We pulled the wagon off the road and found soft grass in the shade of some big oaks and made a place for George while we settled the mule and unsaddled and watered the horses. Mr. McKee recognized my squeamishness about George's injury and put me to work stomping the grass down flat and looking for snakes, or at least making enough noise to scare off most any wild threats. We were near enough the road that we didn't need to worry much about fox or bear or wolves, and far enough from the water that we didn't need to worry about gators or cottonmouths.

Mr. McKee dug into one of the saddlebags and pulled out a flask. He took a sip and handed it to George. "This'll take the edge off, maybe," he said. "Wish I had some laudanum here."

We opened up the basket of food that Mama had packed and ate our supper wordlessly. When the sky turned pewter, I gathered some dry underbrush and we started a small, smoky fire to keep the mosquitoes off, and Mr. McKee took another look at George's leg. I heard the two of them talking real low and saw George shake his head. Mr. McKee handed him the flask again, and this time George kept it for a while.

\* \* \*

As soon as the sun cleared the horizon the next morning—
*deyclean*, George always called it—Mr. McKee and I unloaded the
food and our supplies from the wagon and tied them on the mule
as best we could. Then we lifted George up onto Mazie, careful with
his leg, and gave him the flask for the ride. Mr. McKee rode his mare
and I walked with the mule. We followed the South Edisto for miles,
under grand pines and live oaks dripping with Spanish moss. It was
slow going, but somehow peaceful. Give me an early morning in a
world of green and gray anytime. Give me the scent of salt marsh and
mud, and the tall grass shining gold in the early sun. Give me the
quiet of a morning, just birdsong and insects. My spirit began to lift.

After stopping to eat and rest the horses, we followed the Stono
through marshy, swampy wetlands, still watching for gators and
snakes, and inhaling the sweet, salty scent of mud and oyster and fish.

Midafternoon, we pulled up at the gate of a fine plantation
home belonging to Mr. McKee's cousin Travis Strong.

"Hello to the house!" called McKee.

A few minutes passed, and a tall figure came around the side of
the barn, waving.

"Henry!" he shouted. "Thought to see you last evenin'!"

We rode up the path toward the house, and Mr. Strong surveyed
the situation. "What happened to your nigger there, Henry?"

Mr. McKee told him about the broken wagon axle and George's
leg. I don't like to judge a man I've never met, but it seemed to me
that Mr. Strong was more concerned about the wagon's broken axle
than George's broken bone. I stayed back with George while the men
talked and reminded myself that I'd best stay quiet for the time being.

Mr. Strong called for two of his slaves and sent them back down
the road to repair the axle and retrieve the wagon, telling them
they'd better be back by noon the next day. Then he sent another
of his boys off to fetch a doctor, telling him to be quick, to be back
by dark.

Mr. McKee followed Mr. Strong into the big house. I sat in the shade out in the yard with George and waited with him for the doctor. Two boys peered around the corner of the barn and watched us. George, in need of distraction from his pain, called them over.

"Come here, boys. Need to ask you bout something."

The boys looked at one another, then came out of the shadows and across the yard. They were almost identical in both looks and in the way they moved.

"You brothers?" George asked them.

They grinned identical grins. Almost in unison, they replied, "We twins, mister."

"Well, I'll be. Twin brothers," George said. "How old you boys?"

"We bout twelve," they said.

"What your names?" I'd never known George to be so inquisitive. The flask and the pain, I guess, loosened him up a bit.

"I'm Zac," one boy said.

"I'm Jack," said the other.

I suppose it was combination of pain, whisky, and these matching, grinning boys with their rhyming names, but George, who never laughed, giggled, and his amusement surprised and delighted the twin boys and me. We all four had a good hard laugh.

Zac and Jack wanted to know how George's leg got broken, and what happened to our wagon, and why we were headed to Charleston anyway.

"You ever been in Charleston?" Jack asked.

"No. Have you?"

"We was there once," he said. He and Zac exchanged a glance. "You gotta be real careful there."

"Why? What do I need to be careful bout?" I asked.

Their eyes met again.

"Well," Jack said, in a hushed voice, "sometimes people get hurt real bad there."

"What do you mean?" I asked.

He paused.

"You touch somethin ain't yours, somebody cut your finger off. Or your hand."

"You look at somethin wrong, somebody take your eye out," Zac added.

"You look at a white girl at all, and somebody cut your business off," Jack warned. We all looked into our laps, silent. They seemed completely serious, especially regarding this last observation.

Finally, Jack spoke again. "But maybe you be alright. Maybe you won't have no trouble."

"You lookin at Trouble," George said. "That's this boy's name: Trouble."

"Nah!" said Zac and Jack together.

"My name's Robert," I told them. "Robert Smalls. But sometimes people call me Trouble."

"Why?" Jack asked.

"Just a name my mama use sometimes," I said.

"He's earned it," George added. He eyed the twins for a moment, kind of wistful looking. "You boys got somethin important, bein brothers and bein together. You watch out for each other. You keep each other outta trouble, you hear me?"

Both boys nodded.

"Why you talk so fine?" Zac asked me, after a bit.

"It's just how I talk," I said. "My mama told me it's best to learn to talk fine, so nobody think I ain't smart."

"It ain't workin," Zac said, and he turned and headed up the path to the slave shed.

* * *

We got some rest after the doctor came and splinted up George's leg. Made my stomach roll, seeing him do that and hearing George moan. They gave George something that made him sleep hard, and he was sleepy still when we got him up onto Mazie. The wagon had to stay at Strong's place for the time being, so we headed off with Mr. McKee and George on horseback, and me on that old mule.

The subtle trail gave way to a broad path and then opened onto a well-traveled wagon road, and we began to see other wagons and folks on mules and horses, and lots of colored folk on foot.

As we crossed the Ashley River, I tried to remember all that Mr. McKee had told me about James Ancrum and his wife, Elizabeth, Mrs. McKee's sister. I remembered what I heard the McKees said about Mr. Ancrum's temper.

Mr. McKee made it absolutely clear that I was not to give them any difficulty, and he was particularly emphatic that under no circumstance would he come to bail me out of any further trouble. "Mind yourself," he warned sternly. "Mr. Ancrum is not a patient man."

\* \* \*

We arrived before dusk at a house not too unlike the McKees' house, and Mr. Ancrum met us at the gate.

"Evenin', Henry," he said. "Heard about your wagon axle. We'll make sure you're fixed up good before you head back."

"Thank you, sir!" Mr. McKee was in a good mood, glad to be off the road. "Sure appreciate your hospitality!" He anticipated a good meal, a long drink or two, and a clean bed. I didn't know what to anticipate for George and myself.

"Amos!" Mr. Ancrum called for his houseboy. "Bring Mr. McKee's things in, and then take—what's your name, boy?" He looked at George.

"I'm George, sir."

"Take Mr. McKee's things to his room, and then get George and our boy Trouble over to the barn."

Ancrum turned to Mr. McKee. "When we heard about your boy's leg, we figgered we better not try to put him up any stairs, so they'll be in a stall we're not using, instead of the loft."

"Appreciate it, James. Sure do. "

"Couple of weeks, and he should be well enough to drive you back down to Beaufort."

I busied myself with the horses and mule while Amos took Mr. McKee and his bags into the house.

Amos came back out, and together we helped George into the barn, and into the stall they'd fixed for us. It was a fine barn, and I inhaled the sweet smell of horse and hay, leather and manure.

After I got George comfortable, Amos helped me unsaddle our horses. I watered the horses and curried them down and got the mule situated at the side of the barn. Amos came back with two tin plates heaped full with ham and grits and beans, and George tried to smile. "Best thing I seen in a long time."

"How you doing, Uncle George?" I asked. He'd been awfully quiet most of the day, and I knew he was hurting. I could only imagine the pain of a broken bone, rattling along on these bumpy roads.

"Gonna be all right, I guess. Sure will be good to lie down a bit." He paused, like he had more he wanted to say. I waited.

"Son, those boys back there—Jack and Zac—they got me thinkin little bit bout my brother. I ever tell you bout him?"

"What? You got a brother?" I was surprised.

"Had. Had me a brother. He was smart, and he was strong too. You remind me of him some. Anyway, he thought he was smart enough to speak up when he shoulda kept quiet. And he thought he was smart enough to run north."

He shook his head, slow, like he still couldn't believe it.

"Got hisself hung."

He didn't need to say more, and he knew I'd heard.

We ate every bite, and Amos even brought out lemonade, nice and cold. Maybe a new start would help. Maybe things would be all right here in Charleston. Maybe I could keep myself out of trouble. I fell asleep hearing echoes of the day's conversations. *George and I will stay for a week or two . . . A restaurant . . . Planters . . . A hotel*

*. . . a brother got hung . . .*

I wondered what the morning would bring.

\*   \*   \*

A blast of gunfire startled me from a hard sleep. It sounded like it was just behind our stall in the barn.

"Good lawd!" George tried to sit up, forgetting his leg, then hollered again and slumped back to the blanket on the straw. "Oh, Jesus!" he groaned.

I peeked through a crack in the barn's siding. James Ancrum and Mr. McKee stood a few yards from us, backs to the barn, where they were taking turns shooting at a long gunny sack hanging from a tree across the yard. It was the length and girth of a grown man.

"Better be ready, that's what I say!" Ancrum took aim again and fired his pistol. "Damn Yankees."

"Better safe than sorry." Mr. McKee aimed and shot. "But I don't believe it'll come to that. No point in undoing the Union, after all we've been through."

"They'll take it all away, Henry. Life as we know it. You watch. Just yesterday there was a big article in the *Charleston Mercury.* Just better be ready. That's all I'm saying." He shot again, and I made note of his accuracy.

Both men fired a few more shots, and the dummy swayed, bloodless, from the tree.

For some reason, I thought about Mama and Mrs. McKee being alone and unprotected.

*Jane McKee's Diary*

*October 31, 1851*

> *Today is All Saints' Day. The rector came to call last week, and invited me to today's services. "Mrs. McKee," he said, "I cannot fathom a loss so great as your own."*

*"Nor can I, Dr. Walker," I said to him.*

*He looked on me with great tenderness. Instantly I felt no small shame, as I recalled in that moment that he too had lost a son, an infant child, many years ago, long before we buried Hank. He, however, still has his fine parents, and each of his siblings, and it occurred to me that, though it makes no sense, it is indeed human nature to measure our happiness, or its absence, relative to the pain or gladness we see not only in ourselves but in others.*

*In some strange way, I'm feeling the loss of Trouble, too. Perhaps memories of Hankie are stirring a longing in me. I'm sure my melancholy for that irksome boy will be brief. I'm anxious for Henry to return so we can move on with life.*

*Earlier, perhaps in September, my sister Elizabeth came for a few days' visit. She had been here, of course, for Hank's funeral, but she came back, I suppose, to distract me, and perhaps her own loss of sweet little James compelled her. It had been over a year, but the wound around my heart remains raw.*

*She brought her friend, Mrs. Samuel Kingsman. Julia. Such an unpleasant woman. I've no idea why Elizabeth has cultivated a friendship with her. Charleston must be a difficult place to live. I wonder now how Trouble will fare.*

*On the day they arrived, Elizabeth and Julia announced that they'd like to go "to the quaint shops along the bay." It's the shortest walk to the shops and markets, but they insisted that Elizabeth's girl, Jesse, come along to hold the parasol or to carry purchased items. Lydia was far too busy with dinner preparations to join us for something so trivial. So, I had Trouble come along. Trouble minded himself, and his conversational ability was quite refined. I was secretly proud of him. Elizabeth's Jesse was young yet, and I thought she really should be trained more carefully. And oh my, Mrs. Kingsman's absurd mannerisms! She put on such airs, as if she's royalty.*

*I noticed how Trouble watched everyone, especially Jesse.*

*He's growing up, I thought. That summer on the plantation at Ashdale had put some muscle on him, and some maturity. I was glad we didn't send him back after the funeral. His presence with us here was calming, somehow, and seemed especially to bring some comfort to Henry.*

*On the morning of the funeral, I couldn't think at all, and Lydia was there to help me wash and dress. She was by my side all day. When we got to the graveyard, she stood at the fence with Trouble and George, and some of the other coloreds; she stood there, strong and solid, and when we got back to the house, she stayed close and stood strong for me, as if she knew I couldn't stand on my own.*

*Henry tried, and he was as steady as ever I've seen him, but broken, too, and I could feel his heart's pain. A few days after the burial, a lovely cast iron garden fountain arrived. "A tribute to our Hank," Henry told me. "A symbol of the joy he brought us." It was perfect. Hank would have loved its splashing cascades, the melody of the water, the blue jays and chickadees and sparrows that chase one another off and dart in to splash and play.*

*George and Henry set the fountain just off the front walk, in a spot I can see from the window of our room upstairs. I watched from there as they dug in the sandy yard, and as they placed it so carefully, measuring and steadying and leveling so that it would be just right. Trouble helped, silently moving the soil, and then finally stepping back with the two men to judge their work. Hank would have loved that too, being with his daddy and George, and with Trouble, whom he adored, as they worked and fussed, and finally stood, arms crossed, sweating and satisfied.*

*Well, Elizabeth noticed the fountain right away when she and Julia arrived, and admired its lines and the gentle soothing melody of its water.*

*"I suppose," said Julia, "that it's difficult to get a truly fine*

*fountain in a place like Beaufort. This is sweet, though."*

*Their stay was a bit longer than it ought to have been, though I suspect Trouble may have wished for Jesse to stay a while longer.*

*Well, perhaps at All Saints vespers this evening, I ought to confess my thoughts about Julia Kingsman. And my anger about losing our sweet Hank, and now our boy Trouble. Perhaps. If I can.*

# CHAPTER 19

I laid low in the Ancrum barn during the night, resting and thinking. In the morning, I heard Mr. McKee's call.

"Trouble!"

"Yes sir, Mr. McKee?"

"Let's take a walk, boy."

I remembered Mama saying how things always looked bleak at night and more hopeful in the morning.

We walked through the front gate and turned down the street, opposite the way we'd come in, and looked past a row of fine big houses and out onto a sparkling harbor.

"The Battery, they call it," Mr. McKee told me. "Some of the finest houses—and finest families—in Charleston." We walked down to the waterfront on the boardwalk, which was two or three times wider than the one along the Beaufort harbor.

In the distance I saw a pier, bigger than the others, crowded and noisy, but Mr. McKee stopped before we got near enough to see what was happening. It looked like some sort of open market, and I thought I'd like to come back on my own later and see what all the commotion was about.

We turned again and Mr. McKee told me we were on Market Street, moving away from the waterfront and into the beating heart of Charleston. There were people everywhere, colored people mostly—sweeping streets, driving carriages, washing windows, working in bakeries and livery stables and laundries and shops of all kinds. Three white men in coats and hats crossed the street and stepped into a fine stone building.

"Bankers," Mr. McKee chuckled. "Busy fellows, these days!"

Two doors down from the bank building, Mr. McKee stopped and told me to wait for him while he went inside. I watched an old bent slave man with a broom and shovel clean up after a horse on the street.

McKee came back out and handed me a flat, gray piece of metal with some markings on it and a leather string threaded through a hole punched in the top.

"Tie this around your neck, boy, and don't ever take it off."

"Yessir." I reached behind my neck and tied a knot in the leather cord. "What is it?"

"It's the law, that's all. Just keep it on."

We rounded a corner and McKee stopped in front of the biggest building I'd ever seen. Built of massive stones the rich-brown color of sand after a rain, it wore giant doors painted deep green that appeared to beckon the entire city.

"The Planter's Hotel," McKee said. "One of the finest hotels in the South. Maybe the finest of them all." We admired the wall of enormous windows framed by the same deep green, the glass gleaming in the morning sun. The hotel covered the entire city block, and it seemed to be all doors and windows. *Somebody spends all day cleaning these windows, all this glass. All day, every day.*

"You'll be in the dining room here," McKee said. "The restaurant. Ancrum's one of the owners." He paused. "Robert, you do what they tell you; don't give anyone any trouble, you hear me?"

I couldn't remember the last time he'd called me Robert.

"Yes sir."

"I won't be here, boy. And you're not a child anymore. Things that used to be a little trouble can be big trouble now. You understand me?"

"Yes sir." I heard warning in his words, and concern in his voice. And I knew his ability to protect me had changed, permanently, since the Peter Rhett fight.

He turned and looked me in the eyes. "No trouble, Trouble. I want to be able to tell your mama that you're alright. Alright?" I could see he wanted to be stern, but his eyes gave away the affection that had always been between us.

"Yes sir, Mr. McKee," I promised. And I promised myself. There on the corner of Market and Meeting, I swore I'd keep out of trouble, and keep my mama out of trouble too. I knew if things went bad with me, they'd go bad for her.

We continued walking, seeing more of Charleston so I could learn my way around the city and find my way back to the Ancrums. I felt the energy of this place, felt it coming up from the streets right into my bones and blood. My heart beat faster. I'd be on my own, like a man. I'd go to and from work; I'd walk these streets; I'd find my way. Like a man.

On our way back to the Ancrum house, Mr. McKee reminded me how to wash and dress each morning before work, and how to always walk into the restaurant with a smile. He told me that I should always reply when spoken to, but not to ever speak first to a white person. He explained that he planned to come to town every month or so to collect the money I earned for him. "If things go well, Robert, after a few months I might let you keep a dollar or so."

He repeated his warning. "James Ancrum is a good man but has a temper now and again. Just remember that Mrs. Ancrum is Mrs. McKee's sister, and she's a fine woman. We have to keep those sisters happy, you know."

The first thing I thought about whenever I thought about Mrs.

Ancrum was her house girl, Jesse. When they came to Beaufort after Hank died, I noticed Jesse was growing up. Still delicate, small and graceful, she was rounding in womanly ways, and she moved now in a womanly way too. *Jesse.* Again, my heart beat a little faster.

McKee read me well. "And leave the girls alone." He laughed. "Just leave 'em alone."

# CHAPTER 20

I sprinted up Church Street, praying that I'd not be late. Just two weeks in Charleston, and I had a man's job. The restaurant at the Planter's Hotel had only been open for two months, and when Mr. McKee suggested that I'd have more value in such a place, I felt a window cracking open. At the restaurant, everyone called me Robert, and no one even knew my other name. *Maybe trouble will leave me alone here.*

The Planter's stood at the corner of Church and Dock Streets, just four city blocks from the waterfront docks. The rice and cotton trades were flourishing, and the ships brought sailors and businessmen from everywhere. They came from New York and Boston, but also from France and England and Spain, from the Caribbean and from South America, and from Africa.

It could be worse, this work. My five dollars a month went straight to Mr. McKee, of course, but I got decent food and the chance to observe successful men—planters and bankers, the merchants and the lawyers. I studied them, watched the way they moved, how they walked and sat, how they looked one another in the eye, how they postured when they argued and how they relaxed their shoulders when they laughed together. I overheard conversations about business, about politics, about women. I noticed how they spoke, how they formed their words, how they debated ideas and disagreed agreeably. I noted how they ate and drank, the way they held their forks or where they placed the knife between bites, the way they handled their drinks and the way that drinking seemed to lubricate their conversations.

I savored the possibility of meeting interesting new people from exotic new places. I learned to identify their languages and mannerisms.

All the slaves who worked at the Planter's restaurant reported to the back alley-side door of the kitchen before the bells of St. Michael's finished chiming the designated hour. As I rounded the corner of Church Street and turned up Dock, I heard the first bell ring and slid through the doorway just as the tenth chime sounded.

Mr. Simon Elliott ran an elegant and efficient dining room and tolerated neither tardiness nor sloth. He expected everyone, from the dish boys to the senior waiters, to work with precision and professionalism. He scowled. "Not at ten o'clock, boy. *By* ten o'clock. Don't let it happen again."

"Yessir." *I'm not late.*

"Quality and quiet, boys," he said at least once daily. "Every customer of the Planter's will be astounded by the quality of the food, and by the quietude of the service."

He trained his help, who he called the staff, to greet the diner with a smile but never a grin, and to look a man in the eye but not to hold the gaze too long. It was important, he said, to acknowledge your place and theirs.

*As if we could forget who is who.*

I was twelve years old but had learned long ago to be careful that my face didn't reveal my thoughts. I stood straight and still at the back of the kitchen, listening to Mr. Elliott's daily speech with a benign smile. I listened to the instructions: Ol Sam would be the lead waiter, as always, and the other boys would do as he directed.

Ol Sam lifted his head a bit. He was taller than the other kitchen slaves, and thin, with kind eyes, and he moved with a very slight tilt to the right, as if his right shoulder intended to arrive a bit ahead of the rest of his body.

"We goin ta be busy today. Now, y'all be watchin for when da boss need a drink or a dish, an y'all be quick to fetch it. We goin to be real busy cause dey have lot a boats on da dock today."

When the late winter storms gave way to early spring, the waterfront was indeed busy, and the Planter's Hotel, along with the other establishments in proximity to the docks, filled with hungry pilots and sailors, businessmen and, lately, politicians and military men.

I welcomed the busy days. The variety of diners made the tedious and repetitive work more interesting, and I determined early on to take full advantage of the opportunity to observe and listen and learn. Mr. Elliott's admonitions to "make yourself invisible" allowed me to notice a great deal without being noticed.

\* \* \*

One Thursday morning brought new movement just beyond the door: the hotel maids heading toward the housekeepers' workroom. Something was different today. There were at least five new girls. I noticed girls a lot lately—noticed the way my body responded.

Occasionally, I saw Jesse, Mrs. Ancrum's house girl, when she accompanied Mrs. Ancrum to the tearoom. Jesse always waited at a bench outside, holding a parasol and anything else Mrs. Ancrum might need, and a basket that they'd fill at the market on their way back home.

I watched her from the window on tea days and saw her almost every day in the yard at the Ancrum house, helping with laundry, or sweeping, or mending a piece of clothing.

Sam had seen me looking at Jesse through the window.

"Robert," Sam said. "Son, get your eyes back to work, hear me?"

"Yes sir, Sam." My palms were sweating and my breath had quickened.

I headed toward the pantry, thinking about Jesse, and wondering where the new girls had come from.

* * *

My first task each morning was to carry the plates from the pantry to the dining room, and I made a point of doing it as efficiently as possible. Ol Sam was watching me, and for reasons I couldn't name, I wanted to impress Sam. I worked quickly, and carefully. After placing the dining plates on each table in the elegant room, I went back to the pantry for tea cups and saucers. Within the first hour of my arrival each day, all the tables in the expansive rooms were perfectly laid with dinner, salad, and dessert plates, teacups and saucers, glassware and silverware. Queen Victoria herself would have been satisfied, though I'd worked a full month before learning who she was or where she reigned.

The lunch patrons began arriving shortly after the bells of St. Michael's chimed twelve times. The clock tower, just a few blocks away, stood on what the locals called the "Four Corners of Law," at the intersection of Broad and Meeting Streets. With St. Michael's representing the law of ecclesiology, City Hall was to the north, the county courthouse to its northwest, and the post office and federal courthouse to the west. I quickly grew dependent on the church's bell tower to be at work on time; like a benevolent angel, it told me when to anticipate the busiest hours, and, much later, it chimed the promise that I'd eventually finish the day's work.

As the dining room filled, Mr. Elliott and Ol Sam worked as a team.

Mr. Elliott greeted each customer by name. "Good day, Mr. Benton! How are things at the bank this morning? Top o' the day to you, Mr. Grimke. How are you and those lovely Grimke women?"

Gentlemen came from all over Charleston and from the waterfront, and Mr. Elliott and Sam saw to it that they were made to feel like royalty. As the true Southern aristocracy, most of them were wealthy and influential, and those who weren't aspired to be.

Sam knew and honored everyone's seating preference. Most of the attorneys liked to sit in the front of the room, at or near the windows, where they could be noticed. The bankers liked to sit in the back corners, where they could talk business quietly. The planters and the merchants preferred tables in the center of the room where they could pick up spontaneous conversations with the lawyers and senators about politics and policies, and with the bankers about markets and supply and demand, and perhaps with the visitors from Europe about international concerns.

Every noon and evening, the room filled and buzzed with energy as deals were made or lost, egos stroked or offended, and political views and matters discussed and debated. The presidential election, just months away, consumed everyone. I listened to these conversations discretely, taking care to be inconspicuous.

"Pierce has to go; everyone knows that."

The incumbent, Franklin Pierce, had alienated supporters in the North and failed to assure slaveholders in the South. I learned that the Southern leaders would rather leave the Union than give up their way of life.

Working at the Planter's opened my eyes and ears. The world was big, so much bigger than I'd known in Beaufort, and I resolved to learn something new every day. I wanted to learn a new skill; or, if not a skill, a new word; or, if not a word, at least something of the manner of a businessman or a gentleman. The men who sat at my tables became my teachers, though they never knew it.

\* \* \*

Mr. McKee had warned me more than once to be careful. "Watch who you talk to, boy. Can't know who to trust here." So I kept to myself, mostly. The other boys at the restaurant were older than me and seemed to have their own ties with one another. They didn't pay me much attention. I felt lonesome, more and more.

My room over the barn at the Ancrums' was close enough to the house to hear the sounds of family life, but too far to feel like I was part of it. Jesse was kept busy, as was Amos, and I soon ran short of excuses to be around them. I spent my evenings looking at those hymn books I had stolen and remembering the songs of the church, and trying to make sense of what was in front of me. I knew enough to know that I didn't know who to trust.

What I did know for sure was what I heard at the Planter's, and by keeping my mouth shut and eyes straight ahead, as Mr. McKee warned, I got something that eluded me in Beaufort.

Inside of a month, I began to recognize words—written words. I'd struggled to learn to read since I stole those hymn books back in Beaufort. It was slow going and frustrating. At the restaurant, though, I found a new way to learn. When a diner sat down, after I poured his drink, I'd hand him a small slip of paper called a menu. It wasn't much bigger than my hand, with a list of the day's meals. It named the day's soup or a stew, and a fish dish, and maybe a beef pie or a pork dish. The man would study it and then take a pencil and circle the things he wanted. And most of the time, he'd say the thing while he circled it.

"I'll have the beef stew," he might say as he marked it. Or, "Bring me that crab cake, boy." As soon as I got back to the kitchen, I'd look at what he marked and remember what he said, and pretty soon I could recognize *soup* and *stew, crab, clam, grilled*—lots of words.

If I listened and watched and paid attention to every person and every detail, I knew I could learn just about anything. But I had to do it in a way that didn't look like that was what I was doing. There could be a lot of trouble if they knew I was learning to read, or learning too much about how the world worked.

# CHAPTER 21

I'd been in Charleston a few weeks when, late one afternoon, walking back to my room in the Ancrum's barn, I passed by three young men standing in the doorway of a blacksmith shop. I'd seen them there before, laughing and talking. They'd nodded and I'd nodded back.

"Hey," one of them said this time. "You new round here?"

I stopped, surprised, suspicious. "I guess I am. Bout a month now."

"Where from?" the man asked.

"Does it matter?" I asked.

"Don't you be worried. We just wonderin, that's all. Noticed you pass this way most every day."

"I'm from Beaufort. Not too far off."

"Beaufort! Hey, you know a fella name Abe? Abe Polite?"

"Maybe," I said. "Remind me bout him."

"Big strong fella. I knowed him from the fields, then got traded; sent up here. He a good man. You know him?"

"I believe I do."

*What can this man and his friends tell me about Abe Polite, maybe even my father?* Since meeting Abe, I wondered if there was some way Larry Polite could be my father too.

"My name's Smalls. Robert Smalls."

"I'm Alfred. This here's Billy, and Tombo." He nodded to the others, and they each nodded back.

"We're going inside there, to talk some; you want to come with us?" Tombo spoke like a white boy.

"What kind of talk?"

They exchanged glances. "Prayer meeting," Tombo said.

"Right now?" I asked.

"Pretty soon. We're talking is all." Alfred glanced at the others, hesitated before he spoke again. "They call it a prayer meeting. Friend of ours ended up in jail, beat half to death. We want to figure out what happened, how to keep it from happenin again. How to keep this same stuff from happenin to any of us. It's only gettin worse. Some folks just say pray, but I say we gotta do somethin."

I thought about my mother's prayers, every morning and every evening, always thanking God and all the gods for another day, and always asking for a sign of hope, and looking to "make a way where there ain't no way."

"I guess I could come," I said, curious to see what their meeting was really about.

A few minutes later we heard a bird-like, low whistle from around the side of the shop.

"We go in at the side door," Tombo said, his voice quiet. "This way."

We stepped into a dim room with dark wood floors and dark plank walls. It smelled of fire and metal and sweat. Shutters covered the windows, keeping the light out. As my eyes adjusted, I saw a makeshift altar; it reminded me of the one in Beaufort, somehow. I followed the three men across the room, and we sat on short, dark benches. No one spoke. Several times, the door opened, and a few men walked in silently and took seats near us. I was the youngest in the room.

*I won't say anything, just listen.*

When the door opened again, a man almost as tall and broad as the doorway itself walked in. *He must be the leader of this . . . whatever this is.*

"Brothers," the giant man said softly as he approached us. "My brothers, I have some news from our friends up north. Some good news." No one spoke. He sat on a chair facing the rest of us.

"Garrison and Douglass have made some real progress, and their ranks are growing. More and more of the churches are taking up the cause. And not only that, but some of those churches— or rather, I should say, their denominations—have schools. Fine schools. Universities. And two of them now are admitting freed men. Think of it. Our own brothers learning to read and reason! A tide is turning. It is. But slow.

"Douglass wanted me to tell you to be patient, but not passive, and to be . . . well, the way he put it, to be good, to do the right thing. To continue to choose the way of the gospel of Christ. Like the book says, 'To put on kindness and compassion' even when it hurts. Especially when it hurts."

I heard a few low murmurs, and the big man heard them too.

"I know what you're thinking. 'How can we fight if we can't fight? How can we resist if we can't resist?' And here is what I say to that. Never initiate a conflict. Under no circumstance. And never make something bigger than it is. If a problem is small, keep it small. If someone disrespects you, that's because they're weak, not because you are. Use your strength, but never cause harm. But—" He took a deep breath and dropped his voice so low that all of us leaned forward to hear. "But if you witness cruelty, if you see any person, colored or white or Indian or islander, if you see any person borne harm, use your power to step in. Do what you must. But only when you must."

A deep uneasiness sat in the silence.

"Strength ain't really strength if you can't keep it under control."
Silence again.

"Do you understand me?" He fixed his eyes on every face.
"Alfred, do you understand me?"

"Yes."

"Tombo, do you understand me?"

"I do."

"Billy, do you understand me?"

Billy was silent.

"Billy?"

"I understand your words," Billy said, "but that don't make
no sense at all. How we even goin to survive like that?" His fist
pounded the bench.

A few others nodded their agreement.

"We're not going to survive at all, otherwise. Except as chained
people. Is that what you want?"

"Course not!" His voice rose. "But I already seen too many men
dead, women and chil'en, too. We can't just sit round, bein nice,
bowin down, waitin till kingdom come! Time we take matters in
our own hands, ain't it?"

"And how you suggest we do that, Billy?"

"Good God, Jeremiah. Half of us here are blacksmiths. We
could fashion us somethin, some knives and such, some kinda
weapons, anyways. It ain't like we got no way."

"We could keep em here!" another voice suggested.

"It ain't a bad idea," someone from the other side of the room
said.

I thought about how good it felt to hurt Peter Rhett, and how
I'd like to have a real weapon, how I'd like to return some of the
pain to the ones who inflicted it.

Jerimiah stood and put his hands up to quiet everyone.

"Men, you get to choose. You must choose. If you want to
build yourselves an arsenal, that's up to you. But as for me, I'm

not choosing weapons. You can't have it both ways. You can't make peace with violence."

He surveyed the room, looked every man in the face, and stopped when he got to me.

"Who are you?"

"I'm Smalls."

"Smalls. Well, Smalls, you are welcome among us. Do you understand what I've said?"

"Yes sir, I understand. But can I ask a question?"

"Of course."

"Who are you, a preacher?"

"Not exactly." Jerimiah paused. "I just try to do the right thing, much as I can, whenever I can."

"Is this a church?"

"No . . . no, we're not a church. We're just some folks who want to see a better day. Sometimes we need a sip of hope or strength from one another, y'know? Sometimes we need remindin who we are."

I nodded. *A sip of hope.* I knew I was terrible thirsty.

# CHAPTER 22

Of all the lawyers and businessmen who dined regularly at the restaurant, only one had his own table, permanently reserved and always protected. The table in the far corner allowed him to watch the door while watching his back, and he believed both to be essential. He was deeply disliked, and his distrust of others was mirrored by their distrust of him. But he was a powerful man. He knew it; everyone knew it.

Shortly before noon on a Thursday, just as the tables were set for the midday crowd, in walked Barnwell Rhett. His face, ruddy and beaded with sweat, glowered. Usually an angry man, today he pulsed with agitation.

"Mr. Rhett, good morning. How many will be joining you today?"

"Just Davis, Sam. And don't put anyone at the tables near us, you understand?"

Sam understood and was happy to comply, as Rhett always tipped royally for being treated as royalty. Sam led Rhett to his table, pulled the chair back, and smiled. The restaurant made more on the empty tables around Barnwell Rhett than they could ever make by seating guests there.

"Tea, Mr. Rhett?" Sam always asked. Rhett always grunted and nodded. Today, more grunt than nod. Sam knew to be attentive and invisible.

* * *

Robert Barnwell Rhett had no time for gracious conversation, or for the genteel approach to relationship and transaction on which most Southern gentlemen prided themselves. Other boys had grown up apprenticed to their fathers, watching and learning from those models, for better or for worse or both—learning to come at hard things sideways, learning to charm or cajole. They learned to bully, disguising it as succor. The youthful men of the Southern aristocracy learned subtlety as carefully as they learned to sip their bourbon or seduce their women. Robert Barnwell Rhett had no such tutelage, no role model, no one in his childhood who gave a damn, and he knew it.

Born Robert Smith, he'd been adopted late in his adolescence by an uncle who, without children of his own, was desperate for an heir. The neglected, insecure boy Robert Smith became Robert Barnwell Rhett at eighteen, and at twenty-one stood at his uncle's graveside and whispered a prayer of thanks. It was the first and last time in his life that he felt or expressed gratitude of any kind, and for that he felt both justified and proud.

Sitting at his table, back to the wall, he unfolded his copy of the *Charleston Mercury* and smiled. He'd learned to use the paper, which he acquired at the age of twenty-five, using a fraction of the uncle's money to wield influence and control, not unlike his habit of using his physical bulk to manipulate his wife, his children, his employees and his slaves.

"Can a man get some damn sugar for the tea here, boy?"

"Yessir. Right away, sir." I hurried into the kitchen and back out, with a sugar bowl, spoon, and linen napkin.

Rhett grunted without looking up as I placed the sugar on the table, then the napkin, then the spoon on the napkin.

The street side door opened, and a tall, elegant man floated into the dining room, like a young horse, strong and alive, making it look easy. I sensed that I might learn something from this man.

"Good morning, Mr. Davis," Sam called.

Glancing around the room, the man nodded to Sam and to two men at a table by the window, then strode across the room and to the table in back.

"Good morning, Mr. Rhett."

"Morning, yourself," Rhett answered without looking up from his paper.

Mr. Davis paused as I pulled the chair for him, then sat.

Neither man spoke for a full minute; I stood a few paces away, ready to serve as soon as they signaled me, trying to be invisible until the gesture came. I was still stunned and relieved that Mr. Rhett didn't recognize me. He so infrequently went to Beaufort that I wondered if he'd recognize his own son Peter.

Of course he didn't recognize me; he seldom looked directly at anyone, and would have no reason to notice another slave boy.

"One's as sorry as another," he'd said a few months ago when he was told about the altercation with Peter.

Mr. Davis waited, sitting straight but relaxed. *Like a king. Who is this man?* I liked him and hoped he would be a regular patron.

The two men were as different in temperament as two white men could be, the one rough and rude, the other regal.

Rhett looked up from his paper. "Jeff," he said. "Why the hell are we waiting? How long do we let the Yanks keep us under their boots?"

"You know my position, Mr. Rhett. And I've not changed my thinking. The preservation of the Union is in our best interest. We can find a way through this. It's going to take a little time, and a little compromise, but in the end, we'll be better for it. I'm certain of that."

"You know as well as I do that we don't have a little time, and there's not a South Carolinian alive what's willing to compromise!" Rhett barked with agitation.

"Time is on our side. In fact, time is our best ally right now. They're going to need our cotton, and they know the Brit and French markets are screaming right now. They need our commodities, and they need our labor. Good God, Rhett, Pierce is on our side. Even the abolitionists know it'll be another generation or two before they can legislate this away."

Davis, it seemed, lowered his volume in direct proportion to Rhett's increase.

He nodded my way and asked for a cup of tea.

"Yessir, right away."

"Thank you," Davis said. Surprised, I smiled at the man and he smiled back.

In the kitchen, I told Sam, "That Mr. Davis fella just told me 'Thank you' when he ordered his tea; how bout that?"

"He's a fine man," said Sam. "Lots of talk about him runnin the South. I ain't sure what that means, but he's an awfully nice man, always real polite. Real thoughtful, that man."

I put the tea on a tray and carried it out to the table. The dining room was beginning to fill, but the tables surrounding Mr. Rhett and Mr. Davis remained vacant.

"No point in waiting! Just makes us look weak, that's all. We're taxed to death as it is and legislated right out of business. It's like we're goddam colonies again. It's oppression, plain and simple. We can't allow it, Jeff. It's time to stand up for our rights—for freedom, dammit."

Mr. Davis stirred sugar into his tea, taking his time, thinking. I stood against the wall, invisible again, listening, looking disinterested and distant, trying to put the pieces of the conversation together.

"Rhett, this isn't the Revolution. And the last thing we need is another war. You pursue this—this way—and we'll have men taking up arms, Americans fighting Americans. Nobody wants that. I don't want it. Nobody in Washington wants it."

He hesitated a moment, then continued.

"Rhett, I need to say this to you, and I need you to hear me. You tone down the rhetoric. You're printing things in that paper of yours that divides folks—divides families, even. That's going to get men killed. We've got ourselves a rough road ahead, there's no doubt about it. You and your paper can make it safer, or you can make it rougher. I'm asking you to make it safer. For the sake of the South, Rhett. For our way of life. Show a little restraint, a little moderation. Give folks a way through this that won't get us all killed, for God's sake."

Barnwell Rhett's face turn red, starting just above his tie. His fat neck went red, then his jowls, then his entire face, splotchy red, like a bad peach, too soft and looking like it could make you vomit.

Rhett's gray eyes went cold with anger.

I'd seen that before, up close, in Peter's eyes, and instinctively took a step back, bumping the wall and rattling the gild-framed portrait of Thomas Jefferson.

Rising to his feet, Rhett slammed his fist on the table. "Restraint! That's all I do! No one listens! No one gives me a shred of respect! I'm giving the people the news, the truth, dammit. And you want me to tone it down! I'll be damned if I'll tone it down! This conversation is over, Jeff!"

Barnwell Rhett picked up his paper and rolled it into something resembling a club, and stomped across the dining room, through the door and onto the sidewalk. He could be heard cursing and muttering, pounding his way down the street.

Jefferson Davis, calm and quiet, stood and placed two silver pieces on the dining table, and walked toward the door.

"Mr. Davis," called a man from the table at the window. "Do you have a moment, sir?"

"Certainly, sir," replied Davis.

"Please join us," said the man, standing and offering a chair.

Mr. Davis nodded graciously and sat.

"Mr. Davis, my name is Daniel McLeod. And this here is Charlie Pinckney. We run one of the cotton gins here in Charleston."

"Gentlemen, good to meet you both. I've heard of your gin. I hope business is strong lately." He spoke as if they were at a picnic, as if Barnwell Rhett's tantrum had not just unfolded two minutes earlier.

"Couldn't be better!" Pinckney smiled.

"Mr. Davis," said McLeod, "we couldn't help overhearing your conversation with old Barnwell. Man's a fool. Got to give him credit, though, he says what he thinks!"

"He's harmless," said Pinckney, "but we want you to know that we sure appreciate your position, and we agree with you completely. King cotton's real good to us right now, and our partners in New York and across the pond know it too. This is no time to rile folks up."

"Cotton's good, indeed," Davis said. "And trust me when I say I want our Southern growers and businessmen to be treated fairly. I understand why Rhett's all worked up over the feds, but he's throwing oil on fire with that paper of his. Things can get heated up and out of hand, and he needs to settle down. Nothing I want more than the prosperity of Dixie."

"Don't we all?" laughed Pinckney.

"But," said McLeod, "old Barnwell's right about one thing. If the boys in Washington give in to the Yanks, we'll never be the same. Life as we know it'll be over, that's for damn sure."

"Well, that's not going to happen anytime soon, gentlemen," Davis said. "Far too much to be done, and it needs to be done slowly, real carefully. Lots of folks' lives impacted here, not just our own."

"Mr. Davis, we're just about to have a bite of lunch. Join us? I'd like to visit about something else, if you have the time, sir," said Pinckney.

"Delighted." Davis turned to signal me, and I stepped to the table.

"Yes sir?"

"Do you have that fine split pea soup today?"

"Yes, sir, we sure do. What would you like to drink, sir?"

"Bring me a pint." He looked at McLeod and Pinckney. "You gentlemen ordered already?"

They nodded, and as I turned to go back to the kitchen, Pinckney leaned across the table and spoke, quietly.

"Mr. Davis, I'd sure like your thoughts about this talk of making Christians of the niggers. You probably know where I stand on this, and I'd like to know where you stand."

"Well, Charlie—" Davis paused for a moment as I returned with the beer. He took a sip, and continued. "Looks to me like they've been going to church for a while now, and I'm not sure that's done us any good. Looks to me like it just makes 'em a little uppity. Last thing we need is another rebellion. Nobody's forgotten Stono—or any of the other of 'em."

"But you would agree, wouldn't you, sir, that a more obedient, more—ah, genteel—population would be an improvement? And if the fear of God, and the promise of salvation—or more precisely, the fear of eternal damnation—might keep the rebellious nature in check, then wouldn't it be to our advantage to provide some religious training?"

"I don't know, Charlie. Think about it. How are you going to train 'em? You don't want 'em reading, that's for sure. You're going to have to get preachers on every plantation, every one of 'em, or else you have some that are trained, and some that ain't. That's not a good situation. But I see your point, and you just might be onto something."

He paused again and looked at McLeod. "What do you think, Dan?"

"I'll admit, I'm of two minds on this. Of course, we want our colored folk obedient, compliant. And I suppose some Christian training might help with that. Might even help curb the anti-slave folks in the North, or those damn Methodists and Unitarians." He shook his head in disgust. "But sure as hell, we get 'em churched, they're going to start thinking, and wanting to read, and then what? I'll tell you—then we got trouble. Serious trouble. That's why we had to close all those colored churches in the first place, remember."

I stayed invisible against the wall and strained to hear the conversation. I'd walked past the Emanuel Church a time or two since arriving in Charleston, but the doors and windows had been boarded over for years. I felt a pang of homesickness, thinking about going to the Baptist church with Mama. I didn't miss the church, or the long services or the droning of Rev. Fuller, but goodness how I missed my mama.

Thinking about Mama, I failed to hear McLeod call me to the table. "Boy!" McLeod repeated, sharply.

"Yes sir?" I prided myself on my attentiveness and was embarrassed that I'd daydreamed.

"We're ready for our lunch. Could you see what's taking so long and get it out here, for God's sake?"

"Yessir. Right away, sir." I hurried to the kitchen, angry.

Charleston had opened my eyes, for sure, and my mind too. Sure, things had riled me up in Beaufort, but I couldn't quite say why. Now, with all that I was seeing and hearing, I was beginning to understand the world—mine and theirs. *Get your own damn lunch. I'm hungry too.*

"Now, there's a good example of the dilemma, gentlemen," I heard McLeod say, gesturing toward the kitchen door. "That boy. He may be alright, but he's like all the rest. They can't pay attention long enough to know when the soup's hot. How the hell are you going to train 'em up as some kind of little Christian? And what if you do? Then you got yourself a Brown, or a Vespey, or a goddamn Turner, and then we've got some real problems. No, I say don't take no chances."

They all seemed to forget that we were illiterate—not deaf.

"All due respect, Dan, but some of these boys are bright, real bright. And they're going to push us, some way. I think we're safer, far safer, if they're scared of the same hell we're scared of. Don't you agree with me, Jeff?"

I returned with soup and bread for the table, and Davis waited to respond.

"Look, I don't know Charleston the way you fellas know it. But I know on Brierfield we're good to them, and they're good for us. We take real good care of our people, and it's good for everybody. They're loyal and dependable, and they work hard, and we protect them. I don't think they want to risk that. My God, they'd be lost managing their own affairs. They don't read, they've no experience with financial matters, they've no sense of civic organization. Some may be bright, as Charlie's noted, but that's not the same as capable. I don't see how preaching and such add much value to 'em. As for myself, I'm just trying to do the right thing—keep 'em healthy and productive. It's just good business, that's all."

*"Just trying to do the right thing."* The words echoed as I walked back to my room that evening.

# CHAPTER 23

## 1854

After two years of carrying food and dishes in the restaurant, I grew increasingly restless. I wanted to be out on the water, or at least near it. I missed the life I'd known in Beaufort, being always near the rivers and creeks. I also wanted to make more money—for myself.

At the restaurant, I'd managed to go from five dollars a month to seven, and McKee had agreed to let me keep a dollar a month. I figured that if I could make more money for Mr. McKee, he'd be happy and maybe up the amount I kept.

The men on the docks and boats worked hard, but they also made more than domestic and hotel staff—that I knew for sure. Hard physical labor didn't scare me as I was now almost fifteen and packed more muscle than when I arrived in Charleston.

I walked the docks one afternoon, and the more I walked, the more I longed to spend my days there. So much energy—boats coming from all over the world and leaving for places I'd never heard of. Men loading and unloading, strong, sweating, cursing, laughing. I wanted to be among those men—muscled and sure, making things happen. The sharp smell of fish and oysters, birds, the pine tar used on the boats, the salt in the air, the whistle of steam engines, the slap of sails and lines in the wind, the call of gulls, the constant rumble of cart wheels on the dock. And the water, always the water. I longed to be on the water. Sometimes I could hear Mr. McKee's recitation echoing: *"Of books and boats I sing!"*

The next day, I went back to the restaurant, angry and agitated. *Why should a man not choose his own work? Why should one man tell another where to go, and what to do, and then carry that man's pay home? Why should I carry trays and beer and grits and stew to and from tables of men who never see me, who never want to see me or hear me, who make decisions about people like me, and make money off people like me, but can't even see me as a man?*

I got to the alley side door, the door where people like me came in, and wanted to pull the damn thing from its hinges. I wanted to knock every pot off the stove and throw every fine china plate into the street. I was ready to set the place on fire.

Ol Sam met me at the door with a big, gentle smile. "Somebody here to see you, son."

Not expecting anyone, and still boiling with rage, I snapped at him. "Yeah? Who'd be looking for me? I ain't nobody for nobody. Sam, I hate this! I hate working for people who don't give a damn. Sick and tired of it."

I slammed the door shut, hard as I could, and was glad to hear a few pots rattle.

Sam nodded toward the dining room.

Just beyond the doorway connecting the kitchen to the dining room stood Mrs. McKee. She'd seen and heard my rant, and her expression signaled alarm.

"Robert," she said after a moment. "I need to speak with you."

We stepped toward the corner of the dining room, where she took a seat and I stood, angry still, and now concerned.

"Robert, your mother—"

"What?" I demanded. "What's happened to Mama?"

"Good heavens, boy! What's gotten into you? Please settle down. I've come to Charleston for a few days, and your mother asked me to see how you're getting along. We've arranged for you to come to Beaufort for Christmas. Henry's already talked to James about it."

I looked off to the window, and now my anger turned inward. Nothing good could come of Mrs. McKee witnessing my outburst to Sam. The last time she saw me in Beaufort, I'd just broken Peter Rhett's arm. I knew the strength of her influence in Mr. McKee's decisions, and I didn't need her to think I was always angry, always breaking things.

She spoke again. "You know, we've sold the house on Prince Street. I think Lydia would want you to see our new home."

After Hank's death, the house on Prince Street held more sadness than the McKee family could bear, and they'd finally left it to leave some of the heartache behind.

"Mrs. McKee, ma'am, thank you, ma'am. It would sure be fine to be back for Christmas. I hope you have a fine stay in Charleston," I said. "It's quite a town."

"It is that. Actually, I'm here to see about the Charleston college for Liza Beth."

"Yes, ma'am. Has she come with you?" I realized I missed Liza Beth, in spite of the ways she annoyed me.

"Not this time, Robert. I thought it best that I examine the institution beforehand. It's an important decision, you know."

"Why, yes ma'am," I said, and I wondered briefly if it had crossed Mrs. McKee's mind that Liza Beth and I were the same age, or if she ever wondered if I might be ripe for education as well. For some reason, I thought she might want that for me.

"Are you staying with Mrs. Ancrum?" I asked, knowing the answer but short on other topics of conversation.

"Yes, and I'd better be going. She'll be expecting us for lunch soon." She paused, and I wondered who *us* meant. "I came up with Mrs. Rhett—the new Mrs. Rhett. Peter's going to be attending the Citadel next year."

*Peter Rhett can go to hell.* "Awfully nice to see you, Mrs. McKee. Maybe I'll see you again at the Ancrums' while you're in town," I said. "And give my best to Mrs. Rhett."

Not sure what else to say, I paused, and Mrs. McKee gave me a long look.

"Robert," she started. "The Rhetts have put the past in the past. I hope you'll do the same." She drew a long breath and looked like she wanted to say something more. "Well, I know your mother will be glad to see you at Christmas. You've grown so much I almost didn't recognize you."

"Thank you, Mrs. McKee. It's awfully nice to see you. Please tell Mama I'll be home. I'd best get to work, ma'am."

"Goodbye, Robert." Her smile and her voice were more tender than I remembered. Maybe Hank's death had softened her.

I went back to the kitchen and got a clean apron, and tried to shake off the anger I'd brought in. Mama would've told me, "Hold you head up, no matter how low you feelin." She would've told me, "You ain't who they say you be. You who you choose to be."

*How does a man choose who he's going to be when he can't even choose how he puts himself to work?*

"Everything alright, son?" Sam asked.

"Yeah, Sam. Sorry bout slammin the door." He nodded. I figured this was the right time to say something. "Sam, the McKees want me to come back to Beaufort for a few days at Christmas time. They think I ought to be with my mama. Sounds like it's already decided."

"That's right," Sam said. "They tol me already. Son, you better straighten up. Can't be slammin and throwin things jus cause you don't like the way things is. You understand me?"

"Yes, Sam." *I sure do. And you're part of all this. Being the "good boy," making it even harder for the rest of us to have any say.*

I worked hard the next few weeks, just to show Sam and the boss how I wasn't afraid of hard work, how I saw what needed to get done and then I did it. Every chance I got, I'd go back to the waterfront and watch. I watched how crews tied up their boats at the dock, and how they dropped and folded sails. I watched how they cleaned the decks, how they loaded and unloaded. I watched the way they signaled, coming and going.

I listened hard and heard the men who'd come from India and England, Cuba and Trinidad, Spain and a dozen other places. I listened to their strange words. I noticed they were dirty and hungry, and tried to think how to buy some fruit, oranges maybe, or bananas, and sell to them. I watched and listened and remembered learning from Mr. McKee, on the Beaufort waterfront, which sail was the main, or the jib, what was fore and aft and port and starboard. I watched the tides and learned the rhythms, and noted what happened when the wind came from the south.

I watched the birds and learned from them too; they were masters of opportunity.

Two days before Christmas, just after dawn, I sat on the back of a wagon carrying Mrs. Ancrum and her girl Jesse to Beaufort, eager to see my mother, eat her fine Christmas cooking, and make my case to Mr. McKee.

# CHAPTER 24

## 1854

I'd not seen Beaufort since the fight, and I remembered how lonely I'd felt the previous Christmas, alone in the room over the barn, knowing that Mama and the McKees were together. The Ancrum household had gathered across the yard, and from the barn I heard their singing and laughter and smelled their dinner. That evening, Jesse had come up the ladder with roast duck and potatoes and a big slice of buttermilk pie. She gave me a sweet smile too, and I thought she was the prettiest thing I'd ever seen. I wanted her to stay with me for a while, but she was already back down the ladder before I could think of what to say.

I had plenty to say this season, though, and she did too, all the way from Charleston to Beaufort, and the long ride passed quickly. She told me about the Ancrums, how they'd had a little boy named Jimmie who died the same week as his grandmother, both of them from the same fever. After that Mrs. Ancrum decided that Jesse would move from the quarters into the house and live in the little boy's room.

"I think it's got a haint," she told me. "Sometimes I feel somebody with me there, in the night, just watchin over me." Her round eyes widened. "Sometimes I feel a little pat on my arm, like somebody tryin to say, 'It be alright.'"

The fever and the deaths came about five years ago, just before Christmas, which was why Mrs. Ancrum liked to leave Charleston when Christmas came. The first year, Jesse said, they went to North Carolina where Mr. Ancrum had a brother with a big house. The trip took a full week each way, and Jesse said North Carolina was full of pine trees but too cold. The second year, they went to Washington to be with a cousin. After that, they went to Savannah, she told me. Last year, they stayed home. This time, though, it was just Mrs. Ancrum and Jesse on their way to the McKees. I suppose that mothers who've had to bury children know something about how to be with one another.

Jesse talked on about Charleston, about things she'd seen and stories she'd heard. "You got to watch out about the workhouse," she warned. "Sometimes, they take em to the sugar house, and they don't come back."

I knew about the sugar house, of course, and its role in the correction of insolent or disobedient slaves. In the workhouse, as they called it, was a giant waterwheel, a treadmill powered by the ceaseless work of the slaves turning the wheel by walking, as if they were climbing stairs that never stopped. We'd all heard the stories about the ones who collapsed from fatigue, or slipped on a wet board, and been dragged by the wheel and crushed, as all the others continued marching up the endless steps, powering the wheel but powerless to prevent the slow, mangling death, powerless to not hear the cries for help and the piercing screams.

Jesse whispered that she knew the Ancrums would never send her to the workhouse, even if she disobeyed. "They're so good to me, so kind. I don't never want to do somethin to displeasure them."

I liked the way Jesse spoke—like me. She'd been taught to speak carefully and to adopt the language and vocabulary of her owners. This had served me well working in the dining room, but I missed the sound and the song of Gullah, which I heard so often in Beaufort and only occasionally in Charleston. Both languages lived in me.

* * *

We arrived in front of the McKees' new house just as the sun faded into evening. This house sat even nearer the river, and the tide was out and the scent from the water floated in. *Lordy, it's good to be home.* Mama came flying out the door of the backhouse and wrapped me up in a long hug, laughing and crying.

"Mama, you gettin so little!" I teased her.

"An you gettin so big!"

Mama's fifty-plus years had all been tired, and for the first time in my life, I knew she wouldn't always be there. But we were together for a few days, and that was enough for now.

Liza Beth opened the back door and came down the steps. "Merry Christmas, Trouble," she said, and even in the moonlight, I saw the hint of teasing in her eyes. "Did you come for the food?"

"I work in a restaurant, remember? This ain't just any food. This is my mama's food!"

And Mama didn't disappoint. Mrs. McKee, eager to take advantage of the mild winter climate, instructed George to bring the dining table out to the yard, where we all spent Christmas afternoon eating and telling stories—Mr. and Mrs. McKee and Mrs. Ancrum, and Liza Beth and little Will, almost six now, older than Hank was when he died.

Mrs. McKee wanted everyone together but made sure to arrange the table so it would look proper, with Jesse and George and Mama and me sitting at the end of the table furthest from the street. Mama and Jesse jumped up to go back to the kitchen again and again, bringing platters of ham and duck and shrimp, yams and beans and grits, collards and cornbread. It was a fine feast, and I was glad to be with Mama again, and with the McKees, too, though it was an uneasy gladness. The McKees liked to say they thought of us as family. Maybe so, but we thought of them as wardens—even on Christmas.

"Trouble, tell us some stories about the restaurant!"

Liza Beth had grown into a confident and self-assured young woman, less demanding of attention and more generous with conversation and charm. "Tell us about the antics of the Planter's Hotel!"

"Did you know," I began, "that in fine dining rooms, such as *mine* . . . " I emphasized "mine" and they all howled with laughter. "Well, we attract terribly important people, and so I serve the most important men in South Carolina every day." I paused. "Except for you, Mr. McKee. We keep a table open for you."

He smiled.

"Who are some of those significant personages?" he asked.

"Oh, I don't know their names, sir. I just know that they must be very important if they dine in my dining room!" I didn't want him to know that I'd been eavesdropping on Mr. Pinckney, Mr. McLeod, Mr. Rhett and even Jefferson Davis, that they came week after week and unknowingly taught me how to read. I didn't want him to know what I'd heard and learned of business, and politics, and the murmurs of secession and war.

We laughed and ate and talked all afternoon.

After one of Liza Beth's particularly amusing and well-told stories, I watched the McKees exchange a brief glance, and knew that they were thinking of Hank. His absence would always be present.

Late in the afternoon, after helping Mama and Jesse clear the big table, George and I carried it back into the dining room, and after we'd moved all the chairs inside, I went to find Mr. McKee, who was reading in the parlor. I stood in the doorway.

"Mr. McKee, sir? I wonder if you have time to give me some advice?"

"Certainly, Robert. Let's go out to the porch, shall we?"

I noticed that McKee addressed me as Robert—not Trouble.

It wouldn't do for a man like McKee to have a colored boy in his parlor, under any circumstances, so we sat in the old straight-back rockers on the big porch, just as the sky turned the color of ripe peaches. There's nothing so lovely as a lowcountry sunset, and we both commented on its beauty.

"What's on your mind, boy?"

"Well, sir, first of all, I want to thank you for arranging things in Charleston. It sure has worked out fine." *For you, anyway.*

"Glad to hear it. I hate to think how things might've been had you stayed in Beaufort."

*Yes, either Peter Rhett or I would be dead by now. Thanks to this so-called "way of life" you people have got us in.*

"Yes sir. I s'pose there might've been some trouble." I paused. "Mr. McKee, I've been thinking. You know, you taught me an awful lot about the rivers, and the tides, and about boats and such."

"Yes?"

"Well, sir, I do believe there's some fine opportunity on the waterfront in Charleston. It's a might busy place, Mr. McKee, and I think I could work there, probably make you more money than I'm making in the dining room at the hotel."

I let that sit a moment.

"Mr. McKee, I wonder if you'd see about a place for me on the docks. I could unload ships or learn to clean em up. I'd work hard, sir. You know that."

He looked off over the fountain for a moment, and I wondered if I'd overstepped.

"Well, Robert."

I sat a little straighter.

"I like the way you think, boy," he said. "I hear good things about your work at the Planter's, real good things. James tells me you learn fast and solve problems before they happen. Makes me real glad to hear that, y'know."

"Thank you, sir."

"I know a fella, Simmons. Next time I'm in Charleston, I'll talk to Simmons."

"Thank you, sir." I wanted to ask when he would be in Charleston again.

"Anything else?"

"No sir. Goodnight, sir."

In truth, there was so much more spinning in my head that I wanted to ask.

*Why am I expected to be grateful to live a life that's not my own? Why am I supposed to be grateful when I watch my mama shrinking from endless work? Help me understand this impossible life, this anger and affection. You're not my family. You care about me, but do you care about me? Help me make sense of this.*

# CHAPTER 25

I went back to Charleston the next day, and back to the restaurant, holding the thinnest hope that Mr. McKee would act on my behalf. Hope's a mysterious thing; its absence burdens a man. I tried to remember Mama's words about hope: *"Hope maybe show up on the far side of trouble."*

Mama and I stayed up late, Christmas night, talking about my work at the dining room, and her life at the McKee house. Mama wanted to hear all about the people who were coming and going, and what I was hearing and learning. I told her about the way Mr. Rhett had his own table, and how he huffed around, and I told her about the men who struck me as smart. She laughed when I told her some of the words I'd learned by listening to bankers and lawyers, and she cried when I told her I'd been teaching myself to read.

She told me about the McKees' little boy, Will, and how Liza Beth was becoming a young lady, at last.

"They all had a fine time at the big tea, when she finished at Mrs. Marcham's little school. And it looks like she'll be going on to Charleston or Savannah fore long, for more schoolin. Maybe you'll see her round town!"

I tried to imagine Liza Beth finding her way around Charleston. Of course, she'd have her aunt, Mrs. Ancrum, right there to help her out.

Mama told me she'd been going to prayer meetings at the Baptist church every week on Wednesdays and hearing more and more talk about preparing for some kind of war. She'd heard folks worried about Yankees coming and taking everything away, that people in places like Beaufort could lose everything.

"We ain't got much to lose, son, but lots of white folk, they scared. I guess havin lots means losin lots." She said they prayed every Wednesday for folks to use sense and wisdom. "You can't lose what you ain't got."

*True, but I want the possibility of losing—the opportunity.*

I told her about the meetings I'd been going to with Alfred and Tombo and Billy, and the big preacher-not-preacher Jeremiah.

"They talk like you, Mama, about choosing good, about not fighting if you can help it. That Jeremiah, he's a big man; no one's likely to pick a fight with him anyhow. It's the small ones, like me, get messed with. But I been doin like he says, and it seems to be good counsel."

She just smiled. She never said, "Told you so," even when she did tell me so.

"What else does he say?" she asked.

"Well, he says that Mr. Douglass—remember him?—says he's doing real good work, and things might change for all of us someday."

She was quiet for a long time. We were thinking the same questions. *Could things really change for us someday?*

"Mr. Jeremiah says we have to always be looking out in front of us, let go of what's in back of us. He says when you forgive somebody, it makes you a better person."

"I reckon that's true," she said. "It's awfully hard to do, ain't it? I always want it to change the other person, but I s'pose it changes me most of all."

I was thinking about Peter Rhett and wondered if I'd ever forgive him, and if I did, how would that make me a better person? Seemed to me like he needed the most bettering.

"Mama, do you think the ancestors back in Africa can help us, way over here?" I knew the spirits of the ancestors watched over their descendants, but we were awfully far away. I'd seen a globe in town and figured out where we were and where Africa was.

"I been thinkin bout that too," she said, "and you know, these church people here talk about ancestors too; they just don't call em that. They call em the 'communion o saints.' Did you ever hear bout that? Over at Mrs. McKee's church, specially, they talk about communion o saints and 'great cloud o witnesses,' and when I asked her bout that, she tells me 'they're the ones who gone on before us.' She said ol Mr. McKee, the ol man and the missus too, and even little ol Hank, they died, but their spirits keep on livin, and there's prayers to em, and they lay things on the gravestones, flowers an such, and she says that great cloud o witnesses, they watch out for us! Can you believe that?"

I guess we both found some comfort in the idea that the spirits of the ones we loved could somehow be with us and for us. I wished they'd hurry up and give us help. I needed some direction from them, some guidance. I wished a good spirit would go with me back to Charleston. While I loved all that the big town offered, I knew I'd miss my mama, and she'd miss me. And, somehow, like the way you can smell a storm coming in, I sensed that things would be changing, all things, in ways we couldn't guess or plan for.

*　*　*

It was the week after Easter when the front door of the Planter's Hotel opened and a crisp breeze ushered Mr. McKee and another man into the dining room. I'd not forgotten our conversation, but I assumed he had, all the time working hard and hoping to find some way to get myself out of the restaurant and onto the docks.

McKee smiled and nodded at me as I hurried toward them.

"Mr. McKee, good morning, sir!"

"Robert, this is Mr. John Simmons. Simmons, the boy I told you about. We called him Trouble when he was a boy."

"Glad to meet you!" John Simmons smiled and reached to shake my hand, catching me by surprise. That seldom happened to me, and it sure didn't happen in the restaurant. I liked him immediately.

I led them to a table at the window on the east wall. It was my favorite part of the room; you could see the activity on the street and most of the other patrons in the room, but it was fairly quiet there, and customers stayed a while, which made my work a little easier.

They settled in at the table. Mr. McKee was in a coat, but Simmons simply wore trousers and a heavy shirt with a vest. He wore fine riding boots like Mr. McKee. He turned his chair so that the back was at an angle to the wall, and stretched his legs, looking fully at ease with himself. I'd learned to pay attention when men looked uncomfortable or out of place, and I noticed the ones who seemed to know exactly who they were.

I brought them their tea and left them to their conversation, staying attentive so they could tell me what they wanted to eat when they were ready.

Mr. McKee ordered crab cakes and Simmons wanted roasted chicken, and they both wanted grits. When I brought their food to the table, I saw they were laughing.

"Trouble," McKee said, "how'd you like to be a stevedore?"

"Well, tell me about that, sir," I said, trying to sound like it was the sort of thing I discussed every day.

"A stevedore loads and unloads boats. It's good hard work," Simmons said.

"I can do that, sir."

Mr. McKee smiled. "I'll tell James that you're finished here in the dining room as of today. Mr. Simmons will tell you where to report first thing tomorrow."

"Yes sir," I said. "Thank you, sir. And thank you, Mr. Simmons."

Simmons leaned back in his chair. "Could you bring me a cup of coffee? We need to talk about the details of this arrangement."

"Yes sir." When I came back, he took a sip, and looked me in eyes.

"You'll get fair treatment if you're willing to work hard." He paused. "What's your proper name, by the way?"

"Robert Smalls, sir."

"Well, then, Smalls it is. We can't have someone around the docks called Trouble."

"Yes sir," I said.

"I pay fifteen dollars a month to new stevedores." He was looking at me, but I knew he was telling Mr. McKee.

Fifteen dollars. That was more than twice the pay at the restaurant. Mr. McKee let me keep a dollar each month, and I gave him the rest. Maybe now I could keep two dollars. Or more.

"Be at the waterfront first thing in the morning, by sunup." He rose to go, and McKee stood too, and gave me a smile. I walked with them to the door, and held it for them, against the wind.

"I'll see you in a month or so, son," said McKee. *Son.*

\* \* \*

I didn't sleep at all that night, and was at the waterfront an hour before dawn, trying to figure out where I'd find Mr. Simmons; we hadn't discussed which pier I should meet him on. I walked from one end to the other, feeling stupid for not asking him about that yesterday. At the first hint of light, I saw several men walking toward one of the docks. "Can you tell me where Mr. Simmons is?" I asked.

"Up yonder there." They pointed toward a pier where two big boats were tied up. I thanked them and ran, hoping I'd be there before Simmons.

He arrived about a minute after I did.

"Morning, Mr. Simmons. Looks like it's going to be a fine day." Yesterday's wind had settled down to a light breeze, and the morning was already warm. Spring in Charleston was magic—not too hot or humid the way summer could be, everything green and blooming, like the whole world was being born fresh again.

"Good morning, Smalls. You're going to be working with Gabe here." He gestured to a big fellow near the closest of the steamers. "Do what he tells you."

I introduced myself to Gabe, who was crouched down working on a rope.

"Smalls, huh. You know John Smalls?"

"No. Who's that?"

"You'll meet him; he works here some." Gabe finished with the rope, securing the big boat's loading ramp tight to the dock. *I better learn to tie a knot like that.*

Gabe pointed to a mountain of crates on the dock. "We'll be loading those. Follow me." He led me over the ramp and down into the hold of the boat, low-ceilinged and dark. My eyes adjusted, thanks to the small, round windows up high in the hold letting just a touch of light slip in. The aroma in the damp room reminded me of the pluff mud at low tide back home, smells of fish and food, and decay and grasses, all mixed up together.

We started moving crates, and Gabe showed me how to balance the weight in the hold. "Ballast," he called it. He told me how boats had gone down, sometimes even in a mild storm, when the ballast was "out of kilter" and how the loading crew was blamed and punished when that happened.

Gabe was quiet most of the morning, only speaking when he needed to, instructing me or telling me to watch my step when the ramp got wet.

"Soon as we finish these two, they'll sail, while the tide's up. Four more's coming in."

My shirt was soaked through and sweat stung my eyes as we

finished the first boat. Gabe sat down on the seawall for a quick rest. "Bout two minutes," he said.

We started on the second boat, a cotton steamer called the *Planter*, and spent the next three hours loading cotton bales— twelve hundred. Not yet noon, I was exhausted, but didn't dare let it show.

All afternoon, we unloaded barrels and crates from the four boats that came in at high tide, finishing just after dusk.

# CHAPTER 26

Barnwell Rhett summoned Peter to Charleston the day after the end of the term at Mrs. Marcham's school. Peter had anticipated it; he'd watched as each of his four older brothers' lives were carefully managed. Educational and occupational expectations were well orchestrated, and he was the next in line. The girls' paths had been almost as carefully arranged, lest they marry poorly, in every sense of the word.

Charleston had some fine schools, that was a fact, and Peter looked forward to spending time in the city. Beaufort had grown small for him, and since his mother's death, he itched for a change of scenery. Liza Beth, however, gave him pause. Even though she seldom paid him any attention, he wanted and needed her proximity.

When he arrived at the house in Charleston, his brother Edmund, rather than his father, awaited. The house slave, Saul, met him at the gate with a smile.

"Mr. Peter, it sure is fine to see you, sir!" Saul was old—always ⁿ, seemed like. And somehow, even in that house, so void of ¹aughter or affection, he could make a boy feel welcomed. ⁺le more now, but otherwise seemed unchanged. He

carried the trunk up the stairs, and memories of the last visit came
flooding in.

"You jus holler now, Mr. Peter, if you need anythin, anythin
at all."

"Right, Saul."

Peter stayed at the window, looking out beyond the garden to
the seawall and the water. He'd stood here after Mother died, trying
to ready himself for her funeral, with his fingers shaking so hard he
couldn't button his trousers. He was too old to need her help for
such a thing, and yet he yearned for it. In truth it was Mama Hattie
who'd helped him through every stage of childhood, but he wanted
his mother. They buried her before he ever really knew her.

"Everythin alright, Mr. Peter?" Saul stood in the doorway,
watching.

"Fine, Saul. Tell Edmund I'll be down in just a minute."

"Yessir, Mr. Peter. I sure will."

Peter opened the trunk and pulled out a fresh shirt. The wagon
trip from Beaufort was as dusty and hot as ever, and Father would
never tolerate a soiled shirt at dinner.

Downstairs, Edmund handed him a short pour of bourbon.
"To the graduate!" he said, and they lifted their glasses and drank.

"Let's go to the veranda, see if we can catch a breeze." Edmund
led them outside.

The sea breeze and the bourbon helped Peter relax a bit, but
he still wondered what his father was up to, and what school he'd
determined. Some boys, he knew, had actual conversations about
these decisions. But his father was disinclined to such pandering.

"Welcome back to the city, little brother. I'll bet it feels good to
get out of Beaufort."

"Thanks, Ed. Always good to be here. This harbor makes the
one back home feel awfully small."

"It's busier than ever, too. Ships from all over, money washing
in with the tides!"

He nodded. Edmund was born for business and was happy and successful in the world of commerce.

"Where do you think Father will have me study?" he asked.

"Still prefer the blunt approach, I see," Edmund laughed. "Well, might as well just jump right in, I suppose." He took a sip of his bourbon. "I think he's planning for you to go to that new academy." He motioned to the south. "The Citadel, they call it."

"Sounds like a damn fortress. What do you know of it?"

"Fortress is the idea, apparently. Y'know, we've had to man more arsenals ever since the feds got hot awhile back about tariffs. So, now the South has a proper military academy. Finally."

Peter had heard his father and older brothers, along with uncles and other men, talking about the need for military preparation; they'd been talking about it for years. The threat from the North had been palpable for a long time now.

He hated the idea of being told what to do, where to go, and what to study. He wanted to study architecture, but he was attracted to the image of wearing a uniform and carrying a weapon. He remembered his father's words, from long ago. *"You either make things happen, or things will happen to you!"*

Pacing on the veranda, he tried to figure if he had any say in this. He wanted to design and build things—great buildings and beautiful homes. Charleston and Savannah and the whole damn South were flourishing; everybody had money and wanted to show it. He wanted to be part of that, to have people stand in awe of a grand edifice and say, "Now that's Peter Rhett! That man's an architectural genius." He'd be seen, noticed. He'd leave something standing that said "I was here."

Columbia, home of the University of South Carolina, was the place for architecture. That's where he wanted to be. And it wasn't lost on him that it would put more distance between him and the old man.

"What about Columbia?" he asked, looking at Edmund. "Would he consider the university? I can do architecture there."

Edmund rubbed his chin.

"I heard that the McKee girl—Liza Beth, is it?—will be coming up to Charleston next year." He let that hang in the air, and Peter tried to not let it matter.

Focusing on a long sip of bourbon, Peter hoped Edmund couldn't read him.

*If I want to court Liza Beth, I need to be in Charleston.*

He didn't just want to court her. He wanted to marry her. He'd never assumed otherwise. But he hadn't thought about the geography of the relationship.

*Maybe I could make Charleston work.*

Maybe he could be a man who made things happen. Military rank could be the path forward. Maybe his father could muster up some respect for an officer. And he could study architecture after he married Liza Beth. She'd go anywhere with him. He was sure of that.

*   *   *

Liza Beth and Peter's future had ample support in both family camps. A Rhett marrying a McKee was a union of Beaufort royalty, one that would preserve and augment social status. Mrs. McKee certainly felt that way but worried that the brewing conflict between North and South might upend her grand scheme. Should war befall the South, Charleston would most assuredly be a hotbed of conflict, and Mr. McKee would want to keep his beloved daughter out of harm's way.

*Jane McKee's Diary*

*April, 1854*

> *We dined with the Rhetts last evening. Barnwell's new wife seems perfectly at home. Charleston is a vibrant city, full of commerce and news. I do understand why the Rhetts prefer to*

*spend more and more time at their Charleston home. Still, it's lovely when our friends gather here in Beaufort where life feels quiet and slow, although that seems to be changing these days. Our little harbor is busier than ever, and while I know it is only a fraction of the bustling on the Charleston waterfront, it is a new experience for those who are making their way along Bay Street now. Just this morning, in fact, I witnessed a cart full of fine fabrics being carried to downtown; only last season, we could find nothing so lovely in this little town of ours.*

*Henry has become increasingly concerned about the impending North-South struggle. The reality, it seems, is that the Union cannot operate without our economy. Even now, with these small interruptions in the cotton fields, our English and French buyers are eager to see this resolved so as not to further slow their own manufacturing profits. Surely, those powerful men of Washington and New York can see the futility of their efforts.*

*Henry seems inclined to send Liza Beth to school in Savannah later this year, and I'm more inclined to see her study in Charleston. He believes Savannah will be a safer place if things do indeed become contentious. I love Charleston, and I'd much rather her study there. And of course, apart from the considerations of her education and personal safety, I'm more concerned with the prospects of an appropriate suitor and courtship. After all, what is the point of education in another city if it doesn't result in the finest of pairings for a young woman? She might as well stay here in Beaufort and marry that handsome Peter Rhett! And my goodness, what a match that would be! But I'm confident the Rhetts will send Peter to the Citadel—even though it's still fairly new, and I'm sure they've already identified the families and daughters to whom he'll be introduced.*

*I am trying ever so subtly to persuade Henry that Liza Beth should be in Charleston. He's usually a reasonable man, but my goodness he can be stubborn when it comes to the children!*

*June, 1854*

*I'm so relieved. Henry has determined that exploring Charleston on behalf of Liza Beth is in her best interest after all. (He seems to believe that this was his own idea, of course.)*

*I am now planning to visit my friend Mary in Charleston for a week to explore the fine academies there. Liza Beth is a bright girl, and I'm confident she'll enjoy improving her French and expanding her literary interests as she cultivates and expands her social circles. I must say, I'm a bit envious. Who wouldn't love to be young and carefree again, with young men all about, and the world at your beck and call? It all changes, doesn't it, when we find ourselves running the household, and raising the children, and trying to keep the men from undoing civilization!*

*Oh, I so look forward to being in a city and surrounded by culture.*

# CHAPTER 27

## 1856

For almost three years, I loaded and unloaded boats on the Charleston waterfront every day except Sundays. The back-breaking labor paid off one day when Simmons told me he wanted me to be a deckhand on a boat owned by a man named Ferguson; it was the *Planter*, a boat I'd loaded when I first started on the docks. I wasn't sure what a deckhand did, exactly, but I knew it would be a step up from loading boats all day.

I wasn't disappointed.

Simmons made sure I learned everything about ships and sails and sailors, knots and signals, tides and storms. I learned to make sense of the charts and maps, and came to know every channel of every river and harbor on the Carolina shore.

Simmons taught me how to talk with people; I watched the way he looked a man in the eye, and shook his hand, and I watched the way he handled business. I learned how to give people the kind of attention and honest work that earned trust and respect.

And then I met Hannah.

* * *

We'd taken the *Planter* to Savannah to load rice and cotton and had just returned. I sat on the stone wall of the waterfront to catch a breeze and cool off. It had become my habitual place most days, late in the morning. A great oak provided shade, and from there I could see the entire harbor, and watch boats arriving and leaving. I'd learned the flags they flew—France, Belgium, Spain, Mexico, Cuba. And, of course, the British Empire. Simmons told me the Brits ran the world, that the sun never set on the British Empire. I wondered what the British thought of South Carolina's threats to secede. We'd be a laughably small little empire, but—for some folk anyway—rich in pride.

From my perch on the low wall, I'd learned the patterns of the laborers—of the independent businessmen who exchanged currency without visiting a bank, the net weavers and menders, the butchers and fishmongers. And I couldn't fail to see the trading of men and women and children, hundreds each week. Though the import of slaves from Africa had ended almost five decades earlier, the tragic business continued to flourish—and I hated it.

I watched house slaves come and go, buying fish and produce along the water; that's when I saw Jesse and another girl buying oranges. It had been a year since Jesse'd been traded to a family on the other side of Charleston.

As they turned from the orange stand, she saw me watching her, and I smiled. She ignored me and turned to talk to the girl with her. *Don't act like I'm invisible.*

"Mornin, Miss Jesse," I called out.

"Oh. Well, yes, mornin to you too," she answered.

"And good mornin to you," I said, smiling at the other girl.

"Mornin, yourself." She didn't smile exactly, but her eyes did, and she didn't look back down like most girls did.

"They call me Trouble," I said, holding her gaze.

"I'm sure they do."

"And you?"

"They don't call me trouble. Much." Her eyes held steady. *My goodness.*

Jesse didn't want to hear any more. "Lawd, Hannah! C'mon, let's get on back to the hotel."

"Ladies, I hope to see you again soon," I said with a deep and dramatic bow.

I watched them walk away, Jesse's head shaking.

Hannah looked back.

At me.

\*   \*   \*

Hannah's life had always felt to her like a tangled knot. Every cord, all the little threads that connected her to other people, were twisty and tangled and messy. When she tried to pull any one of them loose to see where they'd come from, all she got was more tangles and more knots.

All she knew for certain was her mama, Sadie. Where Sadie had come from, who her own mama and papa were, were questions they'd find out over Jordan. No living person knew. They maybe came from Africa, or maybe'd been born somewhere near here.

Sadie told Hannah once about a memory, or maybe a dream, where she was with a little boy and a little girl. They were all together crying and hungry and scared, all holding onto each other.

Hannah remembered her mama telling that story because she couldn't forget the rest of that dark day. The gray morning brought afternoon rain, and they'd both gone onto the porch of the big house to stay dry. Sadie rested a big silver pitcher on her knees to polish it. The sea breezes forced constant polishing, and Mrs. Kingsman had no tolerance for tarnish. Sadie handed Hannah a little silver sugar bowl and she rubbed the surfaces to a brilliant shine.

"Mama," Hannah asked, "do they eat out of these shiny dishes?" She knew the Kingsmans' reputation for luxury, and she imagined a huge table covered with silver dishes filled with enough food to satisfy every hungry belly in Charleston.

"Hannah, honey, they got plenty to eat, that's for sure. I s'pose they do indeed use these fine dishes."

After a few quiet minutes, Sadie continued. "Honey, I ever tell you bout how Anansi got his skinny ol long legs?"

Hannah leaned back against her mama, eager to listen to her story, loving the way she slipped back to her Gullah roots, loving the lyrical Gullah words and rhythms.

"Awful long time ago, back in Africa, honey, there live that clever spider. His name was Anansi. Anansi's wife, she was a fine good cook. But always, that Anansi loved to taste all the food what any other body in the village made for themselves and for their families.

"One day, Anansi, he stopped by ol Rabbit's house. Rabbit was his fine good friend.

"'I see you got greens in your pot,' says Anansi, so excited. Anansi, he sure loves the greens.

"'They not quite done,' said Rabbit. 'But soon they be good and done. You stay and eat with me.'

"'Oh, I sure love to, Rabbit, but I got some tings to do,' Anansi say, in big hurry. He knew if he wait at Rabbit's house, ol Rabbit would surely give him work ta do. 'I know,' say Anansi, 'I spin me a web. I gonna tie one end round my leg and one end to that pot o greens. When those greens be all done, you tug on this web, and I come runnin!'

"Rabbit say he think that's a good idea. And so it be done.

"'Now I smell beans,' Anansi say all excited with his nose in the air. 'Fine beans, cookin in the pot.'

"'Come and eat these beans with us!' cry the monkeys. 'They most done.'

"'Oh, I surely love to, Papa Monkey!' say Anansi. So, ol Anansi decide he spin the web again, with one end tie round his leg, and one end tie to the big bean pot.

"Papa Monkey say that's a fine idea. And so it be done.

"'I smell sweet potatoes this time,' Anansi sniff, so happy. 'Sweet potato and da honey, I do believe!'

"'Anansi!' call out his friend the Hog. 'My pot is full o sweet potato and honey! Come share this food with me!'

"'I would love to,' say Anansi. An so gain, Anansi spin the web, with one end tied round the leg, and one end tied to the sweet potato pot.

"By the time Anansi arrived to the river, he got one web tied to each o his eight legs.

"'This is a wonderful idea,' Anansi says to his own self, so proud. 'I wonder whose pot gonna be ready first?'

"Just then, Anansi feel a tug on one leg. 'Ah,' he say. "That be the web string tied to ol Rabbit's greens.' Then, he feel another tug. Then another. And Anansi, he's pulled three way all at once.

"'Oh dear,' says Anansi when he feel the fourth web string pull.

"Then, he feel the fifth web string tug. And then the sixth. Then seven and eight! Anansi felt pulled this way and that way. His ol legs got pulled more and more thin. Anansi rolled and tugged himself into the river. When all the webs got washed away, Anansi pulled himself, all wore out, up on the shore.

"'Oh my, oh my,' sighed Anansi. 'Jus maybe that's not such a good idea after all.'

"And now," Mama said, "to this very day, Anansi the Spider has eight long ol skinny legs. And he never got food that day a'all!"

The rain let up, and they went back out in the yard, where Sadie mended a dress for Missus Kingsman, with Hannah handing her the button or the thread from time to time. When Hannah got sleepy, she laid her head on a little folded-up batch of cloth at Sadie's side.

A searing sting jolted her awake to the screeching voice of Missus Kingsman. "Git! Git your filthy head off that calico!"

Hannah jumped up and backed away from the switch. The next swing just missed, but Missus swung again and caught Hannah's right ear, and she felt the flesh tear and the blood run. "Hush!" the woman screamed, and Hannah bit her lip and willed herself quiet.

As she reached up to her ear, she saw her mama coming at Missus, moving like a mother hen, both arms flying and fire in her eyes. Hannah watched as she lunged for the switch.

"No, Mama!" she tried to shout, but her voice got stuck in her throat, and she saw Missus take another hard swing, and she saw blood running from her mama's eye. She watched, paralyzed, as the switch came down again and again, bloody now, and her mama's voice went silent. Finally, Missus stopped swinging; maybe she decided a blind seamstress might not do.

"Sadie, if you want to see this child live another year, see to it that the both of you remember who you are."

She turned and marched to the big house.

As Sadie lay on the ground, Hannah heard her whisper. "We gonna remember. Yes ma'am. An you won't never forget."

Sadie's eye stayed swollen shut for a long time after that, and when it opened back up it looked kind of sideways. She always closed it to sew, or anytime she needed to see clearly. She said, "Who knew one eye'd be better'n two?" and liked to make a joke of it, but it was always a reminder of that day, and Hannah wondered if every white woman lived with such darkness in her spirit.

*　*　*

One day soon after that, Mr. Kingsman came into the yard and gave Hannah a long look. "You come with me," he said. Sadie was back in the washhouse and Hannah wanted to call out to her, but he told her, "And you stay quiet, you hear me?" He held her by the wrist and pulled her off to the barn and pushed her into the tack room. In the dark she heard him latch the door, and her eyes adjusted and she saw him opening up the buttons on his britches.

"Turn round," he said. She stared at his hand, holding his meat.

"Turn round, you!" he hissed, and let his free hand fly, backhanding her in the jaw, spinning her around. She felt her skirt go up, and her knickers down, and he pushed his knees between her legs, and she felt her flesh ripping and burning. He stayed inside her and slammed hard, over and over. She felt splinters in her forehead and cheek, against the raw wood of the barn wall, felt her own blood on her legs, and she heard him grunt and then a final horrible push inside her, and a moan, then silence.

It happened again a few days later. She saw him from the side yard and started for the washhouse, but he saw her. "You!" he shouted, and she realized he didn't know her name. How was it possible that he didn't know her name? He led her to the barn again, to the same wall, and it happened again, and almost every day after that, except on Sundays. At first it hurt, but then she learned to leave her body, to leave her mind, to simply leave, and it was a faraway thing happening to a faraway girl, a girl she didn't know. Neither of them knew her name, and it was better that way.

He stopped, for a few months, when her belly began to grow. Sadie said, "Maybe now he leave you lone." And he did till after the baby came. And it didn't hurt so bad after that. But Missus Kingsman's anger burned hotter than before. She knew about the barn and she didn't like it one bit, and she called Hannah "Jezebel," and it was hateful the way she said it.

"That's how baby Charlotte come, when I was just a girl myself," she told Robert. "And that's how I got sent into town to work at the hotel. One day, when Charlotte was still little bitty, I heard Missus hollerin at him. 'I will not have it! You get that Jezebel out of here before she gives you another little half-breed! She goes, Samuel, or I promise, I will make every day of your life a living hell.'

"And that was the end of the barn and the beginning of the

hotel. Every morning before sunup I'd slip Charlotte into the blankets with Mama, and then I'd hurry on over to the hotel. My goodness, it was the finest place, fancy and fine, and always seemed like all them folks that stayed there was so happy.

"My job was mostly cleaning the rooms up, and making the beds, and taking the laundry down to the big washhouse behind the hotel. Some days, though, I helped with doin the laundry, stirring those fine white sheets in those giant tubs, tryin to keep the lye out my eyes and nose, cause it burn so. But, in a funny way, I liked that work, that laundry work, as I didn't have to be round so many folk, and some days that was real nice. Just me and my own thoughts."

Hannah stayed at the hotel, and after a few years she was given charge of the laundry room, where she met Jesse. And that was how she met Trouble.

# CHAPTER 28

Late in September, under a full moon, with the Charleston Harbor before them and the grand houses of the Battery behind them, Peter Rhett and Liza Beth McKee stood on the grand terrace of the Roper House, where the cadets had their annual New Term Ball. Peter wore the ring, the boots, the saber, and the gray wool jacket with pride. He'd carried himself like a military man from the beginning; it suited him. He'd been more successful academically than he or anyone else had expected. As he stood in the moonlight with Liza Beth, he savored the taste of genuine personal accomplishment, and it whetted his appetite for more.

Liza Beth, radiant in a blue silk gown, looked into the eyes of her lifelong friend. He'd grown into a handsome and talented man, blue-eyed like his father, and taller. She'd finished two years at Madame Tongo's school across town and was eager for more, eager for a place to stretch her mind and dreams beyond Beaufort.

With no breeze across the harbor, the night air hung hot and humid.

"Liza Beth, we ought to marry after we graduate next year." Peter leaned in tenderly toward the girl he'd loved forever. "We could go on to Columbia and start our family while I study architecture. We could be together. For good." He offered his vision for their shared life, the life he'd dreamed about, the life he'd imagined, the life he believed in.

"Are you proposing, Peter?" she teased gently. "I didn't hear a question in there."

"Is there a question?"

"A question would be nice."

Sweat ran from Peter's temples, down his neck and back.

"Well? Don't you think we should marry?"

Liza Beth looked out over the harbor. She'd feared this moment, but hadn't anticipated it. He'd caught her unprepared.

"Look at the moonlight reflecting on the water. Lovely, isn't it?"

"I suppose it is."

She caught a hint of impatience in his voice. Or maybe she just imagined it. Sometimes with Peter it was hard to tell.

"Peter," she said, without looking at him. "We're not ready to marry. At least I'm not."

"But you'll marry me when you're ready." It wasn't a question. She'd never known him to ask questions. He was a Rhett, and they made declarations.

"No. No, I don't know if I'll ever be ready to marry, but I wouldn't make you a good wife, Peter. I'm not the girl you need to marry."

He stared at her, stunned. "You have to marry me. I've always planned for you to marry me . . . It's why I studied here in Charleston."

"Peter," she said, raising her hand to touch his cheek. He pushed it away.

"Damn it, Liza Beth. Damn it. How can you do this to me?"

"I'm not—"

"You don't know what you're doing. You women. You don't even know how stupid you are." He turned his back and slammed his fist on the balustrade. "It's too damn hot here. I'm getting a drink."

He walked away, leaving Liza Beth in a fog of sad relief.

\* \* \*

On the waterfront below, sitting on the edge of the boardwalk, Hannah and I looked up at the moon.

"My mama's always telling me stories bout the moon and the night gods," Hannah said. "And ol Anansi. She got more stories from Africa than you can magine."

"Oh, my mama's full o stories too. Same thing. Anansi this. Anansi that."

We laughed easily, grateful for these weekend evenings. For over a year we'd spent every Saturday evening together. On Sundays we went to church and spent the rest of the day walking through Charleston or along the waterfront, telling stories and laughing.

I learned about Hannah's daughter, Charlotte, and Hannah heard stories about little Hank. I told her about Beaufort and Peter Rhett and working at the restaurant and now the boats. She told me about the Kingsmans and Charleston and working in the hotel. She was the most interesting person I'd ever met.

"We oughta get married, sugar. We oughta be going back home to our own place together, stead of me sayin goodbye to you every week."

Hannah glared at me like I'd lost my mind. Then she turned and looked out over the harbor. She took a deep breath, tasting the sea air.

"Now, how we gonna do that, Captain?" She kept her gaze on the horizon.

She'd called me Captain since our first night together.

"Robert sound like a cold old man," she'd said, "and Trouble sound like something bad gonna happen. You work on the boats, don't you? Ain't you the captain?"

I'd laughed till my eyes watered. "I sure am, baby. I sure am the captain. They just don't know it yet. And I like the way it sounds when you say it. But how bout when we're round other folks, you just call me Bobby?"

Now she looked at me with that steely look of hers.

"Get married? You think we jus gonna tell your people and my people, 'Hey now, we gettin married!' Can you picture Sam Kingsman's face when he hear that?"

I knew Kingsman from his days at the Planter's Hotel dining room, and from Hannah's stories.

"Maybe the element of surprise would be in our favor," I said.

"Think about it, though," Hannah said. "What if we did get married, and I'm not sayin we could, but what if we did, and then we have us a baby? Then our own baby ain't even our own, he'd be belonging to Kingsman, like my Charlotte does already. How's that gonna work, Captain?"

"I been thinking. And I been savin a little money. Maybe what I do is buy you, then we both belong to McKee. And Charlotte too. That'd keep us together."

"Until it don't! Bobby, all they gotta do is trade one of us off somewhere, and then we ain't together at all!"

"Well, then, sugar." I leaned in, and wrapped my arms around her and held her close. "We find a way out together."

\* \* \*

A few long weeks later, Mr. McKee came to Charleston. I'd practiced my appeal, and explained to him what I wanted to do, and why, and how I knew I could make it work.

"I don't know, son. I'm not sayin' I'm opposed, but ol' Kingsman's a hard man. I doubt he'll give you a chance to even ask. But it's alright with me. If that's what you want to do, you've got my permission."

*Permission to be with the woman I love. What kind of world is this?*

# CHAPTER 29

Times on the Charleston waterfront had been good. Sugar and cotton, rice and indigo sailed out of South Carolina daily, lining the pockets of the planters and breaking the backs of the slaves.

But hard as good times were, bad times could be even harder.

The truth was that the more prosperous the planters became, the better life was for almost everyone. Life was a little less harsh when the cotton prices were up. But it was a different story in the hard seasons; lean times were mean times. And mean people just get extra mean when the economy falls off.

It could get real bad in hard times. Just before picking season in '46, most of the cotton fields were lost to weevils. They descended one day like the locusts of Egypt, and they covered the fields and feasted there. Every man and woman on every cotton plantation worked day and night trying to save that crop, knowing they'd break their own backs picking it if they were successful. They set smoke pots and tended them, working beyond exhaustion, many of the oldest and weakest dying in the sun, but the weevils ate the cotton and reproduced faster than the slaves could push them back.

The dead weevils were almost as bad as the live ones. They died in waves and piles, everywhere, and stepping on them had a sickening effect; the slime and the smell nauseating. But the worst part was how the birds enjoyed them. Thousands of ravens, tens of thousands, followed the weevils, and ate them, and then covered everything with their excrement. The fields, the roads, the livestock, the fruit trees, every vegetable in every garden, they were all covered with slick white splats the size of an oyster shell.

When the cotton crop failed that year, the field slaves suffered even more than if they'd had to pick it. The planters were worried; their losses were immense, and their anger always landed on the slaves, as if they'd conjured the insects or the storms.

Mr. McKee's field slaves were spared, generally, in large part because he traded in rice as well as in cotton, and also because he was, at heart, a man who wanted to be good. I can't say he was a truly good man, because I will never believe that one human can own another and be truly good. But I do believe he wanted to be a good man, and I know he never fully reconciled his desire for prosperity with his desire for goodness. I suppose no one ever does.

These were high times now and moods were much improved. All the crops drew record prices. Cotton and even hemp were in demand in the Northern states now, as well as in Europe, as talk of domestic war grew louder. Rice and sugar markets were exploding. Business on the docks was brisk; planters were making money and building fine houses in the city. And not only in Charleston, but in Beaufort and down in Savannah. Ships moved in and out of the docks as quickly as they could be unloaded and loaded again to sail. Dockhands (mostly slaves) and sailors (slave and free) stayed busy and fed the local economy as they came off the boats hungry and looking for entertainment and companionship. They bought food and beer and bourbon, and more than a few of them looked for a girl to share the night. Money was moving in and out like the harbor tides.

With the rising fortunes came rising opportunities for white planters and free blacks, of course, but also for slaves. Some of us had the opportunity to earn and keep a bit of money ourselves, and I discovered that I could buy five pounds of fruit for a dollar at the market, and sell it for two to the sailors when they came off the ships as they docked.

In the summer of '56, I managed to save twenty dollars, and the summer after that, sixty. I felt like I could be a man, if only I were free to pursue such an opportunity. And I could read a little.

Nothing could stop a man who could read.

And there was Hannah. I'd never known anyone like Hannah, except maybe my mama. Hannah was smart and beautiful and strong and proud. She was all I wanted in this life. I'd met some free blacks who owned other blacks, usually as a way of protecting them, and I'd met some who'd even married. I wanted to do that too.

\* \* \*

A few days after asking Mr. McKee's permission to wed, I took myself to the sidewalk in front of the hotel early in the afternoon. I recalled that Kingsman always ate at the Planter's on Tuesdays, always had two pints, and was always in a mellow good mood when he walked out the door.

I remembered what Mr. McKee had told me about Kingsman— *"He's not to be trusted. You don't know who you're dealing with."*—but I shrugged off the warning.

"Why, Mr. Kingsman, sir, what a nice surprise!" I smiled.

"Afternoon, boy!" Kingsman turned to walk back to his office on Church Street.

"Mind if I walk with you, sir? I'd like your advice, Mr. Kingsman, sir."

Kingsman nodded, and I waited a minute before I spoke again.

"You sure know how to run a business, Mr. Kingsman. I been noticing how you make things happen, and I sure been loading a awful lot of your cotton down on the water!"

Kingsman laughed. "That's good, boy! Cotton's been real good to us, that's for sure!"

"Mr. Kingsman, I noticed your girl Hannah. She's a fine girl."

Kingsman nodded.

"I'd like to buy her from you, sir. And Charlotte too."

Kingsman stopped, looked me over hard, his gray eyes wide with surprise. "Well, now. Just how do you propose that transaction, boy?"

"Well, sir," I said as we began walking again, "Mr. McKee and I have talked about this. I'm working on the water now, you know, and I'm saving me some money. And I found a place where Hannah and I could stay, over a livery where I'd work a little, and make a little more money, and we could live there free, so I'd be saving pretty quick. Mr. Kingsman, I'm prepared to pay you five dollars a month, and on top of that, of course, we'd give you everything extra that Hannah can get, from laundering and ironing and such."

Kingsman pursed his lips the way I'd seen him do in the dining room when he was making a decision.

I continued. "Mr. McKee knows I'll work better and harder if I've got a girl, and I know Hannah will too. We'll be better folks, Mr. Kingsman, good Christian folks. I think we'd make you proud, sir."

Kingsman quickly calculated his counteroffer.

"Tell you what, boy. I'll let you have Hannah for eight hundred, along with the daughter . . . what's her name? Is it Charlotte? You bring me eight dollars a month, and I mean on the first of the month, every month. You miss a payment and the deal is off. After a hundred months, if they ain't paid for, they're mine, and any children you two have as well. You understand, boy?" *I'll take your money and, when it's all said and done, keep the girl. You don't know who you're dealing with.*

We both knew the odds.

"Yes sir, Mr. Kingsman." *I'll make the payments and have Hannah and a family. You don't know who you're dealing with.*

"We'll make you real proud, sir," I said. "And we'd sure like you to come to the wedding!" Neither Hannah nor I wanted Kingsman at the wedding, and we knew he wouldn't want to be there. I smiled.

"Good God, boy! You got yourself some big dreams, don't you? You bring me my money on Thursday, and we'll go from there."

"Yes sir, Mr. Kingsman." I nodded ever so respectfully, and after Kingman turned right at the corner, I spun and sprinted back toward the waterfront. I couldn't wait to tell Hannah.

# CHAPTER 30

I woke up tasting blood; my right arm throbbing. I tried to shake off the pain—tried to remember what happened, tried to understand why I was lying on the floor of a jail cell.

"Boy, you better get up, and I mean now."

I raised myself on my left elbow. That hurt too. Everything hurt. I pulled myself up, leaning on the iron bars of the cell door for support. I knew better than to speak.

"I don't know what you done, but you lucky those Citadel boys left you for dead, or you'd be good and dead, for sure now."

*What the hell is he talking about? Citadel boys?*

"But we gotta hold you forty-eight hours. You musta done something serious wrong."

*Citadel . . . Peter Rhett . . . Damn. When is this war with Peter Rhett going to end?*

"Turn around, boy." The deputy reached through the bars to handcuff my hands behind my back, and the pain in my arm stabbed hard, buckling my knees. "It ain't broken, boy. You got lucky."

*Yeah, that's luck. Beat bloody by rich white boys, and for nothing. Lucky damn shit.*

"Come with me." The cell door opened and I followed the deputy down a dark corridor. We stopped at another cell, bigger.

"You're staying here tonight. If there ain't no trouble, you might be leaving tomorrow. We ain't got space for everybody that gets beat up."

He shoved me into the cell, and the handcuffs came off.

There were eleven of us. Three were sick, vomiting and losing their bowels. The rest were bleeding, or had been. One was just a boy, crying. I remembered my nights in the Beaufort jail after I broke Peter's shoulder with the shovel and moved closer to the boy.

"You alright, son?" I asked. The boy stared at me. "What happened?"

"Horse threw a shoe. Masser threw it at me." He turned his head and I saw the bloody gash. "I didn't see it comin. Woke up here."

One of the older men in the cell spoke up. "They beat us nearly to death, then don't know what to do with us. Gotta get us off the street, cause it make em look like they ain't got no heart. Bring us to jail for awhile. When we leave, we got us a record. Next time they beat us again, they bring us in and lock us up cause we got a record. Ain't no end to it."

I nodded and sat down against the wall. I tried to remember where I'd been. *On the street . . . running . . . Mr. Kingsman . . . Hannah . . . What about Hannah? Was she with me? What happened to her?*

I couldn't remember, didn't think I'd gotten that far. But what if I had? What if they'd gotten Hannah too? They would've beat her, and raped her too, I knew that.

I pulled myself back up and kicked at the cell door.

"Tell me what happened to my girl! My girl! Where's Hannah? Damn it! Somebody, tell me where's Hannah!"

"You crazy, boy? You tryin to get us all killed?" The old man glared. "They'll kill ever one of us; they'll kill that little boy over there, if you don't stop it right now. You gotta stop it now."

I knew the old man was right. I slid to the floor, held my head in my hands, and tried to keep breathing.

*Just trying to do the right thing.*

\* \* \*

When I walked out, the sunlight made me blink, and after I'd walked a block I saw Tombo and Alfred across the street. I crossed over, and the three of us walked toward the waterfront.

"How'd you know I was there?" I asked.

"You missed our Wednesday meeting. We knew somethin happen," Alfred answered.

"What day is this?"

"Thursday, man," laughed Tombo.

"Damn it. Damn it!" My first payment to Kingsman was due.

"What's wrong with Thursday? What's wrong with you, man?" Tombo looked at me, then at Alfred, and shrugged.

"I need eight dollars! I got to meet Kingsman by dusk and I got to have eight dollars for him!" I couldn't miss the very first payment, only days after striking the deal. I couldn't let Hannah down. Or myself. I'd never be able to call myself a man.

"I got half a dollar," offered Alfred.

"What that? You owe *me* half a dollar!" Tombo often found a way to be amused and angry simultaneously. "Give me that!"

"Hold on." I was thinking more clearly now. I remembered I had five dollars under my blankets in my room. "Tombo, I need you to loan me that half dollar that Alfred owes you. Next week I'll give it back to you, and another half on top of it. And if you have any more money, any at all, I'll pay you back double next week."

"I guess I got a little bit," Tombo answered, "but how I know you gonna give me it back?"

"If I don't give it back to you, man, you can tell Jeremiah and everybody else at the meeting house that I ain't a man to trust. You can have my shoes. You can throw me in the damn river. I don't care. If I don't get that money to Kingsman tonight, none of it matters anyway."

Tombo and Alfred traded glances, then Alfred dug into his pocket and gave Tombo a dollar. "I guess I got a whole dollar, after all," he shrugged as Tombo glared at him.

Tombo passed it over to me before reaching into his own pocket. "Here's three. Plus that one. You gotta bring me eight next week. Eight dollars."

"Count on it. I gotta go!" I sprinted back to my room, grateful that I'd have a dollar still to buy some oranges to sell on the docks. I knew I could turn a dollar into two, and two into four, and hoped I could turn four into eight in a week's time.

*　*　*

The Kingsmans' stable slave was hanging a lantern when I arrived at the gate, gasping. I felt like I'd been running all afternoon. "Carver!" I called, and Carver sauntered over to open the gate. "Carver, c'mon, man. I gotta see Mr. Kingsman right away."

Carver laughed. "Slow down, son. The ol man just came in. He prob'ly still cleanin up. I'll tell him you here."

I sat on the lowest of the half dozen steps that led up the little porch and, leaning against the side rail, thought about the big porch on the McKees' house in Beaufort, about how I preferred that big porch, and how I missed what seemed like a whole other life back in Beaufort.

It was almost dark, and I was wondering how I'd get back to my room before curfew, thinking it'd be awful bad to go back to jail so fast, when Mr. Kingsman opened the door.

"You there, boy?"

I jumped to my feet. "Yes sir, Mr. Kingsman. Good evening to you! I've brought you your eight dollars, sir."

"Well, I was beginning to think you'd changed your mind,"

Kingsman laughed. "Try not to wait to the eleventh hour next time, boy." He stuffed the notes into his pocket, turned, and walked back into the house.

"Yes sir," I said to the door as it closed. *What the hell is the eleventh hour?*

I snaked my way back to my room across town, alley by alley, praying I'd not be seen by the curfew watchmen.

# CHAPTER 31

## CHRISTMAS EVE 1857

The McKee home pulsed with energy, and Lydia's own heart beat with anticipation. She'd prepared for weddings before this one. A good wedding spoke volumes about a family, and about a community. And a good wedding reflected on the house slaves.

"Lydia, we may not be the richest family in town, but don't we have the best weddings?" Mrs. McKee's voice sang proud.

The McKees had hosted several weddings for friends and neighbors, and on these occasions Mama cooked and cleaned for days, and then was sent back to the kitchen or the quarters to prepare to serve the guests. She'd never been allowed to actually attend a wedding for which she prepared, but today she hummed with eagerness. Today she would sit on the front row with Hannah and me.

The day she first learned about Hannah, I had been in Charleston for six long years, coming home occasionally at Mr. McKee's direction. Mama always cherished those homecoming moments. Mrs. McKee had a mother's heart and consistently found ways to see that Mama's work accommodated my visits.

Mama heard the horses as they turned onto the street and was waiting on the front porch when I swung off the horse. Her eyes filled with tears, as they always did when I departed and when I arrived home again.

"Mama, you gettin so little!" I said, wrapping my arms around her. As I had grown broad and muscular working on the docks, she'd grown smaller. I kissed the top of her head. Then we walked around the side of the house to the quarters where she'd kept some cornbread warm. She poured me some fresh milk and brought out the cornbread and sat opposite me at the simple table.

After a few bites, she smiled. "What's that light in your eyes, baby?"

"Mama, I met a girl."

\*   \*   \*

A few weeks later I returned to Beaufort with Hannah. Mama told me she was surprised and pleased by the maturity and strength she saw. Hannah carried herself in a way that evoked the stories of African royalty that Mama's mama used to tell. A bit taller than me, and thin, Hannah had dark eyes that sparkled with flecks of gold. But what Mama noticed most, the thing that caught both her eye and her heart, was this girl's confidence. It was clear that in spite of everything, Hannah stood strong.

That night Mama pulled her blanket close and remembered the night of my birth. She remembered the sound of my cry and my body curled into hers. She remembered the moonlight and the sounds from the street and the aloneness. She remembered my first steps, my fevers, how I had adored baby Hank and how I wept at Hank's death. She remembered the afternoon when I broke Peter Rhett's shoulder with a shovel and went to jail, and then to Charleston. Long years, hard years, and they'd passed by so fast.

She rose to stir the fire. She ached as she stood; her bones no longer tolerated the cold, damp December mornings, and her knees cracked and her hips creaked, but today her mind was on the afternoon celebration.

She heard George busy in the barn, feeding the horses early. He'd polished the tack for two days already, but she knew he'd shine it once more before he brought his two finest geldings out. She knew he'd envisioned, for weeks now, the way they'd prance and strut, and he knew the good people of Beaufort would know whose they were. His reputation as a horseman was without equal.

"Mornin, George. Ain't it a fine mornin for jumpin the broom?"

"Gonna be right warm, Liddy. Perfect day for those two."

Mama went through the back door of the main house, and put a kettle on the fire for the McKees' breakfast tea. Yesterday's baking would be today's breakfast, but she was too excited to eat. She brought the basket of breads and a plate of sausage to the table, humming.

"Why, Lydia, you sound like a songbird this morning."

"Yes sir, Mr. Henry, I got a song in my heart today!"

"Don't we all?" said Mrs. McKee. "Fine day for a wedding for those two. What a party we'll have!"

"Yes'm! Fine day indeed!" She brought two cups of coffee to the table, and after setting them down, she took a step back, and paused a moment.

"I jus want to say somethin to you both," she said.

They looked up, and waited, and saw her eyes go wet.

"My boy and me . . . you two been real good to us. I sure do thank you for letting them have the weddin here. I sure do thank you."

Henry and Jane McKee looked at one another and smiled.

"Lydia," Mr. McKee said, "you know you're like family to us. We're just real happy for Trouble and Hannah." He took a sip of his coffee. "We've all been together a long time now, gone through an awful lot, haven't we? You've been good to us, too, Lydia."

He took another sip of coffee and, smiling at both women, returned to his newspaper.

\* \* \*

At three o'clock, under the magnolia tree, as the bells of St. Helena Episcopal Church rang across town, I stood with Hannah in front of Rev. Mansfield French. Mr. McKee had asked the Methodist to officiate after both the McKees' rector at St. Helena's and Beaufort Baptist's preacher apologized that their own schedules rendered them unavailable.

Rev. French smiled, astonished by our audacity and by the diversity of the people that surrounded us in the McKee yard this afternoon. Never had he witnessed a white family hosting a wedding for a slave, and there was no denying the mutual affection. All of the McKees and many of their neighbors and friends shared the festivities. Somehow Henry McKee had convinced Samuel Kingsman to allow Hannah's mother, Sadie, and daughter, Charlotte, to attend. For this, I silently promised to repay Mr. McKee's kindness.

After we spoke the vows, Rev. French nodded to Mama. She stood, solemn and focused, and picked up the short-handled broom from under her chair. She walked slowly to Rev. French's side, and looked Hannah and me in the eyes, and lifted the broom and waved it three times, purposefully, lips moving silently, above our heads. Then she placed it on the ground just in front of us and finally smiled. She nodded once, and I took Hannah's hand and when Mama nodded again, we jumped over the broom together. Laughter and applause erupted and Rev. French pronounced us man and wife.

The guests ate and celebrated until dusk, and Henry McKee remembered it was Christmas Eve, and asked Rev. French to say a prayer.

# CHAPTER 32

## 1860

After I'd been working on the *Planter* for a year or so, Simmons convinced the owner, Ferguson, to make me her helmsman. I had navigated the rivers and channels all around Charleston and Beaufort, all the way past Hilton Head and Savannah. I knew I was good at it, and Simmons knew it too.

Hannah could finally call me Captain.

We had a fine crew:

John Smalls, first mate. Hannah and I liked to call him Brother John.

Alfred Gradine, the engineer, who I knew from Jeremiah's not-a-church meetings.

Abraham Allston, a tall, gentle man with eyes like a sea hawk.

Gabe Turno, who I'd met that very first day on the docks, working for Mr. Simmons.

Abram Jackson, who was older and braver than any of us.

David Jones, who we called Jonesy. He drank a bit and talked too freely on occasion.

They were good men, this slave crew, and I was proud to work with them. They bore untold stories of struggles and hopes and heartaches; you learn to see that in the lines on a man's face, and in the way he moved. We learned to trust one another's strengths and cover one another's weaknesses, as there was no other way to survive life on the water. I learned a great deal from these men and liked to think they learned a bit from me.

* * *

There's no finer sight than the light on the water at the beginning and end of every day—the way it shines and ripples, the way the water reflects the sky and the boats. Sometimes it looks like it even reflects the way things feel.

Late one afternoon after a hard day's work, I sat on the pier mending a line and enjoying the light when I saw a big fellow watching from the sea wall. The sun was behind him, low and bright, and I couldn't see his face, but when he saw me look his way, he waved and came over to where I was working.

*Abe Polite.* I hadn't seen him since that last day on the plantation.

"Afternoon, Trouble!" That big smile of his hadn't changed a bit.

"Afternoon yourself, Abe! What—"

"What am I doing in Charleston town? Bet you're surprised, ain't you?"

"Sure am. Tell me—"

"Why I'm here?" Abe always jumped in like that, talking away before anybody else finished his own thought. "Well, I'll tell ya, I think it was Lydia's idea. I don't know for sure, but I think it musta been, cause one mornin, up come that ol Mr. Palmer, an he tell me, 'Boy! If you got anything, git it now, and come on with me.' So I got my coupla things, and off we go to Beaufort, and then he hand me off to Mr. McKee, and then he—McKee I mean—he hand me off to a fella that belong to them Rhetts, and tell him 'Take him long wit you to Charleston. See if you can find our boy Trouble,' an here I am!"

He paused to breathe.

"Well, I'll be. What are you going to—"

"What am I goin to do? Well now, here's what McKee said; he said I would find you and that Mr. Simmons would know I was comin and he'd be puttin me to work on the water here. How bout that, now?"

I tried to put it all together. Abe would be working for Simmons, which made sense. Abe had a reputation for fine woodworking, and with all the traffic in the harbor, he'd have his hands full. I wondered why Simmons hadn't said anything to me, but then why would he? I wondered, too, how they knew where to find me, but then I remembered that Barnwell Rhett spent more time in Charleston than Beaufort and was sure to see Simmons now and again. Still, it was something—my brother, or maybe my half-brother, right here on the docks, and we'd be working for the same man. Maybe he could tell me more about Larry Polite. He was a talker, that's for sure. If he had anything to tell me, I knew he would.

We went the next afternoon to get his tag. I showed him mine and explained that here in Charleston, if you got stopped without your tag, no matter what, you'd be in trouble, deep. Mr. McKee had given him the money to pay for it for the first year, but I explained he'd have to make sure he paid for it again every year. It had a number stamped on it, and if they picked you up, they'd find your number, and if you hadn't paid your fee that year, you'd be in the jail and hoping that your owner would pay you out.

Abe's tag said *Carpenter*, which didn't do justice to his skills. A little tag like that couldn't do justice to a man's identity. How does a number, or a word, or a piece of metal say who a man is? How can a person be reduced to an entry in a ledger somewhere?

Simmons put Abe to work in the shipyard at the end of the waterfront. He repaired wheels and railings, mended masts, patched hulls. He worked magic with wood. And he was glad to be off the plantation.

We didn't see each other much; our work had us in different places. I was out on the *Planter* days at a time, running commodities up and down the Carolina coasts. But every week or two, we managed to sit a while at the end of the day out on the pier by the shipyard and talk. Mostly Abe talked. He told me that he'd hoped to see Mama when he passed through Beaufort on his way to Charleston, but that didn't happen, and he was bad disappointed. He only saw her, he said, every few years, despite how close by she was. I wondered if Mr. McKee kept them apart deliberately, or if he just never thought about it. Mostly I wanted to hear about Larry Polite; I wanted to find out if he was my father.

"Well, now," he said, after I'd asked him what he knew about Polite. "I don't know much at all, and I sure wish I did. He got sold off and sent to Mississippi long time ago. Don't know if that was before you come along or not. There was a fella on Ashdale that told me once that he thought Polite was the perfect name for him. Said he was a kind soul, a man to trust." Abe looked up at a pelican soaring above. "I don't know, but that always made me want to be that kind of a man, maybe somebody want to say that about me some day, maybe honor the ancestors by being that sort o man."

"Abe, is there anybody else you think my father coulda been? Any idea?"

"Well, I'll tell ya, I thought about that after you left Ashdale. I thought about it a lot, and I don't guess I got a answer for ya. Ya know, we was allowed to go to the praise house now and again, but I never saw our mama there, so I don't reckon she met up with any of the Ashdale men. But I heard another fella say that she came with George sometimes, to the praise house, I mean. Said she rode over with him sometimes, or somethin like that."

"You mean George at the McKees'? Uncle George?"

George. He'd always been there. He'd always watched out for me. And he'd sure been angry when I got myself into trouble. But . . . no, that didn't add up. Why wouldn't Mama tell me if it was

George? Or why wouldn't he?

I was going to have to chew on that, and didn't have the appetite for it just then.

"Anyone else?" I asked. "Is there anyone else you think she might've known?"

He shook his head. "Can't think o nobody. But I gotta tell ya . . . might be just as well. I know who my daddy was, but I never did know the man, and that leaves a kind of a empty place where it seems like there oughta be somebody's life connected with mine, ya know? And now it's just a unconnected kind o place. Maybe it's better to just not have that place at all."

I nodded, but it was because I could see how it felt to Abe, and not because that's how it felt to me. I had that same kind of disconnected place in me, but more and more I wanted to know.

The next week, we met at our same pier near the shipyard, and Abe told me about a woman he'd met. He said he'd loved a girl on Ashdale, and even though he didn't see her much, it just about broke his heart to leave her when he got sent to Charleston. But now he'd met a woman who cooked for a restaurant near the waterfront, and he thought Charleston might be all right after all.

Abe didn't show up at our pier the week after that, and when I saw him the next time his left hand was wrapped up in a big bloody bandage.

"Accident with the big saw," he said. "Coulda been worse, I guess."

He'd lost all of his little finger and half the one next to it, and that struck me as plenty bad. He looked plenty bad too, real pale and weak. He said he'd bled heavy and was awfully tired. They put him right back to work, of course.

Mr. Simmons found me a few days later to tell me that Abe had died; the wound was infected and he'd been found in a fever, unconscious, in the doorway of the tool room at the shipyard.

"I know he was your friend, Smalls. I'm real sorry."

"He was my brother, Mr. Simmons. I appreciate you letting me know."

I knew Simmons would tell Mr. McKee, so my mother would learn, days after the fact and third-hand, of the death of her first son. I wished I could be there with her somehow.

That night, in Hannah's arms, I tried to say how it hit me, how I was just getting to know him, and how he'd been the sort of man he said he wanted to be, a kind man and a man you could trust. I'd thought maybe he'd be able to fill that unconnected empty place, but now I'd lost the closest thing I had to a brother, and I thought about Hank. When I finally fell asleep I dreamed of burying a man whose face I couldn't see. Maybe it was time to bury the questions about my father.

# CHAPTER 33

For almost ten years, I'd overheard the conversations about trouble between the South and the North—states' rights and Northern aggression, the call to arms, and finally secession.

In 1829, Simmons told me, men began bringing granite blocks, shipload after shipload, to create a sandbar at the opening of the harbor, and for more than three decades they'd worked to build the fortification on that foundation. From each of Sumter's five redbrick walls, troops could monitor the passing of every vessel that entered or departed the harbor. From any of its watch points, the command could be given, and from any of its 135 guns, shots could be fired.

Coming or going, every sailor on every ship passed Fort Sumter.

Union troops under the command of Major Robert Anderson had occupied Sumter since the day after Christmas 1860, when the major recognized his troops' vulnerability across the harbor at Fort Moultrie. South Carolina had seceded from the Union just two days before.

We weren't surprised the night those Citadel boys started firing on Sumter; they'd been itching and eager for months, maybe longer.

Back in January, when *Star of the West* headed over there with supplies, those cadets opened up and turned her right around. She wasn't a warship, but they fired all the same, so we all knew it was just a matter of time before a major battle erupted. Now, Anderson and his men were desperately low on supplies of both food and firepower, and they anxiously awaited the provisions ordered for them by the new president, Abraham Lincoln.

I watched most of the battle from the waterfront, along with Simmons and the rest of the *Planter*'s crew. Charleston's wealthiest and most powerful men and women watched from the verandas and rooftops of the mansions just behind us on the Battery.

I guess we all remember where we were that day. April it was, so sunrise came earlier each day, and I always went to the docks before dawn. I heard the shots, just barely, from our room over the livery, and ran out to the waterfront, where the sound carried, and the light too, and those boys were putting on quite a show. For a couple of hours, we watched the explosions over the fort, watched their reflections in the water. It didn't sound like the Union men were returning fire. Just after dawn, though, they began to strike back, too late, and it sounded like thunder, all morning and into the afternoon.

So there it began, in 1861 at the Charleston waterfront, where the Ashley River empties itself from the south and the Cooper River from the north, where the big fine houses that line the Battery wake each morning to the sun rising over the Atlantic, where Forts Johnson and Moultrie flank and protect her, where ships and sailors and cargo of every kind come from every place, where the gate to the entire world stands open.

I watched mortar explode over the water and over the fort, and heard the thunder of the guns in front of me and the cheers of the spectators behind me.

Always in between, always in the middle, trapped between the powerful and the powerless, held between the hands that picked the cotton and the hands that pocketed the cash, caught between the genteel and the cruel. I'd always known I was in between, stuck there, but somehow, now, I saw it in a new way—a place of both danger and opportunity. "Danger and opportunity," I'd heard a sailor say after a voyage from China. "That's what a crisis is, you know, the intersection of danger and opportunity."

\* \* \*

The *Planter* became a warship for the Confederate States of America that April night. They pressed her owner, Ferguson, to lease it to the new Confederacy, and they made it an easy and lucrative decision on his part.

She wasn't much of a warship; she'd started as a cotton steamer, one of the first boats I'd worked on. But she was a fine boat—small, one hundred forty-seven feet long, and thirty feet wide, forty-five in the beam, and a shallow draw, less than four feet of water; built on a live-oak frame, planked with red cedar, two engines, each driving a side paddle wheel; and now equipped with two big guns—a long pivot on the foredeck and another, not quite so long, aft.

She could carry fourteen hundred bales of cotton, but now she'd move men—a thousand at a time—or munitions. She was one of the fastest boats in the harbor and nimble, too, able to reverse course almost immediately when the wheels turned in opposite directions. At first, Ferguson planned to pilot her himself and have the rest of us, all slaves, serve as his crew.

The Confederacy, of course, removed Ferguson, but kept the crew. Our new man, Captain Relyea, took his position quite seriously. He was much impressed with himself in uniform, carrying himself like a peacock, in spite of—or maybe because of—a limp he'd acquired somewhere along the way, another battle somewhere, I suppose. His trademark habit of leaning against the cabin window, arms crossed over his barrel chest, gave him a reputation for arrogance, and it was not inaccurate.

Having been the helmsman already, I was kept on as such, and quite pleased to have the assignment, as I felt most at home at the wheel and on these waters and the rivers that fed them. From the Cooper above Charleston, all the way to Savannah, I knew the lowcountry's marshes and tides as well as any pilot. Our assignments occasionally took us to Port Royal and sometimes Beaufort, where I could see my mother, if only briefly. We carried guns to the forts, and we fortified the Confederate waters with mines and torpedoes to keep the Yanks out.

It's a hard thing, being loyal to the crew you work with and at the same time fortifying your own prison. That's how it felt, every day, on the *Planter*.

We were a good crew, apart from the officers. We liked and respected and trusted one another—life on the water demanded it. Captain Relyea and his officers were all right most of the time. They stayed focused on the assignments and maneuvers, and we executed them. I thought about it all the time—how we were good at our work, but the work was no good.

\* \* \*

Hannah and I were fortunate to be able to stay in the room over the livery in those early days of the war, what with the new baby and another on the way. Our little Lydia—Liddy—had her mama's smile and her grandmother's heart, and I missed her something awful when I was away.

Hannah managed to juggle everything. Except for Mama, I don't guess I've ever known such a strong and determined woman. She sure knew how to keep me focused and could be awful quick to tell me what she thought about most anything. We made quite a team, both of us so strongheaded, but facing the same direction, at least most of the time.

I had to be away for days at a time, sometimes weeks, while she worked hard and took in as much laundry and ironing as she could handle. The war brought plenty of business, that's for sure. More men, more uniforms, more hotel linens, more of everything. She handed an awful lot of cash to Mr. Kingsman's collector every week, more than he'd expected, so it never occurred to him that she was putting some in our own little box every day.

Late one night, after I'd been away for seventeen days, we finally lay together and she told me she'd counted it up. We had ninety-two dollars already, only two months into this. I now understood about war being good for business.

That Sunday, as I walked past the big Baptist church on Meeting Street, I heard fragments of the preacher's message for the morning.

"This war which has been forced upon us by our assailants . . . grounded in opposition to an institution which is sustained by the sanctions of religion . . . The Northerners assume that slavery is a sin and therefore ought to be abolished . . . We hold that it is a Scriptural institution . . . We contend now for the precepts of religion . . . against the devices of the wisdom of this world . . . it is the duty of religious bodies to define their position in this great contest . . . to hold fast to our peculiar institution . . ."

I worked on the *Planter*, helping them to do just that.

# CHAPTER 34

The night Peter Rhett and his battalion fired on Sumter was as exciting and frightening as anything he'd ever experienced. Their commander at the Citadel, Colonel Stevens, ordered them to fire every two minutes, and before sunrise they'd pummeled the fort with cannonballs, red hot. They witnessed the fire-burst and heard the cheers of Charleston's finest, who were watching from their rooftops and windows along the Battery. In his newspaper, Barnwell Rhett described it as a spectacular sight and said he felt God's benevolence serving the South and knew the Divine wrath would conquer the North.

The soldiers at Sumter waited hours it seemed before returning fire. They were so short on powder and cloth cartridges that they improvised with their own socks. Peter wondered what it was like for those Union boys to be trapped out there on that little island of a fort, to have mortar exploding over their heads, to smell the fires, to see their fellow soldiers wounded.

He wondered if now, finally, his father would take note, and approve.

*Jane McKee's Diary*

*Christmas, 1861*

*We must celebrate Christmas in exile this year, although it's anything but celebration. It all happened so fast—the ships, the warning, and then we fled.*

*When our boys fired on Fort Sumter, just before Easter last spring, we celebrated, believing our Cause both justified and successful. It was soon apparent that we were terribly mistaken.*

*Our men saw the need for the forts, off of Hilton Head and St. Helena both, to protect our lovely little sea island from the Yankees, and they'd put most of the slave men to the task. But on that Thursday morning, November 7, we heard the warnings from mounted troops, our Southern sons. "Yanks at Port Royal Sound! Evacuate women and children! Yanks at Port Royal Sound! Evacuate women and children!"*

*I ran to the gate and waved down a soldier. "How soon?"*

*"Leave now, ma'am! They'll be here before dusk!"*

*We took him at his word, and I called for George and Lydia to ready the wagon. I sent little Will up to gather his boots and clothes, while I hurried through the house, gathering what I could of the silver and crystal and books. I soon realized we'd not be able to take it all with us. And how could we salvage the furniture and carpets? What would become of the animals we couldn't take with us? Like everyone we knew, we'd try to get to Charleston, or west into the interior of the state—but where?*

*Henry ran in, just as I was wrapping the candlesticks, breathless.*

*"I've told George to cut an opening in the parlor floor," he said. "We'll hide as much as we can there and leave a few things here. Maybe they'll think they've got it all when they take what they can see."*

*So, I handed the best of the china and the silver platters and bowls down to Henry, down under the parlor, where he rolled them into our finest carpets, and then wrapped those in old quilts and bedsheets. We left the more common carpets on the floors, and a few of the quilts on the beds, and we left most of the books on the shelves in the parlor, which broke our hearts, but there were simply too many and they were so heavy. They cost us too much in weight and space on the wagon. "I cannot live without books," Thomas Jefferson once said, famously, and Henry and I feel the same way.*

*George put two mattresses in the wagon, and Lydia brought out blankets and pillows, just enough, and she put in a few cooking pots and utensils, and a basket full of breads and preserved vegetables, and some oil and flour and sugar. She brought some butter but left the morning's eggs and the milk. I remembered candles and lanterns, and after Henry and I brought out our own trunks of clothing and boots, there was scarcely room for us on the wagon. But George squeezed us in. I held little Reed on my lap, and Willie sat next to me. Reed cried and Willie tried to be brave, asking questions I couldn't answer.*

*Henry, of course, rode out on his beloved Lexi, and I knew he worried that she was too old for the journey, but he couldn't leave her. Both hounds followed us, and we waved goodbye to Lydia and George, entrusting the house to them for now, and joined the sober parade of Beaufort's fine citizens leaving our sweet town, while many others gathered on the steamer taking advantage of the tide rising on the river behind us.*

*And so now, here at Elizabeth's house in Charleston, we can only wonder what has become of our new home, or the sweet old house on Prince Street. Henry and James heard, at a meeting yesterday, that the Yanks have made themselves at home in all of our houses and even the churches in Beaufort—officers living in our homes as if they were their own! And the churches turned to* hospitals! It's a blessing that our own dear parents are no longer among us, as such news would break their hearts. William Bold and John McKee would rise up from their graves, muskets in hand, if they could!

Of course, this will all be over soon, and we'll return to our home, but it can't happen soon enough for Henry and me. At least here in Charleston, we are among family. And Liza Beth is here too, having been requested to stay on to teach French, after finishing her work at Madame Tongo's school. Mme. Tongo tells us that Liza Beth's skills in French are les plus fin, and will be a fine asset to the school and especially helpful to the youngest of her students.

At least Liza Beth's place in life is happy now. She's certainly taken with that handsome Ellison Petigru. What a fine family, although his uncle's questionable loyalty to the state must bring them all no small amount of concern. He, the old uncle James P., resisted secession from the very beginning, declaring, "South Carolina's too small to be a republic, but too large to be an insane asylum." Arrogant man. As I see it, South Carolina is too fine a world to be anything but our home, to be governed as we see fit. Still, surely, it didn't have to come to this.

How good it will be to get back home, to be there for spring and Easter.

# CHAPTER 35

## MAY 12, 1862

After days of planning and praying, Hannah slipped out of the apartment quiet as smoke, a few minutes before dusk, before curfew, just like we'd planned. The sidewalk was empty, the night dark; a heavy cloud cover dimmed the new moon. It seemed the heavens were with us. She told me later how hard she prayed, trying to believe that.

She carried our baby on her hip and held little Liddy's hand. Liddy was sleepy and confused; Hannah had woken her up after she finished nursing Robbie and gave her a little bread. The last thing she needed was a little one crying about being hungry. Liddy was always quiet when she was sleepy, so maybe she'd stay that way.

The two Abes were part of the plan, and Jackson and Allston, along with Sam and Gabe. And William Morrison came too, from the crew of the *Etowah*.

Sam and Gabe both wanted their women, Lavina and Annie, to come, but didn't tell them the plan for fear they'd either expose it beforehand or testify after the attempt. Jonesy decided he couldn't take the risk, and we all made him swear an oath of secrecy. I knew more people could increase our risk, but I also remembered Mama's words: "If you want to go fast, go alone. If you want to go far, go together." I wanted both.

For just over a year, I'd worked with these men, navigating the *Planter* through the channels and rivers around Charleston, and south down past Port Royal and Hilton Head, as far as Florida. We knew each other's habits and behaviors; we worked well together. We trusted each other. But we'd never had to depend on one another like this. If one died, we'd all die. All of us.

Some say there's safety in numbers, but that night it felt the other way around, and Hannah said she worried that more than two or three of us would draw attention. Anytime even a few of us came together, the white folks would call it an "uprising" or a "revolt." Even church was threatening to the white folk.

So, she slipped out, and the others too, a few at a time, hugging tight against the buildings all the way to the docks. They crossed the street two at a time, afraid, moving fast, but not too fast; they knew better than to run. A slow hurry. Seven minutes, maybe, but it seemed seventy.

Fog floated in under the low clouds. Hannah thought about Moses and the Hebrew children slipping out of Egypt, and how God pushed the water back for Moses, and wondered if God could maybe push a little extra fog in over the harbor for a while.

Suddenly Liddy screamed, "Mama! Mama!"

She'd stumbled, and fell hard on her elbow. They were almost there, almost at the dock—but not near enough. Instinctively, Hannah pulled Liddy close into a dark doorway and held her tight to muffle the sound, held her so close she feared she'd suffocate her, or wake the baby, or both. She sang in a whisper, "Hush little baby don't you cry . . ." and Liddy settled down. "I'm not a baby, Mama," she said, and Hannah told her that's right, and big girls like her don't make a single sound till Mama says it's all right. The child nodded, and they crept back out to the street.

At last, they slipped onto the *Etowah*, the boat where they'd agreed to wait until they knew we had the *Planter* empty and ready for them. They waited there while Brother John Smalls and I checked the *Planter* all the way through. Those three Confederate officers had bragged about spending the evening with their women, but it was against protocol, and any one of them could have a change of heart; we had to be sure.

Hannah and the women waited. And waited. And waited.

The minutes ticked on, and Hannah heard the chimes from St. Michael's far off, signaling the start of curfew. She knew we shouldn't be taking so long. She thought of all the things that could go wrong. *If they're not coming, we should leave now. But no, we have to stay.*

The other two women insisted on leaving. "Curfew!" they cried.

"No," Hannah told them. "We couldn't tell you till now, but the men are on their way to us, on the *Planter*. Tonight, we make our run for freedom."

"We doin what? We'll die!" They wept and pleaded, and Hannah feared they'd be heard, and then they'd be right.

She forced herself to stop thinking, to pray.

"Hush now, and pray quiet. God gonna make a way where there ain't no way."

She gathered them close and whispered her prayers, and finally we pulled alongside them. As they stepped across the rail onto the *Planter*, Hannah looked into my face, wondering what had caused the delay.

"I'll explain later," I whispered.

*This is it. We'll find our way to freedom, or die trying. There is no middle way. No guarantee of success. And now—no going back.*

\* \* \*

"Are you sure about this, Hannah?" I'd asked her two nights before. "It'll be all or nothing; we'll make it—or we won't."

I let that sink in.

She let that sink in. "We'll make it. Or we won't." She stated the reality. "Not just the two of us, either. Our children. Our friends, with their children too. Are we mad?"

I was thinking the same thing. "Who are we to put another man's woman and children in peril?"

And then Hannah, my wise and strong Hannah, said, "Who are we not to? If we're running to freedom, shouldn't they have the same chance?"

They'd been in on all the conversations. And they'd all decided for themselves. Even Jonesy, who at the last minute told us he couldn't. That rattled us all; what if he betrayed us? He was a tender soul, but fearful of so much, and we worried he'd inform on us if it meant saving his own neck. He promised loyalty, and we hoped he was sincere, but we wondered, if things got hot, could his good heart stay stronger than his fearful one?

"Our decision will have to be our own, and theirs will have to be theirs. Everyone has the right, the power, to choose," Hannah had said. Hannah never worried much about what other people might do. She always focused on doing the right thing. She's always been braver than me, that way.

She told me later that when they stepped onto the boat, her gut tightened, and she thought she might lose the cornbread she had for dinner.

We'd decided not to tell the other women the plan beforehand because we didn't know them, didn't know if they could be trusted with the secret. Now I told them to trust me and stay quiet, down in the hold. But they panicked, again, and began wailing. "Let us go now!" they cried, and Hannah thought she saw the flash of a watchman's light.

"Quiet!" she hissed. She understood their fear, and she knew that fear could become fatal before they even left the harbor. "Quiet! Trust him. I trust him. You must trust him too!" Her certainty quieted their voices if not their fear.

Hannah remembered how her mama used to tell her, whenever fear gripped tight, to slow down her breath. Slow and easy, she would say, "Breathe slow and easy . . . breathe in strength and breathe out fear . . . Remember the ancestors and ask for their protection."

Hannah asked the ancestors to guide us, and she prayed some of the prayers she remembered from church. And she sang—not out loud, but in a whisper, she sang. She held on to the music, and the music held us all steady.

> *Wade in the water, wade in the water, children,*
> *Wade in the water, God's gonna trouble the water.*

\* \* \*

As we all huddled together on the top deck, against the cabin, hidden in the shadow, I demanded their silence. A kind of courage slipped into me and steadied my heart. I sent Gabe down into the hold, one last time, to be certain it was empty. When he came back up and assured us the boat was ours alone, I sent Hannah and the other women and all the children down to the hold, and told them to stay there, no matter what. I had the men stay up on deck with me, except John and Alfred, who'd be feeding the steam engine.

We'd start by taking the South Channel, and at Fort Johnson I'd give the signal. Then we'd move toward Sumter. I carried all of the responsibility; I had to make the *Planter*'s passage through these waters look routine. The signals had to be routine. I had to stand, wave, look like the captain. *Can I do it flawlessly?*

When we entered into Union water—*if* we entered Union water—we'd raise the white bedsheet we'd brought along as a flag of surrender. If all went well, we'd be free. If not, we'd be done.

We couldn't know what might happen if we made it. What would the Union officers do? Would they even believe a slave crew?

Free. What would that mean? We dared to believe we might make it, might indeed be free. But free for what? Where would we go? What would this passage bring?

I thought, again, about the Hebrews hurrying out of Egypt, through the sea, to the promised land, to their unknown future. After Egypt, seemed like the story got an awful lot worse for an awful long time before it got better. But they followed Moses and they kept on moving toward freedom, and they got there, one fine day. I wondered, *Could their story be our story? How will it unfold?*

The Hebrews followed Moses; now Hannah and the others were following me, trusting my instincts as well as my skill. We'd talked about this for weeks, and of nothing else for the past two days. Once the opportunity became real, we knew we couldn't wait. When a door opens, you have to walk through, or let it close you out. It was the ultimate risk.

If the Confederates caught us, all the men would be executed, no doubt about it. For the women and children, it could be worse— whipped, raped, separated and sold. Hannah said she'd rather take a bullet.

If the Union's boats saw us as the enemy, our little *Planter* would be shredded by lead and fire; we'd burn or drown or both. We were all of one mind, and we'd agreed that if we were seized, we'd light the munitions in the hold. We'd not be captured. We'd not be sold. If it came to that, we'd join the bones of the thousands of other men and women and children on the floor of the Atlantic.

We were already dreadfully close.

We'd planned carefully, and thoroughly. Now it was up to God. And the captain of the *Planter*.

\* \* \*

We'd loaded the boat with weapons and ammunition, and the Confederate troops at Fort Ripley expected them to be delivered just after sunrise. When we finally pushed off from Charleston's southern wharf, only yards from General Ripley's headquarters, I thought about how both the general and the men at the fort would be disappointed, one way or another.

We left so much later than we planned. Now, no turning back.

The boat lurched as it left the dock. We'd get a quiet start and wait for full steam after we'd cleared most of the harbor. That would win us more distance from Confederate eyes, and would, I hoped, get us safely beyond the final barricade by first light.

I wore the captain's straw hat, and his uniform jacket as well. I saw Hannah smile.

"If we're going to do this, let's do it in fine form!" I tried to laugh, nervous. The whole idea had started as a joke one day when Brother John noticed that I was about the same size as Captain Relyea, and Relyea always left his hat and jacket in the pilothouse.

"You could pass fo Cap'n Relyea if you wear his clothes!" I'd played along, standing at the wheel just like Relyea, even walking with a limp. That night I went home and told Hannah what I was thinking.

She said she thought I was crazy. Bold. Both.

The uniform fit almost perfectly, and when I crossed my arms and leaned against the window of the pilothouse, I felt like a captain myself.

The first checkpoint was less than 100 yards from where we left the wharf, and we passed easily. They'd have no reason to question a boat moving within the harbor, as the Confederate troops were constantly moving boats, readying men and supplies.

We kept moving and approached Castle Pinckney. To this day, I don't know why they called that little fortress a castle.

We'd have to stay in the channel that ran between Castle Pinckney to our port side and Fort Ripley to starboard, as navigating anything other than the channel would raise suspicions and the Confederates would send a guard boat out. We couldn't risk that even if the tide allowed us the alternate route.

Which it did not.

Captain Relyea's wide-brimmed hat hid my face, and the jacket of his uniform fit almost perfectly, and though it was too dark to need the protection of a hat and too warm for a jacket, I wore them both, and gave thanks for his habit of leaving them in the pilothouse. I remembered my mama's Anansi stories, and her wisdom: *"You gotta be clever, child."* Was I clever, or foolish? Time would tell.

I called for the signal. Gabe sounded the blast and I held my breath. The return signal came and we passed Fort Ripley without incident.

After we passed Fort Ripley, I called for more steam and we picked up speed, but it felt slow against the heavy rising tide. We'd have to pass Sumter before first light or they'd have troops watching every inch of this harbor, and we'd definitely draw the guard boat. But I knew they could see our steam too, and moving too fast would draw attention as well. I watched as the moon slipped in and out of the low clouds. I'd seldom hoped for poor visibility in open water, but I prayed hard: *More clouds tonight, Oh Lord. Show your poor children a little mercy and hide your big moon tonight.*

The tide was still against us, but we passed Fort Johnson before four o'clock. Soft moonlight, fuzzy in the fog, leaked in through the weathered boards above us. I prayed, searching for words adequate to my fear and trembling.

\* \* \*

The wind picked up, and I tasted the salt spray as I called for the signal to pass Sumter. Gabe's eyes flashed fear. "Too early!" He was right. I waited, listened to the slap of water against the hull, calculated our speed against this heavy tide and the inevitable sunrise—both welcome on any other day, but life-threatening in this dark moment.

Twenty minutes passed, and I called again for the signal. Gabe nodded, and sounded the blasts.

Silence.

A big breeze blew, the clouds parted, and the moon shone bright. *Please, Lord.*

We waited.

Silence. *Have they identified us?* I scanned the water again, but saw no guard boat.

A wisp of a cloud floated across the moon.

Finally, we heard the response signal, and a voice from across the water. "Bring us some damn Yankees, boys!"

"Ay ay!" I called and waved my ungloved hand. Gabe gasped.

I exhaled and wiped the sweat from my forehead and eyes as we kept our steady pace. Only a few more minutes and we'd be in Union waters where the Union Navy would see our Confederate flag and turn their guns our way.

We kept moving, steady, and finally we were out of range of Sumter's big guns.

Directly ahead was the Union's *Onward*, less than half a mile away, turning, positioning her guns, ready.

A man's thoughts run fast sometimes, and I thought just then of all the ammunition on board, just below my family, and all the others who'd put such trust in me. I thought how, if the Union ship fired on us, no one would have even a moment to be more frightened than they already were.

My hands shook like palm fronds in a hurricane as I pulled the line to drop the Confederate flag and feared I'd not be able to signal our surrender before the Union ship attacked. Our fates rested with an old bedsheet.

From across the water, I heard the bark of a command: "*Prepare to fire!*"

I pulled with all my strength to raise the white sheet and braced myself for the cannon blast, wishing I could tell Hannah goodbye.

*Forgive me. God, forgive me.*

Bracing myself for the impact, I heard the voice again. "Hold your fire!"

No shots, no cannon fire.

I waited.

Silence.

The *Planter* was safe.

I exhaled a quiet *hallelujah* of gratitude and steadied myself against the wheel.

\* \* \*

Hannah felt the boat slow as we made it to the Union blockade, but she knew we'd not yet made it to Union protection. She knew I was scrambling to drop the Stars and Bars and raise the signal of surrender. She said the children trembled, anxious and confused, and she trembled too, thinking, *We've come this far, through the gray waters of slavery; now we'll either perish or survive in the deep blue.*

She told me later she tried to pray. She tried to breathe. She sang.

> *Wade in the water, wade in the water, children,*
> *Wade in the water, God's gonna trouble the water.*
> *See that band all dressed in red,*
> *God's gonna trouble the water.*
> *Looks like the band that Moses led,*
> *God's gonna trouble the water.*

# CHAPTER 36

Words fail. It's impossible, still, to describe my relief in that moment, or the great wave of gladness that washed over me.

The sun edged above the eastern horizon and I heard a freedom song, sure and true, a hymn of praise in the very air around us and in the sea below us, a song of jubilation, and triumph, and hope.

I called below, "Come up! Come up! Unlock the hold! Come up! We've made it! Come up!"

Hannah and the others crept up the steps and peered onto the deck, silent, eyes adjusting to the morning light and full of questions.

"It's alright," I said. "We're safe."

They stared at me.

"No," I corrected myself. "Not safe. Free. We're free."

A long silent moment passed, and then an eruption of tears and celebration.

They spilled up onto the deck, crying, praying, singing, dancing in the morning light. I held Hannah close and we both cried our joy. Tears, because there are no words for a moment like that. The children sensed our relief and excitement, and jumped up and down, clapping their hands, and hugging us.

"You're shaking," she said to me, and she was shaking too.

"I nearly got us sunk. Twice." It was hard to confess that to this brave woman, and I swallowed hard. "I called a signal too early back there. And then I couldn't get the flags down and the sheet up. I could see the cannons turning, sugar. They were ready to fire. Close. So close."

We held one another and tried to calm our trembling. She looked into my eyes.

"You did it, Captain. You did it."

"We did it. We did it together." I held her closer.

The *Onward* pulled alongside, her crew leaning against the rail. The incredulity on their faces announced that they had no idea who we were, or how we happened to be there. I saw the big gun in the port, poised.

"Captain!" I called to the officer in charge.

"I'm Captain Nickels," he called back.

"Good morning, sir. I understand this vessel may be of service to Uncle Abe! We've got some of the Union's good ol guns!"

I wondered, even then, at my own audacity.

Captain Nickels and his first mate barraged me with questions, repeating a few of them, grinning and shaking their heads, unbelieving.

"What's your name, son?"

"Smalls, sir. Robert Smalls."

"And how did you happen to come into possession of this vessel?"

"Sir, I've piloted her for a couple of years now. She became a Confederate ship last year, and well—the officers took leave last night, and several of us liberated her this morning, sir."

"You do know, don't you, that you'd been shot if caught?"

"Oh, yes sir. Yes sir, we all knew that."

"Son, looks like you're a free man, and these folks with you."

The captain smiled, took a long, silent minute to think, then turned to his crew and sent six of them to search the *Planter.*

They combed through the *Planter* and we waited, too excited to stand still, talking and laughing and singing, till they came back up on deck.

"She's clean, sir. And full of fine guns and explosives. Good thing we didn't take a shot; she'd be splinters, and that's all!"

Every one of those men just kept shaking their heads and smiling, and I heard one say, "Never seen nothin' like it!"

\* \* \*

We spent the day on the *Onward,* with the whole crew trying to sort out what to do with us and treating us like royalty, bringing food, and asking a thousand questions.

"How did you plan this? Wasn't you afraid? Did you know 'bout all those explosives? What are you folks going to do now that you're free? Where you going to?"

Where *were* we going to?

I knew what we'd left, but couldn't know what was ahead. Where would we go now? We'd heard Beaufort or Port Royal might be all right, and with the federal troops settled there we'd be relatively safe. It'd be awful good to be with Mama, if she was still there.

Captain Nickels and I talked all day long, man to man.

"You know, I suppose, that they'll want you dead now. There'll be a sizable bounty on your head, Smalls."

He was right, of course. Weeks passed before I realized the degree to which I'd humiliated the Confederates throughout the Carolinas, and their thirst for retribution would follow me for decades.

After our talk, Nickels stood and stretched. "Quite a day you folks have had!" He smiled. "We'll be heading on down to Port Royal tomorrow. Meanwhile, we're fixing up some space for everyone to rest a bit. Captain Smalls, Mrs. Smalls." He spoke to us so respectfully. "We've got a cabin for you and the children. Mr. Jansen will take you down. Have a good night." And with that, we went to rest, and sleep, and maybe dare to dream. We were free, at last.

As I removed the tag hanging from my neck, I wondered, *Free, yes, thank God. But are we safe?*

# PART III

*To every thing there is a season, and a time to every purpose under the heaven:*

*A time to be born, and a time to die; a time to plant, and a time to pluck up that which is planted;*

*A time to kill, and a time to heal; a time to break down, and a time to build up;*

*A time to weep, and a time to laugh; a time to mourn, and a time to dance;*

*A time to cast away stones, and a time to gather stones together; a time to embrace, and a time to refrain from embracing;*

*A time to get, and a time to lose; a time to keep, and a time to cast away;*

*A time to rend, and a time to sew; a time to keep silence, and a time to speak;*

*A time to love, and a time to hate; a time of war, and a time of peace.*

*What profit hath he that worketh in that wherein he laboureth?*

*I have seen the travail, which God hath given to the sons of men to be exercised in it.*

*He hath made every thing beautiful in his time: also he hath set the world in their heart, so that no man can find out the work that God maketh from the beginning to the end.*

*I know that there is no good in them, but for a man to rejoice, and to do good in his life.*

*And also that every man should eat and drink, and enjoy the good of all his labour, it is the gift of God.*

*Ecclesiastes 3:1–13*

# CHAPTER 37

## WASHINGTON, DC, 1862

I'd not seen Rev. French since the day Hannah and I stood before him to take our vows four years ago. Now I paced and fidgeted in a fine room in Washington, DC, about to be received by President Lincoln.

"Well, Captain, an awful lot has happened since the wedding in Beaufort!" he said.

"Yes, sir. Sure never dreamed our next meeting would be here."

We both laughed, but I could see he was almost as nervous as I was, the way he played with the buttons on his cuffs, tapping his feet, tugging his left ear. *Try not to do that,* I told myself, *especially in the presence of Mr. Lincoln.*

We waited in a dark-paneled room that smelled of tobacco and old wood. It made me think of the McKees' old barn and George; seemed like a lifetime ago. Three of the four walls were lined with shelves of books, and I remembered Mr. McKee's recitation from that early morning long ago, fishing on the Beaufort River: *"Every man a library, and every man a boat!"*

"You ever see so many books?" I asked Rev. French. "I guess it'd take a lifetime to read all these."

"Books are like friends, Robert. You never want to part with the best ones, and even the less-sure ones can be important occasionally." He paused, thinking. "You read much, Captain?"

"I try. It's real slow, though. Need to work on that." I started to ask him which books he thought I should read, but just then the door opened and a stout man in a morning coat nodded to us.

"President Lincoln will see you now. Please remember to stand until he sits, and when he stands up again, you stand as well."

We both took a deep breath and followed the gentleman into the presidential office.

The great man stood, and though I'd been told of his height, his stature surprised me, and made me feel small indeed. He stepped from behind his desk and extended the long hand of his long right arm.

"It is a fine pleasure to meet you, Captain Smalls!" He shook my hand enthusiastically. "You're a hero, you know. Your name's in all the papers now."

"Thank you, Mr. President. It's a great honor to meet you, sir, a great honor indeed."

He turned to French. "Reverend, it's good to see you again."

"The pleasure is mine, Mr. President."

Lincoln smiled, nodded and motioned for us to sit as he settled back into his chair, which, with his long legs, looked like a miniature. Immediately, he turned to me, amused.

"Son, I've heard about your capture of that boat, but I'd sure like to hear it directly from you!"

I told him how the crew had made a joke about my resemblance to Captain Relyea, and how I'd spent weeks working out a plan to get the *Planter* past Sumter. Right away, he interrupted me.

"Hold on, son." He called to his aide: "Send Stanton in here right away; he's got to hear this!"

Within seconds, it seemed, a distinguished-looking fellow, round in the midsection with a long and wild gray beard, entered. Lincoln stood; French and I stood.

"Ed, this is Captain Robert Smalls, the young man we heard about a few weeks ago. And Rev. Mansfield French, whom I believe you've met."

"An absolute pleasure to meet you, Smalls!" Mr. Stanton shook my hand with both of his, a wide smile growing behind his beard. "And always good to see you, Pastor." He shook French's hand, and slapped him on the shoulder.

"Sit down, please." We sat, and Lincoln continued. "Ed, you've got to hear this. Smalls here sailed that boat right under the noses of the rebels."

Stanton leaned forward. "Tell me everything. How'd you do that? Every detail, son!"

And so I told them every detail—all of it. I told them how the idea emerged when two of the crew members had found Relyea's straw hat and jacket, how they'd put the hat on my head and laughed at how it made me look a little like him, and I told them about all the nights I'd laid awake trying to work out the plan. I told them about how I'd learned to love the water as a boy in Beaufort, and eventually had a chance to work on the docks in Charleston, and finally became a wheelman on the *Planter*. I told them about Hannah and our babies, and how we dreamed of a life as a family, a free family. I told them about rehearsing the signals for passing the forts, and about praying for a friendly tide and cloudy night.

Stanton listened from the edge of his chair, asking good questions, and, more than once, he turned to Lincoln and French with a smile and a shake of his head.

"But what would you have done—I mean, what did you think would happen if . . . Well, let me speak frankly, son. What was your alternative plan?"

"Well, sir, we all agreed that if we were taken, or if capture were inevitable, we'd have to ignite the hold."

They all went silent, smiles fading as they looked at one another, and then again at me.

"You'd have blown yourselves up? You and your women and children?" Stanton asked.

"Yes sir."

He shook his head. "Why?"

"With all due respect sir, to live enslaved is not to truly live. All we want is an equal chance in life. A chance to make our own choices. A chance to make our own way. A chance to make our own mistakes, even. We simply want the chance to live our lives. Without that opportunity, life is already over."

Silence again, and then Lincoln spoke. "Son, you've got that opportunity now. And your family as well. What do you see in your future?"

"Well, I do believe, Mr. President, sir, that the best way to predict the future is to create it." The president smiled a wide smile and chuckled. I was later told that he wrote those very words in his journal that evening.

"I believe you're right about that, Mr. Smalls. I'd like for you and Mr. Stanton here to continue this conversation in a few minutes. You tell him about the future you'd like to create for your family, and for your people."

He turned his attention to Stanton and French. "I see now why you two keep insisting that we ought to let the colored men fight with us. Stanton, I want you to arrange for five thousand men, colored men from—where are you from, son? South Carolina?—just as soon as you can organize them."

He seemed especially pleased to make the first colored recruits from South Carolina.

"And Rev. French," he continued, "you're a Methodist, is that right?"

"Yes, Mr. President."

"You folks are awfully good at schools and such. I want you to see to it that the coloreds in occupied South Carolina have a chance at education, you understand? Not compulsory, of course, but a choice, an opportunity."

"Absolutely, Mr. President."

Mr. Lincoln stood, and we all stood, and he thanked us for our time and shook our hands again, and when we walked back out into the ante-room, I felt like I'd said goodbye to a friend.

* * *

The meetings with Stanton, and later with Salmon Chase, were energetic and efficient. Chase served as secretary of the treasury, and quickly affirmed what I already knew—

nothing of substance happens until the money happens. But they made things happen, and before the end of the month I was back in Union-occupied Beaufort and Port Royal, recruiting for the Union army.

At first, some of the men thought they were trading servitude on the plantation field for servitude on the battlefield, but we explained that their masters no longer owned them, thanks to the federal occupation, and they quickly came to understand that they had a choice, and that they could fight for their freedom and that of their children. It was a true choice, and many chose it.

The men who chose to serve were paid ten dollars a month, and they were trained and fed and clothed, and given all the protections enjoyed by their white compatriots. But perhaps the most motivating factor of all was the hope—the possibility—that they and their wives and children would be free, permanently and forever free.

Those weeks in Beaufort and Port Royal gave back some time with Hannah and the babies too. The Army put us in a little house of our own, warm and quiet, and for those few brief months I was able to hold my little ones in the evening and hold my wife through the night.

We were a family, together and free.

I cherished those days—how Liddy played and sang at my feet as I held Robbie after supper. Robbie laughed at his sister and pulled on my beard or my buttons; he was a busy child, robust and inquisitive.

"Nosy like you was, Trouble," Mama said one evening. I prayed he'd find less trouble and more opportunity along the way.

For the moment, trouble had eluded us and found new residence with those who once administered it. I wondered about both the kindly McKees and the not-so-kindly Rhetts. Were they now on the receiving end?

*Jane McKee's Diary*

*June, 1862*

*We've had to leave Charleston, and how I miss the Holy City—though her holiness has been debased and tarnished so! The fire at Christmas time was devastating, and now this. Even if we could have stayed on with Elizabeth and James, I don't know how we could show our faces on the streets. Somehow everyone seems to know that the stolen boat was the work of our boy Robert, and the humiliation stings. Henry is beside himself. "I taught that boy to sail," he says. "I taught him the tides. We were good to him. We loved him."*

*We believed we were doing the right thing. And we thought he loved us, but now . . . oh, I don't know what to think.*

*A few days after the theft, I encountered M. Chestnut downtown, and she—and only she, I must say—seemed to sense the sadness we bear. "My dear Jane," she said, "you mustn't blame yourselves. That boy wasn't the first of them to turn, he was just, unfortunately, the cleverest. Those officers, Captain Relyea and the others, ought to have seen that. They're the truly guilty ones. Things won't go well for them now."*

*She told me too that the men who stood guard at Sumter that night are being dealt with quite harshly, as I suppose they should be. It was their job to guard the harbor, after all. She said she'd heard that Peter Rhett, especially, is under investigation, as he was the lead commander, giving the signal to pass. He's surely more eager now than ever to destroy Trouble, and he's never been short on that desire. Their own war may have no end.*

*Henry was given a copy of the letter from Lt. Ravenel, and he was so distraught and angry, he crumbled it into a tight ball and threw it across the room. Thinking it might someday mean something, I retrieved it later, and will keep it in my diary here.*

Report of Lieutenant Ravenel, C. S. Army.
HDQRS. SECOND MILITARY DIST. OF SOUTH
CAROLINA,

Charleston, S. C., May 13, 1862.

GENERAL: I have to report that the steamer Planter was stolen from Southern Wharf at between 3 and 3.30 o'clock this morning and taken to the enemy's fleet, off the bar, where she was visible till late in the forenoon. By telegram from Stono this afternoon it is reported that she has gone south. The Planter is a high pressure, light-draft boat, drawing ordinarily not more than 3½ to 4 feet, and has been employed in the Confederate service in the transportation of ordnance, etc., to and from the various posts in the harbor and other localities in the neighborhood. She was under the command of C. J. Relyea as master, Samuel H. Smith, a Charleston pilot, being mate, and Zerich Pitcher, engineer, with a colored crew, eight in number, and all slaves. Neither the captain, mate, nor engineer were on board at the time of her departure, notwithstanding Paragraph VIII, in Orders No. 5, viz:

All light-draft steamers in the employ of the Government will be in readiness to move at once, their officers and crews, when at the wharf, remaining on board day and night.

Four of her colored crew and one of the colored crew of the steamer Etowah are missing, and are supposed to be parties to the theft. The Planter was to have taken to the Middle Ground battery early this morning a portion of the armament for that fortification, which had been put on board yesterday afternoon, viz, a banded rifle 42, one VIII-inch columbiad, one VIII-inch seacoast howitzer, and one 32-pounder. She had also mounted for her own use one 32-pounder and a 24-pounder howitzer, and for use in Fort Sumter a X-inch columbiad carriage, all of which have fallen into the hands of the enemy.

From an examination of the guard in the neighborhood of the wharf whence the Planter was stolen, it would appear that about 8 o'clock last night two white men and a white woman went on board of her, and as they were not seen to return it is supposed that they have also gone in her. The sentinel on post about 50 yards from where the Planter was moored noticed her movement from the wharf at between 3 and 3.30 o'clock, but did not think it necessary to stop her, presuming that she was but pursuing her usual business. The Planter, after leaving the wharf, proceeded along the bay as far, perhaps, as the Atlantic Wharf, where, after a short stoppage and the blowing of her whistle, she was turned and proceeded on her course to sea. She passed Fort Sumter at 4.15 o'clock and was reported by the sentinel on duty to the officer of the day. She was supposed to be the guard boat and allowed to pass without interruption.

I have the honor to be, yours, most respectfully,

F. G. RAVENEL,
Aid-de-Camp.
Brigadier-General U. S. RIPLEY,
Second Military District.

*So, "for the time being" as Henry puts it, we'll go on to the little farm outside of Columbia, and hope for the best, as we brace ourselves for what may indeed get much worse.*

*July 1862*

*Henry has just learned that we've all but lost the eastern seaboard; Savannah is completely blockaded and Pulaski has fallen to the Yanks. Only Wilmington remains. And so we remain here, quite isolated, and with growing concerns. I fear we may never see Ashdale again, or our dear beautiful home in Beaufort.*

*Henry insists that we'll return, and he's promised—"vowed," he says—that if God will see us through this, and return us again to our home, he'll "give back to God." I'm not sure what he plans to give back; neither am I sure that God entertains such negotiations.*

*Willie constantly asks when we'll be with Lydia again, and my heart feels torn when I think of her. She's been a part of our lives for so long, a part of Henry's entire life! She wept with us when Hank died, and I wept with her when Trouble left for Charleston. We are as sisters, nearly, having been through so much together. The wedding, when he married Hannah, was a family affair, and we took her as one of our own, just like Lydia and Robert. Dear Lydia. Does she know, I wonder, of the boy's betrayal? Does she yearn, as do I, for the days of old?*

# CHAPTER 38

Peter Rhett had been put on night post again, still at Sumter. The escape of Robert Smalls had become an embarrassment, a stain on his personal reputation, his family and his school. He was all but a pariah for being bested by a slave—the uppity McKee boy he so hated. And now disgraced, he stood guard at night, forlorn and filled with venom. Had it not been for his father's great influence, a more severe reprimand might have befallen him.

"It wasn't my fault when Smalls stole the *Planter*. Not that my father would ever let me forget. But it wasn't my fault," Peter hissed.

He remembered how quiet it was that night. Fog does that, quiets everything—the lights, the sounds. Like a veil, in a way. So, the lights of Charleston, and the lights on the harbor, were visible but muted, fuzzy. And noises too, including the ship signals. *But that's not an excuse.*

Smalls and his crew got themselves on the *Planter* because Captain Relyea and his crew left their assignments, Peter told his father. Relyea was to blame. They claimed, at their court-martialing, that they didn't know, that the orders to stay with the ship had not been clear, that they were private contractors and not Confederate soldiers.

But any military man would know better. Any thinking man would know better.

*We all knew, of course, that they wanted to be with their women. Can't blame a man for that,* Peter thought. *Their real mistake was trusting Smalls. He'd been with them for some time, and must've tricked them into that trust somehow. He's clever, the worst kind of colored.* Whatever his reasoning, Captain Relyea trusted him, and that was the beginning of the end.

When the *Planter* signaled to pass Sumter, a little after four that morning, the moon was still just a faint light behind the mist. But Peter and his men could see well enough the Stars and Bars flying high, with the South Carolina palmetto flying below it. And the captain in his jacket and that damn straw hat that he wore, day in and day out.

It sure looked like Relyea—the other sentries said the same— the way he stood at the wheel, arms crossed. He always was an arrogant son of a bitch. *It would be just like him to pull out a little ahead of schedule, if only to foster the goodwill of General Ripley.*

Peter wished he could've seen Relyea's pompous face when he got to the wharf just before daylight and found his boat gone missing. And General Ripley, good God, he was furious when he got the report. And then he had to report to Pemberton, and Pemberton to General Lee. There was anger enough for the whole damn South.

*What could I have done?*

The signal, while slightly muted in that heavy fog, was as usual—three long blasts followed by the short blast and the hiss of the steam. Every Confederate boat had a signal book, and Peter never missed an inaccurate signal. The signals were all spot on.

But as first light broke, he saw the tragic reality. Even with the telescopes confirming it, he couldn't believe his eyes. But there she was, the *Planter*, under a Union flag, flanked by the two Union blockaders, one of which was the *Onward*, which he'd watched like a hawk.

*It was enough that he got the* Planter *past us, but how did he get it into the range of the Union boats without being fired on?* That Trouble was clever, yes, but he was lucky too, with that one guard boat out of commission. Once again, he'd humiliated Peter, made him look the fool. Peter wasn't alone in it this time, but he might as well have been. Peter's father was unrelenting.

"How the hell did you miss that, boy?" He emphasized the word *boy*, as if Peter might somehow miss his inference.

"How many times do I need to say, Father? It looked like Relyea. The signals were accurate. Goddamn it, we were expecting the *Planter* to pass; she was scheduled to sail! Why would we suspect anything?"

Both father and son were furious, one blaming and the other blamed.

"You're a disgrace to the South!"

"Jesus Christ himself would've let that boat by! There was no reason to stop her!"

"Quit making excuses, boy! Get out of my sight!"

His father turned to pour another glass of bourbon, and as desperately as Peter wanted more himself, he was even more desperate to get away from the old man. His irrationality wasn't new, and Peter had long ago learned that trying to reason with him was futile.

Peter turned and slammed the front door as hard as he could, swearing he'd never enter that house again. He slipped into the bar at the Mills House and had a drink or two, and tried to think how he'd handle this.

*How will I face Liza Beth, or her father?*

They were reasonable people, but this was personal—he'd let their boy steal a Confederate boat. It didn't matter that it could've happened to anyone; this happened on his watch. How could he face them?

And how could he hold his head up around Charleston? Thanks to the old man, the windbag of the South, it was impossible to be anonymous here. Folks would either blame or pity, and he didn't want either.

He ordered another bourbon.

\* \* \*

The weeks and months that followed were blurred. All the men from Sumter were reassigned, mostly up to Wilmington, all with clear records. Captain Relyea and his first mate were court-martialed, but eventually the sentences were lifted on some sort of technicality.

Smalls was made an officer in the Union Army and detailed to the Navy, and given charge of the boat he'd stolen and a fifteen-hundred-dollar reward and an officer's salary. All the papers up North called him a hero. *A hero? No, he's just a colored boy with power and money.* Peter's father wouldn't shut up about it. Peter avoided him, and the McKees, too, and though he wrote a lengthy letter to Liza Beth, he heard nothing from her for over a year. His brother Edmund made a feeble attempt, "on behalf of the family," he said, to contact him, but Peter's already thin desire to connect with any of them evaporated.

He discovered that hard work and frequent bourbon kept him either busy or numb, and he perfected both.

# CHAPTER 39

## JANUARY 1, 1863

I stood under a towering oak on St. Helena Island where Beaufort planters had once enjoyed their sprawling plantations and their slaves and their fortunes, as Dr. W. H. Brisbane, himself a South Carolinian, surrounded by a handful of Beaufort's white citizens and thousands of eager and illiterate men, women, and children, read President Lincoln's *Emancipation Proclamation*:

*"That on the first day of January, in the year of our Lord one thousand eight hundred and sixty-three, all persons held as slaves within any State or designated part of a State, the people whereof shall then be in rebellion against the United States, shall be then, thenceforward, and forever free . . ."*

After the reading, Rev. French presented the colors—a gift from Northern supporters—to Colonel Thomas Wentworth Higginson, but in the moment before Higginson could respond, a lone male voice surprised the crowd, singing slow and sweet and full of feeling.

"My country, 'tis of thee, sweet land of liberty, of thee I sing!"

Two women joined in, and soon a thousand more, free men and women, claiming the promise and burden of liberty. The proclamation opened the door even wider, with the opportunity for the former slaves to serve in the Union military, promising "that such persons of suitable condition, will be received into the armed service of the United States to garrison forts, positions, stations, and other places, and to man vessels of all sorts in said service."

Beginning in August 1862, I'd quietly recruited and organized the first official colored regiment in the Union army, the 1st South Carolina Volunteers (which later became the 33rd United States Colored Infantry). Col. Higginson not only commanded the men, but cared for them. They served fully aware of Jefferson Davis' pledge that there would be no prisoners of war; if captured, the negroes would be sold at auction, as slaves, and the whites would be hanged.

At the same time, Mansfield French collected donations and books, and convinced a young Unitarian from Pittsburgh to serve as a missionary teacher in the lowcountry, using a small brick church on St. Helena Island as the classroom. They decided to call it the Penn School.

\*   \*   \*

Throughout the war, most of Beaufort's homes housed Union officers; the largest homes, though, and most of the churches became hospitals. Mama was recruited as a cook and was paid two dollars each week for the miracles she worked in the kitchens. She started in the mornings at St. Helena's Episcopal Church, before *deyclean*, preparing food for the officers and medics as well as for the troops convalescing there. Union officers moved into the house on Prince Street, and when they learned that Mama had been enslaved in that home, they requested that she return as a paid domestic worker, for ten dollars a month, the same as the privates in the newly-formed colored regiment. They wanted to pay her more, as she was the mother of a hero, but it wouldn't do for a civilian woman to be paid more than a military man. Nevertheless, Lydia Polite, who had never held money of her own, was becoming a woman of both resources and respect, and she tarnished neither.

She'd shown quiet pride when she learned of our commandeering of the *Planter* and shed tears when I told her about meeting with President Lincoln. After I was invited to speak in New York, she wept again, worried that I'd find the support in the North too attractive to leave, and she worried she'd not see me again. I promised her, "Mama, you know my head's always been turned toward Beaufort."

She'd been so pleased when we came back, and took undisguised delight in Liddy and Robbie, a rapt new audience for all her Anansi stories.

* * *

When Robbie developed a dry cough that next spring, Mama was the one to rub his chest with her warm onion poultice and make him her special lemon and honey tea. She never expected, and we didn't either, that our robust little boy would decline so suddenly. One day he coughed a bit, and the next day he fought to breathe.

And the next day he was gone.

Nothing prepares a man for his child's death. *Nothing.*

I'd grieved for Hank and for Abe, and I'd seen men die, suddenly or slowly, but nothing equipped me for the dark descent and emptiness I felt when Robbie died. It was unthinkable, unfathomable. As I held him in those final suffering moments, as he gasped and struggled, I prayed with all my being that the Almighty could somehow transfer my health to my son, and I would gladly bear his illness and death.

Hannah collapsed with despair, and I feared I'd lose her too. Mama and Rev. French took turns staying with us for weeks after the funeral, and we slowly, slowly climbed our way back into life.

A letter arrived from Washington, DC. President Lincoln,

whose own son, Willie, had died just a few months before our escape on the *Planter*, sent his condolences.

"I know," he wrote, "that our boys are better off in heaven, but it is far too difficult a task to accept such loss."

His words, warm and personal and full of understanding, didn't lessen our grief, but reminded us that we were not alone in it.

# CHAPTER 40

## 1865

Only a few years later, the great man himself was dead, and I like to think that in our enormous loss, he was reunited with his boy and perhaps took a moment to be with mine as well.

Mama never met Lincoln herself, of course, but loved hearing my stories of the man, and of the splendid White House in Washington. When the great emancipator was murdered, she joined thousands in Beaufort to mourn, and to pray for the fragile future.

I noticed, as Hannah and Mama and I bowed together in grief that April, that her energy was beginning to ebb, though she tried hard to disguise it.

"Mama, you feelin alright?"

"Just a little peaked," she'd answered, but I heard the fatigue in her voice, and saw in Hannah's eyes that she'd noticed it too.

"You know, Mama, you been workin awfully hard, just about forever. Maybe it's time to put those weary feet up. Ain't no need now for you to keep goin so hard."

"You sayin I ain't still strong?" She was offended by the thought.

"No, Mama. I'm just sayin maybe it's your turn to sit a spell. Not like you ain't due for it."

Mama had weathered great storms and battles, and like the town itself, had been changed.

*   *   *

Though Beaufort looked much the same after the war, the little town was altered, and was adjusting to a new reality. Unlike most of the beautiful cities of the South, Beaufort had been spared destruction. The occupying forces preserved the lovely houses, and altered our little town's population considerably. More than a few of those Union officers decided to stay, enamored of the town and her lowcountry beauty. Most of the planter families were gone now, possessing neither the means nor the desire to return.

At the tax office, I stood at the window, and handed $600 to the clerk on the other side.

"Good morning, sir. 5-1-1 Prince Street," I told him.

I remembered him from my childhood; he ran the post office and had a small printing business as well. The war had closed his business, and to be honest, I was surprised that he was back in town in any capacity. But here he was, working in the tax office, collecting property taxes from those of us who could afford them, and for that price we took full title to the property.

"Name?" he asked, without looking up.

"Smalls," I said. "Robert Smalls."

His head popped up, and he fixed me with a scowl. "Smalls! You thief—first the boat, and now the house, is it? Well, we'll see how things work out." He turned to the file box behind him, and taking his time, found the document, bludgeoned it with his ink stamp, and shoved it under the window at me.

"Thank you," I said.

The tax clerk's response was not the only, or worst, expression of resentment, but neither was it common, and for that I was grateful. I had known the people of Beaufort to be complex in many ways—proud of and entitled by their wealth, and also generous with it; stubborn and insistent on the right to hold slaves, and also, with a few exceptions, judicious to them as well; profoundly damaged in defeat, and also somehow gracious in pain. I knew that some of these people were proud to claim me as a citizen even as they dealt with the wounds of the war.

I walked the short distance from the tax office to Prince Street, heart pounding. *This house. My house. Our home now.* I walked in, through the front door this time, remembering waiting for permission at the back door only a few years earlier. From the center hallway, I could see into the dining room and the parlor, and back to the keeping room. My hand rested on the stair rail, smooth and cool, and I peered up.

I ascended the stairs for the first time, in the place I'd always thought of as home.

It's a small thing, perhaps, but I was glad that the McKees had sold the house after Hank died, and that the new owners had abandoned it when the federal troops arrived. As much as I loved and wanted this house, it would've been awfully hard to claim it, however fairly, had it belonged to the McKees most recently. It's odd how a business transaction can feel different when somebody's heart and memories are in it. It's odd still, the complicated feelings I have for this family.

\* \* \*

An hour or so later, I found Mama and Hannah at the Episcopal Church where Mama cooked during the war. The white folks were horrified, she said, when the pews were replaced with cots and the big room became home to wounded Yankees tended by colored folk. I knew Mama would be there still cooking, while Hannah helped convert the room from a hospital back to a sanctuary. Although

Hannah was amused by the idea of converting a church, Mama said, in that quiet way she had, "Seems to me like it's a place o healin either way."

"Mama, I got a little surprise for you." I winked at Hannah, who knew where I'd just come from and was giddy about the house.

"Lawd, son. I don't know if this ol heart can take any more o your surprises!" She sat on a pew to catch her breath. I sat down next to her, and Hannah joined us.

"Mama, how'd you like to put your feet up in a fine parlor of a fine house?"

"Sure sounds better than standin on em in the kitchen!"

"Well, we're the new owners of a place I think you're gonna like. In fact, I think you're gonna say it's just about always felt like home."

"What the devil you talkin bout, son?"

"Prince Street, Liddy!" Hannah squealed. "We're goin back to the house on Prince Street, and this time you're livin in it and not behind it!"

Mama stared at Hannah, then at me, eyes wide. "You mean— you mean—you tellin me we gonna *live* there?"

"That's right, Mama. I'm sending some men over this afternoon to start cleaning her up a little, fix a few little things. We're gonna be calling it home in a week or so."

Mama fainted right into my arms.

*  *  *

While we worked to get the house cleaned up, I had lots of time to talk with George. Like Mama, he'd been put to work by the Union officers when they discovered his skill with animals. Beaufort was full of fine horses during the occupation, and George was finally compensated for doing what he loved most. He carried himself a little more lightly than I remembered and whistled more.

He'd heard all about the *Planter*, of course, and pelted me with questions about that night, and about Lincoln, and about various other maneuvers and battles. Sometimes he'd ask to hear one of the stories again, even though I knew he could tell it himself, he'd heard it so much.

One morning, as we took some tools from the barn to the house, he stopped walking and looked me up and down.

"What?" I asked.

"Jus rememberin somethin."

"What's that?"

"Aw, it ain't nothin really. I was just thinkin bout my brother. You never knew him, o course, but he was a good man, real smart." He paused. "I was just thinkin how he'd sure love your stories."

He shook his head, and walked on ahead of me to the house, whistling.

# CHAPTER 41

## BEAUFORT DECORATION DAY, 1868

I spent the morning at the national cemetery moving among the headstones, placing flowers on the graves of men and boys who gave their lives on behalf of the enslaved, before speaking to the gathered community.

"General Smalls, sir, we're honored by your presence today," the town marshal, Mr. Gibbs, declared. "We owe you a great debt, and thank you for your service and leadership."

I stepped to the podium thinking how odd it felt, still, to be addressed as *General*. And I must confess, if pressed, I liked it. They all knew I wasn't a general. But they claimed me as their hero, and that meant so much to the local population that everyone used the title freely and with pride.

General Logan had proposed this day of observance, noting that every city, town, and hamlet in the country had lost fathers and sons, brothers and husbands. General James Garfield was giving a speech at the Arlington cemetery the same hour, and he said I was the obvious man to say a few words in Beaufort. After the drum and bugle corps played "America," a formal gun salute honored the dead. I found it difficult to speak; the words caught in my throat as I named the loss and cost of the great battles.

I'd lost more than a few friends, and had heard the names of hundreds, thousands more. Hannah and I had borne our own griefs too, burying little Robbie after the sudden and deadly cough. So many dark days we'd seen, so many sleepless nights of wondering if we'd survive. And now, on this bright May morning, I recognized that old sensation of straddling two worlds, the wondrous and hard-won life of freedom and the undeniable price of it, evidence of life and reminders of death everywhere.

"My fellow citizens. We stand this morning on holy ground, among heroes. These brave men died that we might live; they gave themselves to the great cause of freedom. They were heroes indeed, and yet they were more! These were our sons and our fathers, brothers and husbands and neighbors. None of us have escaped the pain and tears of grief, the empty darkness of loss, the silence of their absence. All of us owe them a debt which can never be repaid, and yet we must never cease to return their courage with courage, their valor with valor, their sacrifice with sacrifice. They would tell us, I believe, to always stand on the side of truth and justice, to choose—even at great cost—the pearls of reconciliation, and to pursue equality for every child of God! We honor them best by giving ourselves—fully and faithfully—to the cause of liberty and justice for all!"

The crowd's thunderous applause was punctuated by "Amen!" and "Yes sir!" I paused until they quieted.

"Words are only words," I continued, straining to keep my own emotions in check as I spoke, slowly. "And today words mean very little unless we choose to live in a way that makes our words the very accounting of our lives. My friends, this will be a difficult task, and a long one. I implore you, on behalf of this great cloud of silent witnesses who we remember and honor this day, choose to live in a way that preserves that for which they died. Choose! Choose life, choose liberty, and choose justice, for all."

Again, the crowd shouted and applauded their approval and endorsement. We'd been slaves, almost all of us, and shared hard memories, deep wounds, sweet affections, and tender hopes.

I was twenty-nine and keenly aware of my influence, of carrying the great weight of my responsibility to these, my people. And I was weary.

The war years had taken a toll on me and on my family. I longed to return to a private life, a life that revolved around Hannah and our children, a life that put me on docks and boats, a life of relative anonymity. I knew the life for which I longed was impossible, and that the work ahead included uncharted waters. We'd been working hard to secure suffrage, and I felt the pressure, and the obligation, to represent the new citizens in the state legislature as soon as it became possible.

All these things were on my mind as the ceremony concluded and the crowd began to move among the graves, placing flowers and flags, saying prayers, telling stories and wiping tears. I decided to walk the few blocks back to the house on Prince Street rather than taking the carriage.

"I'll see you there in a few minutes, sugar. Just need some time with all these thoughts in my head," I told Hannah.

Preoccupied with memory and sentiment, I failed to notice Peter Rhett emerge from the side street until suddenly he stood directly in front of me.

I stopped, startled.

"Well, it's the nigger general! You look surprised there, boy. I thought you were some kind of damn hero, some kind of military mastermind, some kind of goddam naval genius!" Peter took a long swallow from his silver flask.

"What do you want, Rhett?"

"I want to settle the score, boy. I want to rip you to shreds. I want to hang you from a tree and slice your balls off. I want—"

"The war is over."

"Not between us, Smalls. It's not over between us."

"Go home, Peter, before you do something stupid. Or before I break your skull open. Shouldn't be too hard—nothin in there."

Peter lunged, enraged.

I sidestepped the big man as a dozen uniformed officers, men who'd been at the cemetery, surrounded us.

"You alright, General?" asked the man nearest me. He'd drawn his gun.

As always, I was unarmed. I'd never carried a sidearm, and liked to say it was on principle, but in truth it was a matter of proficiency. My skills were with the big gun boats, and I'd never been much of a shot with a handgun. Now I wished otherwise.

Peter staggered toward me, waving a dagger he'd pulled from its sheath.

"I'll slit your damn throat, Smalls. Don't think I won't do it."

"Want me to fire, sir?" the young officer asked me.

"Not yet, son."

Peter's eyes darted from me to the officers, like a cornered animal. He took a step back, looked at the ground, lowered the hand holding the knife, shook his head.

"Well, I guess you win, Smalls," he said.

I nodded, relieved, and turned to speak to the officer, and failed to see Peter lunge again. I felt the blade go deep into my belly, felt the searing pain, instinctively held my hand against the wound, and watched a river of blood flow through my fingers.

Instantly, seven officers took Peter to the ground and held him there, guns drawn.

"Go ahead! Shoot!" Peter screamed. "Better dead than living with a nigger to run this town!"

A dozen guns aimed at Peter Rhett's head. I heard the clicks of a dozen pistol hammers pulled back, cocked and ready to fire.

A wet spot grew on the front of Peter's trousers, and an animal-like moan came from somewhere deep in his throat.

"I've waited a long time for this, Rhett," I said.

"Please, no! Don't—"

"Why not, Peter? Give me one good reason why not." I looked to the men around me. "Aim!"

Peter soiled himself.

No one moved. No one spoke. They waited for the order.

"Hold your fire," I said, finally, barely able to speak.

"Sir?" the first officer asked, incredulous. "The son of a bitch attempted murder. We're all witnesses."

"He's drunk," I said. "Lock him up. I'll deal with him when he's sober."

"Sir, with all due respect, it's protocol to defend you, sir, by eliminating him."

"What's your name, son?" I winced and held my hand against my belly, soaked in my own blood.

"Prescott, sir."

"Mr. Prescott, I appreciate your service, sir, and your position. But if anyone eliminates Mr. Rhett, I'd like it to be me. And I'd like him to be sober enough to watch me end his life. Now go lock him up. And get me home."

My vision blurred, and the air grew cold and dark and too thick to breathe; I sunk to my knees. "And please call Dr. Johnson."

\*   \*   \*

Dr. Johnson assured Hannah and Lydia that Rhett's knife, though deep, had missed my vital organs.

"He's going to be awful sore for a while, Mrs. Smalls, but he'll be up and around again in a few weeks. Try to keep him away from drunks with sharp blades."

"Maybe I should've shot him, after all," I said to Hannah after the doctor left. "I always end up wishing I'd hurt him worse."

"You two got a lifetime o hateful between you," she replied. "Maybe it's time to put it down."

"You can't mean that. That boy wants nothing more than to see me hang. If I 'put it down,' he'll string me up!"

Hannah shook her head as she walked out of the room, and I heard her say something to Lydia. The pain medication began to work, and I drifted in and out of an uneasy sleep.

My dreams, colorful and vivid and impossible, included Robbie and Hank and Abe and the boy in the fire all those years ago on Ashdale. I saw boats in the sky and bodies in the water and snakes and alligators emerging from the mouths of the bodies and swallowing the boats. The water smelled like fire and tasted like blood. I saw Peter Rhett weeping, holding the body of a dead woman. I saw Liza Beth and Mr. Simmons and Jesse and George all sitting at a table at the Planter's Hotel restaurant, and the waiters were all white boys in Citadel uniforms. I saw my mother talking to the ancestors and laughing.

When I awoke soaked in sweat, I didn't recognize the room. Then I slept again. When I moved, even a little, the pain stabbed and I marveled at the fact that I hadn't been wounded on some battlefield during the war, but was nearly killed after the war around the corner from my home by a boy I'd known all my life.

After three days, I emerged from the fog of the laudanum and asked for Rev. French.

"Captain, what do you need the preacher for? Looks to me like you're gonna be alright," Hannah teased.

Lydia smiled and shook her head. "I don't know. Maybe that preacher can straighten out his soul."

Both women laughed, but I only felt the stab of my wound again and moaned.

Mansfield French knocked on the door after lunch and exchanged pleasantries with Hannah and Lydia for a few moments before sitting down in a chair next to my bed.

"You looked better last time I saw you, General."

"Well, I wanted to look good for the president, don't you know?"

We had mourned Lincoln's death and talked at length after the assassination, wondering what the country's future would bring.

"What can I do for you, sir?" French asked.

"Well, I've got a couple of things on my mind. How long have you got?"

"I'm listening, son, just as long as you want."

I closed my eyes and took a deep breath. "I want to kill a man, Reverend. I almost had him killed him a few days ago, and I wish I had, and I still want to. And I know it's wrong, but it's just about all I think about."

"You've never said a word about it before. Maybe it's just the pain and the medicine talking?"

"Preacher, let me tell you something, something every colored man knows, and you white fellas never think about." I took a sip of water and winced in pain. "We don't talk about—about the anger or the fear or the urge to kill. We don't talk about it or show it, because we'll end up dead before dark if we do. Bein colored means bein quiet, Reverend French, unless we're feelin extra brave or extra hopeless. We have to be calm and quiet just to stay alive. I was just lucky that boy was drunk when he tried to kill me. And he was lucky too, because I'm too proud to gun down a drunk."

We talked all afternoon, and as the light faded, Mansfield French stood and took my hands in his own.

"I'll take care of it, son, just like we talked about."

*　*　*

They kept Peter in jail for two weeks. He didn't remember the first couple of days, except that his head pounded like a hammer and he stank. After he was sober, they let him wash, and his brother brought some clean clothes. He would've given his father's wealth for a swallow of whiskey. Three or four days later, the thirst for whiskey eased a little, and his appetite came back. That's when the preacher showed up.

He'd seen the Methodist preacher around town for a while. They said he was part of a school or something for the coloreds, and Peter reminded himself it was legal now for them to read and write. Seemed like a big mistake, and dangerous too, if they all of a sudden could read, do business and such. No telling what could happen.

Rev. French seemed different from old Dr. Walker at St. Helena's, and he was real different from that Fuller over at the Baptist church. He came in—right into the cell—and asked how Peter was doing, how he was feeling.

"How the hell do you think I'm doing?" Peter asked, and then remembered he was talking to a preacher.

"Peter, you may not want to talk to me at all, and that's alright. But I want you to know, I didn't come here to make you feel bad. I figure you're feeling plenty bad already."

"You got that right. I feel bad about being in here, that's for sure. And I heard that Smalls is going to be alright. I feel real bad about that. Wish I'd killed the son of a bitch."

Peter was at first offended that Rev. French had appeared at his cell. As if he needed some holier-than-thou old man trying to dry him out. Peter didn't want to see him and couldn't think of a reason he'd show up at the jail. So, he asked him, bluntly.

"Well, Mr. Rhett," French began, with a bit of a smile, "that's a good question. I s'pose we'll figure it out together. Why don't you start by telling me what you're doing here."

"That damn Smalls—that's why I'm here!"

"He put you here?"

"No, Father French, I just waltzed my sorry ass in here for the food."

French laughed, making Peter even angrier.

"Well, how is it?" French asked. "The food, I mean."

He came to the jail every day, but never asked about the attack of Smalls. It was the only thing Peter really wanted to discuss, so one afternoon, he asked, "Aren't you going to ask me about Smalls?"

"Hadn't occurred to me," he said, "but yes, now that you mention it. Tell me about Smalls."

"Son of a bitch has ruined my life for as long as I can remember," Peter told him.

"How'd he do that?" French looked genuinely surprised.

"It's pretty obvious, isn't it? A nigger tryin' to be some kind o' big man?"

"And—how did that ruin your life?"

"Are you serious?"

"Just tryin' to understand, son. Tell me more about the life he ruined."

Peter told him about his life in Beaufort, about his mother and Mauma Hattie and his brothers and sisters. He told him about Liza Beth and school and wanting to study architecture but ending up at the Citadel. French asked a few questions, and Peter talked on for days.

One afternoon, Peter told French about Liza Beth's rejection and the end of their courtship. The preacher nodded, and after a moment said. "You haven't mentioned your father."

"What about him?"

"You've told me about your whole life, but you haven't mentioned your father."

"What about him?"

"You tell me."

Peter realized, then, that he didn't actually know his father, that they'd never known one another, but the father had shaped most of the son's life.

"There's nothing to tell, Preacher, except—" Peter couldn't finish.

"Except what?" French asked.

They made him so angry, questions like that. Questions with no answers. He slammed his fists on the table, and paced around the room, while French sat patiently, waiting for him to speak. Peter felt like an idiot. He felt exactly like all those times his father demanded that Peter be someone he couldn't be. Son of a bitch.

French let Peter sit silent, for a long time.

"Do you like him? Do you like your father?"

*Seriously?* Surely, he'd seen the old man for himself.

"He's my father."

"Yes, but what if he wasn't? Is he a person you would like if he wasn't your father?"

"What kind of question is that?"

"Just think about it, that's all. I'll see you tomorrow."

And with that, Rev. French stood up and walked out, calm as could be. Peter thought he might explode.

He steamed and stewed, but eventually Peter actually thought about what he'd observed in his father—the way Barnwell moved through the world, trying to bend it to his will, and the way he used people. Peter began to see him not as his father, but as a man trying hard to do and be something, anything. For the most part, the old man had failed. He'd had his one great, shining moment, when they all signed the secession ordinance, and he thought he'd continue to lead the charge, but Davis prevailed. *And yet again my father played the victim.*

He'd always been angry about something, Peter realized. Anger was Barnwell Rhett's natural state. Anger was his currency. As children, Peter and his siblings thought they'd caused that anger, anger turned toward them or toward their mother. When it found Peter, he'd thought he deserved it. That night in jail, Peter came to the tragic and liberating realization that his father had not ever actually given a damn about anyone else; Barnwell's anger simply manifested his self-absorption. And he was alone in it.

"I wish I could say that I began to have some sympathy for my father, but that would not be true. Pity, perhaps, but not sympathy," he confessed the next week to the preacher.

When the guard opened the door and Peter walked out, he didn't want a drink, and he didn't want to kill a man.

And he wasn't afraid of his father.

\* \* \*

Peter told his brother, years later, "I don't know how to explain it to people, and I stopped trying long ago. But this is what I know; I'm not my father, and I'm not my father's son. He may have sired me, and he sure as hell pushed me to do some awful things, things I did without ever understanding why. But I'm not him, and I will not become him. I may not be a good man, but I refuse to be that man."

Mansfield French became a friend; he was a man Peter could trust, a man to be honest with. Peter didn't always agree with him, but he trusted him. Sometimes they talked, or argued, late into the night. Peter learned that French's wife had died of a fever sickness, long ago, and they talked about loss, and sorrow, and women. Over time, French encouraged Peter to court and marry Sarah Duke, his old acquaintance from Beaufort, and for the next dozen years, when French inquired about Sarah, he'd smile. "I told you so," he'd say. "She's a good woman, and she's good for you."

And he was right. Sarah gave Peter a son, and then a daughter, and she made him a better man.

\* \* \*

Peter Rhett had moved on and was healing, albeit slowly, as were so many in the defeated South. Life for them would never return to normal, but it would return.

I wondered how the McKees were recovering.

*Jane McKee's Diary*

*September 22, 1871*

Goodness, but I miss my dear daughter, though I'm comforted by the portrait of happiness her words painted in her last letter. Pennsylvania sounds lovely, and I do hope an opportunity to visit might become available. Perhaps if Henry's health improves a bit we could make the journey next spring. He is progressing, if slowly, which I attribute to the gradual dissipation of the anxiety and exhaustion of these last years. Leaving Beaufort almost broke his heart, and mine too. The physical toll of escaping to Charleston and then out to Columbia very nearly broke his body. Now that things have quieted down, his strength looks to be returning. His strength of body, at least. His spirit still feels the bruises. I suppose that's true for all of us.

I wonder how it is for Liza Beth there in the North. Do people know of our suffering? Is there any sympathy at all? All we seem to hear these days are sentiments of derision and scorn. I pray that my darling daughter doesn't share such sentiments— that she cherishes the roots from which she came, that she may have yet some pride in being a daughter of Dixie.

She married a smart young man, and so dashing! When the dear Lord blesses them with children, oh my, how beautiful they will be!

I sent Liza Beth word that our Lydia has been ill. Henry received a letter from Peter Rhett, in which he told us, among other things, of Lydia's troubles. Seems she's suffering a rheumatism of some sort. She lives with Trouble and Hannah in our old house on Prince Street! It is almost impossible for me to believe or envision. So many of the homes were given to the coloreds, just for paying the federal taxes. We weren't given any latitude at all. The town has changed entirely. And yet, how I *would love to be there again, along that lovely river, inhaling the honeysuckle, watching the Spanish moss sway from the old oaks.*

*March 4, 1872*

*I received a letter yesterday from Liza Beth, and I find myself both delighted and concerned. She sounds so happy, which makes my own heart happy too. I think mothers and daughters comprehend this special connection as few others can. Above all, I give thanks for her happiness. But I fear her mind has been turned. She wrote in her letter that "the emancipation of the Negro is a good thing," that women are studying in universities, that, hopefully one day soon, women as well as the Negro will be allowed to vote. I fear my naïve little girl has turned her back on her heritage.*

*Has she not considered what shall become of life as we know it if education and suffrage are allowed the Negro? It is one thing that they be free, and a difficult thing at that. But full of knowledge? And with a full voice at the polls? Oh, heavens, that will change everything! I understand—in theory, that is—the romantic notion of "equality," but in practical terms, well, I simply can't imagine how it will work. I pray my dear daughter will think deeply about the consequences of these things.*

*Oh, I must sound so motherly! I'm quite proud of the young woman Liza Beth has become. And perhaps I should take comfort in her assurances that "we need not agree on all things, so long as we agree to love, especially our families!"*

*Her letter makes evident her pride in Ellison and his work. His people have always been so academic and liberal; I suppose I should say "progressive." It earned his uncle a bit of a reputation in S. Carolina. That same old James Petigru underwrote that wonderful school Liza Beth attended in Charleston. That's where this progressive thinking actually worked for good.*

*Liza Beth, I'm so proud to say, was a fine teacher. I remember Mdme. Tongo told me, even before she graduated, that she wanted her to stay on to teach French to the younger girls, and I've encountered some of their mothers in the years hence, and they never fail to thank me for her part in their daughters' mastery of the language. Si vous plais, they all tell me! And now, Liza Beth is head of a language department! When she and Ellison finally have children, how very brilliant they'll be!*

*October 19, 1873*

*Henry has taken ill and deeply wants to see our daughter. I wrote her a letter pleading for a visit and without delay. We will carry him to Beaufort by carriage tomorrow. He insists that Dr. Johnson, old as he is, will be able to provide him some relief, and he says that if that's not the case, he'd "rather be in Beaufort than anywhere else on God's green earth" when he draws his last breath. Oh, I don't know how I can manage if he doesn't improve. I can't bear the thought. I hope Ellison can accompany Liza Beth. I need so desperately to see them.*

*November 6, 1873*

*I received word that Ellison and Liza Beth are on their way and should be there within a week. Glory be!*

# CHAPTER 42

## 1875

I saw Liza Beth and Ellison Petigru waiting just inside the door of St. Helena's Parish Church to avoid the unseasonal chill wind. Just days after Christmas, gray clouds blanketed the December afternoon and threatened a rare snowfall.

As guests arrived by foot and carriage, and a handful on horseback, Liza Beth stepped into the wind to embrace Hannah and then me.

"Mother is in the vestry room, staying warm, but she insists that your family sit on the pews up front with us."

"We'd be honored, Liza Beth." I paused, then asked the obvious question. "That's likely to offend some folks. You sure you're alright with that?"

"Oh, good heavens. Some folks will be offended no matter what. And it will be the same ones that were offended when you two got married! It's their problem, not ours."

"How's your mother, honey?" Hannah asked, gently.

Tears filled Liza Beth's eyes. "She'll be alright. After today."

I took both her hands in mine. "Lydia sends her love. She's heartbroken she can't make it today."

Organ music drew us into the sanctuary, and the vestryman escorted the McKee family to the front pew and signaled our family to follow and sit in the pew behind them. I remembered being in St. Helena's before, visiting wounded troops convalescing in this very room during the war. *A room for the wounded. A room for healing.*

Bits of liturgy and music caught in my mind, like Spanish moss blowing off a branch and catching on a sleeve.

*"As a father is tender towards his children, so is the Lord tender to those that fear him . . . But the merciful goodness of the Lord endures forever . . ."*

*   *   *

A decade had passed since the war ended, and while much had changed, lifetimes and generations would pass before real peace settled here, if it ever did. Peter Rhett sat across the aisle with his father. Barnwell Rhett looked ancient and unwell, and as angry as ever. *The old fire-eater won't give up.* Peter still carried himself with military bearing, erect and stoic. They'd both given themselves, fiercely, to a cause that some could not accept as lost.

*". . . and dark is His path on the wing of the storm . . ."*

We sang the hymns and prayed the prayers and the old rector, Dr. Walker, pulled himself into the pulpit for another homily. How many men and women, children and infants, had he buried? How did a man carry the weight of so much loss and sorrow for so many?

"Truly we shall feel his loss; but we shall honor him best by living up to the lessons which he has taught us. He shared with us his purity of mind and integrity of character, his deep love of nature in all her forms and especially his appreciation of our rivers and marshes and the rhythms of the tides. His heart, kind and gentle, opened to all around him, and he sought the good of all . . ."

*He taught me to fish and to swim, to sail, to ride. He gave me a chance to marry Hannah. I could never be the son he wanted and lost, and he could never be the father I wanted to know, but we gave what we could to one another's lives.*

Memories of practicing knots on the little boat, baiting a hook, cleaning a fish; memories, elusive now, of Hank and the darkness of grief that left its permanent residue; memories of little Robbie, and the kindness of the McKees when they'd learned of his death. Memories of the plantation, of jail, of the first trip to Charleston. Memories of the reversals of fortune, and the sweet pride of being able to help the McKees after the war.

*"I don't know what to say. You don't have to do that, son."*

*"I know. I want to, Mr. McKee. You were real good to my mama and me."*

*"Maybe it's time for you to call me Henry."*

*"Well now, that'll take some getting used to."*

At some point, we finally addressed one another as "Henry" and "son," and we'd enjoyed a friendship born of mutual appreciation these past several years. I'd gone to him to let him know I would be on the ballot to represent South Carolina's 5th congressional district in the House of Representatives, and he shook his head in disbelief. "If it's come to that, son, it might as well be you."

Our friendship proved it could happen—a new way of being men in the world together, even now. Rare, but possible.

"And now as we surrender to thee the frail remains of thy cherished gift, Henry McKee, as the dust returns to dust, while the spirit has already returned to thee, help us to fix our eyes upon our heavenly home."

We left the church in silence and stood around the open grave, huddled close to one another against the cold. Dr. Walker committed the body to the earth and the soul to the Lord, and we all said "Amen" as the sleet began to blow.

Inside the parish hall, we warmed ourselves. I looked around the room with gratitude. These were my friends, my people, my town. Black and white. I'd even been able to let go some of the animosity with the Rhetts, although I doubted they'd say the same.

Liza Beth and her brother, Will, stood next to one another, looking so much like their parents that people took note, commented. The McKees were loved.

A raspy voice broke the warmth.

"Boy, what the hell are you doing here?" The voice, older but unmistakable, belonged to Barnwell Rhett.

"Not here, Father," Peter whispered. The old man glared.

"Not here! I'll tell you about not here! That goddamn nigger ought not be here!"

Hannah squeezed my forearm.

"It's alright, sugar," I said and pulled away, and took a step toward Barnwell.

Barnwell Rhett and I stood toe to toe, and eye to eye. Peter glanced at Liza Beth.

"Don't touch him, Smalls," Peter whispered the warning, "or I'll have to kill you after all."

"No need, Mr. Rhett. I just thought I'd remind your father here that . . . that we're in the house of the Lord." I kept my voice low, and my eyes fixed on the elder Rhett.

*Some things never change. I'm his representative in Washington, but he doesn't give a damn about that.*

"Damn son of a bitch!" the old man snarled. Both Peter and I ignored him.

"He thinks you people are still trying to ruin us," Peter said, barely audibly. "It never stops."

"I'm here to honor Henry McKee. We can take this up another time, but this is neither the time nor the place, sir." I kept my eyes on Barnwell Rhett, who seemed to have lost the trail of the conversation.

Ellison Petigru stepped in. "It's been a hard day, gentlemen. Let's move on, shall we?"

\* \* \*

After Henry died, I thought Mrs. McKee might stay in Beaufort, but she decided to go to Liza Beth's in Philadelphia for a while, and then I heard she did a great deal of traveling. Will had finished at the Citadel, and was going to be studying medicine not too far from Philadelphia. Liza Beth told me that Mrs. McKee felt like no one needed her. Hannah and I thought the travel might be good for her. She had fine friends in so many places now, as lots of folks had scattered from Beaufort when the war began, and some had stayed away, making new homes in new places—Baltimore and Washington, and Boston and New York City and Providence.

I'd had speaking engagements in all those cities after the *Planter*, and they were full of interesting people and wonderful food and music. I myself soon grew tired of the constant movement and missed the gentle pace of the lowcountry, but I believed all that would do Mrs. McKee some good. She deserved some time to enjoy her friends, and Mr. McKee had managed to restore their finances, at least modestly.

And to be honest, I knew that living in Beaufort again after the war had been bittersweet. A few of the old friends had turned cold, in no small part because of me. People blamed the McKees for my taking the *Planter*, and for my efforts on behalf of the Union. A few even blamed the McKees, in a quiet and indirect way, for the fall of the South.

Truth be told, I suspect the McKees were sympathetic to some elements of the Union's cause, even in regard to abolition. That sentiment blossomed in Liza Beth when she married a "progressive" and moved north.

The McKees treated my mama and me with kindness, for the most part, with the considerable and indefensible exception of the harsh truth of our circumstances. How could they not see what they were doing, and continue to declare it fine and proper and Christian?

I think sometimes of that old story about the frog in the kettle, and I suppose the McKees were already in deep before things heated up, and probably couldn't find a good way out. Maybe there were others in the same pot. The Southern way was all about self-preservation.

I'm not saying they couldn't have found some other way; of course they could have freed us, and should have. I'm saying they didn't seem to be able to find a way that worked for them, in this world they were living in at the time, a way that would save their pride and such. That damned so-called Southern pride.

When I was a boy, sometimes I felt stuck right in the middle of two worlds. My life was more comfortable than that of most of my race. But it wasn't mine. And it wasn't good. I lived in the middle, a little bit in two worlds, but not fully in either. Maybe the McKees felt stuck in the middle too.

There's no way around it—their choice to keep slaves was wrong, and I still don't know if I'll ever understand or fully forgive them, though God knows I try. I don't know, really, what they thought and how they felt, and we never talked about it. But they were never cruel, and they helped it work out for me and Hannah to marry, even hosted a fine wedding day in the yard. They watched out for Mama, and—it sounds improbable, I know—I do believe they've loved us, all these years, in their own way. And I suppose we've loved them too. It's a complicated place in me. Maybe it's complicated in them too.

\*   \*   \*

Before Liza Beth and Ellison went back to Philadelphia after Mr. McKee's funeral, we had a fine visit here at the house. I wondered what she would think, being back in the old dining room, as a guest this time. But if it bothered her at all, she never let on. We talked late into the night, all of us, about education, about the power of reading and learning. I even read a little bit for her—it still comes hard to me, but I did my best—just to show her that I could, and when I looked up she was wiping a tear.

"Robert," she said, "I think that's the finest thing I've ever seen."

"Well, now, I'm still working on it, but Lordy, it opens up the world, doesn't it?"

"When did you learn?" she asked. "And how?"

I told her about the hymn books, and working at the restaurant, and all the late nights of trying to figure it out. I told her how glad it made me to send my own children to school, and how they read so well. She listened, nodded, wiped her eyes again.

"Trouble," she said. She'd not called me Trouble in years. "I've never forgotten that day on the porch when we were children. Do you remember? We were looking at a book, and I was showing you how to sound out letters, and Peter came unhinged."

I nodded. I remembered.

She reached across the table and touched my hand. "I've always felt terrible about that . . . how I didn't stand up to him . . . how I let him speak to you like that. I'm sorry, Trouble . . . Robert."

"We were young," I said. "And Peter was a bully. We've all grown some since then."

"I see things so differently now," she said. She looked at Ellison. "You've been instrumental in that, you know." She smiled at him. Their affection for one another was palpable.

Hannah spoke up. "Liza Beth, maybe that day on the porch, maybe that's why you became a teacher. Do you s'pose?"

"Goodness, maybe so. I think we're all teachers, Hannah. And we're all students, too, if we choose—if we choose learning—if we choose to keep our minds open. And our hearts."

"Tell him," Ellison said, nudging Liza Beth, and smiling my way.

"Tell me what?" I asked.

"Robert," Liza Beth said, "my father made a vow, while we were away during the war—a vow that if he ever got back to Beaufort alive, that he would dig up the silver that he'd hidden under the floor at our house, and he'd use half its value for a noble cause. Those are the words he used—'noble cause.' I'd forgotten about it, but when we arrived last week, before he passed, he made me promise to keep his vow."

"It doesn't surprise me that he'd remember, Liza Beth. He took pride in being a man of his word," I assured her. "What noble cause did he have in mind?"

"That's the thing, Robert. He said he wanted us to decide— Will and Ellison and me."

She glanced at Ellison and he nodded. "Go on," he said.

"We think it should support the work at the school, Robert. The Penn School."

I didn't know what to think or say. The school over on St. Helena's Island, dedicated to educating the freed slaves, had struggled from the beginning. But the work mattered, and people were learning to read, and to write. Women and men, and children too, learning about a world beyond the fields.

The four of us sat around that table late into the night, telling stories, talking about books and ideas, about reading and learning and the infinite possibilities unlocked by knowledge.

* * *

In 1870, we'd seen a miracle happen when we passed legislation that mandated education for all of our children here in South Carolina—not just the white children, and not just the wealthy children, but all the children. I got to help write that legislation, and it helped me get elected. We were a long way from seeing statewide education become reality, but, as in so many other arenas, we were making progress.

Liza Beth and Ellison reignited my commitment, and I prayed to see the day that every child could learn to read and write.

# CHAPTER 43

## 1876

For eight days, the skies emptied over the lowcountry, from Savannah to Charleston, saturating the earth, forming new creeks that drained into the rivers and tidal marshes. Travel became treacherous; everyone stayed muddy and damp, constantly. Barnwell Rhett would have been irritated—no, incensed—by the endless unseasonal rains that delayed his burial. He'd been in Louisiana with Peter's sister Sarah and her husband, Alfred, when he died, but he'd made it abundantly clear that his final resting place would be in his beloved South Carolina, as he had secured his position in the Magnolia Cemetery in Charleston decades before.

Nothing about his final journey would have been acceptable to him, and so his life ended as he had lived it—in utter agitation. It was only after his burial that Peter consciously began to release the profound burden his father had heaped upon his life. He'd long been aware, of course, of his father's impact upon the South and indeed upon the entire country. Over half a million lives were lost in the war, and Barnwell Rhett had no small part in it, fueling its flames in every way he could and especially through his cherished *Charleston Mercury*. Because of his newspaper, his sentiments had been swallowed like grits by the people of the South and eventually, briefly, the Confederacy.

"Aye—disunion, rather, into a thousand fragments," he once wrote. "And why, gentlemen, would I prefer disunion to such a Government? Because under such a Government I would be a slave—a fearful slave, ruled despotically by those who do not represent me . . . with every base and destructive passion of man bearing upon my shieldless destiny."

His influence on the rebel cause aside, Peter had for some time now acknowledged his father's influence on his character. Barnwell had been an extraordinary teacher, but in an extraordinarily unconventional way.

\* \* \*

When they finally buried old Barnwell Rhett in the muddy cemetery in Charleston, Peter was able to find a thin gratitude for the lessons learned from his father. Peter learned—by his father's failures and omissions—that he could choose to be like him, an angry victim, or he could live his life, his own life, on his own terms. The old man taught, by his pitiful example, how not to treat people. He taught, as he alone could, about the isolation of a fear-wrapped life.

Mansfield French stood with Peter at the graveside, and when it was time for Peter to speak, the reverend nodded and stepped aside.

"Our family appreciates your presence today," Peter began, "but no one would appreciate it more than Robert Barnwell Rhett." They laughed politely, knowing the old man's need to be the center of all attention.

"He was a complicated man who lived a complicated life. I suppose that's true of us all. His passion—that was his great strength.

And it was his weakness, of course. I suppose that's true for all of us as well. Perhaps his legacy is simply that, to know our passions, and to give ourselves to a great cause."

Peter didn't say what he thought about the cause, or his father's way of pursuing it; he figured people would hear what they wanted anyway.

French finished the service with a prayer, and Peter buried more than a little regret with the old man.

*   *   *

I always hoped that Mama would finally tell me something, anything about my father. That last week as I sat at her bedside, she smiled, and in a feeble little voice told me to pull the chair up closer.

"Trouble," she said, and I noted the deep lines around her eyes, how beautiful they were, the way they deepened when she smiled or worried. She'd done more than anyone's share of both, often simultaneously, and I will always wonder at her ability to hold both life's gifts and griefs so lightly. She was the only person who persisted in calling me Trouble, to the consternation of my wife and children. But she'd become confused lately; she called me Abe twice, and I didn't have the heart to tell her Abe had been gone almost twenty years, so I just said, "I'm Trouble, Mama."

"Where's Abe?" she'd asked, looking distressed.

"He's up in Charleston, Mama," I told her. It was true; that's where he'd been buried.

I pulled the chair up to the bed and leaned in close.

"Mama," I whispered. "I'm here."

"You came on a night full o trouble, son. Did I ever tell you bout that?"

"You told me that's why you call me Trouble, Mama. You told me that lots of times." She made a point, when I was little, to make sure I knew that my name didn't mean that she thought I was the trouble. But she never told me what the trouble had been, and I assumed that she'd been talking about trouble in general, the trouble of life.

"It was the night they hung him, son. The night they hung that man."

"What, Mama? You never told me anything about that." She'd been so muddled these past few weeks, thinking morning was nighttime, and getting our names mixed up. I couldn't tell if this was a moment of confusion or of clarity.

"He'd a been so proud o you, son." Her voice trailed off, and her eyes closed. "So proud." Just a whisper, and I leaned in closer.

"Tell me more, Mama."

She was sound asleep again, peaceful as a housecat, and I dozed in the chair next to her for a while.

\* \* \*

Mama wanted to be buried near the praise house over on the island, where she'd been a child on the old Ashdale plantation, and a few days later, that's what we did. She'd grown so bent and small, and all her strength had left her bones, and finally resided now completely in her spirit. We buried her with the ancestor figures that I remembered from childhood, and with Abe's slave tag, and with unspeakable gratitude and grief. And I buried my unanswered questions about my father. Sometimes you just have to let go.

There are plenty of good people in the world, along with plenty more who aren't. But there are only a few who are better than good, and it's shame there's no name for those. It's tempting to call them saints. I'd like to call my mother a saint, but our Lydia wouldn't like that one bit, and she'd be right. She wasn't a saint; she knew it, and that is, in fact, what made her so very good. She knew her own wounds and losses; she knew her weaknesses and her sharp edges; she knew her capacity for hatred as well as love, which so few ever know about themselves. And because she knew that in herself, she knew how to choose. She knew to choose both kindness and strength, both wariness and warmth, both firmness and forgiveness. She never lost her confidence in the ancestors, and she never lost her hope for the future.

She knew which heart to feed. Hers was a heroic life—unsung, perhaps, but not without impact.

Jane McKee sent a letter when she heard about Mama's passing.

*Dear Robert,*

*Liza Beth sent notice of Lydia's passing, and I send you my deepest sorrow and condolences. I was in Boston at the time, and wished I could make my way instantly to Beaufort. I suppose I simply wanted to be able to say goodbye, somehow. She was special, Robert, as you well know. Only a mother can know the depth with which another mother loves her child. Your mother loved you with all her being. I know you know that, but I wanted you to know that we witnessed it. She taught me so much about being a mother. When Hank died, she cried with me, and told me about the baby girl she'd buried, long before your birth. When you took the Planter—which now I can see helped bring an end to a terrible thing—she was so very proud but she never gloated. Even as a servant, she carried herself with the dignity of a royal, and as a free woman she continued to truly serve.*

*She was my friend, my dear Robert, and I loved her. I grieve with you.*

*Most sincerely yours,*
*Jane McKee*

*P.S. Liza Beth told me of your reading skill, and it pleases me to no end to think that you are reading this letter yourself.*

# CHAPTER 44

## 1882

After his father's death, Peter and Sarah focused on their little farm business, taking advantage of the lowcountry's long growing seasons and pliable soil. Mansfield French saw to it that lots of young colored men found their way to the farm for work, and whole families were often employed. French said it was Peter's part of lifting the dark legacy of slavery, of somehow paying for the sins of his father, and the fathers of the South.

But the new bands of redshirts didn't see it that way. Gun and rifle clubs were forming in every Southern county, with the express purpose of suppressing the negro, especially at the ballot box. They were effective; lynchings were frequent, and without retribution. These men and boys wore their red shirts with pride; the women who made the shirts wore red bows in their hair or red sashes on their dresses. There was no mistaking who was who.

The threats escalated, and only stopped when Governor Hampton finally stepped in, invoking, ironically, Rhett's fine Confederate legacy. Peter and Sarah breathed a sigh of relief, though they still worried over their farm crews, and did all they could to protect them.

The day after little Bethy's sixth birthday, Rev. French asked Peter to meet him at the school out on the island, the Penn School.

"We've got to find decent resources for more of these children, Rhett. You're the only one who can build some kind of goodwill bridge between the whites in town and these families. I want you to meet the teachers and hear what they have to say."

Sarah laughed when Peter told her where he was going.

"Well, Peter Rhett, when you shake off a legacy, you shake it all the way off!"

"Why don't you and Bethy come with me? Christian is in school, and we'll make it a special outing for our girl."

Peter had come to respect French's dedication to the poor colored families on the island, and he'd even come to agree with him that the basic skills of reading and writing would be good for everyone. They still argued about the right to vote; Peter thought it dangerous, but moderate literacy would benefit everyone. And he'd come to appreciate what he'd heard about my work in that regard. Things had changed dramatically for both of us, and Peter had to confess that he respected my courage and determination.

He was motivated, too, by the hope that somehow his old friend Liza Beth might hear about his involvement with the colored school. He'd long ago admitted that they would never have been happy together, but she still held a special place in his heart, and he wondered if she might forgive him for his cruel youth if she knew about his support of the school.

Miss Laura Towne greeted them with a smile on the steps of the Brick Baptist Church that served as the schoolhouse, and they followed her inside and joined Rev. French at a table set with tea. Bethy thought they were having a tea party just for her, and everyone played along, while the adults had their conversation about the school.

"Mama," she said after a while, "I need to go—"

"It's just there," Miss Towne said, pointing across the yard to the little outhouses that served the school.

Peter and Rev. French and the teacher resumed their conversation, but only for a moment.

An explosion, then screams of pain and terror, and the sound of horses galloping away. They ran outside, only to see the billowing smoke. Silence.

\* \* \*

The brief newspaper story described it as a tragic accident, the "disastrous combination of fumes and gases, ignited."

I had arrived just as Sarah and Bethy stepped outside, and the redshirts believed, until the next day, that they had finally murdered Robert Smalls.

Mansfield French spoke at the funeral, but Peter recalled nothing that he said, except "Death can never take what love has given." It seemed to him that death had taken all that love had given, and more.

French stayed with him for most of a week and his brother Edmund came with his wife from Savannah and helped care for Christian for the next month or so. Those days were bourbon-blurred, and it was another year before Peter found the courage to attempt sobriety again.

Love is color-blind, some say. Peter wasn't sure about that. But he knew without a doubt that hate is blind. As Peter aged, he grew to appreciate love over hate.

\* \* \*

That was never more evident than an early morning in 1899 when Peter Rhett knocked on my door, on a quiet Sunday, looking distressed.

"Mr. Rhett," I said. "What can I do for you today, sir?"

The edges of our old animosities had smoothed some over the years, into a kind of mutual compassion, the patina of life's timeworn hopes and heartaches. It's hard to explain to the younger people.

Time had accelerated. I'd become aware of the frequency of the tides, the way each day passed so quickly, and then the weeks and the months. Whole seasons, turning, turning. Entire years had rolled by, and I suppose we both just grew too tired to sustain old wounds as we once did.

"Smalls," he said, and his voice trembled a little. "I've just got word from Ellison Petigru that we've lost our sweet Liza Beth."

He stopped, and I felt my own heart stop as well. The world beyond my front porch turned into a blur, and I felt dizzy and unsure.

I pointed to the rocking chairs on the porch, and we both sat down. Still, I couldn't find my voice.

After a long moment, he spoke again. "He wanted me to tell you straightaway. I only heard this morning." His voice broke. "I loved her, Smalls. Even when she decided she couldn't love me, I loved her."

I tried to put words to the feelings and thoughts that whirled like a storm in my mind and heart but failed.

I thought about my own incredible Hannah, how I'd loved her from the first moment I saw her, and how she'd loved me back. When she passed a few years ago, I thought my own heart would stop; I thought the dark, empty loneliness would swallow me, kill me. The pain never left, but it softened when I met Annie.

I thought about Peter's pain, too. His sweet Sarah and little Bethy, and we both knew they'd died in my place. His grief and my guilt, and nothing either of us could do about it.

"What happened?" I finally asked. "How?"

"It was sudden, that's all I know. A stroke, maybe."

"Sixty," I said. "We're all sixty this spring. Sure went by fast, didn't it, Rhett?"

He nodded.

We rocked in silence.

I remembered all the mornings he came to these steps, stood on this porch, knocked on that door. I remembered the flowers that he held, plucked from a neighbor's garden, usually. I remembered the morning he told me I could never read, and another morning when I'd broken his shoulder with my shovel.

I remembered the morning he beat me half to death in Charleston. I'd thought it was because of the fight in Beaufort, and learned much later it was because Liza Beth had ended their courtship on the same day that I'd been granted permission to buy and marry Hannah. I remembered the morning I stole a Confederate ship under his watch, and our shared commitment at the school, and the day he'd buried half his family. We'd fought each other, challenged each other, and finally respected each other. After being at war such a long time, and sharing extraordinary sorrows, now—in her absence—Liza Beth brought us together once again, and invited us to comfort and befriend each other.

I supposed I could try.

"Rhett," I started. "How's your family doing? You've still got a brother or two around here, is that right?"

He chuckled, a little nervous sounding. "Well, now, I guess I didn't expect that, but I appreciate you asking. Just two left beside me. My sister Margaret is up in New York; I don't hear from her much. And Rob's still up in Charleston, trying to keep our father's—well, let's just call it his legacy—alive. He's the one that might've made the old man proud, if anyone could."

"He was one of a kind, your father," I offered, trying to sound friendly.

"He was just, well, he was always just himself, except there at the end, when he was even more so." He shook his head. "The man always bewildered me, Smalls. I spent three decades trying to emulate him, and one more trying to figure him out and always trying to be seen by him. Finally let it go. Finally, just let it go."

I nodded. "Well, sir, he was never short on conviction; I'll give him that."

Peter laughed. "There's an understatement, Smalls. Conviction.

Often wrong, but never in doubt. That's old Barnwell Rhett." He shook his head. "Your father?" he asked me. "What was he like?"

"Damned if I know, Rhett. Never knew the man, never even knew his name. Had to let that go a long, long time ago."

"No idea?"

"None. I pestered my mama about it for a while, when I was young. I thought I had to know. She always said she'd tell me when the time was right, but then, well, it never happened. I finally let it go."

We rocked for a while, quiet.

"What do you recall most about Liza Beth?" he asked.

*When did he get so talkative?*

I thought about it for a moment. I thought about her love of teaching, and the school, but thought that might be too raw, too painful.

"Did she ever tell you about Hank and his little rabbits?" I asked. He shook his head, so I continued. "You know, Hank, he was the sweetest child, loved every little creature. We built us a rabbit pen one spring, and old Mr. McKee found a couple of rabbits, and Hank put em in that pen. Seemed like no time at all, by the time the salt marsh was green again, we had little rabbits everywhere. Well, Hankie wanted to have those babies in his room, and of course, Jane McKee wouldn't hear of it. But Liza Beth, she loved her little brother, and she didn't mind breaking a rule or two. She helped Hank smuggle a box full of bunnies up to his room."

Goodness, I hadn't thought about that in years. I stopped to wipe my eyes, I was laughing so.

"They stayed hidden for a day or two, but soon enough, there were rabbits and droppings all over this house. Mrs. McKee put her foot down, and out they went. But Liza Beth wanted to be Hank's hero, and she helped him keep one of those little rabbits hidden in his room, for months and months. Everyone—except for Mrs. McKee—everyone knew it. Mr. McKee thought it was hilarious, until that rabbit grew up and hopped into their room one night.

Scared Mrs. McKee half to death. I recall Mr. McKee and Liza Beth laughing so loud I could hear it from the backhouse! Liza Beth, my goodness, she was always watching out for the underdog, that's for sure!"

"Again, well understated, Smalls." Peter was more at ease than I'd ever seen him.

"I wish Liza Beth could be here with us right now," I said. "She'd never believe it."

We both looked out over the yard, past the fountain, beyond the street. A church bell rang.

"Smalls," he said, without looking my direction, "I have plenty of regrets."

"Yessir." *Don't we all?*

"You know you don't need to call me sir."

"I know that. Old habits die slow."

"Ain't that the God's truth."

# CHAPTER 45

Jane McKee stopped at the gate. *This one*, she thought, leaning to rest on the old brick column on which the gate itself rested. *This one*, she told herself, but just as she thought it, she was not sure. *This one? Oh, but it feels good to rest here a minute.* Her feet ached, and she tried to remember when they didn't.

*This one?* The gate looked the same. But that magnolia tree, there on the edge of the yard . . . too big, too wide. *But maybe?*

*How does this work? It slips up and pushes in, or is it out?* She stretched her hand to find the latch, and yes, it slipped up, and she discovered when she give it a little tug that it pushed in. *Yes, of course it does.*

She hesitated.

She exhaled. *Home—finally home.* She couldn't quite recall the journey, why she was away, or how long, or how she found her way back. But now, this enormous relief of being home. The familiar pattern of brick on the path from the gate to the porch. *What did we call that? It's a ziggy-zaggy thing. . . herringbone, yes, that's it.* She always liked the simple elegant symmetry of the herringbone walk.

Simple. Elegant. There was a time of simplicity and elegance, long ago. Or was it a dream? It was too far, too distant now to reach.

Her eyes followed the bricks to the deep porch itself, shaded and open to the breeze. Oh, the caress of the breeze coming off the river, even on a hot summer afternoon. Relief. She exhaled deeply, a sigh, almost a moan.

Just beyond the tree to the fountain. *Yes. That's the fountain we put there after we buried Hank.* She remembered looking out her window onto the fountain, for hours sometimes. Days sometimes. Henry had it brought from Charleston, and old George placed it that very day, with Lydia and Trouble looking on, Trouble trying to help.

*From that window, there.* She tilted her stiff neck to get a better look at the upstairs windows; the windows of her room on the southeast corner of the house. From there she watched Hank's fountain, and knew who was coming to the house, or to the neighbor's house, or walking from Prince Street to Bay Street.

As she looked at the window trying to remember how to get to that room, a man rose from a chair on the porch. She'd not seen him.

He stepped from the shade of the porch to the front steps, then down, slowly, to the walk. He was colored. *Why is a colored man on our porch?*

He moved toward her, and she pushed her matted silver hair from her eye, standing as straight as she could, though her back ached more when she did that. She tried to glare.

The man looked puzzled for a moment, then he smiled, slowly, starting with his eyes.

*Does he know me?*

*Do I know him?*

"Well, Mrs. McKee. Lookee there. Good afternoon, Mrs. McKee."

*How does he know me?*

"Welcome home, Mrs. McKee."

"Who are you?" she demanded, and she tried to sound strong, but when she heard her own voice, she knew better. So she attempted to continue glaring.

He tilted his head a little.

"I'm Robert."

Nothing.

"Trouble. You used to call me Trouble . . . and I guess I was."

*Trouble.* A cloud lifted somewhere in her memory. Trouble. *But he was a boy; this is an old man.*

"Trouble?"

"Mrs. McKee, let's go in and have a glass of tea, shall we?"

She took his arm and they walked slowly into the old house on Prince Street.

The choir in the church around the corner was singing, and the words drifted in.

*Take me to the water*
*Take me to the water*
*Take me to the water*
*To be baptized*

*None but the righteous*
*None but the righteous*
*None but the righteous*
*Shall be saved*

*So take me to the water*
*Take me to the water*
*Take me to the water*
*To be, to be baptized*

\* \* \*

I opened the gate and held it for Annie, and we both walked slowly up the walk, and, even more slowly climbed the steps to the porch. My limp had worsened considerably.

"My legs are burning today." I winced, as I took my coat off. "I thought the rector might've finished up our meeting a little quicker." I sank into the rocking chair with a sigh.

Annie nodded in agreement. "But I think the service tomorrow will be exactly what she would've wanted."

"That Rev. Githens seems like a nice enough fellow. But I miss old Dr. Walker. He baptized and buried most of this old town. I thought he'd outlive us all."

"Shame she was so lost in the head these last few years. Wish I'd known her before," Annie said. "Course, I thought you were lost in the head when you let her in here, put her upstairs like that!" Annie laughed, but we both remembered her anger when I announced that Jane McKee would be occupying a room upstairs in our home.

"Guess I shoulda asked you bout that, huh?" I laughed gently. "I wish I had, sugar. It's taken me a awful long time to get some sense in this old head." I reached for her hand. "Don't know how you put up with me then." I smiled. "Mighty glad you did."

"Well, God knows you had plenty to be proud about, and you were still fighting some big battles then." She looked out over the yard, watched a mockingbird settle on a branch of the magnolia tree, listened to the water in the fountain. "Lot o water under the bridge these last years. Quite a journey."

I closed my eyes, remembering.

\*　\*　\*

When Hannah passed, I'd wondered if I might die too, of heartache, and there were the nights, long nights, when I wished I would. The children had been such help, but they couldn't stay long. Liza Beth and Ellison came, but had to go back to their teaching positions, and Will still had to get back to his medical practice, so they'd all left together for Philadelphia just two days after the burial.

A dozen long years passed after Hannah's death before I met and married Annie, and then had the audacity to bring Mrs. McKee into the house.

"You want me to what?" I can still hear the outrage in Annie's voice. "You telling me I'm supposed to be her house girl? Have you lost your mind, Robert Smalls?" She'd marched out, still talking, and when I caught up with her on the river's edge, she spun around and looked me hard in the eyes. "I'm a teacher, Robert. A teacher. You're telling me I'm supposed to wait on this woman who owned you? Who wouldn't let you read? I'm supposed to bring her breakfast, and clean up after her like your mama did? You married the wrong woman if you think I'm doing that!"

"Now lookee, sugar," I said, taking Annie's hands in mine. I felt her begin to pull away, and tightened my fingers around hers. "I know I married the right girl, and you're right. You're a teacher, not a servant. All I'm saying is, we could make the last little bit of her life a little less lonesome. She's got no one, and I been telling anybody who'll listen that we got to look ahead of us, and not behind us. We got to do this because of the kinda people we want to be, not the kinda people they was."

"The kind of people they were, Robert. Not 'they was.' 'They were.'" She was smiling and I took that as a good sign. "And I don't know if I can be that kind of people you think we want to be. So many wounds still inside of me. And us, just getting our lives together started. I don't know; I really don't. It's one thing to give a person a room for a night or two, but we don't even know how long she'd be with us. Or what kind of sick she could be. Or how much it could cost us. We don't know any of that."

We watched a pair of pelicans glide low over the water, looking for fish.

"Can't ever know what's in front of us, sugar. Only thing we can know is what kind of people we want to be."

The pelicans circled and rose, higher than before, and one of them folded his wings and plunged, straight down into the water, and several long seconds passed before he emerged with his trout, and we watched as he threw his head back and swallowed it whole.

"At least give me a couple of days to think about this, Robert. Tell her she can stay until Sunday. For now."

*   *   *

Sunday came and went and five years passed. My children produced three new grandchildren, one after another. I learned that the McKees' son, Will, had moved back to Charleston after being out west for years, and he considered bringing Mrs. McKee into their home there. But we'd all agreed, in short order, that the frail old woman would be happiest if she could stay in the house on Prince Street. Annie discovered, to her great surprise, a deep affection for Jane McKee and, during the last year especially, spent whole mornings at her bedside, listening to stories. Almost weekly, she listened as the old woman described a boy called Trouble and how he swung at "that awful Rhett boy" with a shovel and broke his shoulder, and how she and Liza Beth and Lydia cried the next morning, and all day and the day after that, when Trouble waved goodbye from the wagon bound for Charleston.

Occasionally, the old woman repeated another story, the story of a young man. "He was our boy, he was!" she cried with indignation, as she remembered the boy who stole a Confederate ship and turned it over to the Yanks.

"I'll never understand it. He was a good boy, and he betrayed us. Just like that!" She always concluded with "Just like that!" and shook her head, with its wispy white hair. Annie never suggested to her that the boy with the shovel and the man with the boat were one and the same, or that she was living in the home of the boat thief.

Sometimes the old woman would tap her head with a bent finger.

"There's some places empty now, you know. I can't remember it all." Sometimes she cried when she said that, and sometimes she laughed. "It's a mystery, it is. I don't know where it went."

"It's the price of a long life, Mrs. McKee," Annie would tell her. "Tell me another story."

"Did I ever tell you about the boy with the shovel?" It was her favorite.

Late one August, Annie found the old woman at the window, weeping.

"What's wrong, honey?" she asked.

"My Hank!" she cried. "My sweet baby Hank! I can't bear it. My sweet boy."

"Oh, here now," Annie said as she wrapped her arms around the frail shoulders. "Let's get you back in bed." And she held her close as she sobbed, then gently guided her to the bed and helped her lie down. "Just listen to that fountain. Isn't that the sweetest sound?"

"Henry brought that for us last week, you know. Trouble helped him. And George. They're awfully good boys, they are." She paused and looked hard at Annie. "Lydia? Lydia, I do believe you're the finest colored woman I've ever known. You are a fine lady, Lydia. And you've been a fine friend to me, yes you have. I sure do thank you for that."

Her eyes closed and she slipped into sleep, where she spent more and more time these days.

I'm a blessed man, to have a woman like Annie by my side.

# CHAPTER 46

## 1904

Five decades have passed. No, six, and now going on seven. Where did the years go?

Five terms in Congress, and fruitful for the most part. Some successes, some failures. Education for all of South Carolina's children finally becoming a reality, though there were setbacks along the way. Children grown, and grandchildren growing. Losses and heartaches.

How much is left? And what will it bring?

On a clear Friday in mid-September, just after noon, Annie and I sat in the pew behind Will McKee and his wife, Claire, with their sons Hank and Rob. Will, the only surviving child of Henry and Jane McKee, insisted on our presence, just as his mother had done when Henry McKee died. *Where did the time go? Seems like we were just here.* I longed for Liza Beth's presence and missed her, thinking she'd be old now too, and that little Hankie, had he lived, would be running a business or holding a grandbaby on his lap. But now it's only Will, a fine man, living up in Charleston, and his family.

The McKees had been away a long time, but Beaufort was their first home, where they'd loved and been loved. A handful of old friends remained, and being loyal people they came to say goodbye to Jane McKee.

The Johnsons came; he's old and bent and she's deaf as a stump; they shuffled and hollered their way through the church and then to the graveyard outside. They found the Dukes there, and stood together, all four of them trying to remember names of folks they saw, till finally the rector hushed them up as the graveside liturgy began.

Will asked Annie and me to stand with the family after the service and the burial. We'd had to talk it through; the little town had healed a great deal, but in a small place with a deep memory such things need pondering. In the end, we did, and I was proud to stand with Annie, alongside Will, our two families side by side, as we'd faced so much of life side by side, through the years, connected even when we all saw things so differently.

Peter Rhett stood on the other side of the grave, his son Christian at his side. Peter looked weary, white-haired and slope-shouldered now. I realized in that moment that, like me, he'd outlived most of his contemporaries. Seems he'd finally begun to move through the world without the weight of his father's expectations and burdens. He'd let go, too, of the old yearning for Liza Beth, and he'd married and then buried sweet Sarah. *Sarah and little Bethy—they should still be here.* He'd blamed everyone when they died—Mansfield French and me and the anonymous men in their red shirts, and I couldn't blame him; now it seemed he'd finally let go of that, too. Most of it, anyway. *Too short. It's all been too short.* Our lives become a long exercise in letting go, and somehow, by grace, we find a fragile peace in all those empty places.

I seldom saw Peter anymore; I knew he ran a big produce farming business and lived over on the island. He gave me a little nod, the kind that says "I see you; I acknowledge you." Sometimes that needs to be enough. It's enough for me these days. Life was only getting shorter now, and I had no time for old angers. I wondered about Peter. No one would say Peter'd become a soft man; but people said he was kinder now, and generally agreeable. He's kept mostly to himself and his business, kind of resigned to things being the way they are and not the way they were. I hope he's beginning to find some peace in his life. I really do.

\* \* \*

After the burial, Peter and Christian extended their condolences to Will and Claire and shook my hand.

"Mr. Smalls," Christian said, "thank you for watching over Mrs. McKee these past few years. Can't have been easy." He turned to Annie with a smile. "And I 'magine you probably did all the work, ma'am." We all nodded in agreement; the past year had been awfully hard and Annie had been a saint.

"She told me an awful lot about your daddy," Annie said, smiling, speaking to Christian but glancing at Peter, "and maybe one of these days I'll tell it to you."

Peter Rhett cleared his throat. "Some of us were foolish back then, Mrs. Smalls. One of us, anyway."

"Indeed we were," I agreed, speaking quietly. "Long time ago."

Annie was restless. "Well, now, let's go to the house for a bit. I have something I want to show you gentlemen."

\* \* \*

Annie and Peter and I settled in the rockers on the front porch, and Will brought out chairs for Claire and Christian and perched himself on the rail. Annie noted how we spend an awful lot of time on the porch these days. A little breeze came up off the river, and one of the boys brought lemonade out for everyone. Late September always seemed to bring relief, a promised retreat of the worst of the summer heat, and we relaxed in the soft breeze.

Annie disappeared into the house for a minute, and returned with a little book tied with an old ribbon. She sat down with the little book on her lap, and put both hands down on it, like she could pull the words right up out of the pages. Annie always loved books, and it earned her a reputation as a fine teacher.

She sat quiet like that till everyone else got quiet too; then she said, "Mrs. Jane McKee left us a treasure here. I just found this yesterday, when I was tidying up some of her things. This page was marked for you, Bobby." She untied the ribbon and handed me the book. "Look there."

Jane McKee's diary. I read, slowly, silently, and they all waited.

*June 22, 1850*

> *Lydia came to me today and asked what I write in my "little book" here. I told her it was just a way of noting things that seemed to matter, or things that made me think; just my way of noticing life. And, truth be told, I do notice life more since I've been keeping this. Anyway, as Lydia stood in the doorway, it was clear she had something on her mind.*
>
> *"What is it Lydia?"*
>
> *"Missus McKee, you known me a awful long time."*
>
> *I nodded. We'd known each other most of our lives, it seemed. I waited.*
>
> *She spoke, and I will try to record it, exactly, here.*
>
> *"I took care of Mister Henry when he was just a boy. Your family's had me longer than I can count."*
>
> *"Lydia, what is it?" I hold great affection for Lydia, and it was true that she'd belonged to the McKees since Henry's childhood.*
>
> *"Missus McKee, I need to tell you something. And ask you something. Something real big, ma'am."*
>
> *"Good heavens, Lydia. What is it?"*

*"Missus McKee, could your write something in your book for me? It's real important to me, it truly is."*

I couldn't imagine what she was thinking about, and she certainly piqued my curiosity.

*"Lydia, what in the world are you talking about? What do you want me to write for you?"*

She looked past me, out the window, over the trees. In a voice low and lonely, she said, *"I need you to write it down about Ruben. About what happened to Ruben."*

She paused. I waited.

*"I been carryin' it here in my heart, every day, carryin' the love and the sorrow, and it just get heavier every day. Maybe if I tell you 'bout it, and you write it down, maybe then I can carry most o' the love and let go some o' the sorrow, an' it won't be so heavy. Maybe if you write it down, Missus, maybe it might be a way for Ruben to still live a little bit, even if it's only in that book of yours."*

Her gaze remained somewhere beyond the trees. The ache of her voice, the simple poignancy of her words caught me by surprise.

*"Well, Missus, you probably already know that our George and Ruben was brothers, but they got split apart when they was real little. George said probly he was five or six and Ruben maybe four year old when they got split apart from their mama, and from each other. George come here, to old Mr. McKee, Mr. Henry's daddy. And Ruben, he got took over to Bluffton to somebody, but then old Mr. Fuller, that preacher's daddy, he bought Ruben when he was 'bout ten, and sent him off to Charleston. That's where he learned to be a blacksmith. They say he was the best blacksmith in Charleston. They say that's why old Mr. Rhett bought him and brought him to his place here.*

*"I just 'bout never saw Ruben, him bein' out at the Rhett's place over 'cross the river most the time. Now and again, we might see one another in the praise house, or over in the*

market, and you know, he was a fine looking man, bigger than ol George—not tall but thick in the shoulders. Strong man."

Lydia paused, like she was trying to pull thoughts from every different direction all at once.

"Real strong."

Lydia's voice dropped so low; she seemed to have forgotten I was there. She was remembering and telling herself this story. I felt a bit intrusive, as if I were eavesdropping on an intimate conversation. But I also felt a strange sort of connection to Lydia; she was telling me something personal, and that felt important to me, and tender.

"Strong and stubborn," she continued, still quiet and detached.

"He always wanted to do the right thing. A dreamer. That Ruben, he was a dreamer.

"Well, like I said, we known each other a long time, real long time, but it wasn't anything to it. And then, that summer night, it was a Saturday night, we was both at the praise house over at the plantation.

"It was one of those rare August evenings, the heat of the day seemed to just lift away and a sweet breeze floated in off the river, and by dusk it was just pleasant as could be out on the waterfront. So, after the prayer service finished up, most everyone stayed there by the water, enjoying the fact that we could rest just a bit. Even the skeeters seemed to settle down a bit; it was just a real fine night.

"Well, I guess it was too good to be true, after all, because even though we was on the island side and not the town side of the river, and even though we was quiet as could be, sure enough the constable and his deputy come chargin' into us on their horses and shoutin' at everyone, "Git home, now, all of you! This ain't no meeting place. Now just break it up and git home now!"

"*They was chargin' around and knockin' people to the ground and scarin' everyone to death, and right away everybody scattered and started headin' back to their little cabins and such. I looked around for George so I could come home with him on that ol mule of his.*

"*Sure enough, there was George unhitchin' his mule, and there was Ruben talking to George, and Ruben was mighty agitated. I heard him say somethin' about 'it ain't righteous' and something about 'no more o' this!'*

"*Well, George saw me lookin' his way, and Ruben saw me too, and I don't know what he said to George, but they had some low angry words and George just threw up his hands and got on his mule and headed off to the ferry without me. I thought he must've been so angry he just forgot about ol Lydia.*

"*So, I figured I'd just take myself on over and come to the house here, and about the time I got to the river, there was Ruben right there with me.*

"*'Let me go over with you, Liddy?'' he asked.*

"*'Fine if you want to,' I said. I wanted him to know I was just fine on my own, thank you.*

"*We walked, quiet like, for a few minutes, but then, right there over by the river with that big moon out and that sweet breeze in our faces, he stopped. He just stopped and looked all round. Turned in a full circle, real slow, like he was seeing it all for the first time, but like he knew it all too.*

"*Bout the time I thought I'd just go on without him, he turned and looked me in the eyes. Looked right into my heart, he did, and he said, 'Liddy, you given your whole life to all this. What's it got you?'*

"*'It just got me old,' I told him. 'Just old and wore out.'*

"*Ain't right. Ain't nothing right about it, Liddy. You're a damn fine woman, you're smart and strong. You're lovely, Liddy. Ain't right for you to have this kind o' life.'*

I stopped reading and rubbed my eyes. "It's still hard for me," I explained, and handed the book to Will. "Could you read the rest?" I pointed to the place on the page where I'd stopped.

Will read, easy and clear.

*June 23, 1850*

*Yesterday, when Lydia asked me to write some things down for her, how could I have known what she was asking? Or what she would tell me? But, I think she's right, it is important. Maybe it's true that everyone has a story, everyone. Maybe everyone needs a word on a page somewhere that says, I was here. I was.*

*I think Lydia needs a way to keep him alive, even though he's been dead a long time now.*

*Henry told me, the day of the hanging, that Ruben was the finest blacksmith in the state of South Carolina, which was why Barnwell Rhett had bought him from that fellow in Charleston. He said Rhett had paid an awful lot, and that was one of the reasons he was so angry when Ruben ran. The story around town was that Ruben had slipped off in a rainstorm, hoping the dogs wouldn't be able to follow the scent. They say he made it as far as Baltimore. He almost made it.*

*They hung him the night Trouble was born, hung him for trying to run. I guess, now that I look back, it wasn't getting caught that killed him, but belonging to Barnwell Rhett. I wonder what might have happened if he'd made it?*

*But he didn't; they caught him, and followed the law in bringing him back, bringing him to justice, if you can call it that; sometimes I don't understand it myself.*

*Lydia never speaks of his death, nor does George. George is just so quiet; as a matter of fact, Henry had to remind me that they were brothers. And Lydia, she's only mentioned him twice, in all these years. I didn't realize at first; simply didn't make the connection. Now that Trouble has grown up a bit, of course, it's more apparent to those of us who do remember him. Now that I think about it, I can see; the broad shoulders, of course, and their stature. Neither of them tall, but they still strike one as big, strong, the way they carry themselves, I suppose, something in the way they move. It's as if they know they have some strength inside, in spite of it all.*

*But most of all, those eyes. Trouble has Ruben's eyes, curious and bright, with those specks of green that flash so.*

*I wonder if Lydia will tell the boy. What good would it do? Or what trouble would it bring? On the other hand, someday he'll want to know, won't he? Don't we all want to know where we came from?*

*   *   *

I looked off into the trees across the street, in wonder.

Peter shook his head, looking puzzled, then stricken.

I began to piece it together: Mama talking to Mrs. McKee in August 1850. The summer on Ashdale. Just a few months before Hank died.

*Mama and Ruben. Me. Ruben and George, brothers. George was my uncle, after all; now I understand his silence. And Barnwell Rhett.*

I looked at Peter. Peter looked at the floor. Neither of us spoke—what was there to say?

Suddenly, Peter jumped out of his chair like he'd been bit. "Good God!" he said. "I'll be right back." He hurried down the steps, with the shuffle of an old man's hurry, and Christian followed, looking both confused and alarmed.

Annie and I watched them go, stunned. Will handed me the book, and I held it in my lap again, trying to grasp what I'd read and heard.

"You alright, baby?" Annie asked. "I thought you should see it. I thought you should know." She got up slowly, and came to me, put her arms around me.

I'd known losses—more than a few. My brother, Abe, and little Hank, who I'd loved like a brother all those years ago. Sweet little Robbie, only three years old. That seemed more than I could bear at the time, but Hannah and I had borne it, and life continued. When Mama died, I'd felt a quiet sadness and a deep loss and the disquieting relief of letting her go. We'd buried her in the old Gullah graveyard on St. Helena, and I'd prayed for her reunion with the ancestors and a long, sweet season of rest, and freedom. When I buried Hannah, I feared I'd lose my mind—life without the feisty girl who'd made me a man, a free man, seemed unthinkable.

Now, I wondered how to both meet and let go of a man I'd never known; an unfamiliar and empty loss, nothing to let go of.

\* \* \*

As dusk fell, and the last of the evening light played off the quiet waters of the Beaufort River, Peter and Christian returned, breathless and sweaty. I'd been so lost in my thoughts and memories and questions, I'd forgotten them.

Peter's hands shook as he held out a small wooden box.

"This is yours." His voice broke as he handed me the box, not much bigger than a matchbox, and old. "I didn't know, Smalls. God, I'm so sorry. I swear, I didn't know."

He nodded for me to open it.

My hands shook too, but I managed to slip the lid off, and stared into the box, touched the gray metal, a slave tag: *Ruben, 479, Farrier, Charleston.*

No one spoke and the sun slipped below the horizon.

\* \* \*

As the tide goes out, the light reflects on both the water and the salt grasses, and sometimes the grasses reflect in the still water so perfectly that the actual grass and the reflected grass are one. The water recedes a little more, the grasses seem taller, then taller still, yellow gold in the winter now, and then a brightening green, and as the seasons turn, greener still and sweet-scented, until autumn, and the green recedes again with the tide, slowly, and the grasses are gold again, then pale, waiting for spring.

When the tide is out, all the way out, you can smell creation—salt and fish and mud, oysters and decaying things: tree roots and the bones of a young deer dragged down by a fast and hungry gator. You can smell it all, taste it almost, all this life, and death too; and it ebbs and it flows, and it rises and it falls, it gives and it takes, it feeds and it destroys, breathing in and out again, never ceasing, always changing: this endless and daily and eternal and faithful rhythm of the tides.

*"My people need no special defense, for the past history of them in this country proves them to be the equal of any people anywhere. All they need is an equal chance in the battle of life."*

Robert Smalls, November 1, 1895

# AUTHOR'S NOTES

This book is fiction. This story is inspired by his.

Rather than a biography, I've attempted to imagine the world in which Robert Smalls lived. I've wondered about the people who shared it, the political and theological contexts that informed it, and the inevitably complicated and challenging relationships therein. What were the hopes, fears, motivations, and aspirations of the enslaved, and the slaveholder? What was it like to be a young man or a young woman, a parent or a child, from a small community in South Carolina before, during, and after the Civil War? How did they navigate the confusing assumptions and expectations? How did they change or adapt or fail when the world changed beneath and around them?

Instead of trying to explore Smalls' military or political career, I've sought to explore his pursuit of courage and freedom, friendship and love, education and self-determination, hope and loss and redemption.

I've attempted to honor the perspectives of a few women and men, black and white, enslaved and free, while recognizing the historical and cultural distances to be bridged. It is the work of human imagination and curiosity that carries our hearts over such a bridge and allows us, perhaps, to be touched by the lives of others. That's what I've sought to do here.

The man changed countless lives. Including mine.

\* \* \*

No memoir of Robert Smalls exists, to my knowledge, nor am I aware of a diary kept by Jane McKee.

There's a great deal of speculation regarding the identity of Smalls' father, but no conclusive evidence.

Robert Smalls did learn to read, if poorly, but we don't know how.

Smalls met Hannah in Charleston and negotiated to buy and marry her, but we know little of their courtship or early life together. Hannah had at least one child when they married, and together they had two daughters, and a son who died in early childhood. Smalls remarried, and his second wife, Annie Wigg, died in 1895, when their son, William Robert Smalls, was only three years old.

A rich legend holds that Mrs. McKee, late in life, returned to Beaufort when the Smalls family resided in her former home; the oral tradition says that she was old and suffering from dementia, and they took her in and cared for her until her death. I want to believe this beautiful story is true but cannot confirm it.

Even the provenance of the surname Smalls is something of a mystery. And his nickname, his "basket name," Trouble, is imagined.

The cotton, rice, and indigo markets fluctuated over the decades, and I may have overstated a crop failure in 1846.

But these things are known: Smalls did indeed commandeer the Confederate steamer the *Planter* and deliver her to the Union navy, serve as a Union pilot through the war, and have audience with Lincoln to advocate for the enlistment of black soldiers. He did return to Beaufort after the war and buy the house on Prince Street, and he had some wealth from the reward money and his salary while serving on the *Planter*. He did serve in the state legislature and five terms in the US Congress, and he not only provided for the education of his own children, but he wrote legislation resulting in free compulsory education for the children, *all* the children, of South Carolina.

Robert Smalls died on February 23, 1915, at his home on Prince Street. Born enslaved behind that very house, he secured his freedom and that of his family, and was instrumental in securing the freedom of countless others.

He was an American hero, and yet most Americans have never heard of this man, this courageous and brilliant unsung hero. I hope this book introduces him broadly.

\* \* \*

**About the other characters:**

Henry and Jane McKee had a daughter named Elizabeth Jane, who was, in historical fact, a month older than Robert Smalls. She did not marry the fictional Ellison Petigru. The historical record shows that she married Edwin Bailey, and lived until 1924. Ellison Petigru is fictional; James Petigru was indeed significant in South Carolina's history and opposed secession. The McKees lost a son at age five (named Hank here), but we don't know the cause of his death. The McKees enslaved a man named George, who was their carriage driver. In the novel, his brother Ruben is entirely imagined.

Very little is known about Jane McKee, and her diaries and correspondence are entirely imagined, although the historical Mary Chestnut (her friend in this book) did indeed keep a diary, which makes fascinating reading.

\* \* \*

The large Robert Barnwell Rhett family had no fifth son named Peter.

Peter Rhett, his fictional youngest son, is entirely imagined, and I hope that his character personifies the possibility of redemptive transformation in the old South. Robert Barnwell Rhett was born Robert Barnwell Smith, and lived most of his life in Charleston. Some sources say he was adopted by an uncle; others say he and his brothers (including a younger brother named Edmund, who lived in Beaufort) changed their surname to Rhett to reclaim their English roots. His own memoirs and his biographers reveal a deeply complicated man. The historical elder Rhett endorsed both slavery and secession, ferociously, and he and his brother Edmund were instrumental in writing the orders of secession. He and his son, Robert Rhett Jr., ran his newspaper, the *Charleston Mercury*, that so enthusiastically supported their views. In this novel, the character Robert Barnwell Rhett is a compilation of both Edmund Rhett and Robert Barnwell Rhett.

\* \* \*

Smalls' first wife, Hannah, was enslaved by a family named either Kingman or Kingsman (the historical records show both spellings) and their words and actions in this novel are purely fictional; the stories about her mother are imagined as well.

To the best of my knowledge, and to honor them, I've used the actual names of the men and women who were part of the crew of the *Planter* the night of the escape.

Laura Towne was one of two teachers recruited to the Penn School. The Penn Center continues today to honor and preserve the history and culture of the Gullah people.

\* \* \*

The "Redshirts" were a highly organized white supremist movement, thinly veiled as "rifle and gun clubs," active after

Reconstruction, and instrumental in suppressing the rights of African-Americans.

As Reconstruction was dismantled and white supremacy regained its stronghold on the South, white political leaders worked hard to diminish Smalls' accomplishments and influence. In 1873, in an attempt to smear his name and diminish his popularity and influence, Smalls was accused of accepting a bribe while serving as a state senator. He was arrested and charged in 1877 and sentenced to three years of hard labor in a state prison. He was released from jail after three days on a pending appeal and returned to Congress. The South Carolina Supreme Court heard his appeal in 1879. Grounds for the appeal included unfair jury selection and the fact that the weak evidence for the case had come from a convicted felon who'd been granted immunity for his testimony. The state Supreme Court ruled against him, and Smalls appealed to the US Supreme Court. But before the Court heard the case, Governor William Simpson pardoned Smalls on assurances from the US district attorney that election fraud charges would be dropped against South Carolinians accused of voter violations in 1878. Smalls was never satisfied that justice had been served. The smear worked and his political reputation had been tainted.

The *Beaufort Gazette*, 100 years after Smalls' death, reported,

> His brand of politics was more local than national. Known as the 'King of Beaufort County,' he secured the first funds for the purchase of what is today the Marine Corps Recruit Depot on Parris Island, raised money for Beaufort's first public school, and was a booster of economic development in a brief period when the county was a center of industry rather than agriculture. Smalls was sitting on the porch of his home when his extraordinary life came to an end at age seventy-six. By then, the political world

had turned against him. Not a word of his death or funeral was reported in *The Beaufort Gazette*.

*   *   *

The story of his heroic life, like so many others, was suppressed, but never fully silenced, and hopefully Robert Smalls will be given the honor due him as an American hero.

*   *   *

This story is inspired by his. Apart from the details above, the narrative is an imaginative work, and I hope it inspires readers to learn more of the man and his extraordinary contributions. The words and actions of the historical figures are imagined, and events referenced are not necessarily chronologically accurate.

*   *   *

Several good resources are available for those who would like to know more about Robert Smalls or Beaufort, South Carolina:

Billingsly, Andrew. *Yearning to Breathe Free* (Columbia, University of South Carolina Press, 2010)

Lineberry, Cate. *Be Free or Die: The Amazing Story of Robert Smalls' Escape from Slavery to Union Hero* (New York, St. Martin's Press, 2017): The author's impressive research and storytelling skill render this a most readable biography.

Miller Jr., Edward A. *Gullah Statesman: Robert Smalls from Slavery to Congress, 1839-1915* (Columbia, University of South Carolina Press, 2008)

Uya, Okon Edt. *From Slavery to Public Service: Robert Smalls, 1839-1915* (Oxford University Press, 1971)

Graydon, Nell. *Tales of Beaufort* (Beaufort Bookshop, 1963) (source of poem "A Town's Peculiarity" by Robert Woodward Barnwell recited by Mr. McKee on the fishing dock)

http://history.house.gov/People/Detail/21764

**Additional resources regarding Robert Barnwell Rhett:**

Davis, William C. and Rhett, Robert Barnwell *A Fire-Eater Remembers: The Confederate Memoir of Robert Barnwell Rhett* (Columbia, University of South Carolina Press, 2000)

Davis, William C. Rhett. *The Turbulent Life and Times of a Fire-Eater* (Columbia, University of South Carolina Press, 2001)

**About the clergymen:**

Rev. Richard Fuller served the Baptist Church of Beaufort, and later became one of the founders of the Southern Baptist movement when it split from the Northern Baptists over the issue of slavery. Fuller and the other Southern Baptist leaders refused to oppose the institution of slavery and preached that it was biblically sanctioned in both the Old and New Testaments. Although he left Beaufort in 1846 to take the pastorate of a church in Baltimore, I've kept him in town as the leader of the Baptist Church a bit longer for the sake of the story.

Dr. Joseph Walker served as rector of St. Helena Episcopal Church from 1823 to 1878. He led a significant spiritual revival in 1831, and helped the congregation restore the church after it served as a hospital for black soldiers.

Rev. Mansfield French was first ordained in the Protestant Episcopal Church but in 1845 withdrew to join the Methodist Episcopal Church. To my knowledge, he did not ever actually pastor the Wesley Methodist Church in Beaufort, although he was in fact a Civil War missionary. He did accompany Robert Smalls to meet with President Lincoln and Secretary of War Edwin Stanton to advocate for the government to allow black men to serve in the Union forces. After the war, French returned to Beaufort and bought the Fuller residence in the tax sale.

I'm grateful to many friends and colleagues who provided remarkable resources regarding African and African-American spirituality, particularly Rev. Dr. April Bristow for sharing her library of resources, including:

Gibellini, Rosino editor. *Paths of African Theology* (Maryknoll, New York, Orbis, 1994)

Proctor, Samuel DeWitt. *The Substance of Things Hoped for; A Memoir of African-American Faith* (Valley Forge, Judson Press, 1995)

I would also like to thank Dr. Yvonne Chireau:

Chireau, Yvonne. *Black Magic: Religion and the African American Conjuring Tradit*ion (Berkeley, University of California Press, 2006). Dr. Chireau and I met, serendipitously, at a family meal in Bethlehem.

The oral tradition of West Africa includes the stories of Anansi the spider god, and Nyame.

**I also found these old documents fascinating:**

DEAR SIR: I have received your communication of yesterday and the enclosed report of Lieutenant Commanding Nicholson, and must again express my approval of the judgment and activity exercised by you and the officers under your command in holding the control of the St. John's River. I leave your future movements to your own discretion.

I have noticed the suggestion of Lieutenant Commanding Nicholson in reference to the destruction of the houses around Orange Mills, but for the present, unless the vessels are fired upon from that vicinity, I do not wish that there should be any destruction of property.

Since Sunday last I have been moving up and down the coast, visiting Charleston, Georgetown, and St. Simon's, arriving here yesterday. I shall be at Port Royal again by Saturday evening.

You have probably heard of the bold exploit of a contraband pilot employed on General Ripley's steamer, the *Planter*. The captain and engineer having gone on shore to visit their families, Robert Smalls before daylight quietly cast off the hawser by which she was moored to the wharf in front of the General's quarters, steamed past Fort Sumter, giving the usual signals and flying the Confederate flag until out of range, when he pulled it down, and hoisting a white flag brought the steamer safely out to the blockading fleet. The pilot is quite intelligent and gave some valuable information about the abandonment of Stone. At my instance Captain Marchand made a reconnaissance, and finding the statement true, crossed the bar on Tuesday last with the gunboats Unadilla, Pembina, and Ottawa. I have no doubt the Charlestonians thought their time had come.

The news from the Mississippi is very gratifying. The whole rebel fleet, nearly, is destroyed on the Lower Mississippi by Flag-Officer Farragut, and in the vicinity of Fort Wright by Acting Flag-Officer Davis, who is now in command, vice Foote, returned to the East on account of his wound. I send you a late paper or two. Please say to Lieutenant

Commanding Nicholson that I have read his report with interest; am glad that he escaped so well.

Respectfully, your obedient servant,
S. F. DU PONT,
Flag-Officer.

## Report of Flag-Officer Du Pont, U. S. Navy.

FLAGSHIP WABASH,
Port Royal Harbor, S. C., May 14, 1862.

SIR: I enclose a copy of a report from Commander E. G. Parrott, brought here last night by the late rebel steam tug *Planter*, in charge of an officer and crew from the Augusta. She was an armed dispatch and transportation steamer attached to the engineer department at Charleston, under Brigadier-General Ripley, whose barge, a short time since, was brought out to the blockading fleet by several contrabands.

The bringing out of this steamer, under all the circumstances, would have done credit to anyone. At 4 in the morning, in the absence of the captain, who was on shore, she left her wharf close to the Government office and headquarters, with palmetto and Confederate flag flying, passed the successive forts, saluting as usual by blowing her steam whistle. After getting beyond the range of the last gun she quickly hauled down the rebel flags and hoisted a white one.

The Onward was the inside ship of the blockading fleet in the main channel, and was preparing to fire when her commander made out the white flag.

The armament of the steamer is a 32-pounder, on pivot, and a fine 24 pounder howitzer. She had, besides, on her deck, four other guns, one 7-inch rifle, which were to be taken the morning of the escape to the new fort on the middle ground. One of the four belonged to Fort Sumter, and had been struck, in the rebel attack on that fort, on the muzzle.

Robert, the intelligent slave and pilot of the boat, who performed this bold feat so skillfully, informed me of this fact, presuming it would be a matter of interest to us to have possession of this gun.

This man, Robert Smalls, is superior to any who has yet come into the lines, intelligent as many of them have been. His information has been most interesting, and portions of it of the utmost importance.

The steamer is quite a valuable acquisition to the squadron, by her good machinery and very light draft. The officer in charge brought her through St. Helena Sound and by the inland passage down Beaufort River, arriving here at 10 last night.

On board the steamer when she left Charleston were 8 men, 5 women, and 3 children.

I shall continue to employ Robert as a pilot on board the Planter for the inland waters, with which he appears to be very familiar.

I do not know whether, in the views of the Government, the vessel will be considered a prize; but, if so, I respectfully submit to the Department the claims of this man Robert and his associates.

Very respectfully, your obedient servant,
S. F. DU PONT,
Flag-Officer, Comdg. South Atlantic Blockading
Squadron.

**Source:**

Navy War Records Office. *Series I, Volume 12:* South Atlantic
Blockading Squadron. (October 29, 1861—May 13, 1862) pp.
802-end. *http://ebooks.library.cornell.edu/cgi/t/text/textidx?c=moa
war;cc=moawar;view=toc;subview=short;idno=ofre0012*

http://www.historynet.com/robert-smalls-commander-of-the-
planter-during-the-american-civil-war.htm

# DISCUSSION QUESTIONS

1. With which character did you most resonate? Why?

2. The title *Trouble the Water* comes from an African American spiritual. Were you familiar with this song before reading the novel? You can search for it online. Here is one of the author's favorites: https://www.youtube.com/watch?v=RRpzEnq14Hs What is the role of music in the book? What is the role of music in your own experience?

3. The novel references scripture, faith, churches, and religions. What is the impact of religion before and during the Civil War? In what ways, if any, has that evolved?

4. Think about Robert's relationship with his mother, Lydia. In what ways did she prepare him for the challenges he would face?

5. What is so important to you that you would risk death? For what would you risk the lives of the people you most love?

6.  The relationships of the characters change and evolve throughout the book. Did any of these surprise you? Discuss.

7.  On p. 278, Robert says to Rev. French, "Preacher, let me tell you about something..." about the realities of being black. Discuss.

8.  *Trouble the Water* explores themes of race, justice, religion, family relationships and more. Which themes did you find particularly interesting? Which challenged you?

9.  Did reading *Trouble the Water* change anything in your understanding of slavery, the Civil War, or Reconstruction? Did it leave you with new questions?

10. Robert Smalls was an American hero, and yet his story remains widely unknown. Why do you think that is the case?

# ACKNOWLEDGMENTS

The journey from story to book, like life, comprises the unpredictable, curious, beautiful, heartbreaking, breathtaking, serendipitous constellation of circumstance, inclination, and people. I'm forever thankful for the circumstances and inclinations, and I'm indebted beyond expression and indescribably grateful for the people who have been part of this adventure.

An old African proverb declares *If you want to go fast, go alone. If you want to go far, go together.* So many hearts, hands, minds, and beautiful souls have shared this journey.

Grateful and endless love to our children: Nathan and Nikki, DT and Vanessa, Robert, Caroline and Sarah Lyn. Had Sarah Lyn not graduated in Chapel Hill, and had we not taken a few days to travel south to the Lowcountry, and had we not jumped on a last-minute carriage tour in Beaufort, when would we have heard those enticing snippets of the story of Robert Smalls?

Had our family and friends and colleagues in Texas not waved us goodbye with encouragement and blessings (and kept their thoughts to themselves when they thought we'd lost our minds) to resettle across the country, how would we have found the courage or energy to pursue this dream? Grateful undying love to Ida and Jerry Dwight, and Wink (who believed and cheered but didn't get to see it happen); to the Robys and the Faubions and the Oliphints, the fine people of FUMCR, and the dozens of other dear ones for whom I give thanks daily.

Had faithful friends not listened and read and edited and cheered, this would have been a far less coherent story. Grateful love to Donna and Leighton, Jody and Dave, Nancy (and Otis), Kim and Cathy and Jeffrey and Michael and each of you who encouraged so generously and patiently.

Had the Pat Conroy Literary Center's Jonathan Haupt not introduced me to Cassandra King, and had Cassandra and Bernie Schein not introduced me to Marly Rusoff and Mihai Radulescu, I might never have had the good fortune to work with such an extraordinary agent, or with John Koehler and Joe Coccaro and their amazing team at Koehler Books. And had Maura Connelly not welcomed me to the volunteer cadre at the PCLC, how would I have met such fun and brilliant and dedicated docents and volunteers and board? Endless and grateful love to each of you.

Because he changed so many lives, including mine, I give eternal thanks for Robert Smalls and his extraordinary legacy. And for all who illuminated his story, I give thanks: grateful love to libraries and librarians, and historians, particularly the encyclopedic Dr. Larry Rowland, and Smalls' generous and gracious great-great-grandson, Michael Boulware Moore.

And had I not fallen in love with the brilliant, charming, handsome, and hilarious man who makes my heart smile every day, none of it would have happened. Ever grateful to and for the great love of my life, Tom Bruff.